GRAY JUSTICE

A novel by

RON W. MUMFORD

3RD COAST BOOKS
HOUSTON, TEXAS
2018

3rd Coast Books
11111 West Little York Rd., #222
Houston, TX 77041

www.3rdCoastBooks.com

ISBN's

Perfect Binding — 978-1-946743-12-1

eBook/.MOBI — 978-1-946743-13-8

eBook/.ePub — 978-1-946743-14-5

Project Coordinator — Rita Mills
Editor & Collaborator — Faye Walker
Text Design — Deena Rae
Cover Design — James Price

Printed in The United States of America

CONTENTS

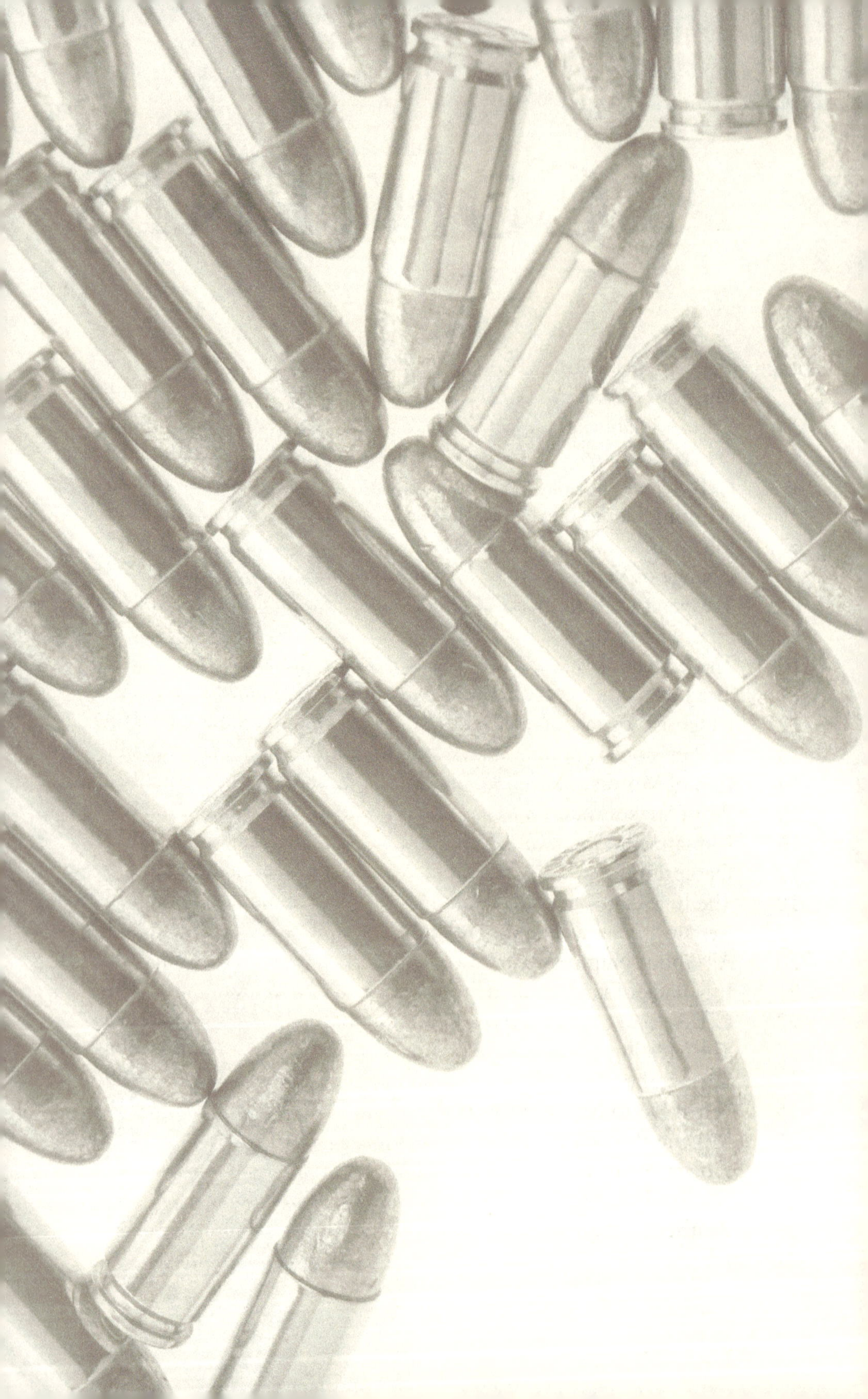

ACKNOWLEDGEMENTS

This book is dedicated to every family in America who has lost loved ones to the devastation and abuse of drugs. Consider this work *payback* for all of the pain, tears and grief that these illegal substances and drug dealers have brought into your lives. There is tomorrow, there is hope.

I would like to thank my God and several people who have made this hope into written reality within the following pages of *GRAY JUSTICE*.

My source of inspiration, God Almighty. Thank you Lord for humbling and choosing me to write this story.

My two encouragers who are now deceased, Fred, my Dad, and Adele, my loving Mom who read every page as it was written and kept me working when life wasn't exactly like living in Camelot.

My legal source, a man among men, Randall "Primo" Fluke who has been fighting drug dealers most of his life—and winning!

Next is my publisher, Rita Mills at 3rd Coast Books, my editor, Faye Walker, Ph.D. who had the faith to publish an unknown writer's first book, and Deena Rae at eBookbuilders for such a great format. I will always be indebted to you all.

Finally, my two former editors and book doctors supreme, Aunie Pierce Thibideaux and Myra Barnes, Ph.D.,co-author of *SOLDIERS OF GOD* and *GIVE ME YOUR WINGS*. Both editors took a first effort novel and turned it into a readable, fast, intriguing, heart-wrenching story. Where would writers be without our editors to make us look as though we know our trade, our calling and our craft?

—Ron Mumford

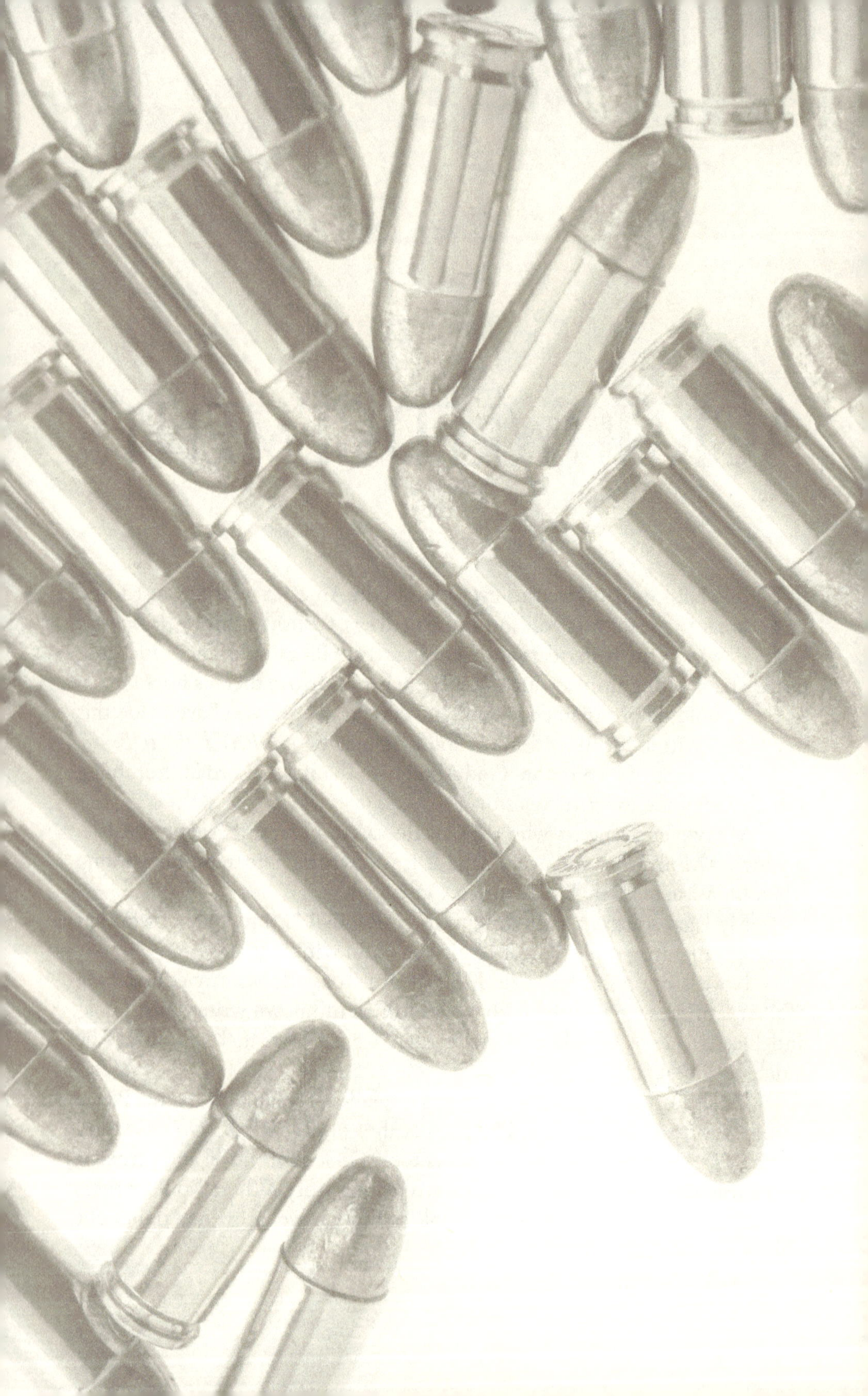

GRAY JUSTICE

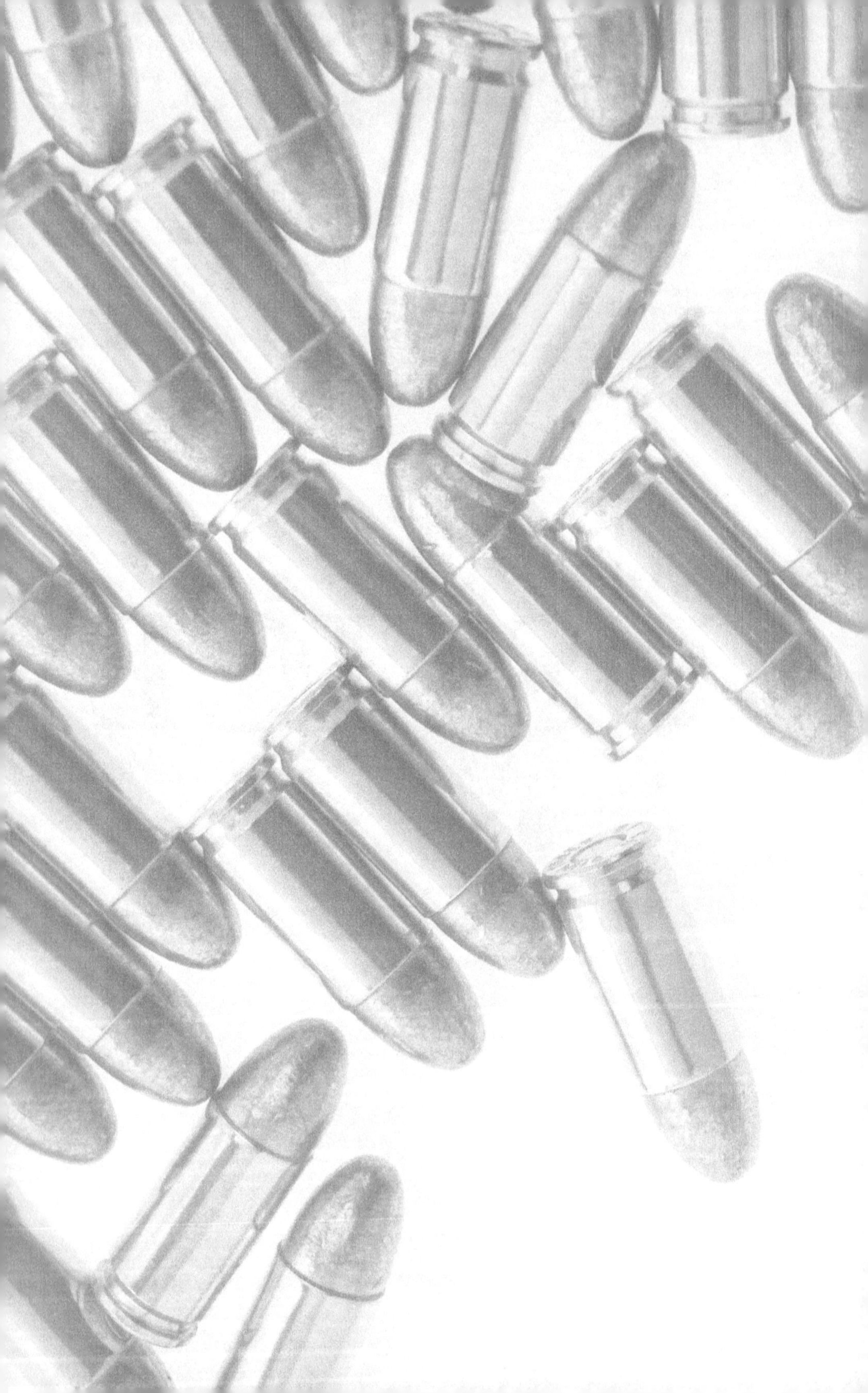

1

MURPHY'S LAW

The ornately carved doors of the study swung open as Dr. Robin Perrone walked out lighting a cigarette, tugging at the stethoscope wrapped around her neck. Her long black hair reflected the light from the huge hallway chandeliers at the Perrone estate.

"How's Father?" Daniel Perrone asked, a concerned look on his face.

"He didn't get the name Nico the Bull for nothing, big brother. He wears his handle well."

"Then he's okay?"

"Father's fine. Chalk his high blood pressure up to the business he's in. You're the one who looks like he could use a couple of aspirin. What's wrong?"

"Some trouble in the Caribbean, family business. You know better than to ask."

Deep down inside, Robin wished that her beloved older brother would never be involved in family business. A business composed of twenty-four families that collectively made up La Cosa Nostra, the American Mafia. She knew Daniel was the heir apparent to the Mafia throne. It was his legacy. She also knew how he detested the killing, the manipulation, and the wrecked lives left in the path of family business.

LATE APRIL, 1:30 P.M., EL PASO, TEXAS

Judd Rayburn pulled the canopy cover off the Christen Eagle experimental biplane and rolled it into the afternoon heat of El Paso, Texas. Within minutes he would be flying at five thousand feet, leaving behind the months of preparation for the largest drug bust in his fifteen-year career with the county district attorney's office. He had grown weary of this God-forsaken pit of narcotics, prostitution, and murder. After making his walk-around inspection of the little two-seater, Judd unlatched the bubble canopy and wedged his five-foot, ten-inch frame into the back seat of the black cockpit. Beads of perspiration began forming on his forehead. The muscles in his neck tightened into achy knots. As he put on the headset and turned on the ignition key. Judd heard the roar of the two-hundred-horsepower Lycoming engine which sent a warm but welcome breeze across his sweaty face. After adjusting his altimeter, radio and cockpit instruments, Judd taxied onto the almost abandoned asphalt strip just outside of El Paso. He completed his pre-takeoff run-up, took a deep breath, and keyed his mike.

"All traffic in the area, November four-four Romeo Mike ready for takeoff on runway two-seven," he said briskly although he knew there was no one in the vicinity to hear him.

As the Eagle screamed down the runway, Judd added a little rudder pedal to correct for crosswind, eased back on the stick and was airborne. Climbing away from the El Paso desert, he maneuvered into a slow roll as if to shrug off the many things on his mind: the looming drug bust, the timing, and the men involved. He yearned for escape to mental freedom.

What could go wrong? he wondered, mentally going over the plan. We've got a good man, Dee Espinoza, inside the Mexican Cartel, telling us every move they're going to make. The shipment of cocaine is coming in next Thursday on flatbed trucks. We know the route and where we'll pull the trucks over. With the combined agencies of the Texas and New Mexico DEA, FBI, and ATF, state and local sheriffs and police departments, the highway patrol and the Texas Rangers, *What could go wrong?*

The agencies had drilled every possible scenario. It bothered Judd that his fears and doubts could not be shaken. Why was it he continued to feel that something wasn't right?

At least once or twice each month, Judd took to the clouds. He had learned to fly when he was in college thanks to the influence of a cute little co-ed he had met named Rikki Rhine. She had had her mind set on being the first female fighter pilot in the U.S. Navy. His path of pursuing her had been straight up. Judd had chased her while obtaining his private pilot's license, instrument ticket, and some aerobatic training before his money ran out. She had been on an aviation scholarship, which paid for most of her flying expenses. Rikki eventually flew off to Navy flight school in Pensacola, Florida, along with part of Judd's heart. With her out of the picture, Judd applied to law school. That was over twenty years ago. Rikki was just a fond memory, one that got away. Now at forty-five, Judd was more concerned about his receding hairline and the fact that his once thick, sandy blond hair was graying slightly around the edges.

Racing skyward, seeking solitude, Judd could feel the cool air blowing through the cockpit vents. He took a deep cleansing breath of the fresh air and felt the tense muscles in his neck loosening up.

"November four-four Romeo Mike!" came crashing across his radio, destroying the peaceful moment for himself, his airplane, and a patch of clear blue sky.

"Four-Four Romeo Mike," Judd answered. "Go ahead."

"Romeo Mike, go to secure."

Judd recognized the voice of Joe Feather, a trusted friend and colleague with the New Mexico FBI.

Urgency and concern were evident in Feather's voice. Judd sensed the nagging return of tension in his shoulders as he picked up his radio and replied in an agitated voice.

"Go ahead, Joe."

"Judd, where are you?"

"Twenty-five miles west of El Paso Inter-national. What's the problem?"

"No time, Judd. I'll meet you at the general aviation office over at International," Feather said quickly.

Judd called the El Paso International tower for landing clearance. Minutes later he lined up for the final approach and settled the Eagle down in a perfect three-point landing. Ground control cleared him to the general aviation section of the airport where a van was waiting to lead Judd into the government owned hangar. As he taxied closer, Judd saw Agent Feather's familiar blue Chrysler sedan. Joe stood impatiently at the back of the car with the trunk open and his shirt off, putting on his bulletproof vest. Something had gone wrong.

"Couldn't take a chance over the radio," Feather said as he handed Judd a bulletproof vest. "I'll tell you on the way. Everything's gone haywire. The trucks will be at the intercept area in two hours; today, not next Thursday. I don't know what happened. I just know we're trying to round up everyone on the task force. Most of 'em are taking a couple of days off. Probably have their cells turned off."

"Slow down Joe. Has anyone heard from Dee Espinoza?"

"Forty-five minutes ago." Feather put the Chrysler in gear and took off. "We just got a quick message from him that said 'Rolling, ETA 4 p.m.,' and then nothing! We didn't know how to contact him. Voice print from the tape confirmed it was Espinoza."

"Did you bring me anything to shoot with?" Judd said feeling under the seat and opening the glove compartment.

"I've got you a MAC 10 or an M-16 with plenty of ammo."

"I hope Dee's all right," Judd said as he tied the ends of the ammo bandoliers together and placed them crisscross, Pancho Villa style, over his shoulders.

"How many guys you think we can get there in time?" Judd asked.

"No way of telling. When I left the office, we had twelve of the local SWAT team members, two Texas Rangers, and four FBI guys on the way from the El Paso office. With you and me, that's twenty."

"Where's the DEA and ATF?" Judd asked.

"Probably the same place the other hundred guys are, out taking a few days off before the bust. Oh yeah, add one more to your total…"

"Who?"

Feather grinned. "Your very own leader himself, the future senator from the great state of confusion, Paul Martinez, Mr. County District Attorney."

"I only thought I was worried before," Judd said as he buried his head in his hands. "Now I'm horrified."

Feather laughed. "How much trouble do you think this can be, anyway? You're letting all those zeroes get to you, amigo. Three flatbed trucks bringing in six thousand pounds of prime Colombian blow with a street value of ninety mil doesn't require a hundred and twenty-five men to stop six to ten Mexican truck drivers out in the middle of nowhere."

"Ambush Pass is not what I call out in the middle of nowhere," Judd snapped. "With twenty men we can't begin to cover the high ground in that mountain pass. I don't like it! I like it even less when I think that Martinez is using this thing to get him into a state senate seat. He'll make a media field day out of it and we'll get our butts kicked."

Judd's concern over their position at Ambush Pass was real. The highway chosen by the Mexican Drug Cartel was literally cut through the southern tip of the San Andres Mountains. At the point where the highway intersects the mountains, steep rocky cliffs lined both sides of the road, a perfect place for an ambush even during the days of the cowboys and Indians. As they approached the area, about two hundred yards in front of them, Judd and Feather could see several unmarked police cars bunched up on the east side of the mountain pass. The drug runners would be heading east, coming from Mexico on the other side of the mountains, through Ambush Pass.

"I don't believe this." Feather let his foot off of the accelerator and coasted the last one hundred yards. "What's that blasted news truck doing out here? It's crazy that we can't round up all of our officers, but we can always depend on someone calling in the news media."

"Chill, Joe," Judd said as he shook his head in disbelief. "Wasn't it about three minutes ago you said all we have to do is to take down a few truck drivers? I mean, you can almost understand this; there's an election coming up in a few months. Mr. DA, Paul Martinez, is running. This is the biggest bust in the history of the state. He's going to milk this right into a state senate seat."

When Judd and Feather got out of the car, Martinez was pointing and directing the deployment of the El Paso SWAT team as the cameras rolled. This wasn't a drug bust. It was a Hollywood production. Judd tried to tuck his anger and concern aside as he walked up to Paul Martinez.

"Paul, did you put anyone up high on each side of the mountain?" he asked.

"No time for that." Martinez was wallowing in his great opportunity. Donald Bonds, the office nose-in-the-boss's-butt, handed Martinez a cup of coffee from his ever-present thermos. Bonds had been in the DA's office for about five years. He was fat, sloppy, foul-mouthed and had bad teeth.

"Rayburn, you and Agent Feather stay with me here at the command post." Local news cameras were rolling, recording the greatest day in Martinez's career. Soon the whole country would see it. "The Texas Rangers are positioning themselves on each side of the highway. You know how Rangers are," Martinez said in a loud, facetious voice, "always wanting to be the macho guys."

It was plain to see Martinez had little respect for anyone but himself. His comments about the Texas Rangers ripped at Judd, his anger forcing him to turn and walk away. Everyone in the state knew Rangers were the baddest cats on the fence when it came to one-on-one confrontations. As the hour drew near, Martinez decided the media had enough shots of him directing the operation and ordered them about twenty yards back with all of their equipment.

Judd kept looking up, searching each side of the mountain pass. Once he thought he saw a reflection of something metallic but put it out of his mind. He was getting too paranoid. As Feather had said, "He was letting the zeroes get in the way."

If Dee's short radio message was correct, the flatbed trucks should be arriving in about fifteen minutes. Judd was glad his good friend Joe Feather was there. He and Feather had worked on many joint cases together over the last fifteen years. They not only had a healthy professional respect for one another, but also a deep personal friendship had developed when Judd's wife and nine-year-old son were killed in a freak car wreck the first year Judd was with the DA's office.

The ill-fated wreck had occurred just across the state line in New Mexico. An over-served Indian from one of the reservations plowed his pickup head-on into Judd's wife's car, killing mother and son instantly. Uninjured in the crash, the Indian had sought refuge inside the reservation. In the spirit of all the Indian civil rights violations going on at the time, the chief of the reservation would not hand over his Indian brother to local authorities. They were ready to fight to defend the guy.

Enter Special FBI Agent Joe Feather, Zuni Indian. Feather single-handedly went into the reservation, climbed over the barricades past hundreds of his painted-face, feather wearing, war-whoop screaming brothers and brought the perpetrator to justice.

"Who's up high, Martinez?" Feather's questions were always short and to the point.

"No one."

"Bad positioning." Feather continued to stare up into the mountains as if to see through and behind the boulders above them. He checked both of his 9-mm MAC 10's dangling on straps under his armpits. It was 4 p.m. Everyone was wet with perspiration under the cumbersome bulletproof vests, everyone but Feather, not a drop of sweat on him. From a distance came the faint sounds of diesel engines.

Show time! Judd thought.

Martinez keyed his radio, "SWAT One, ready?"

"Ready."

"Ranger One, ready?"

"Ready."

"Bonds?"

"We're ready."

Martinez turned around and motioned for the news people to get down and stay quiet. He was shaking.

"SWAT Two, here," whispered in everyone's radios, "I can see three diesel trucks one hundred fifty yards from our position, but…they're not flatbeds, sir; they're tractor-trailer rigs. Kinda funny-looking. They've got rusted steel panels on the sides and tops. The cabs don't have glass, just welded-on steel panels."

"God help us!" Judd remarked in a muffled whisper as he turned and looked at Feather. "I told you I didn't like this."

Joe never acknowledged Judd's statement as he gripped his MAC 10's.

The trucks were still a hundred yards away and traveling at thirty-five miles per hour when the officers lying in wait on the ground heard the sound of the helicopter. It was on top of them in a heartbeat, popping up over the top of the mountain. The loud roar of the engine immediately drew everyone's attention skyward. Dangling hangman style on a rope suspended from the side of the chopper was a bronze naked man kicking and screaming as he grasped frantically at the noose around his neck. Blood covered the lower half of his body and streamed down his thrashing legs. The man had been castrated. The chopper hovered two hundred feet above Martinez's command position, halfway between Martinez and the news truck, blowing desert sand into an almost opaque whirlwind.

Stunned, Feather raised his binoculars. "Oh, God. It's Dee Espinoza!"

At the same moment, someone in the chopper cut the rope. Dee began plummeting to the earth. Releasing his grip on the noose around his neck, Dee's arms began to churn in a windmill motion and his bloody legs tried to walk on air as the chopper pulled out to the left. The mountains came alive with gunfire aimed down from Cartel soldiers. From all directions, strafing rained down on the officers below. Dee's body hit the desert sand below, bouncing twice, then became perfectly still.

With everyone's attention on Dee, no one noticed the three diesels pulling through the mountain pass. They came to a full stop, in line, separating the two groups of officers on each side of the road. Gun barrels from both sides of the trailers burst through slits between the rusted steel plates, AK-47 assault rifles held by more Cartel soldiers riddled the police cars with lead. Hell

Hell itself rained down on the group of officers as squad car windows exploded and tires blew out. There was nowhere to hide. A rocket propelled grenade streamed down from the mountain with a Roman candle-like concussion, hitting one of the unmarked cars. As it exploded in a huge ball of flame, two of the SWAT team members incinerated instantly.

Martinez broke radio silence, "Officers down! Officers down! Ambush Pass. They're killing us; they're killing us!" Martinez screamed, barely able to keep his wits. "Get every officer in the area out here, fast! Send ambulances. Ambushed! Ambus…"

The back of his head exploded. Martinez took a bullet just above his right eye and folded backwards to the ground.

Out of sheer reaction, SWAT team members put six M-72 LAW missile rounds into the three diesel trucks, temporarily putting most of the men inside out of commission.

"I make out about thirty hostiles above us on our side of the mountain!" Feather screamed between bursts of his MAC-10's. "Don't know how many on the north side."

With no time to think, Judd began running and then low-crawling out across the desert-turned-battlefield to Dee Espinoza's lifeless body. Out in the open, away from the car, Judd attracted most of the fire coming from the Cartel soldiers on his side of the mountain. The sand boiled with bullets showering down towards him. As he inched his way closer, the Cartel soldiers' aim got better. He felt a round hit the sand and burrow under his belly.

The remaining officers on Judd's side of the road moved around to the other side of the police cars. The Cartel trucks had been exploded. Another rocket propelled grenade hit near one of the Ranger cars. A few of the officers noticed Judd crawling towards Dee and concentrated on laying down cover fire for him. Judd reached Dee's naked, lifeless body. He grabbed Dee under his arm and started to drag him back. The cover fire helped, but lead was still flying everywhere. Judd inched another foot dragging his buddy with him when the lights went out. His head hit the sand. Movement stopped.

Zigzagging out into the open, Feather raced towards Judd with both MAC 10's blazing into the mountain rocks above. He grabbed the collar of Judd's bulletproof vest. Blood was dripping from Judd's head. Ten yards to cover. A sheriff's deputy ran from the back of Martinez's bullet-riddled vehicle to help Feather; he never made it. Two rounds hit him in the neck and the side of the face. The deputy went down.

Feather finally pulled Judd behind the car, shed his vest, tore off his T-shirt and wrapped it around Judd's head. Officers were falling like flies all around him due to the intense fire coming from Cartel soldiers high above. Joe glanced back at the deputy, only to see a surprised, fixed stare on what was left of his face. The deputy was gone.

The El Paso SWAT team was outdoing themselves against the staggering odds. Two of the SWAT officers laid down a blanket of fire with M-79 grenade launchers; empty 40mm canisters were piled up around them. Two more SWATs were doing the same thing with M-72 LAW disposable missile launchers, single-shot bazooka-looking weapons capable of taking out armored tanks at three hundred yards. Machine gun fire from the mountain became heavier.

With brief upward glances preceded by short bursts from his MAC 10's, Feather saw a group of the Mexican Cartel soldiers moving across the top of the mountain from their well-camouflaged positions, trying to make their way to awaiting choppers that would take them back across the border into Mexico. In the distance Feather heard the rumble of multiple helicopters. As he ducked down behind the car, Joe looked skyward over his left shoulder and saw an olive drab Huey Cobra gun ship and five Huey "slicks." The cavalry had arrived in the form of the Terrorist Assault Group from nearby Fort Bliss. Primarily composed of Green Berets, the TAG team, as they are called, had picked up Martinez's urgent call for help.

Feather, an ex-Green Beret himself, grabbed his radio and dialed the TAG radio frequency.

"This is agent Feather, New Mexico FBI!"

"This is Cobra leader. Looks like you guys could use some help. Where do you want it?"

"Midway to the top of the mountains on both sides of the highway. Friendlies at the base, both sides," Feather shouted, using the military jargon he could remember from his Special Forces days. The Cobra pilot made a ninety-degree turn to the right and then a one-eighty to the left, lining up with both sides of the mountain. Hell suddenly went the other direction. Twin mini-guns from the Cobra pelted every square foot of the mountain to the north of Feather. The pilot fired air-to-ground rockets in salvos as he crossed the highway and started on the other side of the mountain. Completing his first pass, the pilot pulled the Cobra up into a climbing bank, spun around, and pounced on top of the remaining Cartel soldiers again. The mountain was silenced.

TAG teams landed and deployed in a protective line between the remaining officers on both sides of the highway. The Cobra gunship orbited the area and then went over the top of the mountain to the other side, opening up on the few escaping Cartel soldiers.

Four medivac choppers deployed from Fort Bliss landed on the sand as Army medics set up a triage area and began to evacuate the wounded officers.

"Over here!" Feather screamed, as he cradled Judd in his arms. He felt a pulse. The bleeding had stopped. "Hang in there, brother. Hang in there."

Medics bandaged Judd's bleeding head wound and evacuated him to a waiting chopper. Feather wanted to go with them but he knew someone had to stick around, count the dead, and fill out the paperwork. As he walked away from the sandstorm created by the medivac chopper, Feather gazed upon a battlefield, not a drug bust. It was a valley of death. A tear or maybe just a drop of sweat ran down his cheek.

Who was the Judas? Feather wondered. *Who sold us out this time?* The bust had been a carefully planned trap.

Drained, numb, almost lifeless, Feather walked back toward the remaining officers who stood together in a group. They weren't talking. For the moment they didn't hear the chop-chop sounds of the helicopters evacuating wounded or the orders being shouted to TAG team members by their captain. They only heard the ringing in their ears, the screams of fallen comrades and the smell of ammonia lingering in the air from the exploded ordinance.

The smell of diesel-burned flesh seeped deep into their flared nostrils. An officer turned to throw up. No glory on a battlefield, only death. Within minutes, over ninety police cars arrived.

The news crew! Feather was getting back to reality.

He jogged towards the blue and white truck with all the antennas. Erica Stone was easy to recognize. Joe had seen her many times on the six o'clock news. She and the other news people were dusting the sand from their clothes and faces, trying desperately to pull themselves together and be professionals after witnessing such a barbaric event. This was sure-fire Emmy award-winning material and they knew it.

"Ms. Stone, I'm agent Feather. Are you and your crew okay?"

"We think so." She was trembling, shaking, crying.

Trying to do her job, she stuck an unplugged microphone in Feather's face and began questioning him, not waiting for his answers.

"How many men did you lose? Who is responsible for this? What…" She dropped her mike in the sand, covered her face and began to cry uncontrollably.

Feather stepped closer to her, put his arms around her and held her for a moment.

"Ms. Stone, I realize how important this is to you. I'm going to have to ask you and your crew to leave the area," Feather said in a soft voice. She pulled away from Feather with a hard look on her face.

"This is my job!" she blurted out, forcing aside the lump in her throat.

"And I've also got to take your video tape. There may be information on it we can use to identify some of the perpetrators."

Erica Stone looked down at the ground in deep thought, wiping the sand and tears from her eyes. "Tom, give Agent Feather the footage. My editor will probably fire me for this, but then he wasn't here, was he?" she said, trying to speak coherently. Mascara, tears, and sand caked her face.

"I have to ask. Did you do any direct feed of this back to the station?" Feather asked.

"No. You have my word on that. We were pinned down."

Feather handed her his turned to her crew. "Let's wrap up here and go back to the station." She put Joe's handkerchief in her back pocket.

"Need a ride somewhere?" One of the county sheriff's deputies asked Feather.

Feather turned and asked, "Do you know where they took the wounded?" He was without a shirt and beginning to get chilled as the sun set low in the west.

"I'm not sure. We can find out on the way. Specifically, I need to find out where they took Judd Rayburn. He's a good friend of mine." Feather and the deputy got in the sheriff's car, radioed for Judd's whereabouts and drove into town. Joe reached over, turned off the radio, laid his head back against the steel mesh cage and closed his eyes.

2

CORTEZ: DIABLO

The scene outside the Fort Bliss hospital resembled a clip from the movie *MASH*. Medivac choppers landing and taking off, soldiers carrying stretchers in and out of the triage area just outside the hospital adjacent to the chopper pads. Moans and groans could be heard all over the area. Some were police officers, others were Cartel soldiers. U.S. Army infantrymen stood over them with M-16s.

Feather got out of the car and slowly walked inside the swinging doors to the emergency room area. He reached into his back pocket, pulled out his FBI badge and hung it on his belt.

"Who's in charge here?" he demanded.

A male nurse pointed and said, "Colonel Sawyer, sir."

"Colonel, I'm Agent Feather, FBI. Can you tell me where Assistant DA Rayburn is?"

"Come with me."

Feather and the colonel weaved their way through the gurneys in the hallway to an examination room. Judd was lying on his back with his eyes half opened.

"Looks like you're going to live." Feather felt relieved seeing Judd conscious. "How're you feeling, bro?"

"Like I got kicked by a mule. What happened?"

"You caught one when you were playing hero. Luckily, they aimed at that hard head of yours and it just bounced off." Joe cracked a seldom-seen smile. "I'll fill you in when you get out of here."

"That's going to be right now."

Judd pushed himself up to a sitting position with one hand and grabbed his head with the other.

"The colonel released me to a civilian hospital in the area for observation and antibiotics. Can you drive me over to Mercer General?"

Joe lifted Judd up to a standing position and walked him out the door, grabbing a green orderly smock hanging on a hook. Judd was still wearing the clothes he had on but was in his stocking feet and couldn't find his boots. Both got back into the deputy's car.

As they pulled away from the confusion, Judd looked up at Feather in the front seat. "Dee?"

Feather shook his head. "You're doped up now, Judd. Just sit back, we'll talk about that later."

"I'm okay." Judd opened his eyes wide and looked more alert. "Someone set us up. I've got to talk to Paul Martinez. We've got to interrogate some of those Cartel soldiers I saw in the hospital, find out who set us up. What was the outcome of that fiasco, Joe? I don't remember..."

Feather tried to calm Judd down. Then he said, "I don't have an accurate count yet of how many we lost. Most of the Cartel guys are in zip-lock bags. Sit back and quiet down, Judd."

"Dee's gone?"

Joe nodded.

Judd checked himself into Mercer General. The deputy took Joe to Judd's apartment. Joe had a key. After checking in with his office, Feather took a shower and fell asleep on the couch. It was 10 p.m.

At 4:30 a.m. Joe was up and on the phone to the El Paso FBI office. "Let me talk to Agent Richards."

"Agent Richards."

"Glen, this is Joe Feather. Can you give me an update?"

"Joe, we're still putting things together. What we have now is eight dead, eight wounded, one EP-FBI among them, one Texas Ranger, the others are SWAT and local police. You know about Martinez and Dee. On the other side, we've counted thirty-eight dead, ten wounded at the Fort Bliss hospital, and seventeen being held for interrogation."

"Did we get any of the big fish? Do we know who organized it?"

"It was our old friend, Cortez. We ran some of the news video. Cortez was in the chopper that dropped Dee Espinoza. But, to answer your other question, no. All the people we got were just Cartel flunkies, maybe a few lieutenants. We're still interrogating them."

"Glen, can you send a unit over to pick me up?"

"Sure. Need some fresh clothes?"

"No thanks, I still have some jeans I left here on my last visit. I'll borrow the other things I need from Judd."

In the early afternoon, Joe called Mercer General only to find Judd had checked himself out earlier that morning.

Joe's cell phone began chirping.

"Feather."

"How about some late lunch?"

"Sounds good. Where are you, Judd?"

"I just left Paul Martinez's house…they told me at the hospital. I didn't want Pilar and the kids to hear it from anyone else but me. She took it better than I did when I heard…I'm going to miss Paul."

"I wanted to tell you in the car, yesterday." There was a break in Joe's voice. "Didn't think it was the right time."

"I can appreciate that."

"I'm not real hungry. Guess we should eat something, though. Does a burger sound okay to you, Joe?"

"Sure, where?"

"Meet me at *Chompers*. I've been ducking the press all day. I doubt if they'll find us there. Thirty minutes?"

"Make it twenty-five. I just got hungry."

Joe had already ordered when Judd walked in. The lower half of his head was shaved.

"That's a real modern haircut you got there, bro. The kids on the block will like that." Joe took a bite of his two-handed burger.

"If you like this, you ought to see the cat's butt I have over my right ear. I see you waited on me to order."

"You're the one that's not hungry," Joe said with his mouth full.

Judd scanned the one-paged menu consisting of burgers, hot dogs and soft drinks. "Cheeseburger and a diet drink."

The waitress left the table without confirming the order.

"Have you seen the Channel 10 news?" Feather had a serious look in his eyes.

"Yeah, I caught the early news before I left the hospital. Erica Stone didn't sleep much last night."

"It's all over the national news, too."

"I've got to issue a statement before the six p.m. newscast. Oh, I forgot! Shake hands with the acting District Attorney." Judd held out his hand.

"Congrats. I'm glad something good came out of this."

"I'm next in line for the job. Heck of a way to get it though. I've already talked to the police chief, sheriff's department and the military. I need to get some input from your office and issue a joint statement to the media. There's a press conference set up this afternoon. We've got some graphics to show the cameras. So far, we're all in agreement of full disclosure. Short and to the point."

"We aren't going to mention Cortez, are we?"

"Not unless your office wants to, Joe. We'll keep that confidential."

"Good." Joe wiped the mayonnaise from the corner of his mouth. "Who's going to be the speaker?"

"Me." Judd sucked the last drop of diet coke from the paper cup. "I don't want to take a chance of a media botch-up on top of what has already happened." El Paso Mayor Avila made the opening remarks at the press conference. He graciously extended condolences to the families of the officers and men killed in the line of duty and then introduced Judd as the acting District Attorney for Pecos County. Judd gave a detailed account of the events leading up to the bust as well as the facts that followed.

He was surrounded by military leaders, the police chief, the sheriff and the local FBI Agents-In-Charge. After his twenty-minute graphically enhanced speech, the media, now numbering almost two hundred reporters and cameramen, went wild with questions.

Finally, back at his apartment, Judd reached in the refrigerator, grabbed a couple of beers and pitched one over to Joe.

"That shirt looks familiar."

"You need to lose some weight. I can't stand baggy shirts." Feather popped the top on the beer and quickly sipped the foam.

They both kicked back for the first time in two days. For half an hour there was no conversation, only silence.

Judd stared out the patio door. The desert was beautiful at sunset. His head began to throb. He went to the kitchen, poured out some antibiotics and added a couple of aspirins, threw them into his mouth and washed them down with the last swallow of warm beer.

"I'll bet Cortez is having some kind of fiesta tonight, Joe. We've got to get that no good son-of-a-bitch!"

"That's exactly what *we* have to do and fast. While he doesn't expect us. He won't start getting cautious for a couple of weeks." Feather had that steel look in his eyes again. "Cortez will stay drunk that long. I know, we have an E.P.I.C. file on him in detail from the seven months Dee was undercover down there. We know where he is every hour of the day, his routines, who he sleeps with, what nights and how long he lasts in bed. It's all in his file. We need to go down there and get him while his guard is down."

"Sure, Joe! Let's just hop on Aero Mexico, waltz on down there, crash Cortez's party, diddle around with a couple of his señoritas, and put the cuffs on him. He won't mind waiving extradition. Julio Cortez is a wild and crazy guy. I mean, what the hell's stopping us? The government of Mexico shouldn't put up too big of a fuss that a U.S. FBI agent and an acting D.A. decided to skip down there and abduct one of their citizens. Too much paperwork for both sides, right?" Judd was frustrated now. His facetiousness was not aimed at Joe.

"Judd, I've been after the Mob, the Colombian Cartel or the Mexican Cartel most of my life." Now Feather was showing frustration. "I have a great respect for the law, but brother, I'm here to tell you that our system is not working. It protects the guilty as well as the innocent. Cortez is laughing his butt off at us, under the protection of U.S. law. I say it's time to change a few rules and get the job done."

"I'm glad we aren't talking on the phone, buddy." Judd's anger had been picked up and magnified by Feather. Judd had never seen his Zuni friend quite so angry, verbally or otherwise.

"If I can get Cortez on our side of the border, do you have enough evidence to convict him?" Feather was dead serious and wanted a direct answer, not a bunch of legalese gibberish.

Being a lawyer, Judd's first replies should have been "Depends on how we get him across the border" or " If the evidence holds up" or "If the jury sees it our way." He knew Joe. Feather wanted a yes or a no.

"Yes. I can convict him. But how're you going to get him on our side of the border, legally?"

"You just be where I tell you to be at the time I tell you to be there." Feather had a plan, as usual.

"Do me a favor, Judd. Now that you *are* the D.A., don't bring along the news cameras. This one could get a little gray."

"Joe, I want Cortez alive. Gray justice or not."

Joe pulled up to a pay phone on the outskirts of town. He spent ten minutes on the phone and returned to the car where Judd was waiting.

"Joe, whatever this plan is of yours, don't tell me. I can't know and prosecute Cortez."

"The only thing I'm going to need from you, Judd, is an old pickup truck with a camper top on it. Just make sure the engine and transmission are in good shape. We're going to have to make a 250-mile round-trip in it. I don't want it to stand out, but I do want it to run. One other item, an ultra-lite airplane capable of carrying three people. It has to be disassembled and packed in a box in the back of the truck. I'll get the rest."

"I'll see what I can do. I have a flying buddy that has several ultra-lites. So who were you talking to on the phone, Joe?"

"A very close Naval Intelligence black ops friend of mine. You may even know him."

"Why would you get the government involved, Joe? I thought this was covert. So who is it?"

"You said you didn't want to know, Judd. You'll find out soon enough. We're all staying at your place."

At 10:45 p.m., Judd dropped Feather off at the local FBI office. Joe had a lot of homework to do. Judd drove to his office to check on the statements taken from the Mexican Cartel soldiers. He marked the individual files to assign cases to his prosecutors and searched statements for any evidence he could use to convict Julio Cortez if, no, *when* Feather got him back on U.S. soil.

Several long-time members were among the captured Cartel prisoners. Some had been with Cortez for years and knew their boss would get them good lawyers and maybe bust them out completely. Judd knew these few wouldn't talk. His prosecutors would nail their hides to the wall. They were going down for capital murder of police officers. In the State of Texas, that was punishable by death by lethal injection at Huntsville State Prison.

Judd sat down in Martinez's chair in Martinez's office. If he was going to take over the D.A.'s job, there was no time like the present. Turning on the desk lamp, Judd picked up the phone and asked for copies of all statements taken from the Cartel group. A courier brought in a large brown envelope containing the statements. Judd pulled out a yellow marker and began to read over the statements, highlighting the name "Cortez" everywhere it appeared. It was going to be a long night.

A path was developing in the statements. The Cartel flunkies were singing like canaries. The few that had been with Cortez for a long time didn't say much. They didn't have to. The others were saying enough to put them all away, including Cortez. All Judd needed was Cortez on U.S. turf.

"Come in." Judd never looked up from the statements.

A short, cute, buxom brunette wearing jeans and a V-cut sweatshirt walked over to Judd and threw her arms around him, eye make-up running down her cheeks.

"I'm so sorry to hear about Paul and Dee and the others."

Judd pulled her close and held her for a moment before speaking.

"We're going to miss 'em around here, Maureen."

Maureen McAfee, a Jersey girl, had been Judd's secretary for eight of his fifteen years in the D.A.'s office. She was an extension of himself. She knew what documents he needed before he asked. Accredited as a paralegal after working for the sheriff's department for two years, she could make a computer do handsprings.

"I've been trying to track you down for two days, boss."

"Maureen, I'm never going to break you of calling me 'boss.' I guess now it's okay."

"You know that you and Feather are national heroes?" She poured two cups of coffee.

"What do you mean?"

"The news footage of the bust..." Maureen rocked back in her chair, quite pleased that she knew something Judd didn't. "It showed you crawling out to get Dee and Feather running out to get you. How's that hard head of yours?"

"I'm okay. It was only a scratch. Feather said the bullet bounced off." They both laughed.

"I called the hospital and your apartment. Where have you been?"

"Busy, Mom, real busy."

"Don't call me 'Mom,' boss. I'm thirty-four and holding. I'm not your mom."

"I figured that Erica Stone would hit the airwaves with the tapes she got."

"Gotta run, boss. I'll see you in the morning." Maureen left in high gear, her only speed.

Judd continued writing notes on the yellow stick-on pads, attaching them to the statements. He left them on Maureen's desk and put in a call to Feather.

"I'm out of here, Joe. How's the homework coming along?"

"Dee's work is going to pay off. I still have a couple of hours more, then I'll head your way."

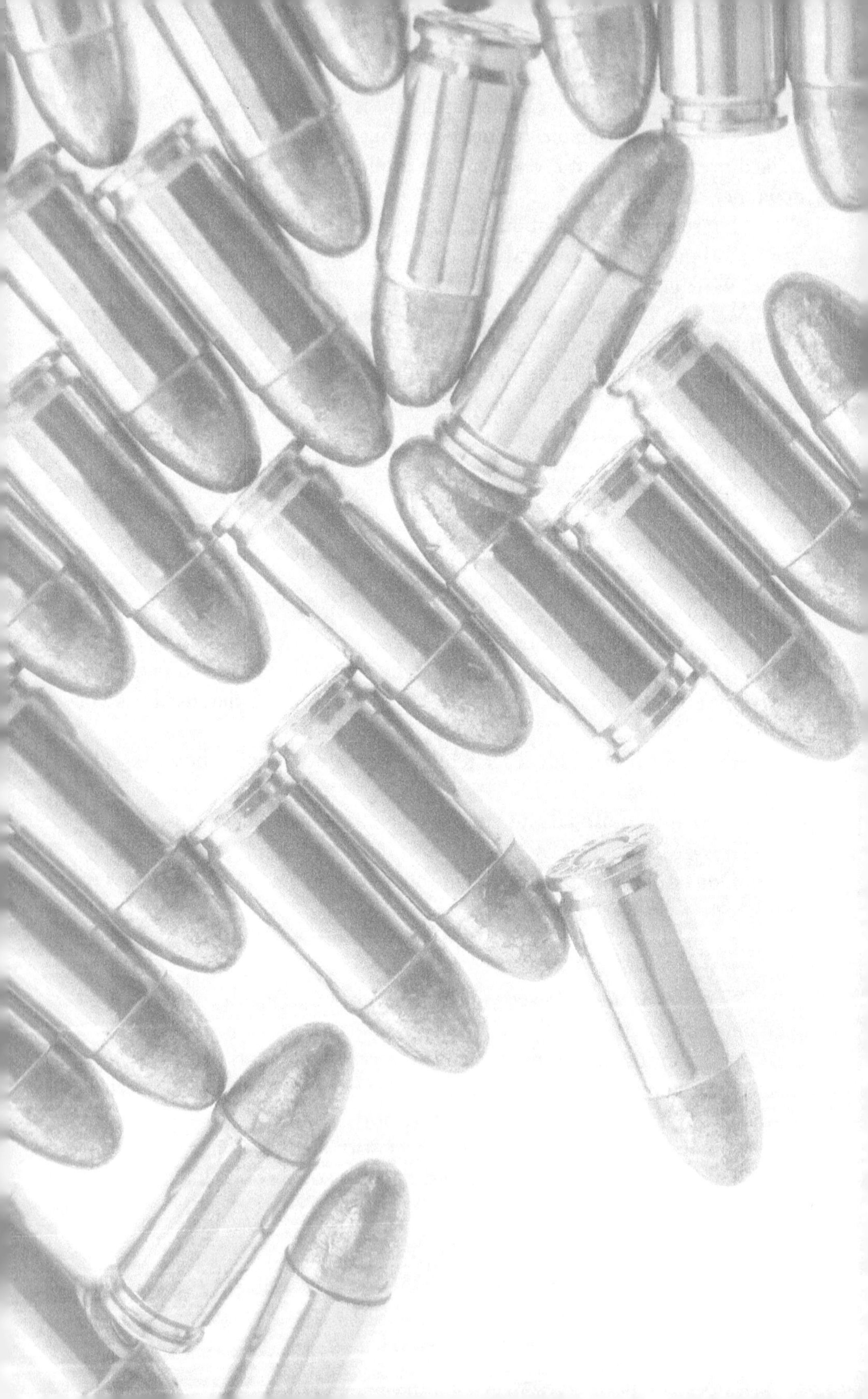

3

"HI, SCHOOLBOY!"

MAY 3RD

Commander Rikki Rhine's plane arrived forty-five minutes late. The sun was still high in the sky for 5:15 in the afternoon, still hot. Judd became concerned that Feather's Naval Covert Activities friend didn't make the flight. He kept waiting for Joe to say, "There he is." But as the plane emptied, still no reaction from Joe.

"You think he's on the flight, Joe?"

"Oh, sure." Feather had a less than confident look on his face. "Probably the last one off."

Finally, emerging from the walkway of the plane as if she were stepping off the QE II was Commander Rikki Rhine, a short, curvy lady looking like the other side of a million-dollar bill. At 5'5" and 110 pounds, her closely cropped, thick brown hair accented her tight, wrinkle-free skin. Judd's heart skipped a beat as he laid eyes on his old college sweetheart for the first time in years.

Rikki walked over to Feather and pinched him on the derriere with her left hand while she extended her right hand out to Judd.

"Long time no see, schoolboy!"

Judd could only muster a nod, feverishly searching for words to respond.

Rikki was wearing a tan suit with a cobalt-colored blouse and gold nugget cufflinks. Her scarf was tan Italian silk embroidered with a stylized hand at the bottom holding a golden sword, the point resting just under her throat.

"I've got a suitcase and a trunk," Rikki remarked. "We need a skycap."

They loaded the luggage and got in the car, which had, by now, an inside temperature of about a hundred and twenty degrees.

"A/C me, fast!" Rikki didn't have a shy bone in her body.

Back at Judd's apartment, Joe took Rikki's suitcase and put it in the spare bedroom. Judd and Feather brought the trunk inside. Rikki opened it and took out a small Igloo lunch kit, putting it in the freezer.

Judd had a puzzled look on his face. "What's inside the lunch kit, Rikki, my ole friend?"

"Party favors for Cortez and his gang. We couldn't pay this man a visit without bringing gifts." Rikki smiled and grabbed three beers out of the box. "I've got to change. Where do you want me?"

Feather pointed to the spare bedroom. Rikki went in, hung up her clothes and came back wearing a pair of cut-off blue-jean shorts and a T-shirt labeled "FLY NAVY."

"Let's get started. I need to be back in Washington in four days. We're working a big deal down in Puerto Rico. Got a flight into San Juan Friday afternoon."

What a bod, Judd thought, remembering how long it had been since their college love affair…remembering how long it had been since he had been with any woman.

For the next three hours, Feather brought Rikki up to speed on the blatant ambush pulled off by the Mexican Cartel and about Dee Espinoza.

At 10 p.m., it was time for a break. Judd put three steaks on the small barbecue pit out on the patio. Feather popped some spuds in the microwave.

"You've sure got a big sky out here." Rikki took a deep breath and looked up at the millions of stars.

"It's good to see you again, Rikki. You look great." Judd began turning the steaks. "How'd you wind up in Naval Intelligence?"

"Long story, Judd. I won Top Gun at Miramar and was given choice of assignment. So, in typical unconventional fashion, I chose Naval Intelligence." She took another sip of her beer. "My first love's still flying, though. I'm an F-18 Hornet driver when I'm not playing a spook for the Navy."

"It always was your first love, Rikki. Who's in second place right now? Feather?"

"Who knows? I always like to keep my options open. Let's change the subject. Beer's not exactly my drink. Got any Zinfandel?"

"In the fridge. I'll get you a glass."

Feather heard the microwave alarm. "Steaks about ready, Judd?"

"I'm taking 'em off the grill, now."

After they finished their meal and all were satisfactorily stuffed, the threesome moved back outside to the patio. Settling into the most comfortable

Wal-Mart-type lawn chair, Rikki looked around the grounds and then over to the apartment next door.

"Have you swept your place for bugs?" she asked.

"Every week. I had this place debugged yesterday." Judd replied.

"You guys got a snitch in the ranks." Rikki sized up situations quickly and was all business, except when she put on her flirting routine.

"We know. But we don't know who." Judd was agitated. "That's why this operation is just between the three of us."

"Divide and conquer."

"What's that?" Feather didn't know where Rikki was going with that statement.

"Joe, the Cartel, whether Mexican, Colombian, or Puerto Rican, works together for a common greed, to make lots of money so they can buy and do anything they want. Money is a great motivator and a heck of a common bond. We, on the other hand, are completely segmented. The FBI doesn't know what the CIA's doing, DEA doesn't know what the INS is doing and so on. What's worse, we don't care what the other agencies are doing. They just want to get on the eleven p.m. news…"

"Ten p.m. news, here," Feather added.

"Like I was saying, we're divided in our efforts to go up against a well-organized opponent. They have a plan and all their guys are on the same page. We, on the other hand, trip over each other. The sad part of the situation is that combined, under a common leadership, we could take these guys out in a year or two." Rikki sipped her wine. "But that's not going to happen, guys. We're going to continue winning a few little battles here and there and get an occasional 'atta boy' from the news, maybe a raise, and slowly watch our nation lose a war to drugs, crime, and money. The Cartel is kicking our butts. For one, I hate to lose anything, especially a war as important as this one."

"It's the same in the FBI," Feather added. "We always get there late and outgunned. Instead of support, we get red tape and paperwork."

Judd jumped into the conversation. "I convict 'em, two days later there are three more pushers on the streets to take their places. In a matter of months, the ones I send to prison get out on some early release program because the prisons are overcrowded."

"On top of it all," Rikki said as she stood up and stretched her tight little body, "the bad guys have the money and threats to suck in our agents and officers. We don't know who the baddies are anymore. Could be the guy next to us in the field, could be the brass up top. There's no communication among agencies because there is no trust between agencies."

"Yeah," Feather agreed, "I've been thrown under the bus more than once. We're fighting a war now that I'm not sure we can win."

There was silence. The unspeakable had been said. They cleaned up the dishes and went to their separate beds.

The sliding glass patio door opened slowly and quietly. Startled, Feather rose from the couch with his PPK aimed at Rikki's head.

"You're getting old, Indian," Rikki said nonchalantly.

"I can't believe I didn't hear you when you left. What time is it?"

"A little after 4 a.m." Rikki was perspiring. "When did you stop running in the morning, old man?"

"I can still take you!"

"Any time you want," Rikki said with a flirtatious wink. Feather smiled and walked into the kitchen. "You didn't make any coffee?"

"Didn't want to wake you, sleeping beauty. What time does Mr. D.A. roll his carcass out of the rack?"

"'Bout another hour. He needs to get some extra sleep." Feather sat down at the table with a cup of instant. "He's got quite a cat's butt over his right ear."

"Yeah, I saw you two heroes on the news. I was worried. That party didn't look like much fun."

"It wasn't."

"You'll like the party I have planned for Mr. Cortez." Rikki took a sip of orange juice.

"Party?" Joe asked.

"Sure! You said Julio is a wild and crazy guy. I want to PAR-TY with that animal."

"OK, no time like the present. What've you got in mind, pretty lady?" Feather was anxious to see what Rikki had in her trunk of tricks.

At 5:15, Judd walked into the kitchen.

"Bro, you ain't gonna believe what this lady has planned for our friend, Julio."

"I'm afraid to ask, so I won't." Judd's eyes were still heavy.

"Have you lined up the pickup and the ultra-lite?"

"Yeah. The truck's a 1992 Ford with a reworked Dodge Hemi engine. Belongs to a bootlegger out of Juarez we caught a couple of weeks ago. As for the ultra-lite, my friend came through. The five-hundred pound capacity is going to be a question mark. He may be able to put a bigger engine in it but that just adds more weight. It's going to be a stretch. Can either one of you fly it?"

"If it has wings or blades, I can fly it," Rikki replied confidently.

Judd dressed and went into the office. Feather and Rikki spent the day at the apartment going over maps, equipment, and photos. Between satellite pictures and flyovers by U.S. high altitude reconnaissance aircraft, they had a complete layout of Cortez's Mexico headquarters located seventy-five miles southwest of El Paso on a lake called Laguna de Santa Maria.

At 2:30 p.m. Judd drove the 1992 pale gray pickup back to the apartment and picked up Rikki and Feather. Next stop was the hangar where Judd kept the Eagle. When he slid open the door to the hangar, Rikki got hot flashes.

"She's beautiful!" Rikki walked over and ran her hand lightly over the multi-colored fabric covering of Judd's bi-plane. "I've seen a Christen Eagle in pictures, but never up close. I've got to fly her."

"She'll be gassed up and ready for you when you get back from wherever it is you're going. Let's figure out how to put this ultra-lite together."

For the next two and a half-hours, they assembled the tiny craft, tore it down, and reassembled it. Rikki cranked it up and made a couple of takeoffs and landings. Then came the big moment. All three of them got in it and on it. There were only two seats. Feather wedged himself between Judd and Rikki. She pushed the throttle full forward as they putted down the runway, gradually picking up speed. The little Honda engine sounded like a large gnat compared to the big two hundred-horse Lycoming engine Judd had in his plane.

Rikki eased back on the stick. The ultra-lite came off the runway, gained three feet of altitude and dropped back down to the runway.

"Gotta have more speed! The pucker factor was ten plus. Feather had a death grip on the tubular frame."

Two more bounces off the strip, each bounce higher than the one before. They were running out of runway. A patch of cactus fifty yards out from the end of the runway was beginning to focus in clearly.

"She's not going to fly with three people!" Judd tightened his seat belt. Feather hadn't said a word.

On the fourth big bounce, Rikki finessed the overweight craft up in the air. "Fly little baby! Fly!" She looked over at Judd and Joe with one of those "Did you ever doubt me" expressions. The boys were pale.

The landing went somewhat smoother than the takeoff. Judd's dislike for ultra-lites went up three notches. He was glad to get back on the ground. Feather still hadn't uttered a word.

They topped off the tank and disassembled the little "widow-maker" as Judd referred to it, and put it back in the crate. Everything was ready.

Joe and Rikki checked over their equipment at the apartment one last time and hit the rack about 6 p.m. One a.m. was zero hour for Operation Party Hearty.

4

PAR-TY

MAY 5TH

At half past midnight Judd, Joe and Rikki were up and dressed.

"I stuck a couple of fishing rods and a tackle box in the rear of the truck." Judd was wide awake. "You could have some trouble getting past the Mexican guards on the bridge going over to Juarez. Tell 'em you're going fishing and give 'em a five."

"Good idea," said Rikki. "Of course you're only guessing where we're going, right?"

"Right."

"Let's move, pretty lady. We may need this extra thirty minutes." Feather was calm and rested.

"Judd, Cortez will be at the border crossing at 6:30 a.m." Rikki was confident. "Make sure there are competent INS people on our side of the border who can recognize him."

"I'm sure the INS would love to give Mr. Cortez a big Texas welcome if he happened to pay us a visit." Judd had several concerns but now was not the time.

"Judd, it's very important that Cortez not see your face at the border. Not that he's going to remember it, but let's not take any chances of screwing this up in the final phase." Feather was still going over the plan.

Goodbyes were no more than silent handshakes. Feather and Rikki pushed the truck out of the driveway so as not to attract any attention, started the Hemi engine and drove off. Judd poured another cup of coffee and sat in the dark of his apartment.

1 a.m. — Rikki and Joe stopped at the U.S. side of the border crossing in El Paso, overlooking the Rio Grande River. Very little traffic for an early Tuesday morning. Feather was driving. INS officials turned off the videotape cameras that recorded ingress and egress across the border.

"State your nationality and reason for crossing," the INS guard said in a very official voice.

"USA. Going to do a little fishin'."

"Good luck." The guard motioned them on.

They drove across the bridge. A hundred yards ahead was the Mexican checkpoint. The night was cool.

"Buenos dias, amigos! What brings you to Me-he-co?"

Feather checked the Mexican side of the crossing. They didn't use video cameras. "We hear the fish are biting at Laguna de Guzman." Feather said in his best Tex-Mex Spanish.

"What's in the back of the truck, señor?" Mexican border guard talk for 'what are you going to give me not to harass you?'

Joe slipped the guard a five, smiled and said, "It's a big tent. If the fish are biting, we may stay a couple of days."

"Oh, gracias, señor, good fishing. You may pass."

1:18 a.m. — They drove through the sleepy streets of Juarez and hit Mexico Highway 45 at the south end of town.

1:50 a.m. — Feather and Rikki made their first checkpoint at Zaragoza right on time and were now south of Samalayuca. Another twenty-two miles to the cutoff and then west to Laguna de Santa Maria. They were busy checking the road ahead, constantly looking into the rearview mirrors. The highway was black; no other lights were in sight.

2:12 a.m. — Feather turned right onto the cutoff road full of potholes and bumps. As Rikki opened the Igloo lunch kit wedged between her feet, smoke from the dry ice cooled her face. She checked the tiny frozen darts inside. Quickly, gently, she closed the lid.

"They're okay."

"How long will the darts stay frozen before they begin to thaw and disintegrate?" Feather didn't remember her telling him that.

"Depending on ambient temperature, about fifteen to twenty seconds. We've got to locate our target and strike in that time span."

Rikki was mentally going over the layout of Cortez's villa.

"The wristband quivers hold twenty darts each and have a tiny liquid nitrogen balloon backing that will keep 'em frozen for an hour after we take 'em out of the cooler. Don't load the dart into the blowgun until you're ready to strike your target, Feather."

"Amazing, those lab men at Fort Belvoir. What kind of mind makes darts out of sugar crystals, then fills them with LSD and knock out drops? How long does the micky part take to put the victim to sleep?"

"Less than a second. It works on the nervous system. Doesn't give the target time to scream, fire a gun, nothing! He drops like a rock. The sugar dart dissolves, and, voila, no evidence." Rikki was speaking from experience.

2:41 a.m. — They reached the intersection of the private five-mile asphalt road leading to Cortez's villa. It was possibly the smoothest road in Mexico, built by Cortez with drug money. There was an unmanned security gate blocking the entrance. Video cameras were mounted on the trellis over the road.

"Remember, there are sensor alarms under the asphalt," Rikki reminded Feather.

They drove past the cutoff for three-quarters of a mile to the base of a mountain.

"Park behind that rock, Joe. We'll put the plane together here, roll it over to the road and fly right over the trellis."

3:01 a.m. — Rikki and Feather constructed the ultra-lite and changed into their black ninja suits. Following exact covert protocol, they checked each other's equipment. Weight was important, as they had experienced in their last ultra-lite plane ride. What if Cortez weighed a lot more than Judd? Records showed him to be about the same weight, barring his drinking half a keg of beer that night.

Rikki and Joe carried only pistols and two extra clips. They couldn't afford to get into a gun battle with the Cartel soldiers who greatly outnumbered and out-gunned them. In zippered leg pockets, they carried two eighteen-inch black blowguns and an electronic battery-powered desensitizer to neutralize alarm systems. Prior to strapping into the ultra-lite, Rikki opened the cooler and handed Feather two wrist quivers and a small flashlight.

Silently, they pushed the ultra-lite plane onto the road, nestled into the tiny craft and fastened their seatbelts.

The little Honda engine started immediately. Feather shined the tiny flashlight a few feet in front of them for Rikki to get a line on the highway. With a quick glance and two thumbs up, they were off. Phase II of Operation Party Hearty had begun.

3:21 a.m. — The takeoff was simple with only two people in the craft. Rikki looked at the small phosphorescent compass she had mounted between the seats to get her bearing. As planned, every fifteen seconds, Feather cupped his Pen Lite and shined it on the compass to keep it glowing. As they climbed to two hundred feet, both began panning for lights of Cortez's villa. They knew a manned gate was located five hundred yards in front of the main house. They would cut the engine and glide to a landing one hundred fifty yards from the gate, alongside the road. Reconnaissance photos had shown plenty of brush cover to hide the craft.

3:25 a.m. — Lights sighted. Rikki cut the engine and glided down.

3:28 a.m. — Out of the plane, Joe and Rikki made their way to within ten yards of the lighted guardhouse, careful to stay in the darkness surrounding the lights.

3:33 a.m. — Rikki held up three fingers to Joe signifying three guards. Feather nodded, keeping his eyes on her for further instructions. She pointed left and then to herself. Feather nodded. She pointed to Feather and then to the right. Feather acknowledged. Rikki pointed to the middle guard and back to herself. A nod.

Slowly, almost without motion, Feather and Rikki took out the blowguns and edged closer to their targets. They opened their wrist quivers and each inserted a frozen, sugar-crystal dart as the clock ticked on the tiny, fragile, laced projectiles. They had fifteen to twenty seconds to make their shot.

As if a track starter's pistol had fired, Rikki and Feather simultaneously puffed into the blowguns. Feather's man went down with a neck shot. The other fell with the dart in his ear. For a second, the third guard laughed, thinking his friend had tripped and fallen. That was all the time Rikki needed to reload. The middle guard grabbed his nose and slumped facedown across his desk inside the guard shack.

3:40 a.m. — Judd looked at his watch. He couldn't get interested in the 1940s late movie he had on the TV and wished he was with Joe and Rikki. Anything was better than waiting and wondering. He had no earthly idea what they were doing.

3:41 a.m. — Rikki and Feather ran and crawled to within fifteen yards of the base of the villa. The two stayed close to each other in order to get and give signals. It was a known fact Cortez was not as paranoid about his safety as some of the other Colombian drug lords. Dee Espinoza had written in one of his reports, "Cortez enjoys astronomy. He loves to look up into the heavens and will not allow his home to look like a prison. Lights would destroy the capabilities of his very expensive telescopes."

Aerial photos confirmed no floodlights had been installed. The villa was built into the side of a small hill. The front of the house had less of a slope leading up to it than in the back where a large pool and deck area, well landscaped, cantilevered over a descending hill.

Two men were standing at the front of the house guarding a Cadillac limo and a stretch Mercedes. As Rikki and Feather got closer to them, they could hear music coming from the pool area in back. Two puffs on the blowguns, two job openings for chauffeurs. Silently, they moved down the front side of the hill and around to the back.

From the looks of things, there had been a heck of a party out around the pool. Beer cans and broken booze bottles were everywhere and loud Mexican music played on the stereo. A naked man and two lovely señoritas were splashing and laughing in the pool. Five guards huddled in two groups near the outer fringes of the wooden decked areas adjacent to the pool. The party was winding down.

3:45 a.m. — Cortez was not outside. Rikki and Joe figured he was probably up in the master suite of the luxurious two-story hacienda. They positioned themselves under the deck after surveying the patio above. The plan was simple: take the group of three guards first.

They aimed. *Puff. Puff.* Feather's target faltered over into the bushes. Rikki's man did not go down. There was only a "ping" sound after she fired at the man's neck. The guard had lifted his left hand to swat a mosquito. The sugar dart hit his ring and shattered, splashing tiny fragments of sugar crystal in his eye with LSD-laced knock-out drops. Instead of laughing like the guard at the gate had done, the third guard in the group wheeled around and tightened his grip on the Uzi in his right hand and walked towards the edge of the deck.

Cunning as she was, Rikki quickly reloaded her blowgun and put another dart into her missed target. Feather waited under the deck as the alert third guard leaned over the rail, Uzi extended in front of him. Feather puffed the blowgun straight up above him, putting the dart under the man's chin. As the guard's knees buckled, Joe reached up over the deck floor and grabbed the Uzi before it hit the wood floor and made enough noise to signal the other two guards on the right edge of the pool area.

Thankfully, they were engrossed in watching the splashing and thrashing of their compadre in the pool who was, by now, engaged in an underwater ceremony that only Neptune himself could have experienced. His two señorita companions were experts in administering human pleasures.

3:53 a.m. — Like silent stalkers, Joe and Rikki moved around to the right to take out the last two coherent guards standing on the grass adjacent to the deck. Feather was feeling confident in his aim by now. He took a shot at his designated man but was about three feet out of range. The dart hit the man's pants leg. In an instant, the guard swatted the place where the dart hit thinking it was just another mosquito. In doing so, he pushed the point of the dart into his leg. The Uzi dropped on the grass, and so did he.

Rikki and Joe purposely left the three in the pool for last. Their intentions were not to drown those two lovely señoritas, just cancel their party. Rikki and Feather moved closer to the edge of the pool, careful to stay in the shadows. Rikki hit the man in the back of the shoulder blades as he went under. The two beautiful ladies followed in underwater, laughing and giggling. Feather and Rikki had to wait until the two lovelies came up for air to turn out their lights.

Feather grabbed the long safety hook at the edge of the pool and pulled the two unconscious girls, one by one, over onto the steps in the shallow end of the pool. As he reached down for Neptune's buddy, he heard a noise coming from the house. Feather released the guy in the pool and moved over to the back entrance of the house. Rikki was already stationed on the other side of the doorframe. Feather looked back at the man floating face down in the pool and then over at Rikki. Both just shrugged. Poetic justice. Let him drown, they decided.

3:55 a.m. — The shrieking noise from inside the house subsided. Opening the door, Feather entered first, crawling quickly next to the wall. It looked like a kitchen, food everywhere, enough to feed half the starving children in Mexico. Luckily, most of the guests had already gone home. Peeking through the swinging door leading into the dining room, Feather could see two men asleep on the couch in the adjoining sunken living room. The house was beautiful. He looked back over his shoulder to motion to Rikki. She was standing straight up in the kitchen, chewing on a chicken leg. Feather couldn't believe the coolness of this lady. Rikki smiled a hillbilly smile at Feather with the chicken leg sticking out of her mouth.

Feather giggled silently as he pointed to the living room. He held up two fingers and then folded his hands together and rested his head on them to tell Rikki of the two sleeping men. She nodded and casually strolled into the dining room past Feather, taking her time as she darted both sleepers.

Cautiously, they made their way up the stairs to the master bedroom, checking each room as they went down the hall. Two more people were asleep in one of the bedrooms. Making sure they didn't wake, Feather played sandman.

Screams cranked up again from down the hallway. There was action in the master bedroom suite. Feather looked under the closed door but saw no light. Rikki pulled a vial out of one of her pockets and oiled the hinges of the bedroom door. Feather slowly turned the knob. It was locked. From another pocket, Rikki took out her lock tools and opened the door.

There was Mr. Julio Cortez, flashing them with his best side. Rikki motioned to Feather to let her shoot. She took a red-colored dart from the quiver. This one had no knock out drops in it, just LSD. She hit Cortez at the base of the skull so the LSD would act faster. Cortez never noticed as he continued his amorous bedside assault on his chosen lovely lady. Rikki watched as Feather low-crawled alongside the bed.

Feather took a dart in his left hand, reached over the top of the mattress, feeling the señorita's derriere, and pushed the dart into her cheek. Standing up alongside the bed, Feather gently kissed her goodnight while looking back at Rikki with a Fonzerelli smile. Dazed under the influence of the fast acting LSD, Cortez did not mind sharing. He saw Feather, looked right at him and smiled. Feather smirked back.

Waiting the few minutes for the LSD to fully grip Cortez, Feather and Rikki went back downstairs and checked the rest of the house. Rikki found the security room where all the camera screens were located and booked one more passenger for the magical mystery tour. The screens showed two guards in suits walking up the hill from the backside of the patio. For the first time, Rikki realized that they could've been seen earlier as they came up into the back pool area.

The two suited guards were still about one hundred yards away from the house, unsuspecting of anything going on because the music outside was still blaring away. The guards were not moving in any defined direction. Upstairs, Cortez was beginning to howl at the moon. The LSD was working its magic.

4:05 a.m. — "Feather," Rikki whispered. It was the first words she had spoken since they got out of the ultra-lite. "There are still a couple of guards back down the hill from the pool. Let's get Cortez and get outta here."

They went back upstairs, put a pair of pants on Cortez as he flailed around the room as if he were chasing butterflies.

"I think Julio is glad to see us, don't you?" Rikki was being her usual charming self again.

Feather didn't talk. He put Cortez's arm over his shoulder and headed down the stairs with Rikki on the other side.

As they walked out the front door with their prisoner, the alarm went off.

"Get him in the Cadillac!" Rikki yelled.

Joe piled Cortez in the back seat as Rikki ran around to the driver's side. The keys were in the ignition.

She looked up, turned the key and took off down the driveway. Just as suddenly, she slammed on the brakes.

"What the.." yelled Feather.

"Don't want those two thugs chasing us." Rikki backed up to the Mercedes, pulled out her pistol and shot out both tires on the driver's side of the Benz, and then took off as the two Cartel guards came racing around from the back yard. Cortez was lying down on the back floorboard. The two guards opened up on Feather and Rikki with Uzis.

Rikki turned around to Feather in the back seat and broke into a wide Cheshire cat smile as she raced down the road, "Check out the bulletproof glass. Don't you just love it?"

Feather shook his head.

The guards jumped into the Mercedes and chased after them on the rims, sparks flying in the night. As Rikki approached the gate, she floor boarded the big Cadillac and sent the gate flying in opposite directions when they hit. Julio Cortez was sitting up in the back seat mumbling something in Spanish. Feather couldn't make it out. Cortez, tripping on the LSD, couldn't quite figure out what was going on, either.

4:10 a.m. — Rikki had a three-minute lead on the spark-throwing Mercedes when she pulled off the road near the ultra-lite plane. She and Feather left Cortez in the car while they ran over to the ultra-lite and pushed it onto the road. The sparks from the Mercedes were getting closer.

"Get him in, hurry!" Rikki yelled as she cranked on the Honda. It didn't start. She cranked and cranked but the motor wouldn't start as Joe loaded Cortez onto the aircraft.

"One more try and I'm getting back in the Caddy," Feather screamed as he unbuckled his seatbelt.

One more attempt and the Honda engine started singing.

"Hold on to him, Joe." Rikki was rolling down the highway.

"I've got him! Just get us in the air! Those guys are almost on top of us!" Feather yelled.

The Mercedes was about seventy-five yards behind them as the ultra-lite picked up speed.

"Shoot out their radiator, Joe!" Rikki pulled back on the stick, trying her best to coax the overloaded go-cart with wings into the air. They started to bounce up and down. Feather got off five rounds at the Mercedes. It began to swerve. He could see steam blowing past the headlights. The bouncing got higher but the overloaded craft came down each time. Cortez didn't seem to mind anything right now. He was just checking out the night.

"Where are they?" Rikki was having a difficult time keeping the bounces on the highway.

"They're falling back," hollered Feather.

"This damn thing ain't going to fly and I'm tired of bouncing. Julio, you fat ass!"

Rikki let off on the throttle and landed the bounce. They were smoking down the middle of the highway doing eighteen miles per hour when the lights behind them disappeared. She turned the little craft back into the wind and finally became airborne at they flew over the trellis and landed near the truck.

4:30 am. — Judd had been dressed for an hour. He couldn't stand to wait in his apartment any longer. They must be on their way back by now, he thought. He got in his car, stopped at an all-night diner for a cup of coffee, and then drove to the bridge crossing.

5:15 a.m. — Judd pulled up to the Immigration and Naturalization Service's offices about one hundred yards from the crossing and walked straight into the office of Willard Harrison, a twenty-five year veteran of the INS and a trusted friend.

"Heard from your boy Cortez?"

"Not a word, but, then, I didn't expect to. I'm just killing some time, couldn't sleep. Got any coffee?" Judd was anxious.

Harrison, wiping the sleep from his eyes, poured the coffee into a styro foam cup.

6:15 a.m. — Rikki, Feather and Cortez were within a mile of the Rio Grande bridge crossing. They had the disassembled ultra-lite packed in the crate and were ending a leisurely drive back to the border. Still in ninja costume, they were having fun with Julio, who by now was spaced out from the LSD.

"Julio, ole buddy, do you like drugs?" Rikki asked.

"Si!"

"Do you like to kill people?"

"Si!"

"Do you want to go to Huntsville and party with us?"

"Si!"

"Well, in about two minutes me and my good friend are going to get out of this truck and let you walk across that bridge up there with all the pretty lights. Would you like to do that, Julio?"

"Si, señora! Then we go to Huntsville and get more girls…"

6:28 a.m. — Rikki stopped the truck about ten yards in on the Mexican side of the bridge. She and Feather got out of the truck, helped Julio out and pointed him in the direction of the border crossing. They taped a ten dollar bill to his forehead. Rikki and Feather stood in the middle of the road watching Cortez trying to negotiate his way to the border crossing, laughing, tears rolling down their cheeks.

Cortez, barely able to walk, slowly staggered himself into the lane leading up to the Mexican guard shack. The same old Mexican guard was still on duty as Julio staggered alongside. He nodded and smiled as he went past the guard. The barely awake Mexican border guard nodded and smiled as he peeled the ten dollar bill off Julio's forehead and motioned him on by.

6:30 a.m. — Cortez hit the guardrails on both sides of the road as he weaved his way over the Rio Grande to the American side. Judd was watching for the truck from Harrison's office window. Harrison was outside at the guard gate.

As the drugged-out Cortez zigzagged up to the INS guard shack, he looked up at Harrison, "I'm on my way to Huntsville. Can you tell me how to get there, Señor?"

"Just step right over here, Mr. Cortez. I'm sure we can show you the way," Harrison said facetiously as he cuffed Cortez, read him his rights, and took him into custody.

When Cortez was out of sight, Judd came running up to the guard shack looking for Rikki and Feather.

"Señor? Señorita? You said you were going fishing. But I didn't know you were scuba divers. I thought you would catch them on the rod and reels." The Mexican guard was baffled as he looked at Rikki and Feather in their ninja suits.

"New style of fishing," Rikki said as she gave the guard a five.

"Sure, amigos, you may cross. Did you catch any fish?" he yelled.

"Just one," Feather said.

"How big?"

Rikki held her arms outside the truck, outstretched horizontally, "About this big."

Judd saw the old truck coming across the bridge. As it got closer, he could see Feather and Rikki grinning ear to ear. He couldn't believe they pulled it off. He couldn't believe that Cortez freely, without reluctance, walked across that bridge.

5

WORKING UNDER COVERS

Before 10 a.m., Cortez was fingerprinted, had his mug shot taken with a big smile and moved to a private cell in the county jail. Judd knew several hours must pass before Cortez would be coherent enough to know where he was. All the warrants and paperwork were in order. No interrogation was done until Cortez had his lawyer present; Judd was taking no chances of a legal screw-up on this one. So far, no announcements of Cortez's incarceration had been made and wouldn't until later that night. Judd returned to his house. Joe and Rikki were just getting up from a short nap.

"How's our party buddy?" Rikki sipped on some orange juice.

"He's feeling no pain right now." Judd poured a cup of coffee. "Mr. Cortez is back in his cell staring at all the graffiti on the walls, happy as a lark."

"Judge Simpson will arraign him later this afternoon, Joe. I've got a press conference scheduled for nine tonight." A thousand things were going through Judd's mind. "It's going to be a busy evening."

"You've got that right. Your turn to do an all-nighter." Rikki yawned. "This crazy Indian and I need to make our exit, don't want any trails leading back to us. I'm hopping a ride out of Fort Bliss back to Washington about 2:30 this afternoon."

"I've got a chopper coming down from Las Cruces at 3:15 to get me back to the FBI offices in New Mexico. Can I get a ride out to the airport?"

"Might be better for you to take a taxi, Joe."

"You're right. I'll be back Friday afternoon. We made all the arrangements for Dee's funeral this morning. It's scheduled for Saturday. Wanted to make it on a weekend so most everyone would be able to attend." Feather had been busy. "I left all the details with Maureen. She's getting the word out."

"Thanks, Joe. I know Dee would have wanted you to handle it since he has no family." Judd looked over at Rikki. "We'll pitch a rose on his casket for you."

When Judd returned to his office, two of the assistant D.A.s were waiting in his outer room.

"We've got more good news," one of them said.

"I'm ready for good news." Judd motioned them in his office.

"We've got the video back from the SWAT team cameraman. He was alert enough to take a close-up of the chopper that dropped Dee." The assistant slid the video into Judd's VCR. "Watch right here. Look who's cutting the rope, Mr. Julio Cortez himself. We've got him cold!"

Judd just watched and nodded his head, gazing out his window for a moment in deep thought.

"Hate to pull rank on you guys, but I'm going to prosecute Cortez, myself." Judd's anger was apparent.

Judd and the two assistant D.A.s walked out of his office.

"I'm going over to the photo lab for a couple of hours, Maureen. Call if you need me."

"Okay, boss." Maureen never looked up from her computer as she typed Judd's announcement speech for the press conference later that night.

As the elevator doors to the parking garage swung open, Judd was startled.

"Hi, Mr. District Attorney."

"Ms. Stone, how did you get down here? The parking area is supposed to be secure from civilians."

"I was coming to see you, but I got in the down elevator and wound up here. Since I've caught you, I did want to talk to you about some missing footage my cameraman shot at the bust. You guys are good. Our video technicians almost never found the cuts. Let's have it!"

"Ms. Stone..."

"Call me Erica," The attractive blonde reporter interrupted as she gave Judd a sexy glance. "Can I call you Judd?"

"Right now, Ms. Stone, eh, Erica, I'm very busy and would rather you not call me at all. There's going to be a press conference tonight at nine. Now, you're the first newsperson to know that. You have a scoop."

"Press conference? What's the topic? Are there new developments in the case?"

"That's all I can say right now. I'm really in a hurry."

"The tapes, we haven't discussed the tapes. I'm not going to let you off that easy."

"I'll talk to you about the tapes after the press conference."

"Fine, meet me at Angelo's Steakhouse at ten. Dinner's on me."

This was not the first time Erica had tried to get close to Judd for reasons other than business.

"Ten sharp." Judd snapped, "Get a booth in the back."

Erica was not hard to look at. Gracefully standing 5' 8" and 128 pounds, she had been a former Miss El Paso and second runner-up in the Miss Texas pageant ten years earlier. She was single and kept herself looking good for her viewers.

Why not? Judd thought, catching a glimpse of her long friendly legs as her blonde hair danced against her sheer blue blouse.

Erica was the one caught off guard now. That was too easy. Either she had Judd over a barrel with the tapes or maybe, just maybe, she had aroused his male interest. Finally!

Judd returned to his office about five p.m. The place was a madhouse. He walked past the hordes of news people in the hallway, sticking microphones in his face, shouting questions, and snapping pictures. The word was out on the upcoming press conference and everyone wanted to be first to get the details. They surrounded him. He was virtually unable to move.

"Wait just a minute! I've told everyone there will be a conference later tonight. That's it until then." Pushing his way through the crowd, Judd entered his outer office.

"Maureen, I need you to type my…"

"News conference speech, yes, sir." Maureen had the speech in her hand, following Judd into his office. "Just make corrections on this." She handed the speech to Judd.

"Messages?"

"Seventy-three."

"Important ones?"

"Judge Ramirez wants to see you in the morning in his chambers." Maureen was sifting through the handful of pink message slips to put on Judd's desk.

"What does the honorable Judge Ramirez want?"

"To talk about the Cartel guys, scheduling, evidence, who's assigned to prosecute the cases, that stuff." She handed the stack of calls to Judd. "By the way, boss, who's Erica? She just called from downstairs and said the reservations are for 10:30 tonight. Is there something you should be telling me?"

"No! Get the schedule ready for me. I want to make a good impression on the judge. This is our first meeting since I became the D.A.."

"Erica, huh? Could that be Erica Stone, famous, gorgeous, TV news reporter with blonde hair down to where her legs come up to? Pardon my grammar," Maureen said tapping her foot with both hands on her hips.

"The schedules, Ms. McAfee."

Maureen headed for the door, paused, looked over her shoulder at Judd. "I'll expect a full report on my desk by eight o'clock in the morning about your date with Ms. Stone, Mr. Rayburn."

At 8:30 p.m. Judd was going over the final corrections on his announcement with Maureen. She had changed into her best business suit and fixed her makeup. She loved to be on TV standing just behind Judd with practically any document he would need during Q and A sessions following the press conferences.

"That's what I want to say. No more changes, Maureen."

"I'm glad we're back on a first name basis, boss. My landlord is the only one that calls me Ms. McAfee, and then only when my rent is past due."

"What time is it?"

"You've got twenty minutes before you have to go out there and face the wolves. Just kick back and relax. I'll give you a five minute curtain call."

Maureen returned to the outer office where a dozen assistant D.A.s, members of the FBI, and others involved in the bust were standing around, suited up for the conference. She distributed copies of the announcement to each one and sat back down at her desk.

"Five minutes till break a leg time." Maureen walked up to Judd and straightened his tie, pulled out her compact and powdered the shine off of his nose. Judd gave no resistance. The entire law enforcement group walked out to the podium as Maureen made the introductions.

"The District Attorney for Pecos County, Mr. Judd Rayburn, will issue a statement updating latest developments in the recent apprehension of several members of a Mexican Drug Cartel, allegedly headed by a Mr. Julio Cortez Villa. Mr. Cortez was able to escape from the confrontation that occurred earlier this week at Ambush Pass where eight members of a combined law enforcement group lost their lives. If you will hold your questions until after

Mr. Rayburn's statement, there will be a short Q & A period that follows. Thank you. Mr. Judd Rayburn."

"At approximately 6:30 this morning, Mr. Julio Cortez Villa, a citizen of Mexico, wanted by the United States and the State of Texas for capital murder and other drug related charges, was apprehended by members of the Immigration and Naturalization Service at the United States entry pavilion on the U.S. side of the Rio Grande River bridge. Mr. Cortez walked through the Mexican checkpoint and proceeded alone and unaided across the bridge to the U.S. side of his own free will. He was read his Miranda rights and taken into custody. Arraignment before a U.S. Magistrate occurred earlier this afternoon, the Honorable Brent Simpson presiding. Mr. Cortez has been arraigned under multiple charges including first degree capital murder of U.S. law enforcement officers in relation to illegal drug activities. That concludes our statement. Questions?"

"Mr. Rayburn, are you telling us that Cortez just walked across the border and voluntarily turned himself in to authorities?" a reporter asked facetiously.

"Actually, as per INS statements from the transcript of their dialogue with Mr. Cortez," Judd said turning for copies of the INS reports. "His exact words were 'I'm on my way to Huntsville. Can you tell me how to get there, Señor?'"

"Was he drunk?" another reporter asked.

"Mr. Cortez seemed to be under the influence. We administered a breathalyzer test to him. Results showed point two eight. In the State of Texas the law states you are legally intoxicated at point zero eight. So, to answer your question, yes, Mr. Cortez was drunk when he crossed the border."

"Did the INS officers help Mr. Cortez out with directions to Huntsville?" Erica Stone asked, laughing.

"I assure you, Ms. Stone," Judd mentioned her name on purpose for the national press she would gain, and, maybe to help him out of his bad position later, "the INS officers will be most helpful directing Mr. Cortez to Huntsville or La Tunia Federal Correctional facility near here as soon as our office is finished with him."

The group of news people laughed and then kept plugging questions.

"Judd!" shouted the CBS affiliate reporter, "How's your head wound coming along? What have the doctors said?"

"My wound is healing very well. Thanks for asking."

Judd had the media in his hip pocket and they liked being there. Their hero was saying just the right things. Cameras zoomed in on the bandage around his head and faded to black.

Questions were still flying when Judd and the other members of his team ducked into the privacy of his outer office.

"Hey, boss, it's 10:15. Ms. Blonde and Beautiful awaits you. You're gonna be late."

"Thanks, Maureen."

Judd left the office and drove to Angelo's. He knew the maitre d' by name and called him on his cell phone.

"Johnny! This is Judd Rayburn. I'll be dining with you tonight. Can you let me in the back? Newspaper guys…"

"No problem, Mr. Rayburn, just knock twice and tell them Johnny sent you."

Judd parked his noticeable black-on-black-in-black Chrysler near the rear of the parking lot. Johnny was at the rear of the restaurant to greet him.

"Thanks, Johnny, I'm meeting a friend. I can find my own way from here." Judd was a little uncomfortable with this meeting.

"I'll show you to Ms. Stone's table." Johnny pointed the way for him. When he walked up to the very secluded, round corner booth he looked over at Erica, stunned. She had changed out of her business clothes into a very low cut, black velvet evening dress. The booth was not the only well-rounded object in the room. Her pearl necklace lay beautifully against her tan chest. The pearl and diamond earrings sparkled against her blonde hair that flowed down over her bare shoulders like a waterfall at sunset.

"You look maavelous, dalink," Judd said, almost out of breath.

"I'll take that as your first compliment." Erica patted the spot next to her so Judd would be sitting close from the start. Johnny poured the champagne as Judd slid around next to her and panned the room for photographers.

"A toast to our future success." Erica said with an inviting look in her eyes.

Judd lifted his glass. The champagne felt cool against his dry throat. He needed the moment to regroup. Sucking down a beer would have been even better.

Trying to make conversation, Judd looked at Erica. "It just dawned on me, who's anchoring the ten o'clock news tonight?"

"Sammy Tate." Erica was looking deep into Judd's eyes with her big blues. "We didn't know how long the press conference would last. I've taped my segment. Besides, I told them I would be working under covers tonight."

"Did you say covers?" Judd blurted out as his champagne went down the wrong way.

Laughing, toweling the champagne from Judd's chin with her napkin, Erica said, "We can either go into the missing footage or, we can have a nice quiet evening, just the two of us. You look like you've had a hard day. Your choice."

Judd wiped his nose and took a moment to compose himself. "Touché. A nice, quiet evening, just the two of us."

Erica poured the next of several glasses of champagne. They laughed, they dined, they drank, and they left. As for the missing footage, it was still missing, at least for the evening.

MAY 8TH

"Good morning, boss. You only have half an hour till your report is due." Maureen handed Judd his morning cup of coffee.

"What report?"

"The report you were instructed to have on my desk by eight a.m. You know, a blow-by-blow description of your evening with the former Miss El Paso. By the way, how'd it go?"

"Very well. Enjoyable."

"She said the same thing in her card." Maureen had that *I know something that you don't* sound in her voice.

"What card?

"The one attached to the single red rose on your desk that was delivered ten minutes ago."

"Are you reading my correspondence now, Maureen?"

"I always have. Besides, coming from Erica Stone, it could have been a miniaturized letter bomb." She handed the rose to Judd and read the card aloud.

"'Dear Judd, thanks for a wonderful evening. You made a good choice, Erica.' What choice, boss?"

"The choice whether or not to keep a nosey secretary around or not. What time is my meeting with Judge Ramirez?"

"At nine in his chambers. I have all the scheduling ready."

"I'm going back to the photo lab on my way to see the Judge. While I'm out, call the district attorney's office in Los Angeles. Have them Fed Ex the transcripts of the Jackson case to me. You know, the case of the videoed police officers beating on the black man that caused all the riots out there." Judd was out the door, still working on his first cup of coffee.

After his meeting with the judge, Judd returned to his office at 11:15 a.m.. It was a madhouse. He walked past several assistant D.A.s and a room full of defense lawyers, most of whom were representing the Cartel soldiers. He entered his office with Maureen right behind him, along with Daryl Thompson, senior assistant D.A.

"Update me, Daryl." Judd knew what was going on, but wanted details.

"So far, three lead defense attorneys have been retained to represent the Cartel soldiers."

"Who?"

"DeGrasse and Jamail."

"That should set the Cartel back a few bucks." Judd was not surprised. He'd been up against this firm many times on drug cases involving the Cartel in Mexico. They were good. "Are they also representing Cortez?"

"No way." Thompson spoke with concern. "Rosen, Jacobs, LaRue is representing Cortez. Rumor has it that they're getting three million up front. Money is going to be transferred sometime today."

"Daryl, intercept it. Call Davis over at the IRS. Have him get his men on this. Cortez is paying Rosen, Jacobs and LaRue with drug money. Have some of our paralegals hit the law books with chapter, verse and case. File briefs with Judge Ramirez. I want Cortez and his bunch represented by Public Defenders as lead whether or not Rosen, Jacobs and LaRue choose to remain backup. Do the same with DeGrasse and Jamail. We've got to walk the tightrope on this one. Thank God for 21 U.S. Code, Section 858. If we can get that drug money, we can use it in our prosecution efforts. I want that money!"

6

DUCK!

Finally back in his apartment, alone, Judd had experienced all the shooting, killing, newspaper reporters, not to mention doctors poking at him that he could handle for one day. Sleep was becoming such a luxury. Judd stretched out on his couch. *When was the pain and misery going to end?* Judd wondered as he drifted off to sleep…

At 9:30 p.m. his phone rang. "Hello."

"Judd? Judge Ramirez. How're you doing?"

Sitting up, rubbing his eyes, "Just fine, Judge."

"I've been thinking about our discussion this morning. I believe we're going to run into several jurisdictional problems."

"I know, Your Honor. I've been going over it in my mind, also. The Feds want Cortez for Dee's death. I don't want any screw ups on this. I was there. I, personally want to prosecute Cortez and the rest of his gang. The Federal Prosecutor's office may nail him and they may not. I want him, Your Honor. What can we do?"

"We all want them, Judd. Let me ask you a very important question that could have a large effect on your future."

"Go ahead."

"Just how important is prosecuting Cortez to you?"

"Judge, Cortez killed Dee with his own two hands. He cut the rope. I had to tell Martinez's wife, Pilar, and his three kids their husband and daddy wasn't coming home again! How important is Cortez to me, Judge? Whatever it takes."

"Would you be willing to temporarily give up the District Attorney job and be designated as a Special Assistant U.S. Federal Attorney?"

Still a little groggy from his two hours of sleep, the Judge's question caught Judd off guard.

"I'm sorry, Your Honor, I'm not exactly on the same page with you. Could you explain where you're going?"

"Judd, you want to prosecute Cortez and the other cartel members we have in custody all at once in the same courtroom, right?"

"Sounds kind of crazy, Judge, but when you think of all the advantages we discussed this morning, it makes sense."

"I've spent the entire day going over all of the points you made, Judd. After careful consideration, especially on not tying up the court for years, plus the money it would cost the taxpayers, I agree with you. However, as District Attorney for Pecos County, that would cross over into federal territory. As Special Assistant U.S. Federal Attorney working for Randall Erin, U.S. Attorney for the Western District of Texas, it could be done."

Judd had only been the D.A. for six days. Now he was confronted with giving it up. Was Cortez worth it?

"Judge, as usual, you ask some very simple, deep questions."

"This particular question I asked requires much thought. I don't want an answer now. I only want you to do some serious thinking. When you have an answer, call me."

"Thanks for calling, Your Honor. You'll be hearing from me soon."

It was 10 p.m. and time for the local news. Judd grabbed the remote and turned on the TV to Erica's newscast. Every other word out of Erica's mouth, it seemed, was "Judd Rayburn."

Halfway through the news, the phone rang again.

"Rayburn speaking."

"Hey, Bro, I heard you have a new girlfriend."

"Joe, what time are you arriving Saturday?"

"Typical lawyer, always changing the subject. You must be taking good care of Ms. Stone."

"She's a separate subject I'll discuss later. So when're you getting in?"

"I'll be in about nine Saturday morning. I'll meet you at the cemetery."

"Let's change the subject again. What do you know about Randall Erin?" Judd asked.

"The federal prosecutor for the Western District?"

"The very same."

"He's a stand-up guy and one heck of a prosecutor, Judd."

"Do you trust him? Have you worked with him much?"

"Yes, to both questions. If the federal prisons were unlocked, his life wouldn't be worth a plug nickel. He's got a very high conviction rate with some bad hombres on his win list. Why?"

"I had a meeting with Judge Ramirez this morning about taking the whole Cartel gang down in one big trial. I can't prosecute all of them as the D.A. of Pecos County, but I can as a Fed."

"Big decision."

"Yeah it is. I'll talk to you about it more Saturday at the funeral."

"Consider something, Judd." Feather said sternly. "The federal level of prosecution has its pros and cons. We hit on that briefly when Rikki was there. Erin is fully capable of convicting Cortez and his people. You've just been made District Attorney and I know how much that means to you. If you go federal, you'll be living out of a suitcase. You'll also be introduced to a brand new type of red tape you haven't dealt with in the past. Cortez is only one drug dealer. There will be more."

"I appreciate your input, as usual. The federal position would be temporary. Dee and Martinez were good men that won't be here anymore. I want Cortez to look up at me when he's strapped down on the table and they put that lethal needle in his arm. I want him to see Dee's picture and Martinez's picture as he steps on that southbound train."

"Sounds to me like you already have your mind made up. Take some more advice and sleep on it a day or two before you decide, Bro."

"I will. See you Saturday. Are you going to stay over the weekend?"

"I think I'd better."

Judd's cell started to ping with a voice message.

"Judd? Erica. How's that hard head of yours? Could there be a little Dom Perignon bubbling from your bandage? Seriously, I did want to see if you were all right. I'll be at the station till 11:30. Call me."

"The rose!" Judd remembered. "I didn't even call her to thank her for the rose." He dialed the phone.

"Erica Stone, please."

"Who should I say is calling?" the station operator responded.

"Tell her it's Dom."

"Dom DeLuise? The movie star?"

"Sure, that's me."

"I'm sure Ms. Stone will be right with you, Mr. DeLuise."

"I'm flattered. It's not every night I get a call from a movie star." Erica's TV voice was sexy and easy to recognize.

"Thanks for the rose. I would have called earlier but I was a bit busy today."

"Thanks for being busy, Judd. You're providing me with good job security. Could I provide you with a back rub?"

"Erica, you're so quick!"

"Aren't you glad that wasn't my line? I could stop and pick up some Chinese on the way, then read you a bedtime story. You must be exhausted."

"I appreciate the offer, Erica…"

"No problem, I'll be over in twenty minutes." Click.

"Erica! Erica!"

As he lay back down on the couch he wondered if it was possible to sleep fast. How does she know where I live? What if the neighbors see her? What if the news media finds out? What the heck, she _is_ the news media. Judd fell asleep.

The phone. That blasted phone. Judd thought as he reached over to pick up the receiver.

"Hey, boss! Are you going to join us for TGIF? This is Maureen."

"What time is it? Judd heard the unexpected sound of water running in his shower as he cleared his throat and tried to wake up.

"Half past eight. Funniest thing, boss, Erica didn't do her morning news at seven. Are we playing hooky from work together?"

Judd was too sleepy to defend himself.

"Maureen, what's on my calendar for this morning?"

"What would you do without me? I've got you covered, at least until ten. Jerry Davis at the IRS wants to see you in your office."

"Thanks, Mom. See you in forty-five."

Erica came walking out of the shower, dripping, with only a towel wrapped around her head.

"Do you have a hair dryer? I can't believe I overslept. What am I going to tell my boss?"

Judd sat up and pointed. "Dryer's in the left-hand drawer." He didn't even remember her coming over.

"It's time for another scoop, big boy. I can't go into work late without something really cushy. Talk to me!"

Judd wanted to talk to her, all right. What had happened? Had they? How did she even get into his apartment?

"Are we plea bargaining, Ms. Stone?"

"Emphatically yes!"

"Will you back off on the footage I allegedly have?"

"For one week."

"A month!" Judd had her right where he wanted her, well, almost.

"Two weeks and that's final." Erica was throwing her clothes on hurriedly.

Judd walked up behind her and helped her zip the back of her dress.

"Okay, three weeks," she said. "Now give, handsome."

"There's a good possibility I'll decide to prosecute them all at once. But, I didn't tell you that. If you say I did, I'll have to arrest you for obstruction of justice."

"If you were the jailer, that could be fun." Erica had the information she needed. "Judd, do be careful, I really care for you. It would be nice if you called me sometimes instead of the other way around."

She gave him a passionate kiss and walked out the door.

"Erica! Last night …? I …?"

"Darling, I promised you a bedtime story and some Chinese food. I dined alone. You were asleep."

"We didn't?" he said with a blank look on his face.

"Not even a bedtime story!" Erica had a smile on her face.

"But the towel on your head?" Judd was really confused now.

"Just wanted to show you what you missed." Her eyes sparkled as she slung the black eel purse over her shoulder and strutted to the car. Erica knew how to handle just about every situation skillfully. Her confidence preceded her. There would be another time for Judd. Confuse and rule, Erica's secret tactic.

Judd showered and hit the bricks. He couldn't believe that he'd slept through what could have been one of the most memorable nights of his life. He would never forget the towel around her head. She was beautiful!

Arriving at his building, Judd noticed the increased security that had been added by Chief Rojas. He pulled into the underground parking area and took the stairwell up five floors to his office.

Sitting down at his desk, he noticed a steamy cup of coffee placed squarely in the middle of his desk pad. He called Maureen on her line, avoiding the intercom, which could be heard by everyone in the outer office.

"How did you know I was here? I need to know. Security."

"Parking lot attendant calls me when you get here. Now you know all my secretarial trade secrets, boss."

"Could you come in with our agenda, Maureen? Maureen! Mau…"

She walked into Judd's office carrying a stack of files.

"Jerry Davis from IRS will be here in thirty minutes. You have time for a staff meeting with Thompson, he's on his way. Here are the latest medical updates on the wounded Cartel guys. Two are not expected to make it. That will put the total to prosecute down to twenty-seven. Five will be in hospital beds. Doctor Colonel Sawyer out at Bliss said they'll be able to stand trial in about two to three weeks. I've also got the information from the L.A. district attorney's office you requested. It's here in these two white boxes. We have more statements compiled from depositions taken from the prisoners at Fort Bliss for your review. Daryl has the rest of the county business assigned to the assistants. I'll let him tell you the details. I won't say a word about Erica, but I would like to know if you go with the feds are you going to take me with you? I'm finished. Your turn, boss."

"How did you know about the federal job? Give, Maureen. This is important."

"Judge Ramirez's secretary lives down the street. We're neighbors."

"Who else knows?"

"No one, boss."

"Good, keep it that way. I haven't decided yet which way I'm going on this one. When I do, you'll be the first to know. If I do go, you'll go with me and thank you for no more Erica jabs. Ask Thompson to come in."

"Good morning, Judd," Thompson greeted Judd as he strode into his office. "We've got more depositions from the cartel guys. I've read over them, and here's how they stack up so far. Of the twenty-six, I'm not counting Cortez or the two not expected to pull through, eleven are hard core lieutenants. We've got good files on them. I figure you'll want to take them down under capital murder charges. Stop me at any time, Judd."

"You're doing just fine so far. Continue."

"Of the remaining sixteen, four are going to be permanently disabled by the wounds they received at Ambush Pass. I think extradition is in order for them. Mexico is going to want some of them back. If we toss them a bone, we won't be out the medical and rehab costs."

"Good call."

"That leaves a dirty dozen. Five are flunkies and are already scared to death. They've been singing for a week and will point fingers at Cortez and his lieutenants with both hands. They just want to go home. We could include them in the extradition package. As it stands now, the Mexican Federales will want some good with the bad. They have charges filed against them on various offenses anyway. Sure will improve relations with our friends down south."

"Continue."

'The remaining seven had their pictures taken by SWAT cameramen at Ambush Pass. We have good shots of the eleven lieutenants also. I total up nineteen for the hot seat, Judd. How's your head?"

"Just fi…"

Glass shattered from the window behind Judd. A bullet hit the rear of Martinez's high-backed, bullet-proof chair with such impact it knocked Judd sprawling across the desk, right on top of Thompson. Both were on the floor on the other side of the desk when Maureen opened the door and came rushing into Judd's office.

"Get down, Maureen!" screamed Thompson.

She dropped to the floor on all fours as another bullet broke through the glass and hit head high into the door, barely missing her. Instinctively, Judd drew his 9mm and crouched up against the back of the desk.

"Are you okay, Maureen?" Judd asked, looking over his right shoulder.

"I think so."

"Stay down and don't move. They'll try to get off another shot at anything that moves before SWAT gets here."

Judd knew police downstairs would be calling for back up. People in the outer office were low crawling out the door into the relative safety of the hallway. Five minutes went by. Everyone held their positions. Finally, sirens broke the silence. Judd surveyed the room to see if everyone was all right. He motioned to Thompson as they crawled over to Maureen, who had assumed a fetal position with her hands over her head. All three crawled into the outer office and out to the hallway. Everyone was pressed against the wall. Two police officers had their service revolvers drawn. Out of the corner of his eye, Judd saw a third pistol and quickly aimed at the man holding it with his back to Judd.

"Freeze! Don't turn around! Don't move a muscle!" yelled Judd as he ran across the hall and took the gun out of the man's hands.

It was Everett Jamail, one of the defense lawyers hired by the cartel. The two police officers had Jamail down on his face putting on the cuffs.

"I have a permit! I'm a lawyer!" screamed Jamail.

"I know who you are." Judd gave Jamail's pistol to one of the officers. "That permit doesn't give you authority to carry a firearm into my office." The two officers raised Jamail to his feet and looked over at Judd.

"Take him down and book him! Hit him with every charge we can think of. I've had enough of this crap!" Judd paused for a moment and let his fear, turned to frustration, pass. "Is anyone hurt?"

No one was hit. For the next thirty minutes everyone stayed huddled in the hall. The elevator door opened, startling the crowd. A sheriff's deputy held out his badge from behind the elevator door. Judd and the other two police officers lowered their weapons.

"Sorry to startle you," one of the deputies said. "Is everyone okay up here?"

"We're okay. Is it clear yet?" Thompson asked.

"Yeah, that's what we came up here to tell you." The deputy holstered his pistol. "SWAT found the room in the building across the street where the shooter was. He must've gotten away. We're still looking."

"Can the IRS be of any help to you, Judd?" Jerry Davis had a worried smile on his face.

"Yeah, buddy, I can use your help. I'll take all the help I can get right now. This is getting ridiculous." Judd was shaking his head again. He escorted Davis into his outer office. "Daryl, get everyone out of here who's not supposed to be here. And ask Chief Rojas to send over some men with metal detectors. I want everyone going above the ground floor frisked for weapons. Maureen, call Fort Bliss. See if they can set us up with offices and quarters for about fifteen people. We're getting out of here! Make the list and start the move. We'll be there for about a month. Get some deputies to go home with you and the other girls. Pack accordingly. We'll probably need accommodations for the families, also. I don't want any more threats."

Maureen acknowledged. Davis and Judd went back into his office, staying clear of the window.

"I've heard of people dodging the IRS," Davis said jokingly, "but I must admit, I've never had a reception like this."

"I hope this is not a preview of what's to come, Jerry. You'll need to think about the security of your agents, also. I'm going to ask you to step on some toes. There may be retaliations." Judd was getting back to business. The IRS was a crucial part of his plan.

"Actually, Judd, we've been shot at before. Goes with the territory. I think you're making a smart move getting your people to Bliss."

"We can't take everyone in the building, but at least we'll try to protect some of the people who continue to work here. The cartel will be after us. I hope the courtroom staff will also be moved out there. These guys aren't giving up easily. They'll probably try again," Judd said as he rubbed his elbow, the fall had ruined another shirt.

For the next hour and a half Judd went over information he needed from Davis and his IRS agents. Part of his plan was to invoke Section 858, to intercept drug money being deposited into defense team accounts by the cartel. The prosecution would be well funded going to trial, bankrolled with cartel money. *Justice,* Judd thought.

Davis left the office with his list of things to do and assured Judd of his complete cooperation.

"Maureen, I know it's short notice but we have to rearrange the funeral arrangements for Dee tomorrow." Judd was trying to cover as many bases as he could. "I want the funeral moved out to Bliss. We can't afford to group as many officers as will be there in one place. Too tempting a target. Also, call Chief Rojas and ask him to get an EOD team over to the garage. I want every vehicle checked for hidden explosive devices before anyone leaves the building.

"Effective immediately, there will be no food ordered outside and delivered into our building. Get the word out to the other offices. Get popping."

"Judge Ramirez? Judd Rayburn."

"I hear lightning does strike twice, Judd. No one was hurt?"

"Luckily, no. I'm calling to make a suggestion."

"If you're calling to suggest that my staff and I move out to the Fort Bliss, I've already made the arrangements. Since Bliss is going through partial decommissioning, there's plenty of room. I've also called the base commander to beef up security and bring in more troops if necessary. General Lawton has put the entire fort on alert. I've got my clerk checking the legalities of holding the trials on the military reservation."

"Glad you brought that up, Sir. You can go ahead and make the call to the U.S. Attorney. I'll accept the federal position."

"You've thought about this?"

"Yes, Your Honor. Right up until the time the bullet helped me clear my desk. One other topic, I will try Cortez and his men as a group."

"In lieu of the events of the past two days, I hope the defense will not waste my time asking for a change of venue. We're going to have a difficult time seating a jury. We'll have to sequester even prospective jurors at Fort Bliss. Once the jury is seated, we'll need to have their families moved within the gates. This is going to be expensive, Judd."

"Your Honor, if the Cartel does what I suspect they're doing, as we speak, the IRS will fund these proceedings for us, in advance."

"I'll see you at the fort."

Maureen marched into his office as Judd hung up the phone. "Boss, funeral arrangements have been rearranged for tomorrow at the fort. I put in a call to Agent Feather telling him of the change of plans. The funeral is still at ten a.m. I've called every office in the building and followed up by writing a memo to advise that no food is to be delivered to the building. All mail, overnight special delivery packages, anything delivered to this building, will be checked out by EOD before being allowed inside. I'm getting my appetite back. How do you propose we eat? Please think about that a minute, boss. I have more.

"General Lawton, out at the fort, has put me in contact with Major Brooks in the Judge Advocate General's office. We can use the military tribunal courtroom for the trial. Major Brooks referred me to Captain Ginther at the housing office. Our staff will be staying in Bachelor Officer Quarters 17. We'll get directions from the sentries at the gate. Not finished yet, boss…

"Ms. Stone called and wants you. I mean she wants you to call her." Maureen was getting back to normal. "Jamail got out on bail and says he is going to sue you. Rosen, Jacobs, LaRue's office called, still wants to meet with you to start discovery. They say you can't keep ducking them like you have for the past two days. I apologized for you and told them you have been a little busy, getting shot at for the past couple of days, then I hung up on that snot-nosed…"

"Be nice, Maureen. You're on a roll. Please continue without getting upset."

"Moving right along, I have trucks on the way to move files to the facilities at Bliss. They will stop at the property warehouse and pick up all Cartel exhibits, including rocket-propelled grenades, assault weapons, knives, pistols, blackjacks, ropes and masks. All forensic documentation is being moved separately. Vehicles will go to Fort Bliss under guard and at separate times. Chief Rojas is coordinating that. Erica says you have her number. I'm hungry. The end."

"How about a killer hot dog down in the basement cafeteria?"

"I wish you'd use a different adjective. If you're buying, I'm flying. Hope there are no reporters in the lunchroom. Wouldn't want to get Ms. Stone jealous or anything. She's bigger than I am."

"Maureen, everyone's bigger than you are. And stop with the Erica jabs for the fourteenth time."

"Touchy! Touchy! Are we getting puppy dog eyes for Ms. Stone?"

"Enough. Get your purse and let's get out of here."

7

CHANGE OF VENUE

SATURDAY, MAY 10TH

It was after midnight when Judd walked into his quarters at BOQ 17. The scene was similar to the mobilization of Operation Desert Storm. Fort Bliss had come alive. Trucks were moving in and out under very tight security and troops were being assigned guard positions all around the perimeter of the huge military reservation, expecting Cartel retaliation. Vehicles with heavily armed military police cruised up and down every street within the fort.

"Hi, boss. You got here in one piece." Maureen had changed into blue jeans and a tight T-shirt.

"I see you've got everything set up." Judd looked around her room. Tables up, phones, fax machines, computer equipment, file cabinets, desk and…a cat's litter box? "Did you bring Posh with you?"

"Of course. Where I go, my cat goes. That's my child. He won't be in the way. Here's a base directory. Judge Ramirez and his staff are in BOQ 5. This file contains a map of the base. They didn't want everyone in the same area for obvious reasons. There'll be four MP Jeeps outside our building at all times. I've got Feather and his agents quartered down the hallway from us."

"Has a Randall Erin called?"

"That was next on my list, your messages. Mr. Erin did call about an hour ago. Here's his number. Said to call him as soon as you got in, he'll be up late tonight. Judge Ramirez wants to have breakfast with you at 7:30 in the morning in his quarters. Feather will arrive about nine; he called to confirm. Cortez will be arriving under heavy guard at the Fort Bliss Hilton Stockade in about an hour and a half. No, Erica has not called. The press hasn't caught on to our move yet and the rest of the calls, I'll handle."

"As soon as you finish over at the chapel, try to get some sleep, Maureen. Good job."

"Will do, boss. You need to catch some z's, too."

Judd went back to his room and dialed Erin.

"Erin speaking."

"Mr. Erin, this is Judd Rayburn returning your call."

"Are you and your staff settled in out at the Fort?"

"We're getting settled. Maureen, my secretary, has got us pretty well squared away."

"I talked to her earlier. She seems very efficient."

"She's been with me a long time. I couldn't do without her."

"You won't have to. I'll be there about nine in the morning with my secretary, Casey. She and Maureen can get all the formalities completed. We need to get you and your staff under federal assignment. Incidentally, welcome aboard."

"Thanks. See you tomorrow."

BOQ 17 was located on the flat valley section of the fort. Judge Ramirez's quarters, BOQ 5, were up on the hill, nestled in the southern-most tip of the Rockies called the Davis Mountains. As the MP drove across the fort and headed up the steeply inclined asphalt road, Judd remembered his ride up the hill twenty-two years earlier, the beginning of eight weeks of sheer torment. Something called Basic Training.

Had it really been twenty-two years ago?

The jeep pulled up in front of a white cinder block building. The sidewalk leading up to the door was lined with white painted rocks.

"I'll be in with the judge for about an hour, sergeant. Could you have someone pick me up then?"

"Roger, sir."

Judge Ramirez stood bare-chested in the doorway wearing a pair of walking shorts and house shoes.

"Good morning counselor."

"Morning, Judge."

BOQ 5 was a senior officers' building with a small patio outside the living room, much nicer than 17. Ramirez had breakfast on the table outside. The morning was sunny.

"Have you heard from IRS on the transfer of Cortez's funds?"

"Not yet, Your Honor. Davis said he'd let me know the minute anything happened."

Judge Ramirez took a deep breath, "I'll be forced to meet with the two firms representing Cortez and his men. So will you, Judd. It could be wasted time, not to mention giving them the right to discovery. Those two firms are going to make your life miserable for the next several months."

"Judge, Davis is monitoring forty-seven bank accounts known to be used by the Mexican Cartel. Those accounts are in five states at twenty-four different banks. When they transfer funds, we'll know."

"How much court time will prosecution need to present evidence?" Ramirez stopped eating and took out his court calendar and note pad.

"Three days."

"Three days?" The judge was expecting Judd to say three weeks.

"That's right, Your Honor."

"Due to the expense and the secure surroundings, Judd, I believe we can go right through on a longer day schedule than normal. These pictures you left with me, are they from the aftermath at Ambush Pass?"

"Yes sir. Your Honor, they're pretty gruesome. I have a feeling the Army cooks are going to have to prepare fairly bland meals that night."

"I'll schedule prosecution time for ten days, just to be safe. Your agenda is aggressive. I hope it works."

"So do I, Your Honor."

"Judd," Ramirez said in a soft, fatherly voice, "go slow and be thorough. No technical errors on this one."

"Thanks, sir. If I get to running too fast, just pull in my reins." Judd got into the awaiting jeep and returned to his barracks.

"Morning, boss," Maureen greeted him. "I've been trying to call you over at the judge's quarters. Davis called about two minutes ago. Here's his number. Oh, yes, Feather is unpacking. He got in twenty minutes ago."

"Thanks. Get Davis on the phone. This is the call I have been waiting for."

Joe Feather walked from the open doorway into Maureen's room. The halls outside were full of staff members from the D.A.'s office. Everyone seemed to be in a festive mood, despite the funeral. Being quartered all together was out of the ordinary.

"Hey, bro." Feather was in his suit, ready for Dee's funeral.

"You look sharp this morning, Joe." Judd was finishing the knot in his tie.

"Did Cortez make it to the fort last night?"

Maureen interrupted, "He's here, boss, no problems with him last night. Davis is on line four."

"Excuse me. I hope this is a three-million-dollar call." Judd picked up the phone.

"Give me good news, Richard."

"Tora! Tora! Tora! Fifteen minutes ago we intercepted a courier carrying a cashiers' check for $3.2 million made out to Rosen, Jacobs, LaRue. I can't believe the cartel was that stupid. The courier walked the check right into their offices. We've been watching banks. Guess they figured we would."

"Fantastic, Richard! You guys do good work. Made my day!"

"We've been ready on this one for over a week. All paperwork and legalities are covered. Rosen, Jacobs, LaRue are going to be hollering to Judge Ramirez and any other judge they can get to listen to them. To take some of the heat off you, my agents waited until the law firm took possession of the check before we confiscated it. I'll file charges against them for being in receipt of drug money. We'll keep those lawyers busy for a while."

"Thanks again, Richard. I knew you'd come through. Randall Erin will be here this morning. He's my new boss. I'll have him call you to work on the details of depositing the check into the proper account. I owe you, buddy."

"Just doing our job. Nail that sucker for us, would you?"

"Guaranteed, Richard."

Judd lowered the phone. Something was finally going right. Judd turned towards the window. He saw a husky fellow, about 5'11" with hair so blond it was almost white. Erin was red-faced and weighed a good 210 pounds, packed solid. The light gray tailored suit revealed a slight bulge under his left arm. Judd figured he wasn't the only one packing heat.

"Mr. Erin, I think you know Agent Joe Feather."

"Hello, Joe. Judd, Feather and I go back a ways."

They continued formalities. Judd took the U.S. Attorney around and introduced him to each member of his staff.

"This is my administrative assistant, Maureen McAfee. My right arm..."

"His left arm, his conscience, and his mom. Glad to see you again, sir. Are you a coffee drinker?" Maureen was trying her best to score points with the big boss right away.

"I've talked with you on the phone, Ms. McAfee. I'll have a cup. Just a little cream, please. Everyone, since we are introducing right arms, this is Casey Phillips, my right arm." Erin stepped back and nudged Casey in front of him.

Casey Phillips was in her late fifties, petite in stature with frosted shoulder length hair, very thin, her tan suggesting the outdoorsy, athletic type. A mother of three, she had been married for over twenty-five years and worked with Erin for sixteen years.

"We should be leaving." Judd checked his watch. "Chaplain O'Connor will begin the ceremony in about fifteen minutes. We have transportation out front. The chapel's only a few blocks."

Feather, Judd, Erin, Maureen, and Casey got into an Army van and led the procession to the chapel. Ranks of law enforcement officers began to enter the white chapel. Police cars were parked for what seemed miles. Chapel bells began to ring slowly, with a lingering resonance that turned the mood somber.

The other fallen officers would also have large police escorts at their funerals. Judd would send some of his assistant D.A.s to represent him. The streets of El Paso would be busy the next day, burying the dead. That fateful day in April would be remembered as El Paso's darkest hour. Ambush Pass would never be forgotten. The funeral was emotionally tough but dignified.

"Erica, it's Judd."

"Where've you been? I tried calling you all last night and most of today."

"I got all of your messages. I'm calling you this time."

"Where are you, Judd? Are you all right? I heard someone tried to kill you yesterday. I've been frantic with worry!"

"I'm still here. After the shooting, we moved the whole operation out to Fort Bliss. And, yes, I'm okay."

"I went to Martinez's funeral. It was moving, well officiated. Judd, I really got worried when I didn't see you there. Pilar did as well as could be expected. She had their whole family there."

"I'm glad of that."

"The station is going to cover the rest of the funerals tomorrow. I guess you won't be at those either, will you?"

"We're going to stay put for a while, Erica. We don't want to give the Cartel another excuse for a shooting."

"Judd, it's hectic at the station. We have every network anchor and syndicated writer in the business here to cover the funerals. Have you been watching the coverage on TV?"

"Haven't had much time for TV. I'll try to catch your newscast tomorrow."

"I'll give you a wink. How can I call you out there?"

"Come to think of it, I don't know. I'll ask Maureen as soon as she gets back. She took Dee's funeral pretty hard. She's with Feather for a little while. I'll get you the number when she returns."

"Have you got Cortez out there or is he still at county?"

"Ms. Stone, ask me no questions, I'll tell you…"

"No lies. I know that line, Mr. Assistant U.S. Attorney. How do you like being a fed?"

"So far, so good. Do you know Randall Erin?"

"I know who he is. That's part of my job."

"Of course, Ms. Know-it-All. As I was saying, Erin is a good guy, I like him."

"How long are you going to be staying out there? I miss you."

"For right now, we aren't going anywhere. I don't have an answer for you on that one."

"Can you get me a pass to come see you?"

"Honestly, Erica, Judge Ramirez's clerk is issuing all entry passes into the fort. I have no authority there. You'll have to contact them."

"And how do I do that? My woman's intuition is telling me we're all of a sudden getting official in this conversation."

Judd heard a single knock on his door. Thompson came storming through the door. "Judd, line 1. It's the President!"

"Erica, I've got to let you go…"

"Did I hear the President is on the line for you?"

"I really have to go, Erica. I'll call you as soon as I can."

"Thompson! Did you say the President? As in the U.S.?"

"Yeah, Judd, for real. On line 1."

Judd wrinkled his forehead and slicked back his hair with his left hand as he took a deep breath, stood up and pushed the blinking line 1.

"Mr. President." Judd had always wanted to say that, but never saw himself actually doing it. "This is Judd Rayburn."

"Judd, it is indeed a pleasure meeting you," the President said. "I've been following the progress of the Cartel proceedings with much interest."

"Thank you, Sir."

"You've become a household name in the White House, too. I thought I would call to see how your wound is healing."

"Fine, Mr. President, just fine. I have a hard head." Judd couldn't believe he said that to the President of the United States.

"Judd, that was a very heroic gesture on your part when you tried to save Agent Espinoza. My deepest condolences go out to you. I'm sorry that I could not be at his funeral this afternoon."

"We appreciate your thoughtfulness, Mr. President."

"After the court proceedings are finished, and I know you will do your best to keep Mr. Cortez behind bars for the rest of his life, I would like to invite you and Agent Feather to the White House. I have the country's highest civilian medal to present to you two. By the way, I was told that Agent Feather was there with you. Could I speak briefly with him, Judd?"

"Mr. President, Agent Feather is currently on the other side of the fort. I know he'll hate missing your call."

"Just tell Agent Feather I will speak to him personally here at the awards ceremony when the trial is over."

"I will, Mr. President."

"Keep up the good work. I'll see you and Agent Feather soon."

"Yes, sir, Mr. President. Thank you for calling." Judd was out of breath.

Even though the hour was late, the hallway outside of Judd's room was crowded with his staff pressing up against the open doorway. Everyone had heard Thompson tell Judd the President was on the line. As Judd stood there wearing nothing but his jockey shorts, with the phone still in his hand, the whole group applauded loudly.

"What's all the commotion, bro?" Joe Feather pushed his way through the crowd with Maureen right behind him.

"Feather! You and I have been invited to the White House to get a medal, from the President, himself. He wanted to talk to you. You missed a call from the President, Joe. The President!"

"Just my luck, Judd. Just your luck to be caught with your britches down. You may want to put on a pair of jeans or something. You're gonna catch cold."

Judd finally realized that he was standing there without pants on and slowly walked over to a chair to put on his jeans. He still hadn't noticed that Maureen and the other ladies on the staff were there, not until they started whistling.

"Give me a break, girls." Heat rose up into Judd's cheeks.

Judd, Thompson, Maureen, Feather, Erin, and Casey were in Judd's room to go over trial strategy. The base information office sent over a DVD player and a TV. For the next three and a half-hours they went over each segment of footage, freezing frames and making notes.

"Maureen, can you bring in the transcripts from L.A. on the Jackson case, please?"

Judd had it down in his mind the way he proposed to prosecute Cortez and company. He wanted to get Randall's opinions before he kicked the prosecution efforts into high gear.

"See how the defense on the Jackson case used the freeze frame on the DVD to their advantage?" Judd underlined passages from the transcript. "By freezing the frames of Jackson lying on his back with his leg in the air, surrounded by officers, obviously protecting himself from the police billy clubs, it looks as though he is preparing to kick one of the police officers rather than defend himself. The L.A. police officers' defense attorneys convinced the jury that they didn't see what they were seeing. Can you believe that?"

"Why do you think they burned down half of L.A., Judd?" Erin added. "No one could believe it. We cannot afford for the defense to use our footage that way. You know they'll try once they see the film during discovery."

"Exactly." Judd got up from the table and walked over to the TV. "That's why we're going to run it at normal speed for half a day, over and over again for the jury. After lunch, I want to spend the afternoon showing a sequence of freeze frames. I want to beat the defense efforts at their own game. I plan to freeze frame the perpetrators, then insert some computer graphics drawing dotted lines from the muzzle of the weapons held by each perp on freeze to the individual police officer in the line of fire. We can establish the murderer of each officer that was killed and the individual Cartel soldier that pulled the trigger. I'll be using three screens. One with focused footage of the perp firing and another with a wide angle panning view to show the officer going down. The third with a reverse angle view."

"Judd," Randall asked, skeptical, "will the footage verify that approach?"

"Yes." Judd walked over to an easel standing in the corner of the room. "Look at this map of the area surrounding Ambush Pass. The Cartel soldiers were up high along the crests on both sides of the highway, here and here. Our guys were down below them in these positions."

Judd walked back to the table and picked up a packet of multi-colored stick-on dots. "These two green dots represent the video cameramen of the SWAT team. This red dot is the location of the news cameras. We've established a reverse angle between these cameras. Now, for the icing on the cake. When the gunships came in blasting, their cameras verified the position of each Cartel soldier and the weapon each carried. By establishing position, we can also determine field-of-fire range on each individual perp."

"How many of the defendants have you been able to isolate using this footage?"

Daryl Thompson joined in, "Randall, we've got positive ID on eleven so far. The lab guys are still working on it."

"Does Cortez make twelve or is he part of the eleven?" Erin asked.

"Cortez is number twelve. He's a no-brainer. We've got him cold when he cut Agent Espinoza's rope." Judd looked satisfied.

Thompson was on the edge of his chair.

"What about the ones you can't nail with the tapes, Judd? I'm guessing you're going to charge them with lesser charges than capital murder, cut some deals and use them as witnesses for the prosecution?"

"Exactly." Judd liked the way the conversation was moving. Working with pros cut time in half. "We'll start off with first degree, then go to second degree murder in cutting the deals. We also have conspiracy to commit murder, drug trafficking and illegal entry. We could return two hundred-page indictments on any of the Cartel guys we have, enough to put them away for about three hundred years on concurrent sentences."

"The cost was high, but I do believe we've got 'em by the short ones this time." Erin cracked a small grin.

Judd was about to lead the conversation in a different direction. "Every time we bust someone, it's only temporary. Have you feds developed any long-range plans for permanently ending drug distribution?"

Erin sat back in his chair, took a deep breath, crossed his legs and stared out the window. "Judd, the think tanks in Washington have been working on that question for years. They've even run hypothetical scenarios of invading Colombia, based on every excuse those highly paid brain-jockeys could imagine. The conclusion is always the same. The United States would be cited for acts of aggression by the U.N. and the world courts, not to mention breaking practically every international law on the books. In a nutshell, laws also protect the guilty. Unfortunate, but true. Short of building a Great Wall of China around the borders of the U.S. and sending the angel of death to Colombia to kill every one of those life-sucking pigs, we're fresh out of ideas. The good news is, we're completely open for any suggestions you might have."

"Randall, I'll let you know the minute I think of something."

Erin stood up and looked over at Casey. "We're going to get out of here and let you people do your jobs."

"One favor you could do for me."

"Name it, Judd."

"Could you contact the FBI Agent-in-Charge in Albuquerque and ask him if I could get Feather assigned here at the fort? I need him as my interpreter during the trial. He was at the scene and knows the Cartel backwards and forwards. I also plan on using him as a witness. He's very important to this case, Randall."

"I'll make the call."

"Maureen, make sure the psychological tests are slated to be complete on the Cartel guys by the end of the week. I don't want insanity pleas hitting us."

"I'm on the tests already."

"Feather and I are on our way to see Judge Ramirez."

"Morning, Judge. Looks like your staff is ready to get to work."

"We worked half the night, Judd. How're you doing, Joe?"

"Fine, Judge."

"I've talked to counsel at Jacobs, Rosen, LaRue," Ramirez smiled. "Richard Davis' agents over at IRS have scared the daylights out of that firm. A courier delivered their official written withdrawal from the case this morning. They're out."

"Good news, Judge."

"I've assigned Lee Wiley and Alex Castenada from the Public Defender's office to represent the Cartel. Both are fluent in Spanish."

"I know 'em." Judd was hoping the judge would assign some rookies. Deep down he knew Ramirez was fair and would assign the best P.D.'s available. Better them than Jacobs, Rosen, and LaRue.

Lee Wiley was a studious looking gentleman in his early forties. Not a man of great stature, Wiley stood about 5' 7" with classic male baldness syndrome.

Alex Castenada was five years out of University of Texas Law School. He had joined the Public Defender's office three weeks after being admitted to the Texas Bar Association. Castenada was a bright law student. Married with three children, Alex's downfall was his wife, a great cook. Alex loved to eat and was suffering badly from pre-mature adult obesity. He was 5' 9" tall with a forty-six inch waistline. In his early thirties now, he had thick black hair and occasionally wore silver-rimmed plano reading glasses in the courtroom, mainly to look older and more experienced before a jury.

"First phase of initial appearance will be tomorrow before me in the military courthouse. Scheduled for nine a.m. Initial appearance has been done once; however, to follow the rules, we're going to do it again under federal jurisdiction, dotting I's and crossing T's."

"I understand, Your Honor."

"Do you have all the indictments in order on each of the defendants?"

"Yes, sir, all in order. Maureen will send them over later this morning. We've added more charges to the original indictments done last week."

"Good. I've scheduled second initial appearance for Friday morning at nine a.m. That should give Wiley and Castenada time to talk to their clients and enter pleas."

"How much time will you allow for discovery, Your Honor?"

This was a crucial time period to the prosecution. Wiley and Castenada were not beginners when it came to digging into the law books to find hidden loopholes for their clients. The longer they were allowed for discovery, the more motions they would file to offset prosecution efforts for a swift and speedy conviction.

"Since you're going to try them as a group, Judd, I'm going to allow two weeks."

"What about time period for filing motions?"

"Two weeks. Unless they know more about the law than I do, we all know the motions they'll file. Two weeks is adequate."

"Jury selection should begin the week of June fifteenth. Trial is set for Tuesday, July ninth. That will get the Fourth of July holidays out of the way before we begin and will also allow us to stay well within the seventy-day time limit from date of arrest. A final caution. Be ready with sound rebuttal on their motions. Burn the midnight oil. Knowing Wiley and Castenada, they'll come out of left field with some of these motions. Be ready!"

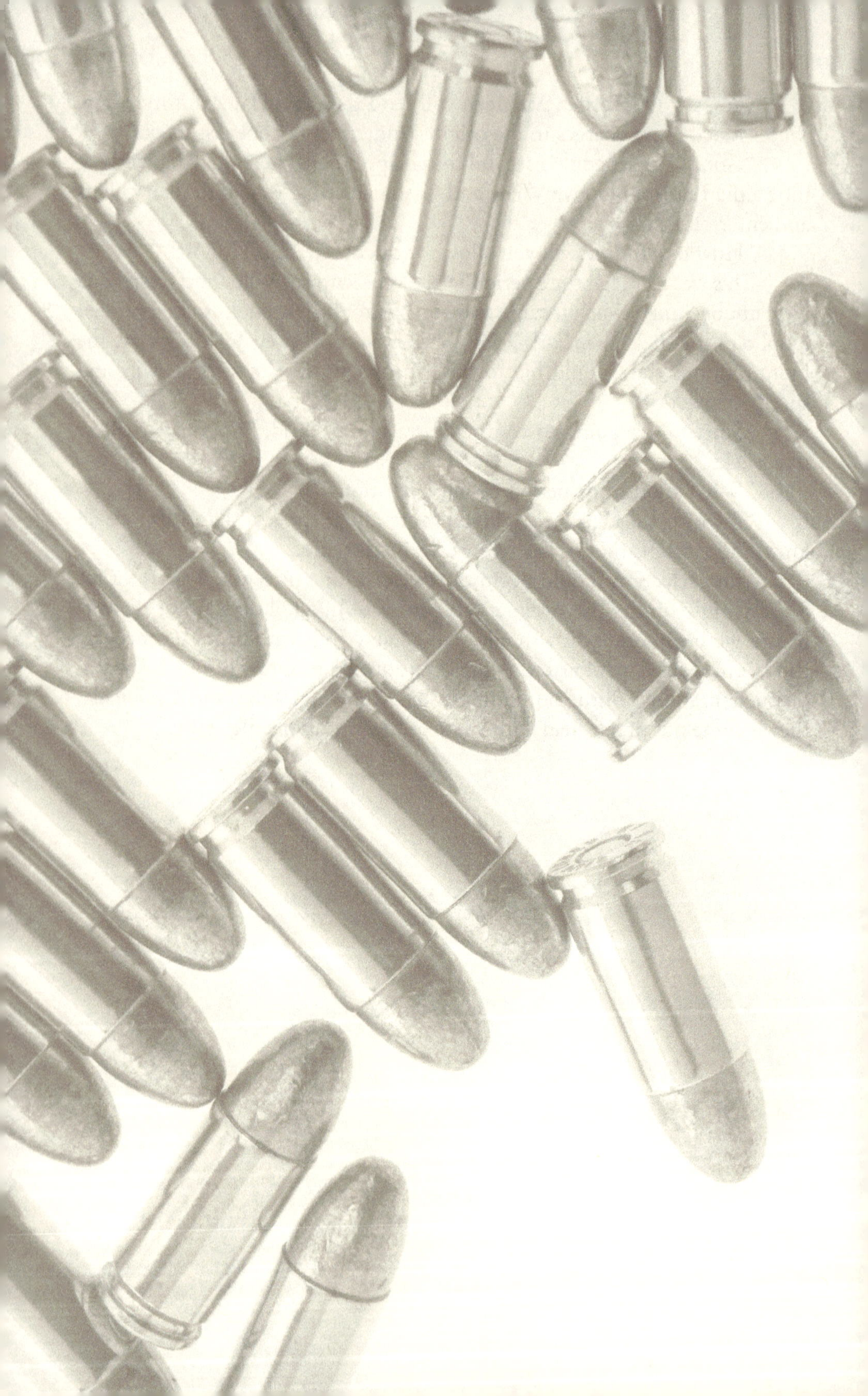

8

TEMPERATURE RISING

Requests for press passes flooded into Judge Ramirez's office faster than his present staff could process them so he brought in more staff. Over a thousand applications had arrived by mail, courier and overnight delivery services from all over the world. *The L.A. Times*, *The New York Times*, *The Washington Post*, AP, UPI, Reuters, *Wall Street Journal*, *London Times*, *Le Monde* in Paris, FNC, BBC, ABC, CBS, NBC, CNN, and practically every newspaper and TV network in North and South America applied. The response to the trial was overwhelming and unplanned. Footage of Ambush Pass became a best seller for audience ratings among all forms of the media.

The road leading up to the military reservation at Fort Bliss was lined with media-owned motor homes, press trucks, communication vans and tents. News that the trial staff had moved to the fort had spread quickly.

General Lawton, Fort Commander, ordered more security for all the entry gates into the reservation. He stepped up roving patrols around the entire perimeter. Every vehicle entering or exiting the base was ordered to be thoroughly searched along with its occupants.

Judge Ramirez had called earlier to request an informal meeting between the prosecution and the defense lawyers. His objectives were for them to view the building he had chosen for the courtroom, and to get suggestions from both sides before base carpenters began construction on the facilities. The trial was getting expensive and it hadn't even started.

"Judd, do you and Agent Feather know Mr. Wiley and Mr. Castenada from the Public Defender's Office?"

"I've known them for years, Your Honor." Judd introduced them to Joe.

"Due to the overwhelming number of press applications and, in the interest of the safety and security of the prisoners and trial officials, I've decided to set up the court in the War Room planning facilities located here in the center of the Fort. Let's go inside."

Ramirez preceded them inside the domed, circular building. "As you can see, the building can seat approximately three hundred people in a semi-circular gallery arrangement. The balcony will handle another hundred and fifty. There are plenty of phones out in the foyer along with a small office for security."

They walked down the aisle to the front of the huge room, which resembled a large, sunken, college lecture hall.

"Comments, gentlemen?"

"Judge, Mr. Castenada, Mr. Wiley, I don't particularly care where I prosecute these murderers. In a cave, in the middle of the desert, under an outhouse. Just so they're given their day in court. I'll prosecute them anywhere, anytime, under any conditions. Let's just get on with it," said Judd.

Judd could feel the moment of truth approaching. His anxieties were running high. He wanted Wiley and Castenada to know from the get-go that he was out for blood.

"I believe we're scheduled for Initial Appearance in my office in about half an hour," said the judge.

Driving back to BOQ 17, Joe saw the fixed determination in Judd's eyes.

"Go slow, brother. Remember what Judge Ramirez told you. Go slow and be thorough."

"I'll be thorough, but slow is not my speed."

"Hey, boss, the hospital just called and said the two prisoners who were not expected to pull through, didn't. Both died last night. After the autopsies are completed this afternoon, the media is going to have a field day. Two refrigerator trucks will take the forty-two Cartel bodies back over the border to release them to the Mexican authorities."

"Pull the indictments of the two that died last night. Incidentally, that did make my day, two less to worry about. Good riddance."

"Do I sense an antagonistic attitude this morning?"

"No Maureen, you sense the beginning." Judd had a strange sound in his voice. "The judge and the defense have their copies?"

"Delivered yesterday." Maureen had never seen Judd so intense.

"Let's go face down our opponents, Joe."

They drove up in front of the judge's office just as the Military Police and U.S. Marshals were unloading their prisoners. Three military ambulances were waiting behind the vans to transport the wounded prisoners inside. Feather and Judd stopped at the doorway and watched the prisoners walk past, holding up their ankle chains with cuffed hands.

There he was, the headliner, Julio Cortez, dressed in gray coveralls and flip-flops, dragging his chains every step of the way.

Looking over his shoulder and not seeing any of the P.D.s around, Judd stopped Cortez just outside the door. Feather grabbed Judd's other arm.

"It's okay," Judd said in a very snide voice. "Just wanted to have a few words with my old amigo, Julio… I hope you're finding the accommodations up to your usual high standards."

Cortez looked away from Judd, not saying a word.

"If there's anything, Julio, I do mean anything, I can do for you, just let me know. I want your last days on earth to be as pleasant as possible."

"Judd, that's enough!" Feather pulled Judd back from Cortez.

Slowly, Judd lowered his arm from Cortez's chest. His fixed stare didn't leave Julio until he was inside the building.

The prisoners were lined up, side by side, against the far wall of the judge's makeshift courtroom. Ramirez was wearing his black robes, sitting at a table flanked by the U.S. and Texas flags, his gavel placed in the right corner of the table. Everything looked very official.

Castenada and Wiley were standing on the far side of the judge's table. Feather stayed close to Judd.

Judd took in several deep breaths and approached the bench.

"Judge, if it pleases the court, we have properly established the identity of each of the twenty-seven prisoners. I realize each of them have names; however, for simplicity's sake, I would ask the court to allow us to refer to them by number. My Spanish pronunciation is not very good and I wouldn't want to offend any of the accused by mispronouncing their names."

There was more than a bit of sarcasm in Judd's last statement.

"Objection, Your Honor!" Castenada was visibly upset. "I cannot allow the prosecution to imply the accused are numbers. They are human beings. It would be a violation of their civil rights."

"They're illegal aliens, Judge. They've come across our borders and killed police officers. They have no civil rights under the U.S. Constitution."

"Objection! I move the preceding statements be stricken from the record, Your Honor. The guilt or innocence of the accused has not yet been established, except by the prosecution." Wiley gave Judd a harsh look.

"Counselors, approach the bench," Ramirez snapped.

Judd, Wiley and Castaneda walked up to the Judge's table.

"I will not tolerate outbursts in my courtroom, gentlemen. If an objection is raised you will both remain silent until I rule on the objection before another is made. Do I make myself understood?" Judge Ramirez had a reputation for staying in control of his courtroom. "You may now step back. I'll rule on the objections before we continue."

Ramirez stared over his reading glasses and focused his look on Castenada.

"I will allow the defendants to go by number instead of name for the sake of expediency. Objection overruled. The court reporter will strike from the record the Prosecution's statement of killing police officers, and that of the Defense stating that the prosecution has already convicted the defendants. Mr. Wiley, before you make further objections in my courtroom, make sure they are objections. Follow with proper rebuttal or remain silent. Do not waste the court's time with unfounded objections. Clear?"

"Clear, Your Honor."

Interpreters from the Public Defender's office were chattering away, giving the defendants a blow-by-blow description of the proceedings. Ramirez tolerated the often-loud conversation until headphones were installed.

"I'll now ask the bailiff to read the indictments. For clarity, and I want the record to reflect this, the charges that will be read will reflect individual charges being brought on each defendant separately, even though the Assistant U.S. Attorney has chosen to prosecute them as a group. Begin reading the charges, bailiff."

"Defendants numbers one, two and three, Capital murder of a law enforcement officer with illegal weapons in connection with drug trafficking—eight counts. Murder in the first degree—eight counts. Murder in the second degree—eight counts. Conspiracy to commit murder—thirty-three counts...

The bailiff paused and poured a glass of water.

"Continuing, defendants four through twenty-seven, Capital murder of a law enforcement officer..."

"Lastly," the bailiff read, "hunting on U.S. government property without a license—one count. That completes the charges against the defendants, Your Honor."

The Public Defender interpreters continued to translate the charges to the twenty-seven defendants. Judd watched the expression on their faces, especially Cortez. Overall, the defendants looked worried, real worried. Cortez, on the other hand, had no expression at all. His face was blank and maintained an "I couldn't care less" look. He was more worried about being inconvenienced than being charged with capital murder.

Feather leaned over to Judd and whispered, "There are some scared hombres in that group of defendants, bro. I think from the way the conversations are going you've got some guys that want to deal."

"How can you hear what's going on over there? All I hear is muffled sounds."

Feather cracked a smile, "I'm an Indian. We hear everything."

Castaneda angrily pushed himself back from the defense desk and began shaking his head, staring up at the ceiling. Obviously, he and Wiley had found the little surprise Judd had waiting for them.

"I was counting on that, Joe." Judd had a confident look on his face. "Defense doesn't know it yet, but I'm going to send fifteen of those idiots back to Mexico. I talked to Randall about it while he was here. We've got some U.S. citizens in Mexican jails that we're going to swap. I've already picked out five of the remaining defendants to cut deals. That will leave the count at twelve."

Pulling his copies of the indictments towards him, Judd sorted through the stack, pulled out the one with Cortez's name at the top and laid it in front of Feather. Written in black magic marker was "Number 1."

It was time to turn the thumbscrews a little tighter. Judd stood and walked halfway to the bench. In a loud, clear voice Judd said, "If it pleases the court, Your Honor, the prosecution will try each defendant for only one charge at a time. We will begin with Capital Murder of a law enforcement officer with illegal firearms during drug trafficking operations. One count for each defendant. Depending on the jury's verdict, the prosecution will go to count two of the capital murder indictment and so on until the court is satisfied that justice has been properly rendered."

"Objection, Your Honor! We could spend our entire careers in this courtroom. This could take years!" Castenada remarked, his anger turning to frustration.

Very calmly, taking his time, Judge Ramirez, without looking up from the stack of indictments before him said, "Objection overruled. Second appearance is scheduled for Friday, June 12th at nine a.m.—"

"Your Honor!" Wiley blurted out.

"Mr. Wiley." Ramirez fired a glance at the PD that could've taken his head off. "You will refrain from interrupting me when I am speaking, now and throughout the proceedings of this trial. As I was saying, at nine a.m. The defendants will be prepared to enter pleas at that time. Take notes, gentlemen. The discovery phase will be completed by Tuesday, June 23rd. Two weeks, Mr. Wiley and Mr. Castaneda."

The two defense attorneys had their faces buried in clenched fists, about to explode. They knew better. The judge's last admonishment had made it clear that they should not say a word, at least for the time being.

"The deadline for filing motions with the court will be Thursday, June 25th."

Judd thought the judge was being lenient giving the P.D.s two extra days from the original two weeks Ramirez had mentioned earlier. The judge's last comment sent Wiley's head to the desk in front of him.

Feather whispered to Judd, "The P.D.s look somewhat perplexed."

Judd continued to smile openly. He was enjoying this.

"Deadlines for changing pleas will be the same as for filing motions, June 25th. Jury selection will begin on Friday, June 26th. I'll allow two weeks. That puts completion of seating a jury on July 10th. Trial will begin at nine a.m., Monday, July 13th."

Judd and Feather returned to BOQ 17 and found all the windows and doors open.

"Bad news, boss! We have a major problem." Maureen fanned herself with a magazine. "The air-conditioning went out about twenty minutes ago. Base electricians are working on it now."

Judd took off his coat and loosened his tie. "Get a couple of fans in the meantime. At least we can put them in the hallways to get a breeze started."

"How about a change of uniform, boss?"

"Yeah, Maureen. Tell the staff to lose the business clothes and go to shorts and T's. It's supposed to hit a hundred and two degrees today. Have the federal regulation books arrived?"

"Came in this morning, boss."

"When everyone gets changed, have the A.D.A.s meet me in my room. We have some reg crunching to do for the next few days. Wiley and Castenada are going to hit us with every motion in the book. I want us to be ready for them."

"Judd, your messages: Ms. Stone found out how to get through to us and has called seven times. Do me a favor and call her back, boss. You can reach her on her cell. Everyone and their brother from the press is waiting on statements from you and wants to do interviews. Thompson passed that message to me along with one more. Your cleaners called and said they cannot clean the suit you brought in. It's ruined. That's all for now."

Judd turned and walked out of the office.

"Erica? This is Judd."

"Why haven't you called me? You said you'd call me right back. Did the President of the United States call you?"

"Yes, he did."

"What did he say?"

"Feather and I are supposed to get some kind of award when all of this is over."

"You mean at the White House? Can I go with you? Purely in an unofficial capacity, of course."

"Erica, calm down. How're you doing?"

"It's a madhouse out here in the press area. I'm not much of a camper. We've done about all the background stories we can think of and the editors are pushing hard to get information. Please, Judd, help me out on this one."

"I can't show favoritism towards you on an official basis, You know that. The really big news is that our air-conditioning has gone out and we're burning up in these pre-Crusades' era buildings. How's your temperature?"

"We stay fairly cool, if you're inclined to call eighty-eight during the heat of the day cool. That is, as long as Pete remembers to put gas in our generator thing-a-ma-jig, or whatever you call it. When are we going to get some news? I'm serious! These national guys are wolves. They'll start attacking you if you don't give us something soon."

"I'll have Maureen prepare a statement of what's happened so far. What have you heard from Wiley and Castenada's office?"

"I should make you wait until my five o'clock newscast. They're both hopping mad. Unofficially, they're saying their clients are being railroaded by you and the judge. We need that statement soon as possible, Judd, for your sake and the sake of the Justice system."

"Thanks for the tip. I'll expedite the statement."

"Thank you, handsome. Let's move on to more important things. When're we getting together again?"

"Honestly, Erica. I don't know when that's going to be. We're all together in one building and no one is coming in or going out until this thing is over. I'll make sure you get a press pass for the trial.

"I'm in your debt, Mr. U.S. Attorney. Stay cool, Judd. Millions of people are watching this case. It could be a big break for you."

"You're about the fifth person that's told me that today. Feather and Maureen are leading the pack in that department. I'll stay as cool as this heat allows without A/C. Talk to you soon."

The next two days were spent anticipating motions Wiley and Castenada would file on behalf of their clients. The cat and mouse game of point, counter-point lawyering. The daytime heat was almost unbearable.

Friday morning finally arrived. Still no air-conditioning in BOQ 17.

"Time for round two, gentlemen," Judd said, cramming the last few papers into his briefcase. "Let's go see what Mr. Wiley and Mr. Castenada have been cooking up for us. Maureen, grab your pad and shorthand every word spoken in there this morning. Don't miss anything."

Judd, Maureen, Feather and three A.D.A.s piled in the awaiting van and headed for Judge Ramirez's office. It was time to see if the two Public Defenders had done their homework. Judd was confident his team was ready. The cool air from the van's A/C felt good.

As the group entered the judge's office Judd looked across the room at Wiley and Castenada to get a read from them. Nothing. The door swung open wide as the prisoners were led into the makeshift courtroom. By the time all were inside the cool air was gone.

"Is counsel for both sides ready to begin Second Phase Initial Appearance proceedings?" Judge Ramirez asked.

"We're ready, Your Honor," Judd said anxiously.

"The defense is ready, Your Honor," Wiley answered.

"By number." Judge Ramirez looked over at the court clerk to make sure all the indictments were in numerical order. "How do the defendants plea?"

"Before we enter pleas, Your Honor, we beg the court to entertain rulings on three motions we are filing with the court." Castaneda placed three half-inch thick legal-sized stacks of paper on the judge's table.

"First motion." Ramirez expected this.

"Your Honor, first motion is a Motion to Sever." Wiley's voice was not very confident, this was more of a formality in providing an adequate defense rather than an expectation of the judge granting the motion without an argument from the prosecution.

"Objection, Your Honor." Judd's voice was calm. "The charges against each of the defendants are the same. They all occurred in relation to the same conspiracy. Evidence is the same. The truth comes out the same way in each case, Your Honor."

"Objection sustained. Motion denied." Ramirez wrote on the first motion, signed it and gave it to the court clerk. "Next motion, Mr. Wiley."

"Your Honor, second motion is a Motion of Change of Venue."

"Objection, Your Honor." Judd expected this one also.

"Objection sustained. Motion denied." Ramirez signed the second motion and slid it to the clerk. "Third motion, Mr. Wiley."

"Your Honor, third motion is Motion of Dismissal of all charges against my clients for Illegal Arrest under the *Posse Comitatus* Act stating that the U.S. military cannot enforce civilian laws." Wiley looked over at Judd. The defense played one of its aces.

After nearly seventy-two hours of trying to out-guess the defense on motions they would file, not one of the A.U.S.A.s, nor Judd, himself, had thought of this one. It was time for the newly appointed Assistant US Attorney to think on his feet. Judge Ramirez stared intently at Judd, waiting for an objection.

"Objection, Your Honor." Judd showed no sign of emotion. He continued speaking in his most confident, courtroom voice. "I beg the court for counsel to approach the bench."

"Approach."

Wiley, Castenada, Judd and his three A.U.S.A.s moved close to Judge Ramirez's table. In a whisper Judd said, "Your Honor, the top-secret Executive Order?"

"Correct, Mr. Rayburn," Ramirez whispered.

Castenada and Wiley looked confused.

Ramirez also whispered, "Mr. Wiley, Mr. Castenada, there is a secret Executive Order issued by the President of the United States and confirmed by congress to allow military intervention during a crisis situation. This cannot be part of the record of the court. If you will give the U.S. Attorney for the Western District, Randall Erin, a call, he can confirm this Executive Order. If further documentation is needed, call the Attorney General in Washington D.C., but I am issuing both of you a formal warning. This Executive Order is classified as Top Secret by the President and the Congress of the United States. If word of this order gets out and is traced by the FBI to either of you, the charge against you both will be treason."

Wiley and Castenada had stopped short of doing all their homework on this one. Statutes were asterisked in the books. They had failed to follow up completely. Wiley looked at Castenada with a "What do we do now?" look.

"Objection sustained. Motion denied." Ramirez peered over at Wiley and Castenada, who were now wearing stunned looks on their faces. "Is the defense ready to enter pleas?"

Clearing his throat, Wiley spoke, "Uh, yes, Your Honor."

Castenada handed Wiley a single typed page.

"By the numbers, sir, defendants one through twelve enter pleas of Not Guilty to the Charge of Capital Murder. Let the record reflect, this is against the advice of counsel. Defendants thirteen through twenty-seven beg the court's mercy to withhold pleas until after a conference with the prosecution.

Your Honor, the Prosecution has been unavailable for consultation and the defense has spent every hour going over the indictments since issued…"

"Prosecution has no problem meeting with defense before pleas are entered on defendants thirteen through twenty-seven, Your Honor. If it pleases the court to so rule." Judd had won round two and he knew it. So did Wiley and Castenada. The flunkies among the captured cartel soldiers wanted to deal.

Cortez and his lieutenants, who had remained calm throughout the proceedings up to now, turned towards their front-line soldiers with looks that could kill.

"So ruled. Counsel and the head U.S. Marshall approach the bench," Ramirez said in a demanding voice. "I want defendants thirteen through twenty-seven kept separate from the other defendants during transportation to and from correctional facilities. This is for their own safety.

"I will also order the prosecution to meet, post haste, with defense in order to settle upon final pleas for the second group of defendants. Second Initial Appearance phase is adjourned until Wednesday morning, next, at ten a.m. for defendants thirteen through twenty-seven. Gentlemen, you are dismissed. Return the defendants to their cells, Mr. Marshall."

The defendants dragged their chains and clanked their way out of the courtroom to awaiting paddy wagons that would return them to the stockade. Judd never turned around to look at them. When the court was cleared, Lee Wiley and Alex Castenada walked up to Judd.

"Mr. Rayburn, when can we meet on pleas?" Wiley was at the prosecution's mercy.

"No time like the present, Mr. Wiley, if you don't mind the heat of our offices. The A/C's gone out."

"We could meet in our offices at BOQ 10." Heat was a four-letter word to Castenada.

"Thanks, Mr. Castenada, if it's all the same to you, I would rather keep all the paperwork in one place. Besides, I'm getting used to working in shorts and T-shirts. About half an hour at BOQ 17, gentlemen? Dress cool." Judd was enjoying his well-leveraged position.

Maureen stood in the doorway, hands on her hips, head down, waiting for the group to enter.

"Judd, Joe? I just heard some bad news on the radio." Maureen looked concerned.

"What?" Judd asked, pulling his tie off.

"The Mexican government just announced it will no longer work with U.S. DEA agents within their borders. The whole program is being scrapped."

"What happened?" Feather questioned in a low, monotone voice.

Maureen was trying to get her facts straight and keep the reply short as possible. "As we all know, Mexican agents have been allowed to work on our side of the border and vice-versa for several years now to put drug traffickers in jail. Well, it seems some of the DEA agents got the goods on a very, I mean, *very* prominent Mexican congressman and asked for extradition for him to be tried in the U.S. The congressman is obviously well-connected in the Mexican government because Mexico City released a statement to the U.S. Embassy stating not only would they not turn the Congressman over to U.S. authorities, but that they are pulling out of the agreements made between Mexico and the DEA to work together in catching traffickers."

"I know the congressman you're talking about, Maureen." Feather was putting two and two together real fast. "This is hard to believe, Judd. The congressman has been under investigation for many years by our undercover DEA agents. They've been walking on egg shells with this guy."

"Why, Joe?"

"Remember the DEA agent that was working undercover in Mexico in 1985? The one that was returned to us in a body bag along with his pilot?"

"Sure, that's the case that started Mexico and the U.S. working together to catch the agent's murderers and bring them to trial."

"Correct." Feather turned and looked away. "The Mexican congressman is connected to those murders."

Silence.

"Years of investigation. Five more undercover agents killed, down the drain." Feather walked to his room and slammed the door.

"Maureen, get changed, then get Erin on the line for me."

"Yessir."

"Erin speaking."

"Randall, what's going down in Mexico?"

"In a word, chaos! We've been after this Mexican congressman for many years. Finally, we have the evidence we need to extradite him. The only legal means Mexico has of not turning him over is to dissolve the narco-trafficking programs. That's just how high up this thing goes."

"Unbelievable! For one man? He must've paid some heavy bucks for this, Randall."

"It's not only the payoffs, it's others in the Mexican government he could implicate under interrogation. Mexico City is afraid the guy will want to cut a deal and spill his guts to us."

"Randall, I've got a meeting in twenty minutes with the defense here at Bliss. How's this Mexican breakdown going to affect our dealing position?"

"Time is very important now, Judd. We've got to swap our prisoners for theirs, ASAP!"

"What's with the immediacy?"

"One of the U.S. citizens the Mexican authorities are after happens to be one of our agents. He's so deep the Mexicans don't even know he's working for us. I don't dare mention his name on the phone, but I will say this much since you're talking on a military-secured line, he's the agent that broke the case on the congressman. Things got so hot in Mexico that our agent made his way up to the border in Juarez, passed himself off as a tourist and purposely got himself arrested for drunk and disorderly to get away from the people in the Cartel and the Mexican secret police who might be chasing him. We don't know if they're on to our guy or not, but we're not taking any chances. That's the reason for the hurry-up. We've got to bring him in before Mexican authorities discover he's not a drunk tourist."

"When do you want to do the swap and how, Randall?"

"Sunday night. As soon as we send the Mexicans your prisoners, they'll begin releasing people we have on our list. We sent them a list three days ago. The Mexican authorities think our guy is down in the interior. We don't think they'll be looking for him in a border town jail, especially as a drunk tourist who got himself hauled in. That was our plan."

"Randall, I've got a total of twenty-seven prisoners. I'm going to prosecute Cortez, his lieutenants and two soldiers and cut deals with two others to use as witnesses for the prosecution. That leaves fourteen for swapping. Will that be enough to trade?"

"Fourteen Mexicans for ten Americans should do the trick. We don't want to give 'em too much of a swap advantage or they'll figure we're up to something. Send the list to me so I can prepare the paperwork. Hurry, Judd!"

"You'll have the names in half an hour."

Wiley and Castenada arrived at BOQ 17 wearing slacks and open white dress shirts. Maureen brought them into the main office. The meeting didn't last long. Judd immediately let the two P.D.s know he was in no position to have to deal. Fourteen to exchange with Mexican authorities. For one of the remaining thirteen defendants he would offer a charge of first degree murder with a life sentence. Federal charges have no parole provisions. Life means life. That one would have to testify for the prosecution. He would point fingers, he would sing to the top of his voice in return for his life.

"Take it or leave it." Judd leaned across his desk, looking straight at Wiley.

"I'll let you know, Mr. Rayburn." Wiley stood up from his chair.

"Let me know now, Mr. Wiley. If you walk through that door, the deal's off." Judd was dealing hard and buying time for the agent in Juarez.

Wiley controlled his anger. Castenada didn't say a word. Feather stared at both of them to apply more pressure.

"I don't particularly like to have this crammed down my clients' throats, Mr. Rayburn," Wiley replied.

"Lee, let's face it. You've seen the footage on TV." Judd softened his tone of voice. "You can send fourteen of your clients home and buy one his life. I'd say that was a pretty fair day's work."

Castaneda was already nodding his head when Wiley looked around at his associate.

"Done!" Wiley knew he had no bargaining position.

"I'll inform my clients. When do they leave?"

"Late Sunday afternoon."

"Which one for life?"

"Number 19, and I'll expect his full cooperation. We want to begin interrogation Monday morning."

"Agreed."

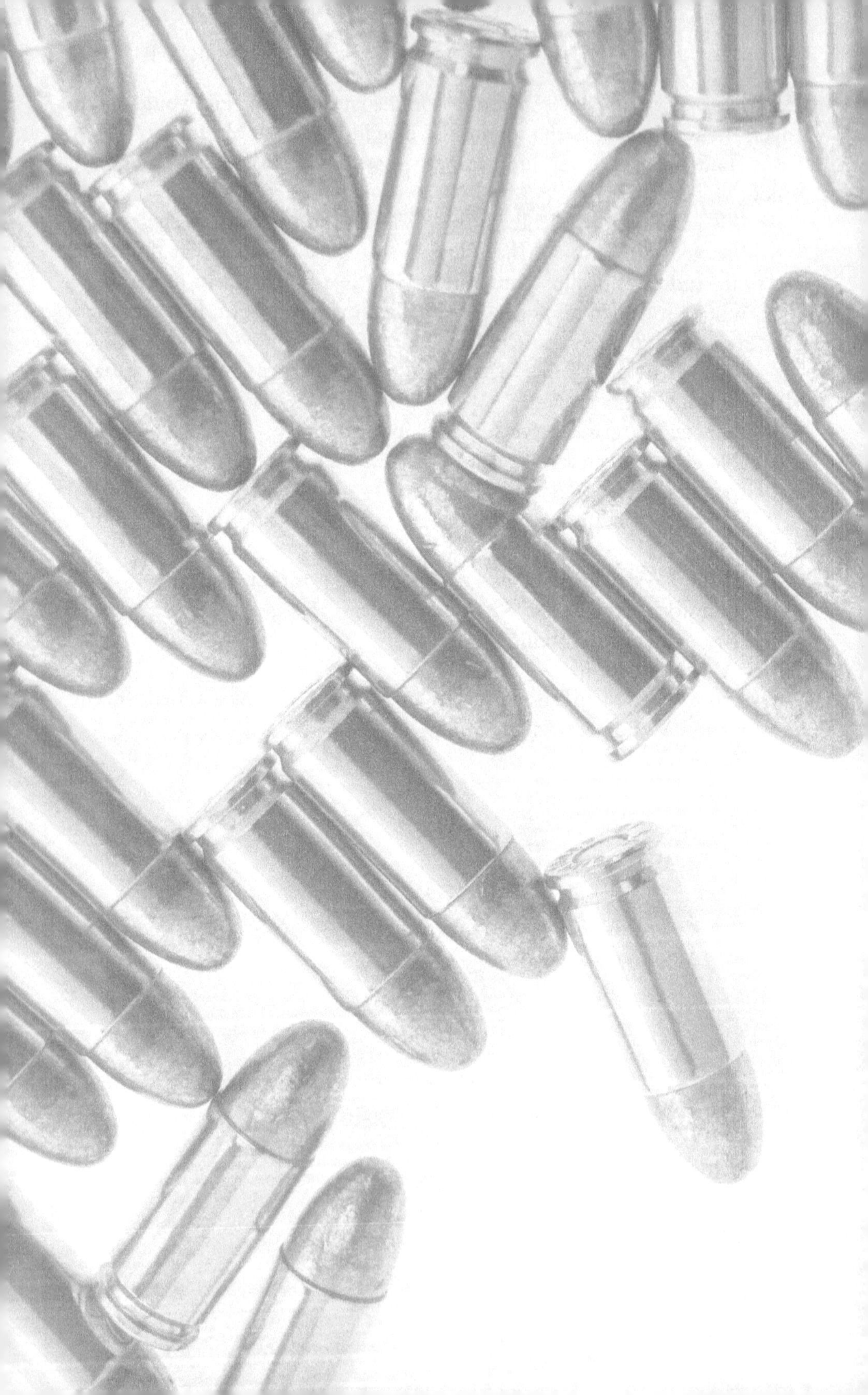

9

HIGH STAKES

The convoy pulled out of the gates of Fort Bliss led by several armored personnel carriers and followed by two paddy wagons full of prisoners. Behind the wagons were three Army medical vehicles transporting the wounded prisoners to the exchange point between El Paso and Juarez. Judd, Feather and two A.D.A.s followed in the black Chrysler. A carload of INS officials along with a man from the State Department were next in line. Another APC covered the rear. Thirty local El Paso motorcycle officers surrounded the nine-vehicle convoy as escort through the hordes of news media vehicles camped just outside the fort.

Every network Sunday afternoon news program cut directly to El Paso for live-feed coverage of this unprecedented event. The convoy continued to the exchange point.

The Mexican officials did not offer to shake hands when they met in "no man's land" in the center of the bridge over the Rio Grande River. They were stone cold.

"Mr. Rayburn, we have seven U.S. citizens for exchange. The other three are being sent across in Matamoros to Brownsville. Do you have the Mexican citizens with you?" The Mexican Army colonel was backed by over two hundred armed Mexican troops. He was not dealing from a position of weakness.

Judd didn't like the tone of the colonel's voice. "I've got fourteen Mexican killers for exchange if that's what you're asking, Colonel. I'm sure your government will treat them as such."

No reply from the colonel. Instead, he turned to his aide for the paperwork and handed it to Judd for signatures. Without moving his stare from the eyes of the colonel, Judd passed the stack of papers behind him to the man from State, a classic "Mexican stand-off" in the making. Papers were signed and exchanged.

"You first, Mr. Rayburn. We will take possession of our Mexican citizens now." The colonel was arrogant.

Judd continued his "stare down" of the colonel. "Get those blood sucking pigs off U.S. tur…"

"Yes, colonel," the man from State was trying to save an already deteriorating situation. "Bring the trucks forward!"

Feather felt that it was time to grab Judd's arm once again. He could see the anger building up as Judd's eyes stripped the colonel of his rank, his dignity and his pride. Too insulting a gesture, Joe thought. Feather stood firm. Judd and the colonel stepped back to let the trucks pass.

When the prisoners were loaded onto awaiting Mexican vehicles, the colonel motioned for the U.S. prisoners to be brought forward. Feather immediately spotted the DEA agent in the group walking under guard to their position. He didn't dare make any sign of confirmation. The swap was completed without further incident, both groups turned for the walk back. No good-byes, nothing else was said.

Halfway back to the guard booth the man from State walked over to Judd. "Mr. Rayburn! You could have blown the whole…"

"I don't want to hear it! Those men I released are killers! Scum! Any way you shake it. You guys from the State Department are too hung up on soft-soaping and smoothing over. You can't call a murderer a murderer."

"That's called diplomacy, Mr. Rayburn. That's what we're paid to do and keep hot heads like you out of foreign relations."

"Mr. State Department, kiss my ass!"

"Judd! We've got some unfinished business back at the fort with a couple of the released citizens." Feather was smiling.

"Meet the Press" was in transition from live coverage at the scene to switching back to their studios. For a three-second period the moderator was on the air, thinking they had cut to commercial. They hadn't.

"Did Rayburn tell the State Department to kiss his ass?" Cut to commercial. It was too late. Thirty million Americans heard the misplaced statement from the mouth of Judd Rayburn and confirmed by the "Meet the Press" moderator.

"Way to go, boss!"

"What do you mean, Maureen?"

"You told the State Department to kiss it. "Meet the Press" screwed up and carried it live. The switchboard is overloaded with calls coming in. Incidentally, in our office opinion poll, we're running ten to one in favor of your statement. The other ten percent is on the phone wanting to talk to you. I mean your boss. Randall Erin is on line two."

Judd rolled his eyes and headed for his room to take the call, not looking forward to it at all.

"Am I fired, Randall?"

"Good show, Judd. I've been wanting to tell State to kiss my ass for years. Don't worry about it. There'll be a little flap. The President may call…"

"Are you serious, Randall? How much trouble am I in?"

"I was only kidding. The President doesn't deal with Assistant U.S. Attorneys. I may get a call from the Attorney General, but you won't," Erin laughed. "Do you have our man?"

"Yeah, he rode over in our car. He's in with Feather now."

"Keep him there. I'm in Dallas. I'll be flying in tonight along with some people from DEA to talk to him. I'll tell you more when I get there. This thing is escalating fast."

"What thing? My statement?"

"Don't worry about that, Judd. I'm talking about the relationship with Mexico and what our agent found out. Can't say anymore over the phone. I'll see you out there later tonight and fill you in."

Erin and two DEA control agents arrived at the Fort Bliss airfield around nine p.m. and drove directly to BOQ 17 to meet with Judd and their DEA agent, Salvador "Sal" Olivares. DEA had put a lot of time and money into getting Sal the right credentials to secure a position as head chef to the Mexican congressman Emilio Cordova. He had worked for Cordova for two and a half years and cooked for the President of Mexico during one reception Cordova held for his boss. Sal's other specialty was electronic surveillance. His lack of noticeable stature, 5'5" tall and weighing 130 pounds, helped him to be almost unsuspected by the Mexican government officials since Sal did not meet the physical requirements of any investigative agency in Mexico or the U.S.

Long hours in chef school trained Sal to get along with very little sleep. Good bakers start around three a.m. preparing the morning pastries. Therefore, no one in the Cordova household thought it unusual to see Sal stirring around the hacienda in the wee hours of the morning. That's when Sal did his best "bugging." Literally every form of communication coming into or going out of Cordova's home was recorded.

Cordova was big on entertainment. At least twice a week he hosted luncheons in his large suite of offices, giving Sal the opportunity to wire the congressman's headquarters, his car, not to mention Cordova's mistress' apartment.

Erin and the two control agents got to BOQ 17 about 9:15. When introductions were over, Erin asked, "Where's our boy, Sal?"

"He's waking up from a little nap," Feather mumbled, eating a cookie out of some C-rations. "That kid had a rough time getting here. By the way, when did you guys start hiring them so big, anyway?"

"It's a long story, Joe." Erin was in no mood for long stories. "Call him in here to Judd's room. I don't want everyone in the building knowing who he is. I'm sure DEA wants to place Sal somewhere else after the bucks they spent on his cooking lessons. Do you have a recorder we can use during the debriefing?"

"Randall, do you mind if I call in Jake? I trust him."

"Jake's okay, Judd."

Ramsey joined the group in Judd's room carrying his ever present laptop. Sal arrived with a thankful grin on his face.

"I believe we're ready for debriefing, Sal," Erin guided the conversation.

"I joined the on-going investigation of our murdered agent and his pilot several years ago, gentlemen." Sal reached for a micro-cassette recorder. "DEA has suspected Mexican government involvement in the murder since 1985. I was planted, at random, for the surveillance of Congressman Emilio Cordova and it paid off. During those two years, I recorded several conversations between Cordova and five other Mexican congressmen that suggested involvement with the Mexican Cartel drug smuggling operations. Three weeks ago, at one of Cordova's pool-side receptions, I recorded conclusive information verifying not only his personal involvement with the Cartel, but solid confirmation that he's working with one Julio Cortez."

That statement raised every eyebrow in the room. The only sound other than Sal's voice was Ramsey's constant pecking on his laptop.

"Cordova was in a particularly good mood during the reception and drank a lot," Sal continued. "About 2:30 one night, after all of the guests had gone home, incidentally, no U.S. officials were invited to the party, Cordova blew it. He placed a call to Cortez and I've got it on tape. Cortez's voice can be verified by voiceprint. Basically, Cordova was feeling bulletproof and didn't want to retire for the night. He wanted an insider-drinking buddy to celebrate some good news that he had gotten earlier in the week. I've got that, too.

"Mr. Cortez arrived from the back entrance of the grounds about 3:15 a.m.. He'd also been drinking. From a voice actuated listening device I'd installed in one of the trees in the backyard I got this…"

Sal placed the micro-tape in the recorder, turned the volume up and pushed the play button.

"Cordova speaks first," Sal was translating the tape…

"Julio, we got a lot of money this time, my friend."

"Close to half a million, Emilio. See, I told you not to worry about that dead agent and his friend years ago. You were so scared someone would find out. We killed him slow, then we made lots of money, didn't we, amigo?"

"Don't talk about that, Julio! Have some tequila and tell me about the deal we swung in Puerto Rico with our pharmaceutical company."

At the mention of Puerto Rico, Feather looked over at Judd without saying a word. Both of them were thinking about what Rikki had mentioned.

"Gentlemen," Sal said as he stopped the recorder, "I could go on translating. We can have that done later. We have what we need. Let me go on and tell you what was discussed between Mr. Cordova and Mr. Cortez. The story will blow you away, my friends.

"Cordova and the other five congressmen are investment partners with a group of people in Puerto Rico. I was unable to get their names. They own a pharmaceutical company down there called Carolina Pharmaceuticals located in the town of Carolina, Puerto Rico.

"Cortez, with the congressmen's help, is actually shipping heroin and cocaine in pill form, properly bottled and labeled, to their company in Puerto Rico to be used as raw materials in drugs they are manufacturing for distribution throughout third world nations. When it leaves their company, it's all legal. Some of the most respected doctors and pharmacists in the third world are their biggest customers.

"It also gives them a vehicle to bring legalized shipments of illegal drugs into Puerto Rico for distribution through U.S. trafficking avenues in Miami, Houston, and New Orleans. They use part of the shipments for pills, the rest are for 'crack' and 'horse' to be sent to drug dealers on the mainland. The big payoff they were referring to on the tape was actually stock dividends from Carolina Pharmaceuticals to the stockholders. Can you believe that? Then, they launder the money through their own legitimate Puerto Rican company."

Sal sat back in his chair to give everyone time to digest what he'd just told them.

"We have some of the facts," Erin began. "Let's get to some of the obvious questions."

"The obvious question is who's involved in the partnership of Carolina Pharmaceuticals in Puerto Rico?" Judd replied.

"Seems like the big question to me," Erin added.

Judd looked back at Feather as if to cue him about Rikki. Judd couldn't mention her name. He wasn't supposed to even know her.

"I've got a friend in Naval Intelligence working in Puerto Rico, name's Commander Rhine," Joe stated. "I've got the number if you want to put in an unofficial call. Maybe Naval Intelligence can shed some light on this. I don't want to take a chance of blowing any cover by going through official channels, though. You never know where a leak may spring up, if you know what I mean."

"Interesting, Joe. Since you know him, why don't you place the call. Can you get him on the line tonight?"

"I'll try."

Feather picked up the phone and dialed the number from memory. He never wrote down phone numbers, especially those belonging to undercover agents, part of his training at "the farm."

"Rikki? Joe. How's the Caribbean climate treating you, dear?"

"Where are you?" she asked.

"Fort Bliss."

Rikki knew that Joe had a reason for the call. She was following the Cortez case closely. Her telephone wasn't guaranteed to be secure.

"What about tomorrow afternoon for margaritas?"

"See you then." Feather turned to Erin. "Rhine will be here tomorrow afternoon."

"Next on the agenda, gentlemen." Erin pulled several Justice Department directives from his briefcase. "These haven't made distribution yet. Let me update everyone on why Mexico is doing what they're doing concerning pulling out of the narco-trafficking programs. I'll read this…'The United States government may kidnap people from a foreign country and prosecute them over that nation's objection, the Supreme Court ruled last week in a ruling called monstrous by dissenting justices. The decision said an extradition treaty between the U.S. and Mexico does not specifically bar such abductions.' End quote."

"No wonder they're pulling out of the agreements!" Judd exclaimed, thinking that the abduction of Cortez was now legal, within U.S. law. "If this scam goes public, half the Mexican government could fall, even the honest Mexican congressmen would be implicated by association."

"You got it, Judd. Plus, there's no telling who we are going to find in the partnership on the other side in Puerto Rico. We're playing with fire, gentlemen! Mexico is not going to be the only country to circle their wagons."

"Sal, you were lucky to get out when you did," Erin was serious. "You stay right here at the Fort, for your own protection. Outside these gates your life isn't worth a plug nickel since we don't know who else is involved in this. Judd, it's conceivable the Mexican Secret Police may try something radical, like trying to get their hands on Sal or even Cortez since he's privy to everything going on. Effective immediately, I'm going to ask Ramirez to declare Fort Bliss closed and on permanent red alert."

"What about the scheduling of the trial?" Judd asked.

"We need to escalate proceedings on the trial, get it done and get out of here. We're too close to the Mexican border. I'll talk to Ramirez about that, too. Gentlemen, consider this the most secret information you've ever received. Effective immediately, no outside calls to family or friends. Official business will be all that's allowed, and only on secured lines. One other thing, Judd. Get the news people with passes inside the gates. Clear the others off the premises. This is still a military reservation. We have the authority to do that, freedom of speech or not. Any contact with other agencies will be done only through me."

"I take it you'll be staying here?"

"You got that right, amigo! We could all be potential targets by Cartel, Mob or Mexican Secret Police. Lord knows who else, depending on the other side of the Puerto Rican partnership and who's involved."

"I'll give Judge Ramirez a call. We should go right on over and update him," Judd mentioned. "You want to go with me, Randall?"

"Yeah, let's allow ourselves forty-five minutes with the judge, then call in Wiley and Castenada. They've got to know the brevity of the situation so they don't put up too big a fuss if we move the timetable up on the trial. The five of us can reset schedules. Do you think they'll co-operate, Judd?"

"We'll find out in about an hour."

Judd and Erin met with Ramirez until midnight bringing him up to speed. Ramirez was already aware of the Supreme Court ruling and knew it would have some bearing on the case. He was now learning just how much.

"Will the prosecution use your undercover agent as a witness?" Ramirez asked.

"Yes we will, Your Honor," Judd answered. "He'll be a cloaked witness, though. We'll put the bag over his head, drape the cubical on the witness stand and alter his voice so no tape ID can be made of him."

"You've got to tell defense what you're going to do."

"Yes sir. We took the liberty of inviting Wiley and Castenada over. They should be here any time."

While they were waiting for the defense team to arrive, Judge Ramirez called General Lawton. The fort was put on red alert. Cobra gunships began regular patrols around the perimeter of the reservation and personnel were moved to their duty stations on a twenty-four hour basis. All traffic in and out of the fort was canceled. Supplies would be transported by helicopter. As soon as press personnel were inside and quartered, Fort Bliss would be officially locked up on alert status.

"Gentlemen, please be seated," Ramirez directed as Wiley and Castenada arrived at the judge's quarters.

For the next thirty minutes Erin and Judd informed Wiley and Castenada of the situation. They listened intently.

"In summary, gentlemen," continued Erin, "you two could become possible targets, but I don't think so. I believe there's a real possibility of one or both of you being contacted by members of the Mexican congress or secret police. They need to know what the prosecution has found out and who within Mexico it may implicate. Wiley, you and Castenada are, from this point forward, sworn to secrecy for national security's sake. No press releases, no calls going out. I'll tell you both right now, your calls are being monitored by FBI and will not, repeat, will not be forwarded to the prosecution.

"We will interview defendant number 19, a Mr...." Erin flipped through the stack of indictments, pulling out one from the stack with `19' written on it in bold black magic marker, "Paco Gomez. We want to talk to him at eight a.m..

"At three p.m. we'll talk to Cortez. I'm sure you two will be present. Two last points. First, go ahead and provide the best defense you are capable of providing, national security or not, I don't want anyone saying they didn't get a fair trial. But, please gentlemen, don't pull anything hocus pocus and petty. There's no time for that. Secondly, give your families a call and get them inside the fort. They can be quartered in your building. Move them in tonight."

The two defense lawyers didn't know what to make of the situation. It was more than they had bargained for.

Wiley and Castenada said very little throughout the briefing.

10

THE NOTEBOOK

Off in the distance the press convoy was moving inside the fort. Military Police had given the media an early wake up call to hand out press passes, move the recipients in and clear out the ones without passes.

"I had Casey and her family moved in last night, Judd," Erin said. "I've instructed her to prepare a statement to the press. They're going to ask a thousand questions about what's happening. I'll issue the statement later this morning and calm them down. I'll also issue do's and don'ts at that time. I'm sure we'll get a few first amendment suits filed against us on this, but we'll deal with them later. As things unfold during the trial, let's hope their patriotism surfaces."

"Glad you're doing the conference instead of me. The media's going to get a little crazy."

"That's why I get the big bucks, Judd," Erin laughed.

"Mr. Gomez you are represented by council…"

"Sorry to interrupt, Mr. Rayburn," Castenada broke in. "Mr. Gomez does not speak English. Do you want your own interpreter?"

"Jake, can you get Feather over here on the double?"

While they were waiting for Feather to get there, Judd passed a list of questions to Castenada and asked him to read them to Mr. Paco Gomez. One of the questions asked whether or not Gomez had ever heard the name Emilio Cordova, from whom, and how it tied in to the illegal drug smuggling operation. Even though Judd did not speak much Spanish, he read eyes very well. When the name of Cordova was mentioned, Gomez's eyes began telling Judd exactly what he wanted to hear. He could see there was a link to Cordova by the fear on Paco's face.

Feather arrived. The list of questions was read to Gomez. The answers given by the very scared individual were incredible. Paco was hooked up to a lie detector by his own consent. Castenada continually urged his client to give true and factual answers, possibly his only chance to escape the death sentence. Paco smoked half a pack of cigarettes during the first hour of interrogation.

"Joe, when we go back in, I've already prepared another list of questions, the same questions we asked the first two hours, only phrased differently," Judd remarked. "We have some hard evidence now that we didn't have before. I want to make sure we have more details. Is there anything in the questions that'll be hard to translate? Do I need to reword anything?"

"Questions are okay, Judd. I'll fill in any blanks we need, plus, Castenada is really helping a lot keeping Gomez cool and on track. Obviously, he's done his homework on the discovery tapes. He knows we've got convictions."

At 11:30 Judd, Feather and Ramsey returned to BOQ 17 for lunch, reeling from the information Paco had given.

"Messages, Maureen?"

"Here's the stack you need to return, boss."

3 p.m. Judd took the same list of questions in for Cortez he had asked Paco. Feather ducked out on this interview as interpreter to watch Cortez through a two-way mirror. Another A.U.S.A fluent in Spanish accompanied Judd. Joe wondered if Judd would remain calm during the interrogation.

"Mr. Cortez, will you consent to a lie detector test?" Judd said in a calm, uncaring voice.

"No lie detectors!" Cortez spoke English very well.

For forty-five minutes, Cortez read the 5th Amendment regarding self-incrimination written out on a three-by-five index card. Judd expected this but wanted to see the expression on Cortez's face when certain times, dates and names were mentioned.

"Tell me about Dee Espinoza, Mr. Cortez. Do you know the man you once called your son?" Judd asked.

"Dee *was* like a son to me," the first verbal answer given by Cortez other than the 5th Amendment, "Then he turns on me. I have no idea why. I always treat him like my son."

"Then why did you castrate him and cut the rope he was suspended from below your copter, hangman's style, Mr. Cortez?" Judd continued.

"I was not cutting the rope. I was trying to pull him up inside the chopper. He seemed to be hurt. I think one of the police officers shot him in the groin," Cortez answered. "I do not know why they were shooting at the helicopter."

"Mr. Cortez, are you acquainted with Emilio Cordova?"

For a split instant Cortez acted surprised Cordova's name would even be mentioned. He quickly resumed a very passive tone of voice.

"I have read the newspapers in Mexico. He is a congressman or something. I do not know him personally," Cortez responded. "Is the Mexican government concerned about my unlawful detention in your stinking jail?"

"Not in the least, Mr. Cortez. What makes you think they would be concerned?"

"I am a prominent land owner in Mexico. I give much to the people and to the government in my country. I am respected in Mexico and have many very influential friends who will protest my illegal arrest. They will see to it that I am home where I belong very soon. How much more are you going to ask me? I am getting very tired of this harassment. I am innocent of any crimes, you will see. I will be back in Mexico within a week and you, Mr. Rayburn, will owe me an apology and will get fired from your job. I wouldn't be at all surprised if your family got threatened for the bad way in which I am being treated."

Judd's expression grew hard. Looking deep into Cortez's eyes but not leaning up from his chair, Judd said, "Julio, I don't have a family. You're dealing with the one and only. Save your crap for someone else. I'm the guy you never wanted to meet and I've got you right where I want you. The entire Mexican army can't get you back."

"You will see, Mr. Rayburn!"

"Julio," Judd said pleasantly without awaiting a response from Cortez. "let me ask you a question."

"Anything, Judd," Cortez responded sarcastically.

"You know you're being charged with capital murder? It carries a death sentence when you are convicted."

"I am completely innocent of any charges, amigo. No one will ever convict me."

Cortez was returned to his cell. Feather came from behind the mirror and met Judd in the hallway.

"You held your temper, bro. I'm proud of you."

"Did you see him flinch when I mentioned Cordova's name?"

"Sure did. Do you think maybe Mr. Cortez isn't telling us everything he knows?"

Feather and Judd chuckled as they returned to BOQ 17.

"Randall! It's Air Jordan time. Slam dunk city!" Judd was excited.

"What did you find out from Gomez and Cortez?"

"Gomez's uncle is a driver for the good congressman, Mr. Cordova. We have the tie we need to him. Paco told us that Cordova has met with Cortez on many secret rendezvous in the last several years. Cordova is in this thing up to his neck. He also gave us the names of the other seven congressmen, not five, who are in on the deal. Paco's uncle has been keeping a record, part of his insurance survival policy."

"Can we prove it?" Randall asked.

"We can if we can retrieve a notebook Paco's uncle has socked away in a safety deposit box just outside of Mexico City. Paco had a key in his billfold when we captured him at Ambush Pass. We've got the key in with his personal possessions in the property room."

"Got to move on this fast, Judd. I've got an excellent LEGAT in Mexico City. If we can get the key to him, we can get the notebook. Who can get down there with it?"

"How about Commander Rhine?" Feather suggested. "Should be here anytime."

"He's real 'white-ish' to be traveling to Mex right now," Randall wasn't too enthusiastic about sending unassigned Naval Intelligence down there.

Maureen came bursting into the room, "Mr. Erin! Captain Perkins of the TAG team is on line 2 for you. There's been a security breech. Someone's broken in to the fort! An intruder!"

"Erin speaking. What's going on Captain?"

"Sir, our ground level scan radar is beeping off the screen in sector twelve. It's been going off for about the last ten minutes. We've got an intruder. But we're unable to find him. I've scrambled a gun ship with orders to shoot on sight. This could be it, Sir. Get your people inside."

"Thanks for the warning, Captain."

"Judd! Red Alert! We've got an intruder inside the gate. Get everyone…"

"Intruder?" Rikki walked into the room with sand all over her cammo pants and FLY NAVY short-sleeved sweat shirt. "I get an invitation for margaritas and this is the reception I get? Being called an intruder?"

Erin reached for his Glock.

"No, no, Randall! This is Commander Rhine! It's okay!" Feather blurted out as he dashed between them.

Rikki stood there with a sexy smirk on her face. It took a couple of minutes for everyone to calm down.

Erin walked over to Rikki and stuck out his hand, trying to hide his look of disbelief, "I've heard a lot about you, Commander Rhine. Looks like the joke's on me. I expected to see some big burly brute, not a..."

"A female? Sorry for the confusion," Rikki said with a snide chuckle. "I would've been here earlier but I had to set off the radar on the other side of the fort before I walked through the main entrance. Then, I thumbed a ride up here..."

"You thumbed a ride?" Judd had a perplexed look on his face.

"Yes," Rikki continued, "the company jet was unavailable in San Juan, so I had to take a commercial flight to El Paso. The guards wouldn't let me in the fort. I couldn't just tell 'em I was Naval Intelligence. I'm not supposed to be here, anyway. Besides, it was kinda fun. No one told me the fort was on alert. I really think you have a security problem. That was too easy. Where can I stash my bags?"

As usual, Rikki had made her entrance. Erin called Captain Perkins to stand down, explaining the intrusion was a security check, which he failed miserably.

"Feel like doing us a little favor, Rikki?"

"I feel wonderful, slept most of the way here, Indian. What kind of favor?"

"Simple. Just put this key in a safety deposit box, open it and bring us a little black notebook."

"Sounds simple, where's this safety deposit box?"

"In a little branch bank outside Mexico City. Here it is on the map." Feather spread a road map of Mexico on the table.

"Give me time to get showered and changed. By the way, has anyone got any cash? I left in a hurry," Rikki pulled her left pocket out of her cammos, empty.

There was no way of telling how much money she had in her purse. No one asked. Ramsey went to the safe.

"How much do you think you'll need, Commander Rhine?"

"Couple thousand should do."

"Commander Rhine," Erin gave Rikki a piece of paper. "I have a good Legal Attaché, or LEGAT, in Mexico City, you can trust him. If you need his assistance, this is his number."

Rikki glanced at the name and number and then gave the piece of paper back to Erin. "Thanks, big guy, I'll try not to bug him. This shouldn't take long." Ramsey looked over at Judd. Judd nodded. Ramsey got the cash and gave it to Rikki. She left that night in a first class seat on Aero Mexico.

"How'd the press conference go, Randall?"

Judd could see that Randall was about ready to call it a night.

"Just about like we expected." Erin sat back. "They wanted more information than I gave 'em. They accused us of holding back and covering up, the usual. I had one of the reporters from a rag tabloid thrown out of the fort. That'll be our first lawsuit. It served as a good example to the other reporters though. They calmed down after that. Oh, yes, Erica Stone wants you to call her. She gave me her number. Attractive lady!"

Judd took the note without reply.

TUESDAY, JUNE 9TH

Maureen walked into Judd's room still wearing her night gown and terry cloth housecoat. She put a steaming cup of coffee on the nightstand beside his bed. He was still sleeping as his alarm rung out the last few dings.

"What time is it?"

"A quarter 'til six. Thought I'd let you sleep an extra fifteen minutes. Tell me about Commander Rhine. You were smiling in your sleep. Who is she, anyway, boss?"

Judd reached for the coffee, took a sip and sat back against the wall, no headboards on Army beds.

"An old college flame. She's the girl that started me flying."

"Looks like you're still flying. She must've been special to you."

"She was. I enjoyed seeing her again, catching up on old times. Did you know she won the trophy at Top Gun?"

"Impressive. When do I get to meet her?"

"Soon."

"Boss, when can you fix me up with our Army driver?"

"Never."

"Come on, boss. He's beautiful!"

"He's dangerous."

"He's intriguing."

"He'll steal your heart and leave you hanging."

"My heart belongs to three other guys already, boss."

"You'll just be another notch on his bedpost."

"Maybe he'll be one on mine."

"Company ink, Maureen."

"Commander Rhine is ink."

"She's special. We're not talking notches here."

"Are we talking double standards here, boss?" Maureen smiled as she sat further back in the chair, pulling her robe down around to cover her ankles.

"Thanks for the coffee and the wake-up, Mom. Now, would you clear out and let me get dressed?"

Judd was putting on his sneakers when Erin knocked once and entered the room.

"We got problems, Judd. I got a call from my man at the embassy in Mexico City. Secret Police down there have a Mr. Robert Jones, that's right, Jones, in custody. They've had him for three days. He's a tourist from Houston, literally. They're convinced he's our inside guy for some reason. His family reported him missing yesterday to Houston PD. Mexico wants to deal. Side note, Commander Rhine just leveled the little bank outside Mexico City, it's a pile of rubble. Has anyone heard from her?"

"No. We probably won't until she gets back. Jones?"

"Believe it, Judd. At this point it doesn't make any difference whether it is our man or not. The Mexicans are convinced he is. I'm sure they've banged him up some. Jones may be telling them anything they want to hear to keep them from hitting on him anymore. Who knows?"

"What kind of a deal do they want, Randall?"

"They want Cortez back!"

"No way!"

"I agree. However, they've got a U.S. citizen in custody. Whatever we do to Cortez, they're going to do the same thing with Jones. That's the way the game is played. Mexico is highly hacked about the Supreme Court decision anyway. Couple that with half the Mexican congress being mixed up in this Puerto Rican pharmaceutical scam and we got big problems prosecuting Cortez.

"There's more. It is imperative we know who makes up the other side of the partnership in Carolina Pharmaceuticals before we nail Cortez. As of now, the Mexicans don't know we have any knowledge whatsoever of that deal."

"Looks like discovery is going to take on a whole new meaning in this case, Randall."

"I just hope Commander Rhine makes it back with that notebook. That'll give us more chips to play in this poker game. I'm anxious to know what she's found out in Puerto Rico, also. We should've debriefed her before she left. She's got to get that book."

"She will. The lady's good, a bit colorful at times…"

"We've still got two weeks for discovery. Have you got your ducks in a row here, Judd?"

"We're finishing up our video presentation. We've got a couple of local witnesses to round up, but for the most part, we're ready to go to trial."

"The minute Commander Rhine gets back, we've got to go over the notebook and debrief her on Puerto Rico. Based on what we find out, you'll probably have to go down there and dig out the other side of the partnership. We've got to know who we're dealing with before we plunge into this trial. I've got a call in to the Attorney General in Washington. We're getting the State Department in on this Jones thing ASAP."

1:30 p.m.. The press corps had received word from their Washington affiliates that something was stirring with Mexico. They knew the name of Robert Jones. Houston reporters surrounded the Jones' residence trying to get information from the family. State Department personnel were already there with the Jones' to keep a lid on the situation.

Members of the press at Fort Bliss were getting impatient at the silence from Judd's office. They were sure of a tie-in with Cortez and wanted details. BOQ 5 and 17 were strictly off limits to them as stated when they were first brought inside the fort; however, phones in 5 and 17 weren't off limits. They were ringing off the hook.

"I'm not trying to tell you how to run your business, boss, but someone better tell the press corps something soon. They're getting hostile." Maureen was serious.

"Randall and I are preparing a statement now. Call over to the press building and set up a conference for 3:30 this afternoon. Have you heard from Rikki?"

"Not in the five minutes since you last asked me, boss."

The statement to the press was being carefully coordinated with the State Department who had two men on the way to Bliss to help with the press corps problems.

2:30 p.m. "Boss, Commander Rhine just called, she's at the airport. She's still on the phone."

"Welcome home, lady. Am I glad to hear from you! Got the notebook?" Time was running out for Judd and the statement to the press.

"Piece of cake. You want to send a chopper over to get me?"

"It's already there. Go to the military information desk there at the airport. Get here fast. We need that book."

Judd, Randall, and Feather were waiting on the flight line at the fort when Rikki's chopper sat down. The two men from State were waiting back at BOQ 17 preparing several scenarios of statements, leaving blanks to be filled in after talking to Judd and Erin. They didn't know of Rikki's involvement, just that someone was coming in from Mexico with new information.

Rikki sensed the urgency in Judd's voice. She'd been around long enough to know something big was stirring. She raced from the chopper and got into the black Chrysler. Judd reached for the notebook. Rikki pulled it back and gave it to Feather.

"It's all in Spanish, Judd. Better let Joe fill you in. I read some of it on the plane coming back but I didn't want to flash it around too much. Never can tell who else on the plane may have wanted it. To give you a thumbnail, it's a diary-form chronolog. It gives names, dates and places. The details will knock your socks off. Half the Mexican government is in there. That's got to be the hottest notebook in the western hemisphere. I'm dead serious."

"Fantastic work, Commander," Erin said. "We've got a press conference slated in less than an hour we're coordinating with the State Department. Don't worry, we haven't blown your cover. They don't know you're here. We've moved your things next door to BOQ 16. The Mexican Secret Police have a John Q in custody in Mexico City and they're claiming he's one of our agents. Things have gotten tense since you left."

"Now they want to deal for Cortez. Right, Randall?"

"You're real quick, Commander Rhine. By the way, how'd you get down there and back so fast? I figured you'd have some trouble."

"I've got a great travel agent."

"Sure, Commander."

"What exactly happened at the bank?" Erin asked.

"Details," Rikki crossed her legs and cracked a smile. "I hadn't planned to blow the whole bank. Guess I sorta mis-figured the strength of the C-5 explosives. Anyway, getting inside the bank was easy. I neutralized the instant alarm system with all the bells and hooters. I figured there must be some heavy bucks in that little bank because of the sophistication of the alarm system and the vault. That only means one thing, drug money! The system had a delayed alarm on it. I didn't have time to disarm it. When that C-5 went off…" Rikki started to laugh, "It doggone near blew up the whole block. Pesos and diamond rings were flying everywhere. There's some nouveau riche in that neighborhood. You should've seen those people grab that money. Where the bank was is now basically a vacant lot. It was hilarious. No one got hurt, either!"

"The whole bank, Rikki?" Judd couldn't believe it.

"Hey, Judd. I got your blasted old notebook, didn't I?"

Feather hadn't been listening to the story of the bank. He was going from page to page in the notebook.

"Gentlemen, I believe we hold the fate of a nation in our hands with this book. It's all here, everything we need to topple the government in Mexico. It goes pretty high up."

11

THE JURY

Press corps personnel packed the conference room adjoining their quarters. The speaker's podium had at least forty microphones duct taped around the edges resembling an AT&T trunk station.

Maureen walked up to the podium as a hush fell over the group. She was surrounded by an entourage of prosecution trial staff, along with Erin and the two men from State.

"Mr. Randall Erin, Special U.S. Attorney for the Western District, State of Texas, will issue a statement updating the progress in pre-trial proceedings in the Mexican Cartel case. Q&A will follow when this statement is completed. Ladies and Gentlemen, Mr. Erin."

"Good afternoon." Randall wiped the perspiration from his forehead. "I'll try to be brief as possible and begin with updates in the trial proceedings. You have been given charges against the defendants along with their names. The prosecution has decided to try the defendants on one charge at a time beginning with Capital Murder which carries a death sentence. The defendants will be tried as a group. Judge Ramirez has denied motions of change of venue and a motion to sever.

"Jury selection will begin in about a week and a half. Jury members will be sequestered during the entire proceedings. Trial is scheduled to begin Monday, July 13th, as earlier planned. Prosecution will ask for the death penalty if guilty verdicts are rendered by the jury. That concludes my statement. Questions? You, there. I can't read your name tag."

"Mr. Erin, Sam Clark, US News. Is there a connection between Mr. Jones' arrest down in Mexico and the Cartel members about to go to trial?"

"The U.S. Attorney's office sees no connection whatsoever." Erin was keeping his answers short as possible. "The lady over there."

"Erica Stone, ABC News. Will the government of Mexico use Mr. Jones as a bargaining chip to secure the release of Mr. Julio Cortez and the other defendants in the Cartel trial? And part two of the question, will this affect the critical path chosen against the defendants? I mean, seeking the death penalty?"

"In answer to the first part of your question, Ms. Stone, we have no indication that Mexico seeks any kind of release of the defendants. We believe the government of Mexico is anxious to see that justice is done concerning the defendants. Part two of the question, trial proceedings will go as scheduled. No change in strategy. You there."

"Jeff Townsend, NBC News. Why was the media moved inside the fort if there is no immediate danger from retaliation by Mexican officials on the capture of the Cartel members, and was there a breach of the base's security yesterday and what was it?"

"The Honorable Judge Ramirez ordered the press inside the fort for your own protection, from the snakes and scorpions, not from any expected Mexican retaliation. I believe the Red Cross reported two cases of snake bite by sidewinder rattlers and three scorpion stings the first two days of the media's encampment outside the fort. Your protection is from the elements, not from any foreign government.

"The base has been put on alert status by General Lawton, Base Commander, as a matter of standard operating procedure since so many civilian personnel are inside the fort. Security has been beefed up to secure the ongoing protection of defendants, also standard operational procedure. The lady in the blue jeans, there."

"Clara Johnson, CNN. Mr. Erin, do you really expect the members of the media to believe all this hogwash? There's a lot more to this than you're telling us. What's the U.S. government trying to cover up this time?"

From that point, the press conference went downhill fast. Erin closed out the Q&A.

"I'm going to issue bullet-proof vests before the next news conference," Randall said. He knew the media was not going to be content with the information put out. However, he didn't expect such a level of hostility to begin so soon. "Maybe someone from State should do the next conference. They're a lot better trained in lying than we are." Judd's contempt for State Department officials continued.

"Judd, it's important to keep State out of this thing as much as possible…"

"Sorry for interrupting, Randall," Judd blurted out. "But, depending what we find out in Puerto Rico, I'd just as soon keep everyone out of this. I mean State, CIA, FBI, the President, Congress, the whole shootin' match, with the exception of Feather and Commander Rhine, that is. I've been shot and shot at. I'm getting real uncomfortable about this. I believe we're going to see some names on that partnership list in Puerto Rico that are going to raise some hairlines, much less eyebrows. We've got to keep this under lock and key until then. No more involvement by outside agencies, period!

"One other thing, I want to know who is running this show. We're playing with fire here, Randall. I trust you, but that's as high up as it goes. I don't mind the heat as long as I know who's stoking the fire, if you know what I mean!"

"I'm not sure I do know exactly what you mean, Judd. Obviously you've got more on your mind."

"What happens if the names on that list turn out to be U.S. government officials? I haven't played the game in Washington, but I'm not dumb. People get dead for turning over the wrong rocks."

"I've played the game in the DC, Judd. Your concern is justified, believe me. My position is this; we do keep the proceedings of this case under lock and key. I'll front for you keeping the other arms of government out of your hair. It's your case, Judd. You have my word on that. You direct the investigation. I'll do my best to separate Mr. Robert Q. Jones off to the State Department. That should keep them busy. However, you know that Mexico is going to want Cortez. State is going to try their best to get right in the middle of our business of convicting, sentencing and needling Cortez. That's coming, Judd!"

"I know it's coming, Randall. That's where my trust in you kicks in. I want Commander Rhine assigned to this case as officially as we can make it to the point at which she is not, repeat, *not* obliged to tell her superiors at Naval Intelligence everything she knows. Next, I want my own team. By that I mean a carefully selected team of technicians, like a small Delta-Force team: experts in communication, assault tactics, covert activities, demolition, electronics, the whole bag. Can you arrange that, Randall?"

"That's a tall order, Judd. To stand here at this moment and guarantee you all of this. I can't right now. I'll prepare a plan, a checklist, and work with Commander Rhine and Feather to see what we can put together. That's the best I can do for now. You're talking black ops that is blacker than black. We're putting ourselves on real shaky ground here, Judd."

"I told you I trust you, Randall. That's good enough for now. Let's go next door and finish debriefing Rikki and let her in on what we're going to do."

Judd and Erin walked over to BOQ 16. An Army sergeant brought in some sandwiches from the mess hall. It was going to be another long night.

"I like it, Judd." Feather had changed into shorts and sneakers. "Our own group, independent of interagency leaks, ready to act at a moment's notice. It's the only way to go. Otherwise, someone could get killed and no one would ever know. We have to watch each other's backs from God knows who."

Rikki was eating yogurt, following the conversation.

"We've got to have a code name for the group. "Rikki said. "How about The Jury?"

"Code name Jury it is, gentlemen," Randall confirmed.

"I've got a retired agent friend," Rikki continued as she put the yogurt down, "who has a two hundred acre ranch back in the hill country around Con Can, Texas, west of San Antonio. He's got a barn and a couple of hangars along with a four thousand foot asphalt air strip out there. I'm sure he'll work with us on this thing. He'd be helpful in training, too, since he put in thirty years with the CIA. He's forgotten more than most of these guys know. What do you think? Con Can, Texas? Headquarters for the Jury?"

Judd looked over at Erin. Randall leaned forward, "It does need to be in the middle of nowhere. Con Can, Texas is Nowhere USA, all right. There's a state park near there with lots of campers. That should help our traffic in and out of the place to blend in real well. Give your friend a call, Commander. Let's do it!"

"We should start the list of applicants for the team right here at the fort," Feather took charge of putting the team together. "There're some good men on the TAG team; we've seen them in action. I'll talk to the General, feel him out on this, then screen the list. Inter-agency communication could pop the lid on this in a hurry."

"Yeah, you're right, Joe," Rikki pitched the yogurt container in the trashcan. "I can get some ex-CIA'ers that I know. How many guys are we going to put on this jury anyway?"

Judd cut his eyes towards Feather. "Joe, can you come up with a logistical list of who we'll need to round out the team?"

"Sure. I'm guessing about thirty max."

Randall had said very little during the planning stages.

"Boys and girls, we could get ourselves in a lot of trouble for this. You know that, don't you?"

Everyone in the room acknowledged. They had just chartered a very exclusive club, one that bordered on illegality and high treason. But they were paid to enforce law and the law was losing almost every battle. They needed a win at any cost.

"Let's let The Jury thing mull over in our minds for a while," Erin said. "We need to start taking some notes on what you've found out in Puerto Rico, Rikki. We're going to need an easel, markers and paper."

If anyone wanted out, now was the time to speak up. Glances around the room confirmed that they were all in.

Rikki walked up to the easel and began the session.

"No law, gentlemen. I'm telling you there is no law in Puerto Rico! You want to talk drugs coming into the island. Let me tell you about drugs. Every citizen in PR knows about the drugs coming in, where they come from and who is involved. But to whom are they going to complain? To the cops? I don't think so. I could go on and on. I believe you get the picture. We cannot count on any help from local law enforcement when we get down there. I'm not going to say that all the cops are crooked. They believe they're up against overwhelming odds. They don't know who is into what. They don't trust, therefore they do not act. Sound familiar, guys?

"We're going to be solidly on our own. And, Judd, we'll be looking over our shoulders from the time we arrive until we get back on the mainland. After that, who knows?"

"I had no idea," Erin exclaimed with a bewildered look on his face.

"I ran checks on several of the policemen in Puerto Rico. Some are living a little over their means. I know they're receiving kickbacks. But bear this in mind: Getting a few dollars more for turning your head is a way of life down there. Can you blame them?"

"I can blame them!" Erin never minced words when it came down to guts and glory. "When they put on a badge, they're sworn to uphold the law."

"I hear you, Randall. I also agree with you. But it was mainly a terrorist group calling themselves *El Prevision* that Naval Intelligence had an interest in. That group was on my investigation list."

"You've made your point, Commander," Erin inserted. "No law!"

"We've got another faction down there, also." Rikki yawned. It was 2:30 a.m.. "The mob."

"Why doesn't this surprise me?" Judd yawned. "What part is the mob playing in the drug trafficking?"

"Without solid evidence, I would have to venture a guess based on mob involvement on drugs here in the States. I'd guess they're laundering the bulk of the money, Judd. The old timers in the Mafia are and have been against the distribution of drugs for decades. Drugs affect children. Contrary to what many believe, the Mafia is very family oriented. I don't mean to sound cute, either. The younger generation La Cosa Nostra, or LCN, see the big money and want to get heavily into drug sales. Some are distributing now. However, as long as the Perrones control the alliance of families in the States, direct involvement in the distribution of drugs will be kept to a minimum."

"So, Commander, have you made any connection with the partnership involved with Carolina Pharmaceuticals?" Erin pressed.

"None. When Sal mentioned the name, it was the first time I'd heard of it. I've been checking on the terrorist group based in the mountains, *El Prevision.* The home office wants to know if they are a threat to U.S. security."

"Are they?" Feather asked.

"Not as far as I can determine. After the short time I spent in Puerto Rico, I've come to the conclusion these terrorists may be helpful to our efforts. They just hate the government and corruption down there."

"Looks like we've got some digging to do, Rikki," Judd remarked. "We need to go to Puerto Rico and dig out the partnership in the pharmaceutical company."

"That's a good place to start, Judd. One problem. Your face has been plastered on every news program in the free world. They'll recognize you immediately." Erin closed his notebook and rubbed his eyes. It was now 3:30 a.m..

"I'll arrange transportation, Randall." Judd had an idea, killing two birds.... "We need to arrive in Puerto Rico unannounced."

12

La Cosa Nostra

At seventy-one years of age, Nico Perrone was the most powerful Mafia boss among the twenty-four U.S.-based families of La Cosa Nostra. He was first generation Mafia, a World War II-era gangster. Nico had worked side by side with Al Capone, Charles "Lucky" Luciano, and Frank Nitty, all Mafia hall of famers. He had grown up in the mob and was involved in the development stages of turning trainloads of street hoods into Mafia businessmen. His father fought in the '30s mob wars. Nico later carried out his father's dream of organizing the families into a powerful, close-knit working organization. He accomplished this with tact, finesse, and paid assassins. It was Nico's way or meet your Maker, flowers included.

Nico Perrone was the founder of legitimacy in the mob. He organized labor unions, put up part of the money to build Las Vegas and made the almighty dollar more important than the bullet. He hired the best accountants and businessmen dirty money could buy. Perrone believed in long-range planning, unheard of during the gangster days of the late '30s. He was smart. Perrone played to the power and money weaknesses of the other family leaders by showing them huge profits on paper if they worked together instead of fighting each other for turf.

By controlling the ledger sheets and the plans, he controlled the entire mob and everyone was happy. They made a lot of money and maintained more power and respect than anyone had ever expected. His organization also curtailed the families from killing each other. That part was particularly appealing to some of the older generation bosses like himself. Nico organized the Council of Families where members voted him chairman for life, a position he would soon pass on to his son, Daniel.

Now almost completely bald and at least thirty pounds overweight, Nico was always immaculately dressed, soft-spoken and obviously well-fed. His six- foot, one-inch height commanded respect. He traveled extensively and was always accompanied by an entourage consisting of Benny "the Hat" Pizzuli, his enforcer, Robert Cotter, his *consiglieri*, Daniel, and at least four lieutenants who doubled as drivers, personal valets and gofers. Nico owned several vintage Cadillac limos ranging from the thirties to current day. All were black, in perfect condition and complete with bulletproof glass and fully stocked bars. Some even had the original running boards alongside for bodyguards. He maintained traditions of the old days which was one reason for his popularity among the old school family leaders.

Standing beside one of the family Hawker corporate jets just outside their hanger at JFK airport, Nico gave Daniel, last minute instructions.

"Daniel, my son. When you arrive in San Juan, wait at the hotel. You do not have to call anyone. They will know of your arrival. Let them come to you." Nico spoke softly, as usual. "When they do call, put them off. Tell them you are vacationing. They will know better and will get very concerned. After three days, invite Miguel Torres and his son, Tito, to dinner at the hotel. Do not ask them why the amount of money we launder has fallen off fifty percent; they will bring it up and begin to make excuses. Your presence will tell them of my disappointment in recent revenues from our operation down there."

"Yes, Father," Daniel carried on the tradition of respect, speaking only during a break in his father's instructions. "I will follow your plan exactly. I'll be visible around the hotel and the beach area while Mario and Joey do some snooping around."

"Keep your guards close to you, my son. Something is wrong in Puerto Rico. We must find out why. These are ruthless men so do not turn your back on them."

Daniel hugged his father and boarded the twin-engine jet along with Joey Verocchi, Mario "Uzi" Uzelli, and three of his own lieutenants. As the plane taxied away from the hanger area, Nico watched with pride. His only son was more than he could have ever expected. Educated in the finest schools in the U.S. and Europe, Daniel had a Bachelor's degree in Business, a minor in accounting and had received his JD, law degree, from Harvard. Now forty, Daniel had coal black hair which he combed straight back and closely resembled his father in height. He had deep blue eyes and a strong build. Nico saw himself back in the '40s every time he looked upon Daniel.

After refueling in Miami, the multi-passenger jet headed south towards San Juan, Puerto Rico. The thirty-minute stop was welcomed by Daniel and his men, giving them a chance to stretch their legs and use a real bathroom. During refueling, the men stayed close to the aircraft. The aircraft was known by all the federal agencies as belonging to the Mob. Daniel had expected to be rousted by Miami DEA agents. Fortunately, the Hawker was not searched before their departure. A good sign, Daniel thought.

Once they reached their designated cruising altitude, Daniel called Joey Verocchi and Mario Uzelli over to the small conference table.

"When we arrive in San Juan," Daniel said softly and authoritatively, "I want you, Joey, to hit the streets, take a cab, make a buy. Talk to some of the street peddlers, find out how drug sales are going. Also, try to pick up on any new names we aren't familiar with. Joey, this is a fishing expedition. I need to find out who is cutting in on the family business in the Caribbean."

Daniel turned to Uzelli.

"Mario, tomorrow morning, I want you to drive out to Carolina Pharmaceuticals, meet with Alberto Vega, the general manager, and ask him to take you on a tour of the facilities. Tell him you are vacationing. Check out the inventory levels. Are they high or almost non-existent? This information is crucial. Keep your ears open for any shoptalk around the company. Read Vega. Tell me if he seems uncomfortable with your presence. Is he holding back anything? You know the procedure. Take a small concealed camera with you and take pictures of everyone sitting in the lobby, in the conference room, people in the hallways dressed in nice suits, especially any Italians or Anglos in the facility. Be sure your visit in the morning is unannounced, say, about ten a.m.."

Daniel was precise in his information gathering. He'd been trained at one of the finest law schools also by an organization that specialized in knowing what was going on all over the world through a network envied by the CIA and the now extinct KGB alike. Daniel had learned to read body language from his father, Nico. He could spot a lie in a heartbeat, usually the person's last. He detested people that lied to him.

The Hawker jet lined up on final approach to the San Juan airport. Daniel and his associates had a limo waiting to take them to the family-owned San Juan Hotel.

SAME DAY, WEDNESDAY, JUNE 10TH

Judd was having the ride of his life.

"Will it be dark when we land?"

"We'll get in just before dark, schoolboy. It'll be beautiful." Rikki was in her element. "I wish I could let you fly this baby. I'd like to see if you've improved your flight skills over the years. Unfortunately, there are no controls in the back seat of an F/A 18-F Hornet."

The ride, the feeling of power and speed was almost overwhelming. Judd's excitement had not diminished since they took off. "I'd probably get white-knuckled like a two-hour student, forget everything I'd learned and crash us."

As the sun lowered in the Caribbean sky, they could see tiny lights just off their port wing.

"What carrier is that, Rikki?"

"CVN-77, The super carrier, *George H.W. Bush*. It's on a training cruise."

Rikki lined up. The double row of lights that grew further apart the closer they came to the carrier looked as though they were on a small harbor buoy, not a carrier. The closer they came to the deck, the more Judd didn't think they would make it. He grabbed the handhold and pressed his helmet back into the headrest. He wanted to scream but he knew better. Like all first-timers making a nighttime carrier landing with an instructor, he couldn't look. In an instant, he heard the thud of the F-18 plummeting down onto the deck and felt his butt go up around his shoulders.

The canopy opened and a Caribbean salt-water breeze hit him in the face. Judd had enjoyed the experience of the flight but was grateful to be down. An elevator lowered the craft to the hangar deck. Rikki climbed down the ladder from the cockpit and snapped a salute along with a smile. Returning the salute was Captain Cody Bennett. Rikki had been assigned to his carrier group when she was selected to go to Miramar for Top Gun school. She was the first aviator, male or female, from his carrier to win the coveted trophy. They'd been close friends ever since.

Bennett was short and stocky, gray hair, red-faced from years on the seven seas. Wearing a perpetual grin, he was respected by his men and fellow officers. It was obvious he was glad to see his star aviator.

Rikki pulled off her white flight helmet with an Indian Mohawk haircut painted across the top.

"Scalper! Welcome aboard, baby," Bennett hugged her. "Who's your rear?"

"This is Judd Rayburn. Judd, meet the best carrier captain in the Navy, Captain Cody Bennett, my ex-boss."

"Nice to meet you, Captain." Judd shook hands.

"I've seen your battlefield two-step on the news Judd. Your reputation precedes you," Bennett said with his usual grin.

"Captain, Rikki told me on the way over that you could tell me how she got her call sign of Scalper. She said you gave it to her."

Bennett took off his cap and rubbed the perspiration from his forehead, "That was a long time ago, Judd. It happened at her one and only trip to the Tail Hook convention held annually by naval aviators in Las Vegas."

"Yeah, Captain," remarked Judd. "That convention got a lot of bad publicity for you guys. I saw the investigations on the news."

"That's the one." Bennett was somewhat embarrassed. "She made her walk down the now infamous hallway flight-deck at the convention and the second guy that tried to grab her butt paid the price."

Bennett began laughing and remembering.

"The story goes, Rikki kneed him in the balls, then hit him with an upper cut. The guy was out cold. She reached in her purse, grabbed a small pair of scissors, and whacked his hair off, right there in the hallway in front of everyone. Since that time she's been known as 'Scalper'. Every pilot in the Navy knows her call sign, now," Captain Bennett added.

After dinner, Judd and Rikki informed Captain Bennett of their mission, why they were there, and how he could help them in the next few days. The immediate future was unclear.

THURSDAY, JUNE 11TH

Judd and Rikki arrived quietly and unannounced in San Juan, Puerto Rico, on a Navy motor launch from the ship. Rikki rented a car and the two of them drove through the hotel district of Isla Verde, past the San Juan Hotel, towards her high-rise condo in Condado, a continuation of the tourist district with turquoise water leading up to snow white sandy beach-front real estate properties.

"Nice place you got here, lady." Judd was impressed. "The view is magnificent. Not only the sand and sea, check out the bikinis down there on the beach."

"Part of the *image* of being an ad scout. Word gets around fast here on the island. I've always got a bunch of Hollywood hopefuls lounging below my patio hoping I'll discover them." Rikki handed Judd a pair of binoculars.

"Speaking of work." Judd walked into the guest bedroom where Rikki had her computer and electronics gear hooked up. "We need to get to it."

Rikki pulled a backup CD from her briefcase, inserted it into her laptop and pulled up the pertinent information.

"If we can't trust any of the government people here on the island, Rikki, my question is where do we start?"

"It's like I mentioned in the debriefing session back at Bliss, my original mission was to determine whether or not this terrorist group, called *El Prevision*, which means 'The Foresight' in Spanish, is a threat to our national security. So far, my determination is that they're not a threat to the U.S. Rather, they're against the corrupt government in Puerto Rico and have been labeled as terrorists by the administration currently in power here on the island. Personally, Judd, I think we should make contact with them. They have eyes and ears here that we don't have. The shortest distance between two points is a straight line."

"Tell me about their history, Rikki." Judd was not ready to commit to a plan of dealing with suspected terrorists.

"*El Prevision* is led by a guy named José Irrizarry. He's third generation in this group. His grandfather, Ramon, was a sugar cane plantation owner back in the fifties when the governor of Puerto Rico instituted the 936 Tax Free status on the island and began the process of getting U.S. investors into Puerto Rico. This is an island, land is limited. The sugar cane plantation owners held land that was very important for U.S. investment and manufacturing expansion. The governor tried to buy the land from Ramon, he wouldn't sell, so, as the story goes, government lawyers drew up some hokey document calling for vast amounts of money from Ramon in back taxes, which he didn't owe. Then they used government troops to confiscate the land from grandfather Irrizarry."

"And granddad was hacked, right?"

"So hacked that he and his workers, numbering over two thousand, headed for the protection of the mountains in the central part of the island. First to escape being killed by the troops. Second, to set up this *El Prevision*, to constantly harass the government and try to get their land back. Granddad died of natural causes about two years later in the mountains but not before he put together a fairly sophisticated group.

"What happened to Ramon's son? You haven't mentioned him."

"Frederico Irrizarry succeeded his father as leader of the group. About eight years ago, the governor's own squad of secret police caught Frederico in a little mountain roadside beer joint after a two-month stakeout and blasted him in cold blood. Enter José, his son of twenty-four years and, oh yes, his daughter, Leticia, or Leti for short. Here's a picture of Leti and her brother, José."

Judd looked at the eight by ten. Leti was beautiful, in a deadly sort of way. She had long reddish brown hair, large dark Castilian eyes and a slim figure. She wore jungle fatigues and combat boots. The picture had been taken at their camp in the jungle. She and her brother José were posed holding AK-47 assault rifles, a weapon that no self-respecting terrorist would be caught without. José was average height, thin, with a face that showed worries and responsibilities far beyond his years.

Judd lay the picture down. Deep in thought, with Leti's piercing dark eyes refusing to leave his memory, he walked over to the sliding glass door leading to the small patio overlooking the beach. Bikinis were no longer on his mind. He stared out to sea seeking the right answer.

The brief moment of silence was interrupted. "Your call, Judd. I know some people that can contact Irrizarry for us if you want."

"Rikki, the question that keeps going around in my mind is whether or not they are involved or have knowledge at such high levels here on the island," Judd was still agonizing over the right approach. "If they can't help identify members of the group specifically involved with Carolina Pharmaceuticals, then, all of a sudden we are dealing with biased individuals looking to overthrow a government that is a Commonwealth of the United States. That's a pretty big can of worms to open up. Once we talk to them, unless they will be helpful to our focused cause, we won't be able to walk away without them singing to all the newspapers of our meeting. That's a big chance to take."

"Let's just go a step at a time."

"What do you mean, Rikki?"

"Let me make some initial contact with some of the lower echelon members of the group. Depending on what I find out, you can make the decision from there. What do you think?"

"That'll be fine. What time is it getting to be? My body clock is haywire and I didn't reset my watch."

"It's time for a bite of lunch, Judd. I'll run down to Burger King and grab a couple of burgers. We need to go to the grocery store. Then, I'll start making some contacts. You can just crash here 'til your clock gets rewound. One last thing, a reminder. Don't use this phone to call anyone. There're no bugs here, but someone could put a tap down line somewhere. Just being cautious, schoolboy."

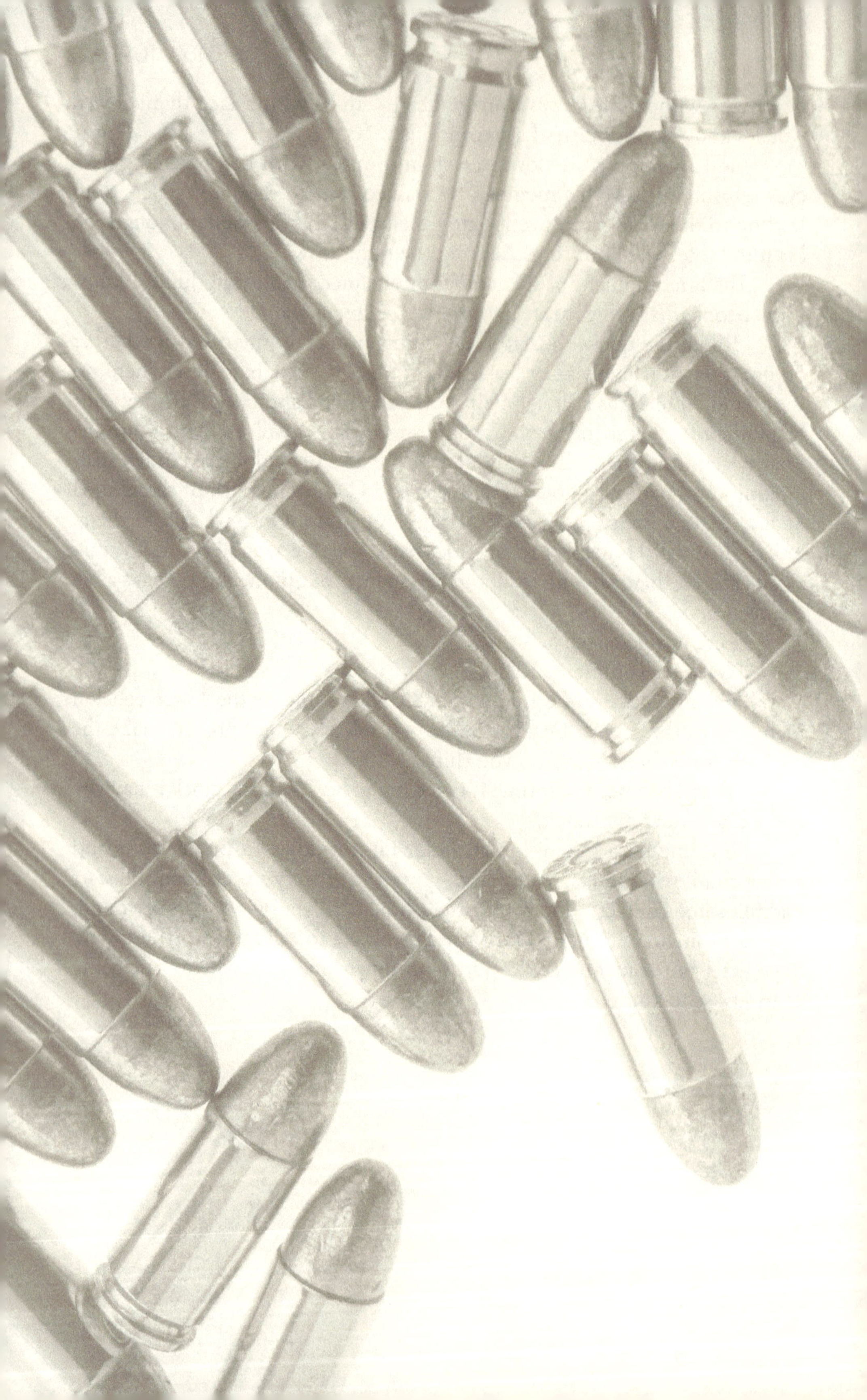

13

EL PREVISION

Mario "Uzi" Uzelli returned to the San Juan Hotel just after one p.m. with his digital camera. His drop-in visit to Carolina Pharmaceuticals had been very productive. He was anxious for Daniel to see the pictures.

"How was your tour, Mario?"

"Interesting, Daniel. Take a look at these. Do you recognize anyone?"

Daniel took the camera and looked over the pictures slowly. Each photo presented a new problem. Worse than he had expected. He immediately recognized two U.S. congressmen, one from Illinois, the other from Florida. Both, he thought, had been recipients of healthy campaign donations from the Perrone family. Several of the other pictures revealed known Colombian Cartel lieutenants. The next picture caused Daniel to shove the camera into Mario's hands.

"Rigozzi!" The Sicilian Mafia boss who controlled drug trafficking operations in Europe.

Daniel walked over to the window of the luxuriously furnished penthouse suite.

"You know who they are?" Uzelli asked sheepishly, knowing Daniel was mad.

Daniel continued staring seaward. "Find an office supply. Buy a scanner and plenty of paper."

"We have that down in the office of the hotel." Mario said.

Daniel spun around casting a glance at Mario that could kill. Mario left the room, quickly, just as Joey Verocchi came in.

"So what's the word on the street, Joey?" Daniel could almost give the report himself. He had a good idea what was happening from the pictures Mario had taken.

"Drug sales are booming, thirty percent increase over two months ago."

"Two months ago." Daniel was putting the puzzle together. "That's when our revenues began dropping."

"Another thing," Joey said. He could see that Daniel was very concerned about something and having been friends with Daniel since they were both in the first grade, Joey didn't hesitate to dive right in. "The peddlers were very tight-lipped other than what I could drag out of them. Something's going on here, Daniel. They were very cool to me. No respect!"

Again, Daniel didn't answer but continued to stare out the window. He must speak to his father, Nico. Their earlier suspicions were beginning to be realized. His father had told him before they left there was a possibility of the Colombian Cartel hooking up directly with the Sicilian Mafia.

The Sicilians manufactured and controlled all the heroin going into the European countries. The Cartel manufactured and controlled the distribution of cocaine. Cocaine was in higher demand in the States due to its more user-friendly characteristics, smoking the drug instead of the choice of shooting-up with a needle, offensive to potential newcomers of the thirty-something generation. Cutting out lines of coke on a mirror surface and using rolled up one hundred-dollar bills to snort the cocaine was also considered a cool thing to do. If these techniques sold cocaine over heroin in the U.S., it was a matter of time before cocaine would become the number one drug in Europe. The price of cocaine was higher in Europe than in the U.S., meaning higher profits.

"That must be what they are doing!" Daniel was thinking out loud.

The other Perrone lieutenants in the room remained silent as they waited for instructions, prepared to do anything, absolutely anything, Daniel asked of them.

"Ms. McAfee. This is Erica Stone, you know, the reporter who is making your boss a hero throughout every household in America. Now for the fourth time, where is Judd Rayburn? I want to know!"

"And for the fourth time, Mssss. Stone. Mr. Rayburn is out of the office. I don't know when to expect him." Maureen was building up a dislike for Erica. "I know perfectly well who you are. What I don't know is when Mr. Rayburn will be able to return your call."

"Ms. McAfee, this is a fort, a military reservation! One does not leave his office out here, one leaves the fort. Is Mr. Rayburn even within the fort?" Erica's blue eyes were turning stormy black.

"Ms. Stone, Mr. Rayburn's exact whereabouts are not known to me at this time." Maureen's brown eyes were turning a vicious red. "I will give him your persistent, persnickety, poignant messages the minute I see him. Is that coming through to you loud and clear?"

Maureen took great pleasure in slamming the phone down with every bit of strength she could muster.

"That blonde-haired bi…"

"Temper, temper, little sister." Feather loved to see Maureen get mad. He was fascinated by her range of emotional ups and downs, so unlike his own personality. "We mustn't let these reporters get to us."

"Well, she damn sure isn't getting to you, Joe. It's me she's getting to. I think she just has the hots to see Judd. She's jealous as slop over Commander Rhine if you ask me."

"I'd rather think she is trying to stay on the payroll as a reporter, Maureen. There ain't been that much news happening around here the last few days. She's going through reporter withdrawal."

As usual, Joe had a calming effect on Maureen. That's the reason she loved him like a brother.

"Have you heard from the boss lately, Joe?"

"No, I doubt seriously if we will for a couple of days. They can't be sure of talking on a secured line down there."

Rikki had been gone for hours. Judd was getting concerned. He had the number of the LEGAT in the San Juan office that Erin had given him but hesitated to cry wolf so soon. Rikki was street wise and could take care of herself. It was just the icy feeling of being in a strange place, not knowing what to expect, not knowing who, if anyone, to trust. Judd would give her until midnight before calling the number for help.

Another hour passed. Judd heard a key rattling in the door. He instinctively reached for his 9mm given to him on board the USS Bush. The door opened.

"I was getting worried about you. Thought you may've been abducted by one of those hot Latin hunks, as you call 'em."

"Had a real interesting meeting, Judd." Rikki said pulling a folded newspaper from her back pocket. "You know, we get a lot of our information from newspapers. About a month ago, one of the local papers did a piece on a Father Molina, a priest that lives in a small mission in the jungle near a place called *Los Tres Picachos* or `The Three Peaks' in the Corazal Mountains. The article implied that Father Molina knew of *El Prevision* and was sympathetic to their cause."

"Being a Catholic priest, he can say that and get away with it, right?" Judd added. "I've noticed the abundance of Catholic churches around here. There are three Catholic stations on cable TV that run twenty-four hours a day."

"True. Puerto Rico is a Catholic stronghold. These people are devout. You don't knock the church."

"So did you see Father Molina?"

"Yes, I did. He confirmed what we talked about earlier and described *El Prevision* as being modern-day Robin Hoods. I told him why I was on the island, to investigate the so-called terrorist group. I told him what I had read in the papers and heard from the people on the streets. To some they are terrorists, to others they are heroes. I put my cards on the Father's table and told him that you and I wanted to talk to José and Leti Irrizarry in person, alone, in secret and without warrants."

"That's being direct. You think that was the smart thing to do?" Judd could see Rikki's reasoning. She'd taken a big chance, as usual.

"I believe I gained Father Molina's trust by showing my hand. If *El Prevision* is a non-terrorist group, now is the time to decide. Otherwise, they know I'll talk to government officials in Ponce, the capital of Puerto Rico. They also know that I'll side with the government and they'll have more trouble. This time with Uncle Sam."

"Good approach. What now?"

"We meet with José and Leti tonight at eleven p.m. at the Father's mission." Rikki looked quite pleased with herself.

"Did you ask Father Molina about Carolina Pharmaceuticals or talk about drugs at all?"

"I started to but the Father cut me short and told me to ask José and his sister. He said they would be very helpful."

"How long to get there?"

"The mission is south of the town of Manati, about forty-eight miles west of San Juan. We need to leave about 9:15, so grab a jacket. It gets cool up in the mountains at night."

The toll road west out of San Juan resembled a freeway in Los Angeles, well lit, multiple lanes, smooth. When Judd and Rikki turned left onto 149 the smooth surface quickly gave way to a winding, twisting, pothole-filled blacktop road that led into the jungle hillsides of the mountains.

"Could you slow down a little, for heaven's sake? I'd hate to go over the edge before we get to the mission." Judd had never seen a jungle setting like this in West Texas.

"We're going uphill, Judd. This little rented four-banger can hardly handle the incline as it is. I've got to keep us going forward so we don't go down backwards. Just close your eyes and hold on, buddy."

The jungle road was pitch dark. The headlights only lit up the road to the next curve, which was about every ten feet. Judd had a lot more questions for Rikki before the meeting at the mission, but he figured that it wasn't the time to engage in a deep conversation.

After another twenty-five minutes, Rikki took a sharp right as if to turn into the mountain itself. There, tucked fifty feet back into the jungle terrain and about half-way up the mountain with a single light showing was the little concrete mission, complete with a covered porch and small bell tower. Father Molina stood under the porch light wearing old jeans, sandals and his short sleeved black shirt and priest's collar. He was in his fifties with small features. His face bore the lines of a hard life in the jungle, most likely complicated by the problems of his poor parish.

"Father Molina, I'd like you to meet Judd Rayburn with the U.S. Justice Department." Rikki was very courteous to the priest.

"Nice meeting you, Father," Judd said respectfully.

"A pleasure to meet you, Mr. Rayburn. The TV doesn't do you justice. Oh yes, I've seen you on the television at the bishop's residence. We have no TV here, but I enjoy watching it when I go in to San Juan for my visits with the church officials there."

They walked inside the small sanctuary; there were only nine rows of pews. The pulpit was surrounded by burning candles below a chipped statue of the Virgin Mary. A large cross made of twisted vines from the jungle hung on the back wall overlooking the pulpit. The mission was dimly lit with two windows on each side. No glass had ever been installed.

"I've prayed many hours for such a meeting, Mr. Rayburn." Father Molina spoke with a very concerned, reverent voice. "I believe the way to put aside our differences is for honest men to sit down together and work out their problems face-to-face. I sometimes think finding those honest men is the biggest challenge." Father Molina cracked a fretful smile.

"I have the same challenges in my profession, Father. Getting at the truth," Judd agreed.

"Our other guests should be here shortly. I wanted to take a few minutes to talk with both of you and get to know you," Father Molina continued. "I have known José and Leti most of their lives. Personally, I believe they have been chosen for the life they live. Contrary to what you may have read, they are good and decent people. They provide for their followers the best they can, sometimes at the expense of others who have more. Their hearts are in the right place, I am convinced of that. I don't approve of all that they do or the way that they do it, but then, maybe I have been chosen to minister to them. That is what I believe."

"Belief is important, Father." Judd could feel the priest's warmth and sincerity.

"I can see belief in you, Mr. Rayburn. I will summon José and Leti now."

Father Molina took one of the unlit candles from the altar and walked towards an open window. He lit the candle and set it down on the sill and returned to Judd and Rikki.

"They will be here soon. If you are carrying firearms, please take a moment to put them in your car. I do not allow any weapons in God's house. José and Leti know that, also. You are in no danger here."

"We have no firearms on us, Father," Rikki responded.

The single rough oak door opened. Judd and Rikki could see the shadowed figures of two people standing in the doorway backlit from the porch light.

"Come in José. Come, Leti. It is okay."

Father Molina stood up from the front pew where he had been sitting and walked towards the door with his arms outstretched, meeting José and Leti, embracing them and walking them back to the front of the sanctuary. "Miss Rhine, Mr. Rayburn, please meet José Irrizarry and his sister, Leticia."

"Please, call me Judd, this is Rikki. We're honored to meet both of you."

Judd shook José's hand firmly, a gentle squeeze for Leti. He was taken aback by her rough look and natural beauty. Even in the dimly lit sanctuary he could see the deepness of her brown eyes, the reflections of candlelight upon her long bushy dark hair. She did not smile. Neither did her brother.

"I am José. Call my sister Leti."

"I will prepare some tea while you get acquainted." Father Molina walked through a doorway to his small quarters behind the back wall of the sanctuary.

For the next half-hour José told Judd and Rikki what they already knew. He was fighting against the corruption of local government. He emphasized his loyalty to the United States and to the working people of Puerto Rico. Leti said nothing.

"As we said earlier, our presence and our purpose here on your island is as secret as your camp, José, Leti."

"José, what can you and Leti tell us about drug trafficking operations here on the island?" Rikki asked.

"Drugs are a real problem for our people." José stood up from the pew. "*El Prevision* detests drugs; we are not involved. Two months ago, our island was visited by a Mr. Carlo Rigozzi. He is Sicilian Mafia and controls drug trafficking throughout Europe."

"We're familiar with Rigozzi, José." Rikki looked startled to hear the name associated with Puerto Rico and looked over at Judd, only to see the same reaction on his face.

"We have had Colombians, Venezuelans, Mexicans, Jamaicans and Dominicans on our island for a long time," José reflected. "Puerto Rico has been more of a staging area for the further transfer of drugs to other places than a central distribution point. However, we have four million people here. They began selling the drugs to our people as well as shipping them out of here. We at *El Prevision* are very concerned about that."

Rikki and Judd said nothing.

"Two months ago when Rigozzi arrived, things began to change in the trafficking operations. People on the island who had been involved with the trafficking operations in the past all of a sudden began turning up dead. *El Prevision* was blamed by the government. We did not do the killings, but we didn't mind these drug dealers were being killed. We thought it was some kind of gang war and allowed it to continue. It saved us a lot of time and bullets.

"That was not the case, though. When Rigozzi got here, he brought some of his own people. They began meeting with the Colombians outside of Manati. Manati is a well-known trafficking stronghold here on the island. Local police stay clear. They just give people traffic tickets there if you know what I mean?"

"They turn their heads?" Judd inserted.

"A proper description, Mr. Rayburn." José continued to show Judd and Rikki proper respect by not calling them by their first names.

"José, the people who are getting killed, who did they work for before Rigozzi came to the island?" Rikki asked.

"Different groups. Mainly local peddlers. The most powerful of these groups was headed by a man in Ponce, where the governor of Puerto Rico lives. The man is still alive but in hiding. We believe he may be affiliated with Mafia families on the mainland. Information has been sketchy at best. They have never been well organized. Now, with Rigozzi and the Colombians meeting practically every week, they are becoming very well organized."

"Are they meeting in Manati, José?" asked Rikki.

"No. They stay in the finest hotel in Condado, the Condado Tower. This hotel got into financial difficulty not too long ago. Rumor around Hato Rey, our financial district outside San Juan, is that one of Rigozzi's organizations in Italy bought the hotel. Maybe that is what brought him to the island in the first place. They meet at a company in Carolina, just east of San Juan. The company name is Carolina Pharmaceuticals."

Judd whipped his head around towards Rikki. The only sound was coming from the *Coqui* frogs outside in the trees. Their shrill voices became deafening. The link was established!

"Did I say something to startle you?" José looked puzzled. "To the contrary, José, you just said the magic words, Carolina Pharmaceuticals. We thought the New York Mob, called La Cosa Nostra, may be involved there along with several prominent people from Mexico." Judd pulled his notebook from his jacket pocket.

"We have many people loyal to our cause working there, Mr. Rayburn," Leti entered the conversation. "It is becoming a puzzle to us."

"What do you mean, puzzle, Leti?" Judd looked deep into her almost black eyes.

"We know everyone who goes into the pharmaceutical company from our people who work there," Leti went on. "Over the last two months we have seen pictures of people we do not know taken by the gate entry cameras. Some appear to be prominent Anglos. Some are European and several others wear lapel pins that appear to be flags of nations we do not know."

"Can you get us copies of those pictures, Leti?" Rikki had to hold her anxieties back. She needed those pictures. They could break the whole mystery open.

"I have copies with me, Miss Rhine," Leti said. "I will give them to you before you go. It would not be safe to send them by any form of messenger."

After their third cup of very weak, lukewarm tea served by Father Molina, José summoned the pictures from some of his men waiting in the dark jungle just outside the mission. They agreed to stay in contact with each other through the good Father. Rikki took the brown folder containing the pictures. They shook hands. She and Judd walked back to their car.

EARLY FRIDAY MORNING, JUNE 12TH, 2 A.M.

Daniel placed a call to his father, knowing the phones were not secure. Anticipating this, he and Nico had worked out a code for letting the other know someone may be listening to their conversation.

"Hello, Dad," Daniel never called Nico, "dad." This was the signal of unsecured conversation.

"Hello, boy," Nico's acknowledgment. "How is the vacation coming along? Are the beaches beautiful as ever?"

"I'm having a wonderful time. Did you receive the gift I sent you?" Daniel was referring to the pictures Mario had taken at the pharmaceutical company.

"I got your gift, son. Thank you. I should get a lot of enjoyment out of it as soon as I learn to use it. Maybe Cotter can explain it to me," Nico acknowledged the receipt of the photos and would have his *consiglieri*, Robert Cotter get right on it.

"I'm expecting guests for dinner tonight. I look forward to the conversation." Daniel let Nico know that he had been contacted by Miguel Torres and his son, Tito, and would be having dinner with them later that night.

"I know you are enjoying your stay, son. Call me tomorrow." Nico cut the conversation short knowing Daniel was okay. He would talk to him later and cipher out what Cotter was able to find out from the photos.

Rikki turned right on highway 22 heading east towards San Juan. Both were glad to be off the winding, dark, jungle road and back on the well-lit toll road. Judd pulled the stack of photos from the brown envelope. With the help of a penlight flashlight, he began to look over the pictures.

"You aren't going to believe some of the people in these pictures. We're talking Super Bowl here. Take a look at these."

Judd held up three pictures for Rikki to get a quick glimpse as he continued to look through the rest.

"This is an odd mix, Judd. The only thing these three have in common is they are all in congress: Congressman Frank 'Frenchy' Fuselier, Louisiana, Agricultural Committee; Congressman Thomas 'Tommy' Zapata, Florida,

Budget Secretary of the Finance Committee. And last but by no means least, the honorable Senator Joseph Capriatti, Illinois, co-chair of the Senate Foreign Relations Committee. He's a really big fish around the district. If the President kept very close tabs on these three, he probably wouldn't sleep well at night. I don't know exactly what we have here, Judd, but I'm thinking Watergate won't touch this."

Judd looked over the half dozen pictures of the men wearing flag lapel pins.

"What do you make of these? Recognize any of them?"

She looked closely at each photo wracking her photographic memory to tie a name with a face.

"I don't recognize any of the faces, Judd. I do know that the pins are from the Russian republics. This pin is the flag of the Ukraine. This one is Belorussia. The big guy here is wearing the pin of 'Mother Russia' herself, the Russian Republic. Here's Latvia, Kazakhstan and Uzbekistan."

Judd turned around to check out the cars near them. It was late and not many were on the toll way. Still, he had an uncomfortable feeling about what they were going to find.

"I don't think Super Bowl will adequately describe these players, Judd. More like the World Cup. We need a program of participants, names, and oh yeah, a copy of the rule book would sure come in handy. We don't even know what game this is."

"One thing's for sure we do know, Rikki. We've got to hop Hornet Airlines later this morning and get these photos to Erin. By the way, surely *big brother* tracks your aircraft. How do we get away with this?"

"I'm a Top Gun winner and I'm in Naval Intelligence. Of course my flight path is monitored. No one jumps in an unauthorized $60 million aircraft without filing proper flight plans. I do this all the time, I'm authorized and I couldn't agree with you more about the photos. I've seen a lot of puzzles during my years in Naval Intelligence but this one may just turn out to be the best yet. U.S. Congressmen, Russians, drugs. Strange bedfellows. Something doesn't compute here."

Rikki swerved onto the shoulder of the highway and then back on the road.

"I can't put this together. These guys have nothing in common that I can see. It's driving me crazy."

"I heard the crazy driving part, Rikki. Give it a rest."

"Exactly what we need. How about a nightcap at the beautiful sunken bar at the San Juan Hotel? They've got an oval chandelier hanging over it that's something to see. That place never sleeps. What say? A glass of orange juice for the road? Catch a couple hours of sleep and then back to Bliss?"

"Fine with me, lady, long as we keep the photos in the briefcase along with the heat."

3:15 a.m. Daniel couldn't sleep. His phone should be ringing off the hook. His associates on the island should be wanting to get together for a drink. He'd received only one call, an expected call from Torres, that snake!

Daniel got out of bed and walked into the living room of the suite where two of his men were playing cards.

"Get Mario and Joey up," Daniel demanded. "Tell them to get dressed. We're going down to the bar for a drink. You guys get some rest."

As the elevator opened Daniel caught a glimpse of several Puerto Rican ladies, dressed to the nines, laughing and walking to the bar. Daniel looked back at Mario. Mario smiled.

"I believe it is time to mingle with the locals, boss. Should I find us a table and invite some over?" Mario asked Daniel.

"Why not?"

They walked over to the hotel concierge. He knew exactly who Daniel was and seated them at the best table in the bar area. Mario soon joined them with three ladies, introducing the best looking of the group to Daniel and seating her next to him. Two waiters immediately surrounded the table as they ordered drinks and hors d'oeuvres.

Rikki pulled the car into the circular drive of the hotel, flipped the doorman a five and told him to hold the car near the door. Judd got out carrying the briefcase containing the photos and a 9mm. Rikki had a more feminine .380 auto under her blue blazer.

"Beautiful hotel, Rikki! Did you say the La Cosa Nostra owns this place?"

"I don't know if they still own it. Rumor is that they built it back in the 40's or 50's."

The sheer beauty of the entrance was put to shame only by the magnificent foyer of the hotel itself; pink marble floors, high dark walnut wood, metal-carved walls and a beautiful mural painted on a domed ceiling that Michelangelo might have been tempted to replicate.

Rikki led Judd over to the sunken bar near the registration lobby of the hotel.

"I see what you mean. That chandelier must've cost a hundred grand, then or now." Judd did a 360-degree turn, checking out the craftsmanship of the hotel. "We ain't got nothing like this in West Texas. How much are the drinks?"

"Tonight, schoolboy, they're free. The OJ's are on me."

As the two of them walked towards the sunken bar, a man and a woman were leaving the bar area.

Judd and Rikki quickly grabbed the two empty barstools.

"Judd, check the group over in the corner. You know who that is?"

Judd reached into his jacket pocket and put on his round, black wire-rimmed glasses.

"I've got his picture on my bulletin board. That's Daniel Perrone, himself! He's looking this way. What do we do? He's seen us, Rikki!"

"I've been known to turn a head or two. Best thing to do in a situation like this is to get a table and invite him over for a drink."

They moved from the bar to a table about twenty feet away from where Perrone and his group were sitting. When the waiter came over to get their drink order, Rikki instructed him to deliver a message to Perrones' table. They waited as the waiter walked over to the other table and began talking to Daniel. Perrone looked over at Rikki and Judd as if he didn't know who was sending the message and gave a slight nod, scooted his chair back and walked over to join them.

"Mr. Rayburn, so glad to meet you in person. I've seen you on TV. Terrible thing that happened out there in Texas." Daniel was cool and dignified in his greeting. "Miss, I don't believe I know your name, I'm Daniel Perrone."

"Rikki Rhine, Mr. Perrone. Won't you join us for a drink?"

Across the room, Joey and Mario cut the small talk with the ladies. They fixed stares on Rikki and Judd. One wrong move and there would be openings in Naval Intelligence and the Justice Department.

"You've picked a lovely setting for some rest and relaxation. The island is beautiful, yes?" Perrone led off. "You are here for vacation, are you not?"

"Of course," Rikki quipped. "You're vacationing also?"

"I love it here. The beaches, fresh air, the ladies," Daniel turned to look back at his table where the three girls were sitting. "Much too nice a place for business."

"What business are you in, anyway, Mr. Perrone?" Judd asked. He couldn't wait to hear the answer.

Rikki stepped on Judd's foot under the table signaling him to get off the subject.

"Hotel business, Mr. Rayburn," Daniel answered nonchalantly. "You're a district attorney back in Texas, right?"

"Something like that, Mr. Perrone. Here, I'm just your average tourist soaking up some Caribbean sun."

"You will be prosecuting the Mexican fellow in the helicopter soon? Must have an open and shut case to be vacationing so close to the trial date," Perrone parried. "Papers say you will nail him with the death sentence."

"If you read it in the papers, Mr. Perrone, it must be true," Judd countered.

The discomfort was beginning to show around the table. After shaking hands with Judd and Rikki, Daniel thanked them for the drink and returned to his table. Each knew the other was fishing. The meeting ended in a draw, nothing lost, nothing gained, other than both knew the other was there for a lot more than a glowing Caribbean tan.

"Rikki, Daniel Perrone never gets too far outside of New York or Chicago unless it's an occasional trip to Vegas, or his yearly trip to Italy. The FBI watches him like a hawk." Judd was so tired, he was almost thinking out loud. "La Cosa Nostra frequents Puerto Rico on a regular basis, mainly lieutenants working for the Perrone family. The fact that the old man, Nico, sent his son down here is significant. I don't know how, yet, but, mark my word, it means something."

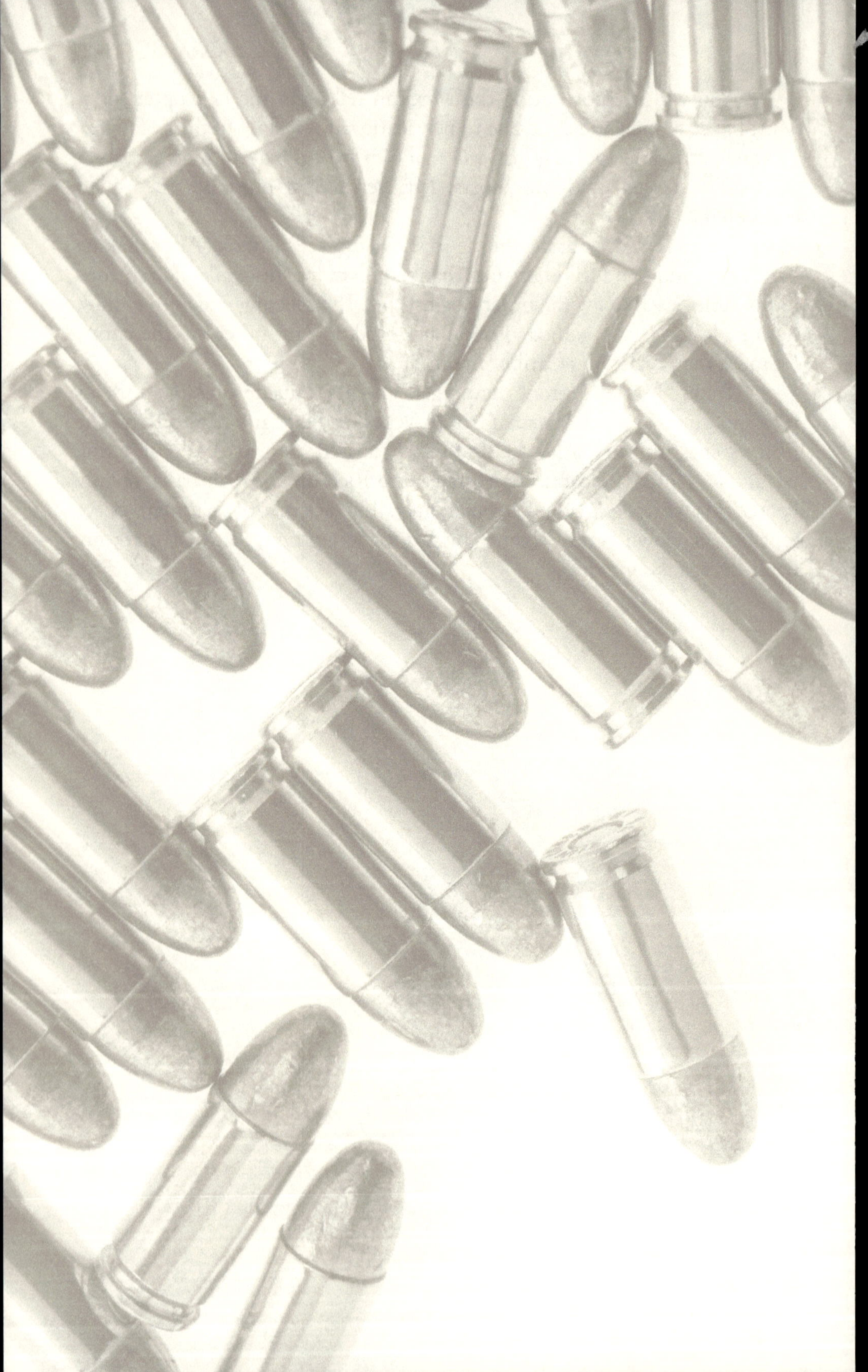

14

CAN OF WORMS

Just after ten a.m. a single F-18 catapulted off the USS *George H. W. Bush's* deck bound for El Paso. The oxygen felt refreshing to Judd and had a reviving effect. The island was beautiful but held so many mysteries. It felt good to leave…

Feather hung up the phone and turned to Maureen, "Little sister, has a Boyd Dixon called this morning?"

"About forty-five minutes ago. You sure have been talking to him a lot the past few days. Who is he anyway?"

"Just an old friend. Did he leave a number where he can be reached?"

"He said you had the number. He's at his ranch, wherever that is."

"Thanks."

Joe went back into his room and dialed Boyd's number.

"Hello, Boyd?" Joe thought he recognized the voice but wanted to make sure before talking any further.

"Joe, I called earlier to let you know that three truckloads of equipment arrived here late last night. Everything's about ready for you guys to move in." Boyd Dixon's voice was full of enthusiasm. "I've contacted seven of the company's best exes. They're on their way from all over the country."

"Great. Can you have dossiers on each one of them for me to study when I get there?"

"Some of the guys will bring them when they arrive. I assure you, Joe, these are some sharp individuals. When're you coming out to join us?"

"I have twenty men from the TAG team on loan from General Lawton. We really had to do some dancin', but in light of what's happening with Mexico, the General consented and is willing to keep things under his hat for a while. I should be in Con Can late Sunday night with the men."

"I'll be looking for you."

"Good, Boyd. See you Sunday night, and thanks."

As soon as Feather hung up, his intercom buzzed.

"Joe?" Maureen's voice came across the intercom.

"Yes, Maureen."

"Judd's calling you and Mr. Erin on a secured line. He's somewhere over the Gulf of Mexico. Line 5."

"Hey, Judd, I've got Randall standing here. Go ahead."

"I'm about to drop a bomb in your laps." Judd's voice was muffled speaking into the oxygen mask radio from thirty-eight thousand feet over the Gulf.

"Bombs away, Judd," Randall returned.

"Rikki and I met with the terrorist group, *El Prevision*, early this morning. In a word, they're basically freedom fighters. Good guys far as I can tell. They gave us a stack of photos taken of visitors out at Carolina Pharmaceuticals. The guest list is puzzling. I'm going to need your help."

"Did you recognize any of them?" Erin asked.

"For starters, Congressmen Fuselier, Zapata, and Capriatti."

Erin looked up at Joe, covering the phone, "Judd's got pictures of three U.S. Congressmen visiting the pill factory in Puerto Rico."

"Are you still there, Randall?" Judd questioned after not hearing a reply."Still here, Judd. I don't know exactly what to say to that. Is there more?"

"Much more, Randall. Here comes the bomb, Russians!"

"Russians?" Randy repeated Judd's remark for Joe to hear. "What Russians?"

"That's why I need your help. Rikki identified the lapel pins the men were wearing in the photos. She says they're small flags of six of the Russian Republics, but we don't think they're political figures or KGB. We don't have a clue... Randall, are you there?" Judd asked in a loud voice.

"I'm here, Judd." Randall's voice contained a note of dejection that could be picked up even at thirty-eight thousand feet. "I'm just wondering where this thing is leading, buddy."

"There's more. Rikki and I bumped into Daniel Perrone at one of the hotels in San Juan last night. Rigozzi of the Sicilian Mafia is also in town for a little fun in the sun. Put that together."

"I'm afraid you've caught me speechless, Judd," Randall remarked. "Just get here with those pictures. This is gettin' crazy."

FRIDAY EVENING, JUNE 12, 8 P.M. EST

Guest services and dining room waiters had just finished setting up a lavish buffet-style meal out on the patio of Daniel's top floor suite. Customary for the Perrone family, the entire floor went exclusively to Daniel and his men. Elevators were keyed, allowing only exclusive access. Visits to the top floor were by invitation only.

Daniel walked into the living room where Joey, Mario and the other three lieutenants were sitting.

"I've just talked to my father," Daniel spoke in a dry tone of voice. "It is imperative we find out from Torres and his son, Tito, exactly what is happening to our operation. They may or may not be enjoying their last meal. Do I make myself clear?"

Everyone acknowledged.

"Mario, call down to the front desk and inform them not to send anyone up here. We may have some loud music playing. I'm sure the hotel manager can make excuses to any guests who are disturbed."

"Right, boss." Mario dialed the front desk.

"Joey, on my signal, grab Tito, it will be after dinner. We will start on him while we question his father, Miguel. They do not leave without telling us what we want to know. Does everyone know what to do?"

The phone in the suite rang.

"Torres and his son are down in the lobby, boss."

"Go down and bring them up," Daniel instructed. "Take Lugo and Frankie with you. Make sure they are clean, no weapons, be thorough. On second thought, make them wait another twenty minutes, then go get them."

"I take it we may be going for a moonlight flight over the Caribbean, huh, boss?" Joey had kicked more than one into the sea.

Miguel Torres and his son entered the suite. Daniel greeted them with the usual Mafioso embrace. Miguel looked repulsive to Daniel; he always had. Torres had bug eyes that lacked a defined color. Torres' daily drinking faded any hint of color in his eyes except red. He had a potbelly that protruded from his frail, slump shouldered frame. Barely standing 5' 6" and weighing about one hundred forty pounds, Miguel wore fine clothes and lots of gold jewelry. Son Tito had the same slithery features. They were both snakes in

Daniel's mind. One of the snakes would probably never live long enough to turn gray like the other.

They ate a hearty meal and started on their second bottle of wine. Conversation during dinner was not specific. Tito said very little, Miguel was evasive. Daniel was reading the situation very well. His frustration during the casual dinner chitchat prompted him to look forward to what was about to happen. Daniel was going to get very specific, very quickly. He nodded towards Joey.

Tito was seated to Joey's left, next to his father. Torres was sitting first chair next to the head of the table where Daniel dined. Under the tablecloth Joey put on some brass knuckles over black leather gloves. He swung his left clenched fist backwards towards Tito. Joey landed the full force of the brass knuckles squarely on Tito's mouth, knocking out all of his front upper teeth. Tito went sprawling backwards onto the concrete patio floor, his head hit the surface like a watermelon. Blood gushed from his mouth. Like lightning, Mario, sitting across from Miguel, pulled an Uzi that had been taped under the table and put it in Miguel's face.

Slowly, Daniel pushed himself away from the table, taking his glass of wine with him, as he walked around and stopped near Tito. Joey was squatting down by Torres' bleeding son and had a switchblade gently inserted into one of Tito's nostrils. Daniel began.

"Miguel, let us understand one another." Perrone's eyes were ablaze. "I do not like you, I never have. You are sloppy, untrustworthy, and worst of all, you take the Perrone Family for fools. You have the misconception that we believe these lies you tell my people when they visit you down here on the island. You have no respect for my father, Nico Perrone, and we live by respect. Some people die for the lack of it. Understand me, Miguel?" Daniel was in his face.

Miguel could not talk, just nodded vigorously as he cut his eyes sharply towards his son lying on the floor. Tito was bleeding profusely, with the blade in his nose, gurgling, trying to breathe.

"I am going to ask you questions, now, Miguel. You will answer quickly, without hesitation, or Joey will practice plastic surgery on Tito. First question. What is Rigozzi doing in Puerto Rico?"

Torres hesitated, Joey pulled the razor sharp blade through Tito's nostril as one of Daniel's lieutenants turned up the stereo to blank out Tito's screams.

"Too slow, Torres. I told you not to hesitate. Now, again, quickly, the answer to my question."

"He's here talking to the Russians! Please, let my son go, I will tell you what you want. Please let Tito go," Miguel was losing it, completely overcome with fear. He began to cry fitfully.

"Next question, Miguel. Why are the American congressmen here?"

Immediately, Miguel responded as Joey placed his blade in Tito's other nostril.

"Same reason. They are working on some kind of deal, Daniel. I'll tell you what you want to know, see?"

"You are doing well, Miguel. Next question. What deal?"

"To get drugs into Russia. Please don't hurt us anymore..."

"Okay, Miguel. Now let's finish this. Next question and I remind you, I am in no mood to play your games, answer quickly. What is the involvement of the American congressmen?"

"I swear, Daniel, I do not know! On my mother's grave I do not know!"

Joey looked over at Daniel for a signal to slit the other side of Tito's blood-covered nose. Daniel motioned to hold up as he took a sip of wine and walked over to the edge of the patio, looking down onto the beach below. Tito's crimson face was wrenched with fear. He was breathing heavily and shaking from shock and loss of blood.

"Let's back track, Miguel. Several of my associates here on the island have turned up missing. I'm guessing they are dead. Who ordered them killed?"

Without any hesitation, Miguel blurted out, "Rigozzi! He's taking over the island, Daniel. That's the truth! The men working for the Perrone family down here in Puerto Rico have been given a choice of working for Rigozzi or being killed. They had only seconds to decide. Rigozzi also does not tolerate hesitation just as you do not, Daniel. I wanted to call you and tell you, but I feared for my life."

"By your own statement, Miguel, you said Rigozzi only gave seconds for those people to make up their minds. I see you and Tito are still living. I take that to mean you decided to work for Rigozzi, too."

"I had no choice; he would have killed us on the spot. You must understand! Please understand, Daniel! We are dead either way. I am relieved that you are here now. I kiss your hand. I have respect. You will see I have respect."

Daniel nodded and kept staring out onto the beach. He motioned for the music to be turned down and continued his stare.

"Joey, help Tito up. Get him a towel, clean him up. Pour Miguel a glass of wine. We have more talking to do. Miguel is going to prove his respect for our family."

Miguel managed a half smile as his eyes panned the room, trying to anticipate the next move by Daniel's men. Would they kill him? Maybe Daniel needed more information. Miguel was ready to say anything, anything that would allow him and his son to walk out that door.

"I understand you have a very beautiful daughter, Miguel. What is her name?" Daniel asked.

"Oh, she is very beautiful, Daniel. I will get her for you. Do you want my daughter, Looma, to come to the hotel? Anything you want, Daniel!"

"You are disgusting, Miguel! You would pass your own daughter around to me and my men? Have you no pride? Yes, I do want you to get your daughter up here, fast! However, she will be treated with respect, something you are going to learn if it kills you. I mean that, Miguel. She will remain here with us as our insurance policy while you do some work for my family."

"I meant no disrespect, Daniel. I knew you would treat her right. She is a flower, a dove, such a wonderful girl, the joy of her father's life. I will get her here quickly, just as you ask."

"Tell her she will be my escort while I am here on the island. Have her pack an overnight bag. I will buy her any clothes she needs downstairs in the boutiques. As long as you do what I ask, she will be safe. You know what will happen to her if you cross me?"

Mario put the phone in front of Miguel, whose hands were shaking. Miguel managed to dial the number of his daughter's condominium in Condado. He put on his best telephone voice so as not to alarm her. She would arrive in forty-five minutes.

"Now, Miguel, here is what I want you and Tito to find out." Daniel slid a hotel note pad and pen over to Miguel. "Write it down. Make no mistakes, Torres! First, I want to know about the involvement of the U.S. congressmen. Second, I need to know specifically who each of the Russians are, their backgrounds and their positions within the Russian republics. Third, are you getting all this, Miguel?"

"Yes, Daniel." Torres' writing was scribbled. Each question took up a whole page.

"As I was saying, third, is the Rigozzi family working with the Colombians to move cocaine into Russia or Europe? Have you got this, Miguel?"

Miguel, still writing, nodded, looking up at Daniel.

"The last question I need answered is very important." Daniel walked over to Torres and bent down face-to-face with him. "Why is Rigozzi killing my people? What is his plan for the Perrone family?"

"I will find out all of this, Daniel. It will take some time."

"You have until Tuesday of next week."

"I will get the information to you, Daniel. You have my word on that."

"No, Miguel. I have your daughter's life on that."

Back at BOQ 17, Judd was walking out of the shower. He hadn't eaten and the jet lag and cramped cockpit of the F-18 was catching up to him. Feather walked into his room with some leftovers of Sal's press banquet the night before. Sitting on the side of his bed in cut-offs and the wet towel still around his neck, Judd dove into the plate of food.

There was a knock on the door. Randall, Rikki, Jake Ramsey and Sal walked in.

"I see you're enjoying some of Sal's cooking. How're you feeling?" Randall said with a smile.

"A little tired, but otherwise, fine. I'm glad to be out of Puerto Rico for a while. There's a lot happening down there. I didn't get much sleep."

"Do you feel like hashing this thing around or do you want to wait 'til morning?"

"No, let's get to it. On the way I studied the players list and may have come up with a theory. There's still some holes in it but it may be a place to start." Judd reached for his leather briefcase. "Rikki, could you bring the easel in here for me?"

Judd pulled out several yellow note pad sheets and spread them on his bed. Rikki returned with the easel and a package of colored marking pens.

"The first thing I did on the flight back was to arrange the players into teams, who was on whose side, as nearly as I could tell." Judd walked over to the easel.

Taking out a red marker, he wrote the names of the congressmen, the Colombian Cartel, Sicilian Mafia, Mexican congressmen, Carolina Pharmaceuticals and the Russians. On the left side of the tablet, he picked up a green marker and wrote La Cosa Nostra and under it the Perrone family, all based in the U.S. The group in the room copied the scorecard onto their tablets as Judd continued to fill in the names on the easel.

"Let's start with what we know," Judd continued. "We know that Rigozzi represents the Sicilian Mafia and that they control the manufacture and distribution of heroin worldwide. We know they have worked with the Colombian Cartel exchanging heroin for cocaine, which is manufactured and controlled by the Colombians. The Sicilians have set up permanent headquarters in Venezuela to be closer to the Colombians.

"Hypothesis number one: the Colombian Cartel and the Sicilian Mob are working a big deal together.

"Now, let's switch to the Russians. We don't know who these guys are. That alone is significant. They aren't KGB, they aren't political figures. What's left? Answer? Free enterprise. Entrepreneurs, gentlemen. These guys are trying to make some bucks. That's hypothesis number two."

"That's a good place to start the computer checks, Judd," Randall interrupted. "Jake, can you tap in to the computer in Washington and see what we can find out about these guys?"

"Right, sir."

"Hypothesis number three." Judd resumed his brainstorming. "The Mexicans and the Puerto Ricans are involved solely for the money. They provide transportation of raw materials and manufacturing capabilities to get the drugs ready for distribution to other parts of the world, like Russia. That's where Carolina Pharmaceuticals comes in. Not that hard to figure out. I don't believe their involvement in the overall plan goes much beyond that. Next, gentlemen, is the sixty-four thousand dollar question! Why in blazes are the three U.S. congressmen getting into this snake pit? Each of them is wealthy. They've been in the House and Senate for many years with fairly quiet records of performance. They don't need the extra income. We may want to run financials on these three to check their current status."

"Good idea," Randall responded looking over at Jake banging away on his laptop. Jake acknowledged.

"Continuing with the congressmen, gentlemen, I can't tie them into this thing. Makes no sense to me. Can anyone add anything at this point?" Judd asked as Feather stood up, walked over to Judd and took the blue marker from him.

"Maybe a good approach to the congressmen would be to break them down individually. What are their responsibilities on the committees they seat?" Feather mused. "I've been doing some digging. What I've come up with is that Fuselier from Louisiana is on the Agricultural Committee in the House. Maybe the Sicilians want the Colombians to start growing poppies next to their cocoa plants. They could use some advice from the Ag department on how to get the greatest yield on their crops of poppy seeds and cocoa bushes from the land that is available."

"We can run with that, Joe. Write it down," Judd directed.

"Then there's Zapata from Florida." Feather took out another colored pen from the pouch. "He's budget secretary of the all-powerful Finance Committee in the House. One of the biggest problems in the old Soviet Union has been the non-acceptance of the Russian ruble on the world market."

"So enter Mr. Budget Secretary, Zapata, to figure out a way to convert their rubles to world currency, right?" Rikki questioned.

"Makes good sense to me," Erin said. "Let's put that down as another hypothesis."

"Now the biggest fish of all, Senator Capriatti, multi-millionaire and co-chair of the Foreign Relations Senate Committee. He has the power to open the doors to any country in the free world. Between him and Zapata, they can suggest Preferred Nation status and loan amounts for the asking."

"So Capriatti opens the path for the drugs to enter Europe and the Russian republics?" Judd was thinking out loud again. "But for what purpose? That is the question! These three guys are taking the unnecessary chance of being prosecuted for something they don't need. There's no country in the world where they could hide if this conspiracy hit the press. The risk is just too great."

"So where does that leave La Cosa Nostra and the Perrone family, Judd?"

Rikki stood up to stretch her bare, shapely legs. "Looks to me like it leaves them sucking hind tit."

Rikki temporarily broke everyone's train of thought to size up the situation.

"I think the correct phrase is between a rock and a hard place," Judd added. "That's the position of Perrone and the LCN. They've got the Sicilians infiltrating their U.S. operations due to us Feds putting their Americanized bosses in jail at an increasing rate. They're filling the ranks with their Sicilian brothers who may be trying to take over La Cosa Nostra operations through attrition.

"On the other side of the fence, the Sicilians are taking over La Cosa Nostra's money laundering operations as well as their limited heroin distribution operations in Puerto Rico. They've got the FBI closing in on them from one side and their good brothers, the Sicilian Mob, hitting them from the other side and within. The Colombians are obviously siding with the Sicilians. That leaves the Perrones, along with the other twenty-three U.S. mob families, without many friends."

"Didn't you say that you and Rikki met Daniel Perrone last night in Puerto Rico, Judd?" Randall asked.

"Yeah, we did. He's very polished, very polite. Under different circumstances I think I'd get along with the guy."

"Then," Randall stood, "that's the reason for his presence there. He's also wondering what the heck is going on, wouldn't you guess?"

"Sounds logical to me," Judd concluded.

"I think we have plenty to work on," Randall summarized. "I'll buy us a drink over at the 'O' Club if everyone's up to it. Judd, that honey of yours, Erica Stone, has really been looking for you. To the point of causing great suspicion on the media side of her brain. It caused us some problems, too, in hiding your whereabouts. An appearance at the club would take some of the heat off by letting the media know that you're here, conducting business as usual. What do you say?"

"A tall, cool one sounds real good." Judd disappeared into his room and reappeared in jeans and a t-shirt.

Judd led the group to the van outside. They piled in and drove away.

On the way to the Officers Club, Feather spoke up. "I think we left something out of the 'what if 'session we just concluded."

"What's that, Joe?" Randall asked.

"The obvious is sometimes the most blatantly overlooked."

"You're thinking about where this situation leaves us, right?" Judd inserted.

"That's business as usual!" Joe added. "The only difference we have in this situation and the other cases I've worked is that it was always *us* against *them*. Most of the time we knew who the enemy was. Now we don't know if the enemy is within or without."

"We need to have a meeting with Judge Ramirez in the morning," Randall added. "I believe he can give us the insight we're searching for. Until then, we'll just keep it quiet and talk to no one. Agreed?"

"Agreed."

Judd turned the van and once again headed for the 'O' Club. As they walked in, Erica's eyes fixed upon him. With an almost robotic reaction, she left her table of fellow reporters and walked over.

"Hello, stranger. I've missed you."

Judd was a little embarrassed at her opening remark in front of his colleagues.

"Hi, Erica. I've been real busy lately."

Grabbing his arm, Erica pulled him away from the others. "Could we sit over here, just for a minute, and talk?"

"Sure," Judd answered looking back at Erin.

"Where've you been? Don't tell me you've been shut up in your room somewhere because you haven't!" There was concern as well as inquisition in Erica's voice. "Us newsies haven't had much to do around here for the past few days. We've been keeping busy watching the F-18's take off and return. You took off Wednesday and just returned a few hours ago. Where've you been?"

"If you weren't a friend, Erica, I'd have you removed from the reservation for a demand like that."

"Then, Mr. Special U.S. Attorney, you'd have to kick all of us reporters out. I'm running cover for you and you don't even know it! That table I left over there is full of the best investigative reporters in the world. Some are with the *Washington Post*, others are syndicated columnists that have been busting government butts for years." She was not smiling.

"Erica," Judd took a pull from his longneck, "I appreciate your running interference for me, I really do. Even though you are a trusted friend…"

"That's all? Just a friend?" Erica was burning. "Can't you see I'm trying to protect you? These people have the power to destroy you and your career. They made you a national hero overnight. They can bring you down just as quickly. Don't you realize that, Judd?"

"I can't, Erica. I can't."

For the first time since she had seen Judd in the D.A.'s office, Erica noticed a crack in his voice.

Erica's anger turned to compassion. She completely disregarded everyone else in the club, what it would look like or what people would say. She reached over and took Judd's hand in hers.

"It's bad, isn't it?"

Judd nodded, "Yeah, it is."

"I won't press you on this anymore, Judd. How can I help? I care about you."

"I know you do, Erica, and that means a lot. I don't know what you can do. I don't even know what I can do. That's what I'm wrestling with now."

Erica squeezed his hand and gave him a smile, slid her chair back and rejoined her group of associates.

Judd took another swig from his beer and returned to the table where Erin and the others were sitting.

"Suddenly, guys, I'm not much in the mood for the club scene. Think I'll catch a ride back to 17."

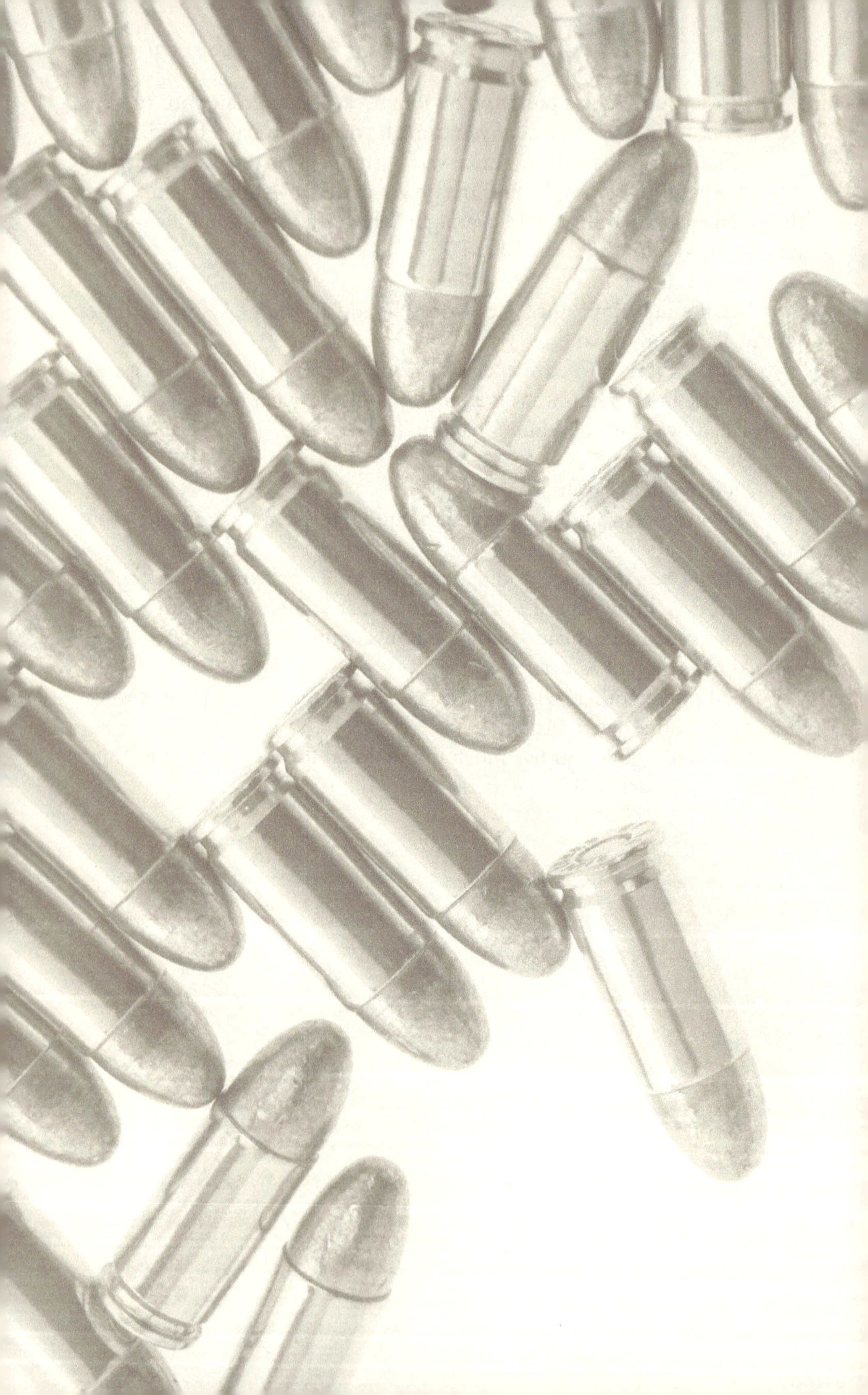

15

Pit of Snakes

The prosecution group huddled around Maureen's desk in preparation for their meeting with Judge Ramirez. Everyone except Jake Ramsey was ready. He was back in the computer room receiving information from Washington.

What Jake read both thrilled and confused him. He was reading as he entered Maureen's office where the others were anxiously awaiting the news.

"Maureen, could you call over to Judge Ramirez's office and inform him that we may be about thirty minutes late. There's some last minute information that we need to go over." Jake was still thumbing through the pages.

The group adjourned to Judd's room.

"What have we got, Jake?" Judd asked, popping three more aspirins and washing them down with his fourth cup of coffee.

Everyone pulled out their tablets and turned to fresh pages.

"It says here that thus far there are no unusual financial activities taking place for the two representatives or the senator. I'm still checking," Jake was scanning the stack of papers as he spoke.

"Washington has identified the Russians. I knew that should be fairly simple, just had to match up pictures…" Jake continued to read. "Here it is, we were very close. All but one of the Russians in the photographs are in private business in the Soviet republics. One is an assistant deputy director in their equivalent to our Food and Drug Administration, a Mr. Sero Muscovia. Here's a list of the others. I'll make some copies."

Within a couple of minutes, Jake returned and handed out copies.

Judd focused on the handout best he could. The document was very complete and listed names, ages, birthdates, hometowns located in the newly formed republics, party affiliations, schooling, complete physical descriptions, arrest records, family members including children and their backgrounds along with complete work histories of the individuals.

"Impressive!" Judd said as he continued reading.

"Thank you!" Rikki remarked. "We do our best to keep you suits informed about what's going on in the rest of the world."

"Let's go over the names and occupations, gentlemen," Randall directed, "Then we can see if our earlier theories will hold up. I'll read. Ivan Poparov, age fifty-one. He's cut some deals with U.S. fast food chains. Those could be distribution points. Next is Yuri Korikin, age sixty-one. He's taken over most of the government-owned shipyards in the Russian republics."

"Laborers and the possibility of labor unions," Rikki inserted. "We believe unions are beginning to organize. He could be another Hoffa."

"Good point," Erin continued. "Ilya Dubrovnia, age forty-three. He's running a commuter airline service between major cities throughout the republics, subcontracting from the government-owned airline, Aeroflot. There's how they get the drugs around the country. Next is Yakin Stolski, age fifty-five, clothing manufacturer and owner of a string of high fashion boutiques."

"Who better to sell drugs to than the Russian rich?" Judd added. "Half the people I've busted in the U.S. come from wealthy families. That part makes sense."

"I agree, looks like we've not been too far off in our hypotheses," Randall read on."Notka Nuriev, age thirty-eight, a young tyke. Look at this! He owns pharmacies in every major city in good ole Mother Russia. We can surely be creative with this guy."

"Over the counter drugs!" Feather joked.

"Not only that, he could sub-distribute those drugs through every prescribing doctor in the Soviet Union."

"Correct, bro, and that guy Muscovia, the assistant deputy director of their FDA, could type out inspection schedules of what trains, boats and aircraft are not to be checked for illegal drug entry through the network of his associates."

"I think we have part of what we need to brief Judge Ramirez," Judd said, placing his copy of the information in his briefcase. "We shouldn't keep the judge waiting much longer. What've we found out about our Mr. Robert Jones, the tourist the Mexicans have?"

"We may have Mexico stalemated on that one, Judd," Erin remarked. "The Mexican Secret Police have probably figured out by now that Mr. Jones is not an agent. Our legal attaché in Mexico City is not communicating with their State Departamento at all with the exception he told the Mexicans if one hair on Robert Jones' head was ruffled, we'd hit the press with news that would be very damaging to some very high officials of their government. That seemed to shake them up. We feel that Mr. Jones is probably ordering margaritas and telling jokes to his captors right now. It's just a matter of time until his release."

The van pulled up in front of the judge's quarters. The prosecution team entered and began their briefing.

"How was beautiful Puerto Rico, Judd?" Ramirez questioned.

"Parts were beautiful, Your Honor." Judd thought of Leti standing in the jungle. "Parts were pretty bad, sir."

After going over the complete findings with Judge Ramirez, they could see his experienced mind working overtime. Upon hearing the story involving so much more than taking a drug pusher to trial, Ramirez got up from his desk. He walked around the room and then outside his quarters, finally returning. He sat down behind his desk and said nothing for ten minutes. The silence and anticipation were maddening. They knew Ramirez would know the course they should take and waited patiently for his reply.

"Feather, when will this 'Jury' be operational?" Ramirez asked with wrinkles forming on his brow.

"Tomorrow. Almost immediately after everyone gets to Con Can. The equipment and the C-130 are already there."

"In that case, gentlemen, I suggest we contact Mr. Wiley and Mr. Castenada and once again move the trial date. This time we move it up. We need to go ahead and get Mr. Cortez and the other defendants through trial as if nothing unusual is going on."

"I agree with you, Your Honor," Randall affirmed.

"Next, Judd," Ramirez continued, "we need further evidence gathered on the three congressmen involved in Puerto Rico. We need to know their connection to the Russians, the Cartel and the Sicilian Mob. You've got to return to Puerto Rico."

"I figured that."

"Randall, you can coordinate with Interpol as soon as Judd gets the information we need. Commander Rhine, will the Russian republics cooperate with us on this?"

"Maybe if we can get to the right people, Your Honor. Nowadays it's difficult to tell who does what over there. Putin calls all the shots."

"I'll contact Wiley and Castenada to reset the trial date, gentlemen." Ramirez removed his reading glasses. "I'm assuming the prosecution is ready for trial?"

"Yes we are, judge."

"Judd, I'll give you a week longer in Puerto Rico to see what you can dig up. And, gentlemen, I don't have to tell you about confidentially on this subject. We are playing very high table stakes, here."

"We understand," Judd responded, "and appreciate your direction.

"I hope we're all breathing when this is over!" Rikki added.

The meeting was adjourned. They all felt better that Judge Ramirez was part of the team, a small consolation to the uncertainty they faced.

Ramirez had been a former prosecutor himself. He had been the protégé of the former San Antonio District Attorney, Maxwell Perkey, who later went on to be a federal judge. His nickname was "Mad Max" Perkey because he always handed out maximum sentences to all murderers, rapists and specifically, to all drug felons. While working in San Antonio, Ramirez had been threatened many times by drug bosses. Even after Mad Max was assassinated by the drug lords, Ramirez had refused to succumb to their demands.

SATURDAY NIGHT, JUNE 14TH, 11 P.M. CST

Erica Stone was no spring chicken when it came to investigative reporting. Her intuition was now racing at mach three. She knew something big was going down and knew she had to be there when it did. She made a late night call to her news director at home.

"Dave? This is Erica. Hope I didn't wake you."

"No, Erica, just turning in for the night. What's up?"

"I had a brief conversation with Judd Rayburn last night. Dave, this Cortez trial is just the tip of the iceberg. Something much bigger is going on. He told me that much."

"Told you what?"

"He wouldn't or couldn't say, but it's got him shook up bad. I know him well enough to tell."

"So what can I do to help?"

"I know for a fact that Judd left the fort last week on a military F-18. Where he went I don't know. What I do know is that he was visibly upset when he returned. I have a feeling he'll be going back to wherever he went in the near future. I've got to know his destination. He flies with Commander Rikki Rhine, the lady Navy pilot in Naval Intelligence. We know the number of her aircraft and when she takes off. Can one of our communication satellites track her aircraft, at least enough to give us a bearing on the direction she flies?"

"I don't think they can track an aircraft. Wait a minute! I have a brother-in-law that's a flight controller in Houston. I know he can't tie up his radar to track her flight from beginning to end but he may be able to give us a fix and a direction once she straightens out. From there, we'll take a map and see where the line crosses and formulate a sophisticated wild ass guess."

"Great, Dave! I'll call you when I see her aircraft being refueled. That'll give your brother-in-law a little advance notice. When you guys decide on a location, then I'm out of here."

"Can you get off the fort, Erica?"

"Yeah, no problem."

"I'll alert the news desk to watch for your call, Erica."

"Judd Rayburn is going to get me a Emmy if it kills both of us. I'll call you soon as I see the Hornet pull out of the hanger."

SUNDAY, JUNE 15TH, 10 A.M., EST

"Daniel, Miguel Torres is on the phone for you."

"This is Perrone."

"Daniel, my friend. I trust you slept well?"

"I always sleep well, Miguel. What do you have for me?"

"I cannot say over the phone, Daniel. I would like to visit you. How is Looma?"

"You play games with your daughter's life, Miguel."

"I am sorry, Daniel. I do not understand what you are saying."

"Last night our room service attendant was someone different. I think the new man was your cousin, Porfi."

"Oh yes, Porfi has been working at the hotel for many years."

"Untrue. He started last night. 'Last night' is the key phrase, Torres. He tried to pass a pistol to Looma."

"Oh, Daniel, you must believe me, I had nothing to do with that. He must have thought his cousin was in danger and acted on his own. I promise I had nothing at all to do with that."

"Miguel, tell your family to plan a funeral for Porfi. He will not be present."

There was silence on the other end of the phone.

"Serves him right, Daniel. He did not think. But my daughter… is Looma all right? She had nothing to do with this. Please!"

"Looma is indeed a flower, Miguel. I have taken an interest in her. She is fine. However, anything, I repeat, anything else that happens and she will join Porfi. Do you understand, Miguel?"

"Oh yes! Thank you, Daniel!"

"Be here in half an hour. I await your information. It had better be good."

Looma walked out of Daniel's bedroom into the living room and poured herself some dark, rich Puerto Rican coffee.

"Looma! Put on a robe! Get dressed. I don't want my men seeing you like this!"

Mario looked across the room at Joey. Joey was staring at Looma's black, sheer negligee. Mario shook his head at Joey telling him to look the other way. It was plain to see that Daniel had in fact become very interested in Looma. Joey's stare could become very unhealthy for him if Daniel noticed.

"Your father will be here in half an hour, Baby. Mustn't give him the wrong impression," Daniel changed his expression and smiled at her as he spoke.

"Anything you say, darling," Looma casually walked back to Daniel's room, barefooted, scantily dressed, drinking her coffee.

"Dave! This is Erica. The F-18 is about to take off. I'd guess ten to fifteen minutes. Ask your brother-in-law to track it."

"I'm on it. Stick close to your phone. When we determine where they're going I'll book the earliest flight for you. I'm gone!"

"Miguel's downstairs, boss."

"Bring him up, Joey, this should be interesting."

Looma had finished dressing. Daniel ordered breakfast on the patio. The regular room service attendant set up the meal, shaking a bit but smiling, always smiling. He didn't wait for a tip.

"Have some coffee, Miguel," Daniel was in a good mood. "The white carafe is American, the black is Puerto Rican coffee."

"I prefer Puerto Rican coffee, Daniel."

Joey poured the coffee for Miguel and then returned to the other side of the table opposite him. Miguel was uneasy enough as it was.

"You look very well this morning, Looma."

"As do you, Father."

"Looma, could you go down with Frankie and do some shopping?" Daniel was polite.

Looma and Frankie left the room.

"Now tell me, Miguel. What news do you have for me?"

"Erica, it's Dave, they're heading for Puerto Rico! I've got you a flight leaving El Paso in forty-five minutes connecting with American in Dallas then direct to San Juan. Can you make it?"

"I've got a driver outside with the motor running. I'm packed. I'll make it!"

"Pick up your tickets from Carlo at the American counter."

"Why Carlo? Why isn't John going with me? It isn't fair to him."

"No time for fair, Erica. John's a great cameraman but Carlo speaks Spanish. Call me when you arrive."

"Your information on the Russians is very good, Miguel," Daniel was impressed.

"I have a cousin who's a clerk at the CIA in Washington, Daniel. He is very thorough."

"Entrepreneurs. All but one." Daniel read the report that Miguel had carefully typed. "This Muscovia, he will allow the drugs into Russia. A very good plan my Sicilian brothers have contrived."

Daniel read on through the report.

"Rigozzi is in fact working with the Colombians. He will want to offer cocaine as well as heroin to Europe and the Russian republics. Now I need the answers to my two final questions. What is the involvement of the American congressmen? And, why is Rigozzi killing my people?"

"Daniel, my sources tell me that the Sicilians consider Puerto Rico a very important staging area for the distribution of their drugs to Russia. Of course, the flights out of Puerto Rico will not go direct. They will go to Argentina after packaging is complete, then on to various entry countries before finally entering Russia. Rigozzi must have full control over the island here. He cannot contend with outside involvement, even from the American Mafia."

Daniel nodded, looking towards the beach. "The American congressmen?"

"I swear to you, Daniel, I do not know. It is hard to figure them out. No one is paying them, at least no one here on the island. We have checked and double-checked. I still have until Tuesday, remember? You have given me until Tuesday."

"You will have these answers Tuesday, Miguel, no later. Now leave me and begin your investigation."

Daniel stood up from the table on the patio. He walked over to the edge overlooking the beach and took a deep breath of the sea breeze coming off the beautiful Caribbean, in deep thought.

"Mario, get my father on the phone!"

Rikki's F-18 touched down on the deck of the USS *George H. W. Bush*. Judd and Rikki immediately took the launch over to San Juan.

"Hey, it's Sunday afternoon, Judd. There's a custom in Puerto Rico not to work on Sundays. How 'bout a drink over at the Condado Tower patio? It sure helps get rid of the lags." Rikki smiled.

"Sounds good to me."

During the first hour on the hotel patio they carefully surveyed the other guests. Rikki ordered their third drink. Judd was just starting to relax.

"Got to go powder my nose, schoolboy. I'll be right back." Rikki walked into the hotel to find the nearest ladies room.

Judd pulled out cash to pay for the drinks not wanting to leave a credit card trail, when the waitress arrived.

"No, señor," the waitress refused his money. "The gentlemen over at that table have bought these drinks for you and your friend."

Judd glanced over two tables. Four men dressed semi-casually looked his way and tipped their drinks. Judd smiled and nodded his appreciation, wondering who they were. Two of the solidly built, middle-aged men walked over to his table.

"The governor of Puerto Rico welcomes you to our island, Mr. Rayburn," one of the men said.

"Tell the governor I appreciate his welcome." Judd did not even know the governor's name. "And who do I have the pleasure of meeting?"

"I am Special Agent Bennazar and this is Special Agent Acevedo. We work directly for the governor."

"Nice to know you, gentlemen."

"Señor, the governor would like to have the pleasure of your company this afternoon. We have been sent to take you to his hacienda," Bennazar said with a smile.

"I would love to meet the governor, Mr. Bennazar. I'm waiting for a friend." Judd felt something was wrong. The governor couldn't have known of his arrival.

"Unfortunately, Mr. Rayburn, the governor instructed us to bring only you. Alone." Bennazar's voice was firm but polite.

Trying to buy time until Rikki returned, Judd looked up at Bennazar.

"I can't leave my friend until I let her know that I am going to visit the governor. Could I see some identification, sir?"

Bennazar's smile disappeared. He pulled open his jacket to reveal an Uzi hanging underneath his arm. Acevedo did the same, gripping Judd's arm.

"I must insist you come with us quickly, Mr. Rayburn. We wouldn't want anyone to get hurt." Bennazar turned to see if anyone was watching.

"Slowly, Mr. Rayburn. Stand up and walk quietly with us or I will kill you where you sit. Don't lift your hands." Acevedo moved in closer to Judd.

They walked into the lobby of the hotel, no Rikki. Within forty-five seconds they were getting into a black Lincoln stretch limo and driving away from the hotel.

Rikki returned to the table. "Señora. Señora! Have you seen my friend who was sitting here with me?" she asked politely.

"No, señorita. Maybe he went back to his room."

"Oh, we're not guests of the hotel." Probably in the *banos*, as the Spanish referred to the bathroom, Rikki thought.

Thirty minutes passed. She knew something was wrong and made several trips to each of the men's rooms located in the lobby. She asked the bell captain and most of the bellmen if they had seen a man fitting Judd's description after putting ten bucks in each of their pockets. No one had seen Judd. Judd was someone's prisoner and Rikki knew it. She walked back to the patio and sat down at their table, once again panning the crowd seated outside. She began back tracking her memory. Who was still there? Who had left. Rikki remembered the table of four men. They were gone.

"Señora!" she summoned the waitress. "The four gentlemen seated two tables over, have they left?"

She looked in the direction Rikki was pointing.

"I do not see them there anymore. I guess they left."

"Do you have a copy of their tab, Señora?"

"No, they paid in cash. I'm sorry I cannot help you."

"Señora, do you know their names or where they work? Anything?"

"Sorry. As I said, I cannot help you."

Typical, Rikki thought. *No one sees anything*. She began to develop a plan of action to locate Judd…

16

KIDNAPPED

The afternoon sun was low in the West Texas sky, bringing on the cooling process in the desert. Erin, Feather, and Maureen were sitting outside BOQ 17 talking, reading the Sunday newspaper, and waiting for Judd and Rikki to check in, generally, just taking the day off and relaxing.

"Randall!"

"Yeah, Casey."

"Commander Rhine's on line 1, says it's an emergency. She needs to talk to you ASAP."

Randall ran into BOQ 17 with Feather and Maureen right behind him, as a gust of wind scattered their big Sunday papers all over the yard.

"Erin speaking. What's the problem, Commander?"

"Judd's been kidnapped, Randall, about an hour ago. We were sitting outside the Condado Towers Hotel having a drink, I went to the bathroom and when I got back he was gone. No one saw anything. I'm contacting *El Prevision* for their help in locating him…"

"Slow down, Commander! Give me a minute to think." Randall's expression was obvious. Feather and Maureen knew something bad had happened.

Covering the phone, Erin turned to Joe and Maureen. "Judd's been abducted."

Maureen broke, "Oh, my God!"

Feather just stood there, stone-faced, waiting for more information from Erin.

"Where are you calling from?" Erin asked.

"I'm on board the *Bush*. They're secure here."

"Good!" There was a long pause while Randall ran options through his mind. "Don't call the State Department. Repeat, don't call State. We don't know who we're dealing with yet. Do you have any theories about who may've taken him?"

"It's got to be the Sicilians or the Puerto Rican governor's secret police, or a combination of both."

"What about the Cosa Nostra? Didn't you say Perrone is down there?" Randall questioned.

"Perrone is in a bad position with all the above. His fight is going to be with the Sicilians. Same as ours for once."

"Commander, first contact Father Molinas and see what José and Leti can find out."

Randall tried to remain calm while working with Rikki to formulate a plan. They had to act and act fast. The longer the abductors kept Judd, the less the chances were of getting him back alive.

"If *El Prevision* drags their feet, Commander, then talk to Perrone. I figure he definitely has an interest in this."

Feather tapped Randall on the shoulder. Randall covered the phone and looked over at Joe, noticing the tears rolling down Maureen's face. "I can be down there tomorrow afternoon with The Jury," Joe looked serious. "I can get at least thirty men ready."

Erin nodded and uncovered the phone.

"Feather says he can be down there tomorrow afternoon with about thirty men. We can land on the *Bush*. Alert Captain Bennett that The Jury is on its way. I'll get things going from this end. Commander, call me back after your meeting with José and Leti. I'll remain here at Bliss to coordinate."

"I'm outta here, Randall. Talk to you soon."

"Be careful, lady. I don't want to have to start looking for you, too."

"I'm gone."

Randall put the phone down and turned to Maureen.

"Maureen, Judd will be okay. Right now, I need you to pull yourself together. I need your help and so does Judd."

"I know, I know," Maureen was trying hard to stop the tears.

"I'm going to hop a ride to Con Can. I'll be there in two hours. We'll be ready to leave tomorrow afternoon," Joe said. "I'll have time tonight and in the morning to brief the guys and get the equipment together. Let me know if we'll be landing a different type of aircraft in Con Can or whether we can go on the C-130."

"I'll arrange transportation, Joe," Randall said. "I'm also going to drive over and tell Judge Ramirez what's happening. Re-emphasize the obvious, gang, keep this thing quiet."

Blindfolded, gagged and handcuffed, Judd sat in the back seat of the limo. No one spoke to him. He figured they must've been driving for the better part of an hour and had no sense of whether it was daylight or dark. The closed windows and air-conditioning prevented him from detecting odors. He could feel only the road becoming bumpier. They were turning a lot. He remembered the ride he and Rikki had taken down route 149 through the jungle to meet with Father Molinas. Maybe they were driving on such a road. But which one? What direction were they going?

Daniel had spoken to his father on the phone earlier in the day. Most of the conversation had been idle chitchat, "It's beautiful here in Puerto Rico, having a wonderful time, wish you were here," sort of talk. Nico read between the lines of the conversation. He knew that his son had information but didn't dare discuss it over the hotel phone. Nico understood Daniel would write down the information and send it by his private fax. Daniel was just making sure his father would be at home to receive his communication.

As he sat at the desk in the living room of the hotel suite, Daniel tried to compose all the facts into the briefest, most concise letter he could write. He decided to write the letter in cablegram language, in Italian. The translation of the communiqué read:

Father,

Sicilians killing LCN in PR. Working deal with Cartel for Russian distribution.

Beware Sicilian brothers inside LCN. Have Miguel's daughter, have Miguel working for us. Congressmen Fuselier, Zapata, Capriatti with Sicilians. Involvement not known. Need information. Five Russian businessmen involved, in PR. One Russian FDA assistant official, no problem. U.S. Attorney Judd Rayburn in PR. Investigation will help us. LCN operation in PR non-existent for time being. Beware, advise, I await. Daniel.

When Erica and Carlo walked off the American DC-10 into the terminal in San Juan, it was 9:15 p.m. EST. They walked down the hallway that opened to the large baggage area near the front of the airport. Both were tired and looked forward to checking into the hotel, taking a bath and getting a good night's rest before figuring out what Judd and Commander Rhine were doing in Puerto Rico.

"If Judd and that Navy bitch came down here for a quick shack, I'll, I'll…She'd probably kill me, Carlo. I hear she's some kind of karate expert. Dammit! Dammit! Dammit!"

After claiming their baggage, Erica and Carlo hired a skycap to load it into one of the many taxis waiting outside the terminal. The heat and humidity engulfed them as soon as they walked outside the air-conditioned terminal. Within five minutes the taxi was pulling around the circular drive to the magnificent San Juan Hotel.

MONDAY, JUNE 15TH, 6 A.M. CDT

Rikki contacted Father Molina and met with the good Father, Leti, and José during the wee hours of Monday morning. José and Leti broke their standing rule of allowing no one other than a bona fide member of *El Prevision* to know their location. They took Rikki's predicament as a measure of good faith and allowed her to spend the night at their camp in the mountains. After collecting additional details from her they put out a message to their members to find Judd. Now came the waiting.

El Prevision had no prior knowledge of the abduction. This gave Rikki cause for concern. The capture of Judd had been well planned and kept secret. How did they know the two of them would go to the Condado Tower for a drink? Rikki had to deal with the present problem, save Judd's life, get him back. After deciding it was time for her meeting with Perrone, Rikki drove back into San Juan.

Impatiently, she walked into the lobby of the San Juan Hotel, picked up one of the house phones and asked for Perrone's room.

"I'm sorry, señorita, there is no one here at the hotel by that name."

Rikki was in no mood for games. She was ruffled from her night in the jungle camp. Members of *El Prevision* lived a hard life without modern conveniences. She walked over to the registration desk, flashed her Naval ID and asked to speak to the hotel manager, now!

The manager walked up to Rikki in less than a minute and escorted her into the privacy of his office, not knowing the reason for a Naval Intelligence agent needing his assistance. Rikki knew she had blown her cover, if it had ever been a cover. She felt the cat was out of the bag and everyone on the island knew she was an agent.

"You have a Daniel Perrone staying in this hotel!" Rikki was not being tactful. "I know who he is and what he is. I'm not after him. I do need to talk to him. Get him on the phone for me now unless you want me to pick up the phone and have half the IRS agents in Washington auditing your books for the next ten years!"

The well-dressed Puerto Rican hotel manager sized up the touchy situation in a hurry and dialed Perrone's room. "Mr. Perrone, please. This is the hotel manager calling." There was a brief pause while Joey got Daniel on the phone. Mr. Perrone, I am sorry for the disturbance. I have a Commander Rikki Rhine of Naval Intelligence standing before me demanding to speak to you. Will you speak with her, sir?"

Daniel figured she was CIA or FBI but was not sure. Why would she blow her cover? Why did she want to talk to him?

"Put her on the phone!" Daniel commanded.

"This is Daniel Perrone, Miss Commander Rhine. How can I help you?"

"Mr. Perrone, I need to speak with you about a matter that may be beneficial to both of us. I have no interest in you or your family," she remarked hurriedly.

"This is unusual, Commander. Are you saying that this is an unofficial visit?"

"Where you and your family are concerned, Mr. Perrone, it's very unofficial."

"I am having breakfast on the veranda. Perhaps you would like to join me?"

"I accept your invitation."

"Commander, would you put the hotel manager back on the phone?"

Rikki handed the phone to the manager.

She left the manager's office and positioned herself near the battery of elevators. She stood there with an anxious, stern look on her face. Her clothes were dirty, she had on no makeup on and she hadn't slept at all.

Rikki knew that Perrone would keep her waiting while he hid everything, anything that could be incriminating. Rikki's impatience was reaching an all-time high while she waited for the bellman to return with the elevator key. For the fifth time the elevator doors opened, releasing tourists anxious for a good breakfast and some Caribbean sun.

"Fancy meeting you here! Is this the real Commander Rhine or am I just imagining this?"

Rikki was completely caught off guard as she stood face to face with Erica Stone.

"Hello, Erica. Vacationing?"

"I might just ask you the same question? Is Judd with you? You look like you didn't get your nap last night."

Erica picked up on Rikki's surprise right away.

"Hey, when you're on vacation, why waste time sleeping?"

"You didn't answer my question, Rikki. Is Judd with you?"

"No!" Rikki looked around for the bellboy; she didn't need this questioning, especially from Erica.

"I see," Erica's reporter mind began spinning. "Where is he? He flew here with you yesterday. You left Bliss about 10:30 a.m. in an F-18. Don't lie to me, bitch! Where's Judd?"

The bellboy showed up just in the nick of time to stall out Rikki's interrogation session with the now jealous, explosive, Erica Stone.

The elevator door opened. Rikki and the bellboy walked in, Erica followed.

"Wait, Erica! You can't go with me, understand? Besides, you need to take some time to work on your very limited vocabulary, not to mention your wild imagination."

"No, I don't understand!" Erica could get just as belligerent as anyone when she smelled a story or, especially when her love life was being threatened. "Why don't you help me understand, Commander! I'm all ears!"

Rikki literally pushed Erica out of the elevator and motioned to the bellman to close the doors. She knew she should've used more finesse on Erica, especially Erica. She was tired and didn't need a Q & A session. Erica had followed them to the island snooping for a story; that was obvious. Rikki knew she'd be waiting for her when she returned and would deal with her after the conversation with Perrone.

The doors of the elevator opened up into Perrone's suite on the top floor of the hotel. Joey was standing in front of her as she was escorted out onto the veranda where Daniel was seated eating his breakfast. Daniel wore a robe and slacks and looked just the opposite of Rikki, well-groomed and well rested.

"Please be seated, Commander. Have some fresh fruit?" Daniel was being polite as usual.

"Just coffee. I'd like to speak with you privately."

Daniel motioned for Joey to leave the patio. His other men were already stationed on each side of the living room in the adjoining bedrooms, listening to every word, watching every move.

"Now what can I do for you? It is not often that I get a visit from a professed Naval Intelligence agent."

"I'll get right to the point. As I said earlier, I have no interest in you or your family. I know exactly why you are here; your operation on the island has been taken over by the Sicilian mob."

Daniel neither confirmed nor denied Rikki's statement. He continued to express an unconcerned but attentive expression.

"They're running La Cosa Nostra out of Puerto Rico, killing any of your men that will not be loyal to them. They're going to run drugs into Russia. You know that and I know that." Rikki looked Daniel squarely in the eyes as she spoke. "The way I see it, Daniel, interestingly enough, for once we may both be on the same side of a thorny fence."

"I'm sorry, Commander, I do not follow this train of thought." Daniel continued his uninterested look.

"They plan to run you off of this island." Rikki was attacking, laying her cards on the table once again. "Your own organization in the States has been infiltrated with Sicilians. Just about now, Daniel, you have to be wondering just who you can trust within La Cosa Nostra and whether or not the long-time relationship with your Sicilian brothers is about to self-destruct. Matter of fact, you're probably planning to give them some swimming lessons."

Being very evasive, Daniel interrupted. "Commander Rhine, pardon my return to formality, but I do not know what all of this has to do with me or my family, who incidentally are in the hotel business."

"Then I'll be very clear about the reason for my visit."

"Please do."

"Judd Rayburn, whom you met last week, has been abducted, yesterday evening at the Condado Towers Hotel…"

"I had nothing to do with his abduction!" Daniel blurted out.

"I know that! You have no reason! We're actually helping you on this one, don't you know that! I need your help in getting Rayburn back from the Sicilians and the Puerto Ricans. Let's stop with the games, Perrone. I certainly wouldn't be talking to you like this if I thought you had him."

"Strictly as a concerned citizen of the United States, Commander, I will offer any help that I can in freeing an agent of the government in Mr. Rayburn's position."

"Perrone, let me try this another way." Rikki sat back in her chair, sipping coffee, trying to relax from her sudden outburst. "I could write a book on your father, Nico. We know what he's trying to do with the organization.

It's his dream. He wants to legitimize the entire organization, to move away from the punk killing power-struggle days of the early Mafia. For once, the U.S. government and La Cosa Nostra share a common wish, to end organized crime, as we both know it. If you will help me now, who knows? Maybe we can help you later. Do you see where I'm coming from?"

"An interesting concept, but what assurances do I have that you are not employing a different tactic to gain knowledge of me and my family's business? The government has been harassing us for decades. Am I to think we are about to enter into a truce?"

"Daniel, I'm giving you the best and only assurance that I have, Judd Rayburn's life. It may be in your hands."

That got a reaction out of Daniel. Commander Rhine was leveling with him, now. The congressmen! Neither he nor the commander had brought them into the conversation. Both knew they were playing high level stakes. At the present, the other side had the upper hand. The Cartel, Sicilians, Puerto Ricans, Russians and, oddly enough, the U.S. congressmen had formed a very powerful team. *Perhaps*, Daniel thought, *it was time to bring in some reinforcements.* Rikki calculated that Daniel might respond to having his nemesis handed to him on a silver platter.

"I think you are sincere and very concerned over the safety of your friend, Judd Rayburn." Daniel's look of nonchalance turned to business. "I will see what information I can get. Where can I get in touch with you?"

Rikki wrote down the number at the condo, stood up from the table and stuck out her dirty hand.

"A very symbolic gesture, Commander," Daniel said. "Longtime adversaries sharing a common bond." Daniel shook her hand.

Rikki walked towards the elevator. On the way down to the lobby, she remembered Erica. "You knew I'd be waiting for you, Commander. C'mon, give a girl a break. What gives?" Erica questioned, knowing that Rikki's lack of sleep rendered her vulnerable. She decided to use a more gentle approach.

"Let's find a table in the lobby, Erica," Rikki said, seeming to give in to her demands. "You and your cameraman are in danger here. I can't go into details, Erica, believe me, you have to leave. Immediately! I'll escort you to the airport and stay with you until you board. That's how dangerous this situation is."

"Oh yes, Commander, are you suggesting that I tell my editor that I got scared and came home. That'll get me a spot in the unemployment line."

"You don't understand, Erica…"

"You said that earlier, Rhine. It's you who doesn't understand. Danger goes with the turf in my job, just like yours. We're not leaving and that's final! Where's Judd?"

Rikki's frustration level had never been as high.

"Then, Ms. Stone, you leave me no choice; I'm placing you under arrest. You have the right to remain silent. Anything you say…"

"Wait a minute! Are you serious?"

"Dead serious!"

"What's going on here, Rikki?"

"I'll tell you on the way to the airport."

"I didn't say I would leave. You can't arrest me because I won't leave and I'm damn sure not leaving! Now, what gives and where's Judd?"

"Erica, just listen and don't interrupt until I finish. Get your cameraman and check out. I'm taking you to the ship."

"What ship?"

"The USS *George H.W. Bush*. It's a carrier anchored out in the bay. You'll be safe there."

"I don't want to be safe. I want some details, like where the hell is Judd?"

Rikki stood up and attempted to cower over Erica with her most fearsome look. Unfortunately, Erica was taller than she was.

"Now!" she bellowed.

Erica got the message. Carlo walked over as they went back to their rooms to pack and check out. Rikki called ahead for transportation to the *Bush*.

"Captain Bennett, this is Erica Stone and her cameraman, Carlo. If you don't mind, they'll be bunking in with you guys for a while."

"I beg your pardon, Commander. I don't 'bunk in' with anyone!" Erica had been briefed on the ride out to the ship but still didn't like any of it.

"The Commander looks tired, Ms. Stone. I'm sure she meant to say you will be our honored guest on board my ship," Captain Bennett said, smoothing over Rikki's choice of words.

Erica looked over at Rikki and then back to Captain Bennett without acknowledgment. She felt like she was now *inside* on this developing story and content to be there.

"I'll place you in her care to show you around the ship."

"How nice of you Captain," Erica said snidely. "This should be interesting. Maybe we can have a little slumber party and talk about our old boyfriends."

"Ms. Stone, our old boyfriend may be getting his butt kicked as we speak. He may not be alive." Rikki was pleasant and sincere.

Erica realized how childish she sounded and shut her mouth.

"Captain, when's Feather getting here?" Rikki asked.

"ETA is 20:09 this evening. Ms. Stone, that's military time for 8:09 p.m. EST."

"I knew that Captain. Thanks anyway."

"Captain, I've got to go back to my condo. It's not safe, but that's where Perrone and *El Prevision* know to contact me. I've got to be there." Rikki was forming noticeable bags under her eyes.

"This is completely unofficial, but I'm already involved. I'm assigning three of my SEAL team members to go with you. They'll also take some radio equipment so we can communicate over secured lines," Captain Bennett said.

"Could you do me one more favor, Sir?

"Name it."

"Could you monitor government transmissions coming out of Puerto Rico. We may intercept something we can use to find Judd." Rikki was tired, but thinking.

"Good idea. We'll get right on it. I'll call you by radio if anything turns up."

MONDAY, JUNE 15TH, 1 P.M. EST

Judd spent Sunday night on a dirt floor with no idea where he was. His captors removed his gag so he figured it would do no good to scream for help. He was stiff and felt dirty, otherwise, so far, so good. The handcuffs dug into his wrists and his eyes watered continuously from the masking tape placed over them for hours. The heat convinced him that it was daytime. No one had spoken a word to him. He could hear several men talking outside. Some spoke Spanish, others spoke in Italian. Judd had a pretty good idea who his captors were.

He heard a vehicle drive up and voices but could not make out what they were saying. Judd was not bi-lingual except for the limited Spanish vocabulary he still remembered from his freshman and sophomore classes in college.

Rigozzi had come to the camp. Because he was blindfolded, Judd had no idea who else had arrived. He heard multiple footsteps approaching. One of the men entered Judd's hut. Two other men picked Judd up off the floor and threw him onto a folding chair. Rigozzi stood directly in front of him.

"Mr. Rayburn."

Judd could only tell he was being addressed by someone with a heavy Italian accent.

"I trust you slept well?"

No reply from Judd.

"I'm sorry that your vacation accommodations had to change so abruptly."

"I'm assuming I'm speaking to the Governor," Judd replied facetiously.

"I'm afraid the governor had other plans. He's a very busy man, you know. From here on out, Mr. Rayburn, I will ask you questions and you will only speak to answer those questions. Unfortunately, you will be beaten every time you fail to respond, do you understand?"

Judd made no reply. He felt a crashing facial blow that knocked him out of the chair onto the dirt floor, almost knocking him out completely. He was roughly picked up and put back in the chair. This time held upright by one of his captors. Judd felt a deeper pang of fear travel throughout his body and settle in his stomach. It overshadowed the pain from his cheek. He felt he might be going to die. He needed to focus, he had to.

The questions continued, the beating continued. Judd was near passing out and could barely feel his own blood dripping down his face. He continued his silence. For some reason he thought about his dentist, Dr. Morgan, back in El Paso. He was definitely going to need some dental work.

"Mr. Rayburn. Mr. Rayburn! You only make it hard on yourself," Rigozzi said. "We will find out what you know eventually. Spare yourself this beating. Once again, what do you know of our operation? Why are you here in Puerto Rico? Tell us and we will return you to your friends."

Sure you will, you scumbag butt wipes, Judd thought. Nearing unconsciousness, he pretended to be out cold. They splashed his face with a bucket of water. The water felt good on his battered face.

"He's out," one of the men said.

"If we had more time I would shoot him up with heroin and make him beg to tell me what I want to know," Rigozzi said angrily. "I must know what he knows, quickly. Our whole operation could be jeopardized. When he wakes up, start on him again. He will break."

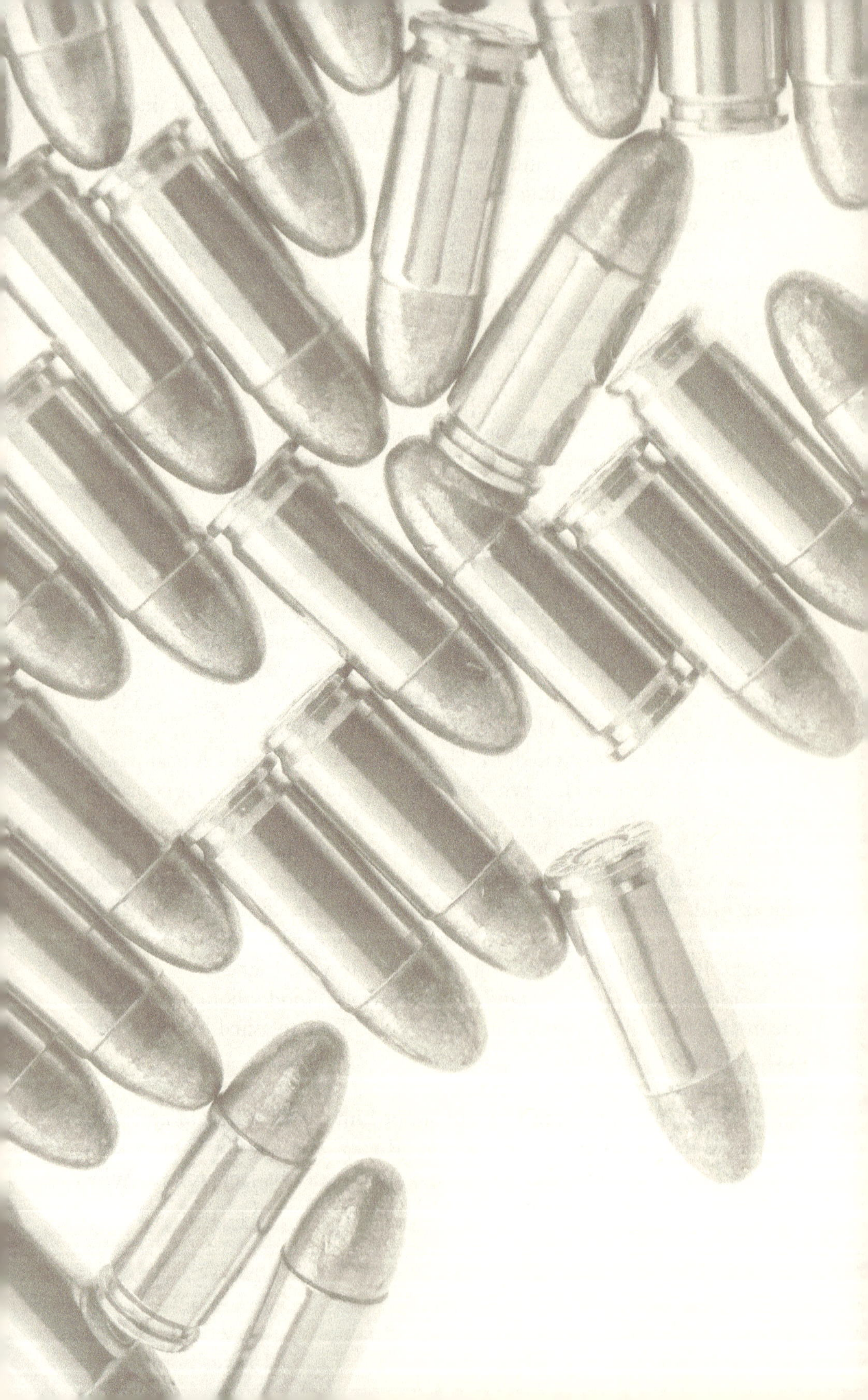

DECEPTION

Daniel summoned Miguel Torres to his hotel suite.

"Miguel, I have another job for you. Don't speak! Just listen!" Daniel's eyes blazed a glance towards Miguel that told him to take special note. "The Sicilians have abducted a Mr. Judd Rayburn. Do you know where they have taken him?"

"No, Daniel, I swear I do not."

"I am sending Mr. Verocchi with you to find out where Mr. Rayburn is being held," Daniel looked over at Joey. "Joey, assist Mr. Torres here to find out the location. I want to know before dark tonight. Now, leave me. Oh, yes, Miguel, if you do not return or anything happens to Joey, I will cut Looma's heart out and place it in your lap."

Miguel nodded his head vigorously and left with Joey Verocchi. The fax machine in the suite began to ring and a page rolled out. Translation:

Daniel,

Board of Directors meeting held midnight last. All subsidiary presidents in attendance. Problems evaluated. Layoffs underway. Three outside consultants not, repeat, not under contract. Will attempt to bargain price with them. Urgent hand-carried message on way by Robin. ETA 6:45 p.m. EST today. Meet at airport. Specialists ready to assist you in PR. Request if needed. Be Safe. Nico Perrone.

Daniel read the fax twice, ciphering his father's message. Nico had told him that all twenty-four family heads of the La Cosa Nostra had met in secret. His father had told them of the Sicilian action in Puerto Rico. "Layoffs underway" meant only one thing, the most violent killing spree since the St. Valentine's Day Massacre back in the thirties. The American based La Cosa Nostra would purge the organization of all their Sicilian brothers. The war had already begun. Daniel knew that only his father could have commanded the respect from the other Mafia leaders to order such widespread hits on the Sicilians within the U.S..

The next part of the message confused Daniel. The "three consultants" his father referred to in the fax were clearly the three US congressmen. Daniel could have sworn he'd seen money go to them. Nico was telling him they were not on the take. *Clearly*, Daniel thought to himself, *they must be on the Sicilian payroll.* Last, why was his father sending his sister, Robin, to Puerto Rico? Nico always kept the women of the family outside the business circle. It could be only one thing. Nico was having a trust problem when it came to the safety of his only son. Daniel remembered the deep love between himself and his father. He was the only reason his father would risk putting Robin in danger.

Miguel drove Joey away from the hotel to a purple colored building located in San Juan. Painted in yellow across the face of the single story cinder block structure were the words "La Cha Cha." There was a large pothole-filled parking lot in front. It was strip joint controlled by La Cosa Nostra, a distribution point for drugs, prostitution, and to launder money from the many "men only" tourist groups that met in San Juan each year. Locals, especially affluent locals, frequented the place year round.

"Why are we here, Miguel?" Joey asked. "Your daughter's life depends on getting the information on Judd Rayburn's location back to Daniel before night."

"Joey, my friend, I do not really think my daughter's life is in any danger. The ladies that work in maid service at the hotel are some of my many cousins. They tell me that Daniel truly likes Looma."

"How do you know that?" Joey asked.

"They change the sheets!"

Instead of being scared, fearing for his life and that of his daughter, Miguel appeared to be very confident.

"Come inside, Joey, relax. We can have a drink, see the pretty girls. Then we will speak to some people who can give us the answers that we need. That is the way things are done here on the island. Just sit back and enjoy."

Joey had always been loyal to the Perrone family. They had given him a lifestyle that was very appealing. He had only two vices, drinking and pretty girls. Miguel knew that and ordered the waitress inside La Cha Cha to keep Joey's glass full and make sure the prettiest girls in the club sat at his table.

Hours later, the door of the dimly lit club opened. The sunlight revealed silhouettes of four men walking over to their table. Joey was already half drunk as he flirted with the four women seated around him.

"Ladies," Miguel said with a smile on his face, "please let us discuss some business. You can rejoin us later."

The girls left. The four men, all big, wearing suits and obviously armed, walked over to the corner table.

"Allow me to introduce some of my friends. This is Joey Verocchi of the New York Perrone family," Miguel called each of the men's names out to Joey. They shook hands.

One was Rigozzi. Joey had seen his picture back at the suite. However, Miguel had introduced him by another name. Joey was getting scared.

Rigozzi, or Totelli, as he was introduced, began to speak. "Mr. Verocchi, it is a pleasure to finally meet you. I have heard so much about the good work you do for the Perrone family. You have much respect. I like that. Because respect is so important, I am going to make you an offer you should consider carefully…"

Here it comes, Joey thought as he remembered his favorite line from the movie, *The Godfather*.

"Before I make you this offer, Joey, can I call you Joey?" Not waiting for an answer, Rigozzi continued. "I must tell you of our plans. They are great plans that will make us more money than we can imagine, and with money comes power. Your boss, Nico Perrone is a very good man, a man with vision. He wants to turn La Cosa Nostra in the States into a legitimate business. I think that is a wonderful idea; however, being Sicilian from the old country, I feel it is my duty to maintain our decades of tradition. We will always need a powerful brotherhood to enforce our business ventures. I represent that brotherhood as well as our traditions. Do you agree with me, Joey?"

"Of course, brotherhood and tradition are important."

"Good, good, Joey. I knew you still had respect for our way of life," Rigozzi said as he took a sip of the red Italian wine that was placed in front of him. "Nico is going one way, our brotherhood and traditions are going the other. You must choose, now! Whether you will support our traditions and our way of life or whether you will break those traditions to live a different lifestyle. What is your decision?"

Joey had been around the organization long enough to know that his life hung on what he said next. The music in the club got louder. Joey knew what could happen.

"I choose brotherhood and tradition."

"Excellent choice," Rigozzi smiled. "It is just a matter of time until the Sicilian Mafia runs the show in the United States. Perrone is getting old, and it will be time for a change. You will play a very important part in our takeover. I may even make you head of all the families, but first you must prove your loyalty to me."

Joey was trying to save his own life. The thought of becoming the "Don" overall the U.S. based families was overwhelming. He knew the strength of the Sicilians and knew of their increasing numbers within the families in the States. He would switch his loyalty. He would prove himself to Rigozzi.

"This is what I want you to do for me," Rigozzi looked deep into Joey's eyes. "We have Mr. Rayburn. We are holding him deep inside the jungle near Cayey. I want you to continue working for Daniel. Give him the information he needs. That will prove your continuing loyalty to him. Here is a map. Lead him there along with Mr. Rayburn's friend, the Naval Intelligence agent, Ms. Rhine. We know that she has been having secret meetings with *El Prevision*. She will enlist their help in obtaining Mr. Rayburn's release."

Joey looked surprised. This was news to him.

"I, through my sources on the island, will ask the governor to call the President of the United States. He will tell the President that *El Prevision* has captured Mr. Rayburn. He will request the Delta Force to be flown to the island immediately to help local authorities secure Mr. Rayburn's release. There will be a huge battle between *El Prevision* and the Delta Force. Of course, the highly skilled Delta Force will eliminate *El Prevision*.

"We will allow the Delta Force to reclaim the body of Mr. Rayburn. Yes, Joey. I mean for you to kill Mr. Rayburn during the battle. That is how you will prove your loyalty to me. You will also kill Daniel and Mario at the same time."

Joey had expected to have to kill someone to show his loyalty since this is the way of the Mafia. He hadn't expected it to be in the middle of a battle. He could not show Rigozzi any weakness or he would be dead on the spot.

"As you ask, I will do." Joey spoke firmly.

Daniel took Mario and Lugo with him to the airport to meet his sister, Robin. She flew commercial so as not to draw further attention to the Perrone family's presence on the island.

Dr. Robin Perrone looked radiant walking out of the terminal. Her coal, straight, silky hair that normally reached her waist was pinned up in a bun with a multicolored scarf around her head. She was tall, 5' 7" with big brown eyes, late 30's, and an athletic figure. Even though her family was notorious for taking lives, she had wanted to be a doctor since the age of three. Robin had been a practicing surgeon for many years.

Although her father tried to get her married to "some nice young man" from a prominent family, Robin had a mind of her own. She rejected her father's requests to settle down as she pursued her calling with blind determination. Robin was going to make her own tracks. Daniel taught her to shoot a pistol at the age of fourteen. She respected weapons and was a better shot than her brother and most of the men hired to protect her family.

Robin's unexpected visit to the island comforted Daniel. He loved her so. "Sister, how was your flight?" Daniel said, kissing her on the cheek and taking her carry-on bag.

"Perfect," she answered holding Daniel next to her. "Can we send the men back to the hotel in a cab? I need to talk to you alone."

Getting into the limo, Mario drove. Lugo and the others left in a cab. Daniel rolled up the opaque partition window between Mario and the back part of the limo.

"What's so important that father sent you to tell me?"

"Father has instructed me to tell you that the other families are eliminating the Sicilians from their ranks. The decision to do this weighed very heavily on all the family heads. It was not easy to convince them that the Sicilians planned to completely take over La Cosa Nostra."

"Only father could have done that, Robin. I know it was difficult for him to even suggest such a drastic move. "

Robin dug in her purse, pulling out a pack of cigarettes and a gold lighter. She smoked like a chimney.

"Daniel, Father said to watch those who are closest to you, Mario, Joey and Lugo. He said that Rigozzi will try to recruit them or kill them. Most likely, they will continue to work for you while they are siding with Rigozzi. Father said not to take your eyes off them!"

"Thank you for telling me this. As usual, father is thinking. I had not even considered the possibility until you mentioned it," Daniel said as he stared out the window of the limo. "Oh, I almost forgot. I brought a 'friend' for your protection."

Daniel handed Robin a nickel-plated, pearl-handled .380 automatic with a full clip. Robin put it in her purse.

"I have a new roommate, Sis," Daniel said with a sheepish grin. "Her name is Looma. She's Miguel Torres' daughter."

"Another toy, big brother?"

"No, Robin, I really like her."

"I'm sure I will, too. It's time you got married and have children."

"Not so fast. I said I really liked her, I didn't say I was marrying her."

"You have the look, big brother. I think you have finally found the one who will have your children. Women can tell these things, even when you men cannot."

Back at the hotel, walking into the suite, Joey was anxious to show Daniel the map he had obtained with Miguel's help. Mario took his things out of the adjoining bedroom to the suite so Robin could use it and be closer to Daniel. Robin began unpacking.

"Daniel, the Sicilians have Mr. Rayburn. They are keeping him out in a jungle location near Cayey. Here is a map of the location," Joey said handing the piece of paper to Daniel.

"Good work, Joey," Daniel said, thinking, *that was too easy!* Maybe Joey was the Judas. He would watch him carefully. Surely not Joey!

"Mario, order up some dinner for us. I'm sure Robin is hungry. I have to make a call."

"Commander Rhine," Daniel said from the privacy of his bedroom. "Would you care to join me for dinner in about half an hour?"

"Thanks for the invitation," Rikki said, knowing that Daniel had some information for her regarding Judd's whereabouts. "I'll see you in thirty minutes."

Daniel emerged from the bedroom with Looma who had been putting on the finishing touches before meeting Robin.

"Mario, knock on Robin's door and ask her to join us in the living room. There's someone I want her to meet."

Robin walked out of her room, having changed into a backless sundress with her hair brushed out.

"This is my sister, Robin," Daniel said with pride. "This is Looma Torres."

"You are as beautiful as my brother said, Looma."

"You are more beautiful than your brother could describe. I have been looking forward to meeting you."

"Ladies, we will be joined for dinner by Ms. Rhine, an old friend of mine."

18

THE JURY CONVENES

MONDAY, JUNE 15TH, 7:55 P.M. EST

"**M**other, this is Juliet three zero, on approach to your location from two eight five degrees, altitude two zero thousand. Do you copy?" The C-130 pilot carrying Feather and The Jury was approaching the carrier and called for landing clearance.

"Juliet three zero, we have you on scope. Come to a heading of two seven zero, descend to seven zero. Winds are zero nine at one five, weather clear, advise prior to landing. Mother out." The flight controller aboard the USS *Bush* was fully briefed on the incoming C-130. Everything was ready.

"Commander, scramble the rescue choppers," Captain Bennett ordered. "The flight deck is cleared?"

"Aye, aye, sir! We're ready for them," returned the executive officer.

The C-130 pilot turned into the wind as the pilot made his approach to the massive carrier. He had clearance to land. The tail hook caught on the first attempt as the large aircraft turned off the glide path and came to a stop. Joe Feather was the first one to de plane.

"Agent Feather requesting permission to board, sir."

Bennett returned Feather's salute. "I think you have boarded, Agent Feather. Permission granted."

"Hi, Joe. You look cute in your cami's," Erica said, seeing the surprise on Feather's face.

"ABC must have some stroke for you to be here, Erica. Why are you here?"

"Long story, Joe."

"Captain Bennett, any word on Judd's location?" Feather asked.

"Possibly. Commander Rhine called when you guys were on your way down. She's got a meeting with a Perrone guy in San Juan. May have more information soon," Bennett escorted Feather downstairs to the flight deck to join his men.

"Ms. Rhine, allow me to introduce my sister, Robin. And, this is a friend of mine, Looma Torres."

When Rikki first saw Robin, she did a double take. Robin was graceful, poised, stunning, even through the eyes of another woman.

"Pleased to meet you Robin, Looma."

"Mario, the four of us will dine alone on the patio," Daniel said, excluding his men from the meeting.

After dinner, Daniel leaned over to Looma, kissed her on the cheek and whispered something in her ear. She smiled and dismissed herself from the meeting, which was to follow.

"Ms. Rhine, I have a map of Mr. Rayburn's location." Daniel got right to the point. "I must qualify my statement with the fact that this map was very easily obtained. It reeks of a set up."

"I'll take that into consideration, thank you," Rikki took the map and looked at it closely. "Cayey! Rugged territory around those mountains, heavy jungle surroundings."

"I believe he is really at this location, Ms. Rhine. I have no idea how long they will keep him there," Daniel continued. "If you have the manpower, I would suggest you and your men get there fast, before daylight tomorrow."

"I have the manpower, Mr. Perrone."

"I will accompany you. I'm bringing Robin, Mario and Joey with me. I have a very vested interest in how this thing shakes out," Daniel said, not asking, telling.

"That may cause some problems, Mr. Perrone."

"No! Ms. Rhine! That is my deal for securing the location for you. We will accompany you and your men. I know you are working with *El Prevision*. I have no quarrel with them. I do have a score to settle with Rigozzi, but I'll handle it."

"So be it," Rikki said with some reluctance. "*El Prevision* will get us to the location and provide outer perimeter cover. They will not go in and make the rescue. I have my own group for that, trained specialists in this sort of thing."

"Delta Force?" Daniel asked.

"Uh…Similar. Get some sleep, Mr. Perrone. I'll contact you by messenger in a couple of hours with the details. Be prepared to come with my man when he contacts you." Rikki's mind was going a hundred miles an hour.

Back at her condominium, Rikki instructed one of the SEALs to drive over and contact Father Molinas. Instructions were to have José, Leti and ten of their men meet them at four a.m. just off of the Autopista, near Cayey, at the small park near the bronze statue commemorating the "Workers of Puerto Rico." Everyone on the island knew the spot. At that time of the morning it would be completely free of tourists and locals. Sunrise was 6:28 a.m.. The rescue would be set for 5:20 a.m..

"Get Captain Bennett on the radio, Chief," Rikki said to the SEAL radio operator.

"Got him, ma'am."

"Captain, this is Scalper."

"Go ahead."

"Are Feather and the Jury on board?"

"Affirmative."

"I have Judd's location. We have to hit early in the morning. Tell Feather and his men to copter over to the Navy pier at 0300 hours. Do you copy?"

"Roger, zero three hundred at the Navy pier," Bennett responded.

"Captain, we're going to rappel down from the choppers into the jungle. We'll need five choppers with full muffler soundproofing, four rappel ropes per chopper with 200 feet of length each. Can you handle it?"

"What else?" Bennett shot back. "Do you need a radar jam chopper? Just in case?"

"To be safe, that'd be a good idea. We still don't know what part the Puerto Rican government may play in this. This location looks iffy at best. We could get caught with our britches down. It could be a trap, but we have no choice. We've got to move fast if we want to get Judd out alive."

"Potential problem, Scalper," Bennett said. "Some sort of atmospheric glitch caused our decoder receiver to go down for approximately 45 minutes earlier today. So far we have intercepted no messages out of the government or military facilities located on the island. I'll contact you if we hear anything. Out."

Rikki sent another SEAL team member to the San Juan Hotel to get Perrone and bring them back to her condo. When they arrived, they were dressed in their finest Dockers khakis and Gucci cammo tops.

Before they left the San Juan Hotel, Joey ducked into Robin's room to make a quick call, thinking that his absence had been unnoticed. Daniel saw the door close behind Joey.

Judd was lying on his side in a corner of the hut in the jungle with his knees drawn up tight against him. His face throbbed from the beatings. Every bone in his body ached and mosquitoes were ravaging him. Still blind-folded, he heard footsteps approaching the hut once more. He mustered every ounce of courage he had left. How long would the beating last this time? He had told them nothing, he had survived the initial shock of being beaten and had endured the pain. Now it was survival. His determination was strong and getting stronger. While the Sicilians beat him he spit blood on them. Defiance kept him going. The blows only hurt afterwards, not during the beating. They hit him, he spit on them, they hit him, he spit again until they would beat him into unconsciousness.

"Eat, pig!" one of the Sicilians said. "You must stay healthy so I can punish you more."

The guard laid a bowl of rice and beans on the ground in front of Judd as he removed the cuffs from behind him. Spite, not energy, forced Judd to forego the much needed food for just one chance to return some of the anguish he had suffered since his abduction. Judd put everything he had into a roundhouse right fist that caught the Sicilian squarely on the chin and sent him crashing through the opposite wall of the hut. Two other guards came rushing in. The butt of one of their assault rifles struck Judd on his forehead just above his hairline, knocking him unconscious once again.

"Carlo," Erica said, "We've got to figure out a way to get some footage on this rescue. It's Emmy for sure if we do."

"Tell me!" Carlo confirmed.

"I overheard Feather briefing his men," Erica was scheming. "Their choppers are going to be full. We need to find some flight uniforms and pass ourselves off as technicians on the radar-jam chopper. It's our only hope."

"I know where they keep the flight gear, Erica. What size flight helmet do you want?" Carlo said with a grin.

TUESDAY, JUNE 16TH, 2:15 A.M., EST

The deck of the *George H. W. Bush* was bristling with activity, choppers doing their run ups, groups of men staging for chopper assignments, last minute equipment checks.

Erica and Carlo, dressed in flight gear bearing SEAL insignias, walked over to the radar-jam chopper with helmets on and their faces painted with camouflage stick.

"SEAL camera team!" Carlo said to the pilot with a commanding voice. "We're going with you guys."

Erica and Carlo boarded the chopper with no reply from the pilot. No one questions a SEAL!

Under cover of darkness and muffled exhausts, the six copter assault group lifted off. Maps had been copied, distributed and studied. Feather and Captain Lewis knew their men were ready. It was time to do it.

Arriving at the Navy pier, one chopper landed. Rikki, her SEAL team, Robin, Daniel and his men boarded. They were on the ground for no more than two minutes. The chopper lifted off quickly and quietly to rejoin the others orbiting above them. Gaining altitude for the flight over the mountains, they headed for the meeting site to pick up *El Prevision* members.

"Jury flight leader, I have multiple radar contacts! Contact one, bearing one-seven-zero degrees, two thousand feet descending, one hundred miles out," reported the radar operator on board the *Bush* to the lead chopper pilot. "Contact two, multiple. Bearing two-one-eight degrees, two thousand feet, one-five miles your position, paralleling your course, over."

"Roger, Mother! Will monitor on our scopes," replied the lead chopper pilot. "Do you have flight origins or type of aircraft, over?"

"Jury flight leader, this is Mother. Origin on contact one appears to be from the mainland. Aircraft type is C-130 transport, non-scheduled. Origin of second contact is the island of Culebra. Aircraft type appears to be some old Huey's, over."

"Roger, Mother, track and advise. Jury leader out."

That uncertain feeling began to creep into Feather's gut. He sensed something was going wrong, Indian intuition.

"Jury one to Jury two, over!" Feather was calling Rikki.

"Jury two, go ahead."

"What do you make of the radar contacts, Jury two?"

"Damn the torpedoes, Jury one! Jury two out."

The six choppers landed on the parking lot beside the Workers Statue near Cayey at 3:30 a.m.. José, Leti and their men were waiting. Feather, Rikki and Daniel met with the group from *El Prevision*. Enlarged typographical maps of the area obtained from the ship's map center were spread out on the ground. Feather's men had already been briefed. For over an hour, plans were explained to Perrone and *El Prevision* while Rikki's SEALs guarded the entrance to the parking lot.

"Jury flight leader, this is Mother."

"Mother, go ahead."

"Update on radar contacts. The C-130 transport is orbiting two-zero miles your location at one-zero thousand feet. The choppers have gone off screen five miles your location. They're too small for Huey's, over."

"Roger, Mother. Keep us advised. Jury flight leader out."

"Feather, I hear that tone in your voice, again. What do you think is going on? There shouldn't be activity out here this time of the morning." Rikki was worried.

"Can't figure it. This could be a set up. I can understand the choppers nosing around. They're probably gun ships waiting to blow us to bits. I can't get a grip on the C-130 coming from the mainland."

"We'll just have to wait and see on the transport," Rikki said. "I'm calling Captain Bennett, I'm sure he can deal with the choppers. This is getting crazier by the minute."

Joe nodded. It was precisely 5 a.m.. The six Jury choppers lifted off for the short flight to the drop point near the jungle location where Judd was being held.

19

RESCUE

"Jury flight leader, this is Mother."

"Go ahead, Mother."

"Choppers back on screen. Unable to contact. Status friend or foe unknown. Hornets airborne, contact on one-one-eight point three. Call sign, Knife. Will cover your position, over."

"Roger, Mother. What about the C-130?"

"Jury flight leader, this is Mother. Transport ascending to five thousand, closing your destination. Unable to contact. Friend or foe status unknown, over."

"Mother, Jury flight leader out," The lead chopper pilot changed radio position to contact the F-18. "Knife, this is Jury flight leader. Do you copy?"

A voice came back over the pilots headset. "Jury flight leader, this is Knife, over."

"Knife, cover our butts. Besides door gunners, we're unarmed, over!"

"I'll take good care of you guys. Knife out." The F-18 continued to orbit high above the six choppers.

"Jury one, this is Jury flight leader. Go time in two minutes. Do you copy, over?"

"Two minutes, copy," Feather confirmed.

At exactly 5:20 a.m. the five choppers carrying the Jury were hovering silently over their rappel sights as they descended into the jungle below. Rikki and the second group followed. Robin never batted an eye when it came her turn to slide down. *El Prevision* made ready for their descent as Jury members secured a position on the ground.

"Stand in the door!" said Delta Force commander, Lt. Colonel Billy Williamson, thinking he and his men were about to tangle with some renegade Puerto Rican terrorists and attempt a rescue of a hillbilly West Texas assistant U.S. Attorney. "Green light! Go! Go! Go!"

The Delta Force was on their way into the jungle.

"Jury one! This is Mother! We've got multiple, repeat, multiple metal objects parachuting from the transport! Do you copy, Jury one? Do you copy?!"

"Mother, we copy! We're taking aerial fire from bogey choppers!" Joe screamed into the radio as the dawn erupted with tracers blistering downwards on their position.

"Jury one, this is Knife! Hold tight, I'm on `em!"

Knife was too close for air-to-air rockets. Switching to guns, he pulled the F-18 into a tight right turn to line up on the two choppers firing down on the Jury.

"Adios, hombres!" He said as his index finger squeezed the firing button.

He flamed the first chopper immediately. It exploded in mid-air. The fireball was spectacular in the pre-dawn Caribbean sky as the pieces of the chopper fell to the barely visible jungle below. Knife was closing too fast to get the second bogey and had to make a 360-degree turn for his second pass. By the time he finished the 5-G low altitude turn, the second chopper was running for cover.

"Thanks, Knife! We'll take it from here. Jury one out," Feather said as he pulled his face from the dirt of the jungle floor and looked over at Rikki. "So much for the advantage of surprise. Half of Puerto Rico knows we're here. Let's get Judd. Now!"

The Delta Force had chosen the clearing to the east of the camp as their drop point, the Jury's extraction point.

Jury fighters began making their assault on Rigozzi's camp. No time for tactics now. They went in with heavy M-60 machine gun cover fire. All hell was breaking loose!

Inside the hut, Judd had managed to peel the over-used duct tape from his mouth. He knew Feather and Rikki were there to get him out. He began yelling to give them his position.

"I'm here! I'm in here!" Judd yelled, barely audible over the cracking automatic weapons fire.

The main body of the Jury forces split into two groups: one on the right side leading up to the hut where Judd was screaming, one on the left side. They set up a corridor for Feather, Rikki, Perrone, and Joey to enter the hut. Dr. Robin Perrone was right behind. The enemy positions were much stronger than expected. There were at least forty to fifty men firing back at them, all with automatic weapons. The Jury team picked the weakest enemy position and concentrated their fire.

Feather entered the hut first. He saw Judd, standing on his knees, bound in back by the cuffs.

"I knew y'all would get me! Thank God! I knew y'all would come!"

Feather and Rikki grabbed Judd by each arm and started back through the doorway, bullets ricocheted all around them. The Sicilian soldiers had time to take up defensive positions and fired back, en masse. Daniel, Joey, and Robin followed them from the doorway of Judd's hut with their backs towards them, guarding their exit. Joey was between Robin and Judd. In the midst of the confusion and gunfire, Joey lifted his .45 automatic and pointed it to the back of Judd's head. He was going to prove his loyalty to Rigozzi.

Out of the corner of her eye, Robin saw Joey's pistol level on Judd. She spun around and without hesitation pumped four rounds into Joey, oblivious to the surrounding chaos. Rikki and Feather hit the ground with Judd, falling on top of him for protection as the battle continued. Joey slumped to the turf with a heavy thud.

Part of the Sicilians force was caught in a crossfire between the Jury team to their immediate south and *El Prevision*, who were firing back at them from the north. Something had to give.

"Get me the hell outta here!" Rigozzi screamed at three of his men. "Where is the damned Delta Force, anyway?"

Shielded by the three men in front, Rigozzi ran towards Perrones' position. Daniel was at the rear of the group going back into the jungle. The dawn allowed just enough light through the trees for Daniel to catch a glimpse of Rigozzi as he ran towards him. Daniel planted both feet firmly and stood straight up as bullets whizzed past him from Rigozzi's men. Perrone raised his Uzi and sprayed the three men in front of Rigozzi and then emptied the balance of his clip on Rigozzi. Jury snipers provided cover fire.

With death grips on his arms, Feather and Rikki continued to drag Judd out of the line of fire about twenty yards from the hut, back to the original command post.

"Jury flight leader, extract! I repeat, extract!" yelled the SEAL radioman just as they began taking automatic weapons fire from their east flank. This plan was definitely not going according to Hoyle. The Jury was taking substantially more fire from the Sicilians than had been expected. Now they were getting hit by God knows who on their right side.

"Give me that radio!" hollered Feather. "Set it to one-one-one point one. I just figured out who these guys are."

Feather knew the Delta Force frequency from FBI cipher books.

"Delta Force! Delta Force! This is FBI Agent Joe Feather! Cease fire! Stand down!

Both sides stopped firing momentarily. The only gunfire being exchanged was between the Sicilians and *El Prevision*.

"Who's in charge, Delta Force? I say again, this is FBI Agent Joe Feather. Who is your commanding officer?!"

"Sir, we're getting something very strange over this radio on our Delta frequency," The Delta radioman screamed to Col. Williamson. "Some guy claiming to be an FBI agent. A Joe Feather, sir!"

"Cease firing!" Commanded Col. Williamson to his elite group as he grabbed the mike from his radioman. "You'd better be the Joe Feather I knew in New Mexico or you're dead meat mister!"

"Who is this?" Feather yelled over his radio.

"Col. Williamson. What's my first name? You've got exactly three seconds to reply!"

It couldn't be, too coincidental. Feather thought. He had worked a military case with a lieutenant, a Williamson in Special Forces. *What was his first name?* Feather tried to remember.

"Billy! Your name is Billy!" Joe yelled.

"Stand down! Hold your positions! Cease fire!" Commanded Col. Williamson to his Delta Force team.

With no more fire coming from their right flank, the Jury pushed their attack forward. *El Prevision* saw a great opportunity for some pay back and began hitting the Sicilians with everything they had. Within two minutes no one between the Jury and *El Prevision* was left alive.

Cautiously, Feather waved a white handkerchief over his head in the direction of the Delta Force. They did the same. Slowly, Feather stood up and walked towards Williamson's position.

Col. Williamson and about twenty other Delta Force members leveled their weapons on the figure walking to their front. Williamson saw Feather's face as the sun began peeking above the horizon.

"Agent Feather, what in the hell are you doing here?"

"I could ask you the same thing, Williamson," Feather smiled a smile of relief. "Who called you guys into this?"

"The governor of Puerto Rico called the President. We were supposed to rescue this Rayburn fellow from some terrorist group. What gives here?"

"Billy, this is a big SNAFU based on bad intelligence." Feather said. "I'll tell you about it on the way back to the clearing. You've got to keep this whole thing TOP SECRET. As far as your superiors are concerned, you got Rayburn and the bad guys are all dead. Deal, Billy?"

The jungle was quiet except for an occasional moan coming from the group of Sicilians, last gasps. Cautiously, José, Leti, and the *El Prevision* members stalked towards the blood-covered camp from their positions inside the jungle.

"Ms. Rhine, is Mr. Rayburn alive?" asked Leti, bending down to touch Judd's swollen face.

"He's going to make it, Leti. Thanks to you and your brother," Rikki responded as she removed the cuffs from Judd's swollen wrists.

Robin rushed over and knelt down beside Judd on the other side of Leti. A medic ran over to join them. Robin grabbed the medic's bag and took over, wrapping gauze bandages around his head where the rifle butt had caused a serious gash. Judd was in and out of consciousness.

"Billy?" Feather motioned for Col. Williamson to walk over to him. "I want you to meet the people you thought you were going up against. This is José and Leti Irrizarry, they lead *El Prevision*. They've been helping us locate Judd."

The Colonel shook hands with both of them as they stood surveying the dead and wounded. Smoke from the gunfire still hung heavy in the air.

"How did you know it was the Delta Force on your right flank, Joe?" Williamson asked.

"The real give-away was the para-sails. Nobody in the military uses para- sails but jump teams like the Army's Golden Knights and the Delta Force or Special Forces. It had to be you guys."

"Joe," Rikki said wiping the dirt from her eyes "Believe it or not, we only have minor wounds here. Most of the guys came out of this without a scratch. Can't say the same for the Sicilians. Not one of them is going to make it."

Feather turned to Col. Williamson, "Billy, could you mop this thing up for us? We're not an officially formed group. Our involvement in this thing could raise a lot of eyebrows. We need to get pictures and ID's on all these rascals, then we need to bug out of this mess."

"I'll take care of the details here," Williamson said authoritatively. "You better get your people out of here."

Rikki called the choppers back in, said her good-byes to Leti and José and loaded up her group for the return back to the ship. She had no idea that the whole conflict had been professionally filmed by Carlo and Erica, who had already returned to the ship with no one the wiser.

As the choppers landed on the deck of the *Bush*, Erica, Bennett, and five medical personnel ran over to the chopper carrying Judd. That was the first time they saw Robin. Blood soaked and dirty, she held the bag from the

I.V. she'd put into Judd's arm. Jealousy began to overshadow concern as soon as Erica saw Robin. Judd was going to make it.

"Daniel, why don't you, Robin, and Mario stay overnight here on the ship? I'm sure Judd will want to thank you when he comes to," Rikki said.

"This whole thing, me working with the FBI and Naval Intelligence, it's a crazy feeling, Commander, but for some unknown reason, I feel good about it. I accept your invitation," said Daniel. He looked tired. He knew Robin would want to stay with her patient a while longer. She had that look in her eye, also. Daniel could tell.

One night turned into three aboard the ship. Judd had lost a lot of blood and had been bitten by a host of exotic insects. He was completely drained. Twenty-eight hours passed before he awoke. His eyes opened slowly, unfocused. He could see the image of someone leaning over him. As blur turned into focus, he saw Robin. She was truly an angel.

Still groggy from the medication, he continued to stare at her. "Where am I?"

"On board the USS *George H. W. Bush*, Mr. Rayburn. Welcome back to the world of the living," Robin smiled down at him. They were alone in the small cabin.

"Who are you?" Judd could only muster a few words at a time, still weak and confused.

"Dr. Robin Perrone."

Judd managed a dazed, partial smile, "I've been looking for you Dr. Robin."

"No, Mr. Rayburn. You have been looking for my family."

"I don't know your family. I've been looking for you…for a long time…" Judd slowly closed his eyes and drifted back to sleep as the medications worked on his battered body.

20

ALL ABOUT NUMBERS

Robin slept in the upper bunk in Judd's cabin. For the first two days on board ship, Robin doctored him back to health and allowed very few visitors. Even though she was doing an excellent job as Judd's personal physician, she made Erica feel that she was being shoved out of Judd's life.

Robin was intuitive enough to know that something more than casual interest existed amongst Judd, Erica and Rikki. Her interest in Judd was more than casual. She hovered over him, talked to him, got to know him. Robin decided that she would not allow anyone else to have him. She fed him and watched his swollen face return to near normal proportions. He was still badly bruised.

"Sis," Daniel said to Robin, leaning into the cabin. "We'll be leaving the ship in about an hour. I'd like to speak to Mr. Rayburn privately before catching the launch back."

Robin placed her hand on Judd's cheek, smiled a girlish smile and gave a little wave. She left, walking about six inches above the floor.

"My sister is infatuated with you, Mr. Rayburn. Could be your TV heroics which have been all over the news…That concerns me," Daniel said firmly.

"I understand she saved my life there at the camp. Killed one of your closest friends?"

"Joey turned. I would've done the same."

"Let's drop the formalities." Judd said, gathering his wits. "After all, we've fought together. Now, at least for the moment and through unusual circumstances, we're on the same side. Your enemies are my enemies. How can we go forward? It's important for me to know, Daniel."

"Matters of the heart often overshadow everything else, wouldn't you agree?" Daniel said matter-of-factly.

"True. I can't be part of your life, you can't be part of mine. The question is, can Robin be in both?" Judd asked, raising himself to a sitting position on the side of the bunk. He had seen her look and she had seen his.

"A difficult question. I am not sure I have the answer."

"Let's look for one. That is, if you're willing?"

"I began searching for a solution the first time I saw Robin look at you. She is very dear to me, Mr. Rayburn. I've had three days to think. All I've been able to define is where we are now, not where we can go from here."

"Daniel, tell me how you see the whole situation now; the Cartel, the Sicilians, the whole group. I believe we both have the same information. At least Rikki seems to think so and I trust her judgment."

"If we have this discussion, I must be assured that it is strictly between us. No wires, no tapes, no nothing…completely off the record."

Sluggishly, Judd stood up from the bunk and pulled off the workout bottoms he'd been wearing. He stood before Daniel wearing only his Navy supplied skivvies.

"You do the same."

Without hesitating, Daniel accepted Judd's challenge and stripped down to his black shiny boxer shorts.

"Now!" Judd said, "We have nothing to hide. Let's talk."

"The way I see it, " Daniel was standing straight up in front of Judd with his hands on his hips. "You have done my family a favor by temporarily interrupting the deal between the Cartel from Colombia, the Sicilians and the Russians regarding distribution of cocaine into the new Russian republics. That association would have formed a strong bond between the Cartel and the Sicilian Mafia. But it is only temporary. The Sicilians probably have Rigozzi's replacement negotiating with the Cartel as we speak."

"Allow me to interrupt, Daniel. I'll add what you cannot say," Judd had been briefed earlier that morning by Feather as to what was going on inside La Cosa Nostra back in the States. "Your father, Nico, has convinced the other families to purge themselves of Sicilians within the organization. They're disappearing in large numbers. You neither need to confirm nor deny that, Daniel. I have my sources. I know what's going on."

Daniel looked somewhat stunned by Judd's information.

"I do not see a formal war beginning with our Sicilian brothers. These things happen. They took a shot at taking over the organization in the

States and it backfired. We are honorable men. We seek profits, not wars. Our relationship with Sicily will cool. They will go their way without our intervention and vice-versa. Neither of us wants our problems to disrupt business. They will accept their losses in the States. We expect no recourse from them."

"So as far as you're concerned, La Cosa Nostra is back to square one. Business as usual. Right, Daniel?"

"Right. And square one dictates that you and the FBI are still our adversaries, not the Sicilian Mafia or the Cartel."

There was a long silence. Judd's head began throbbing. He couldn't leave the conversation hanging. He had to think of a way.

"We've defined your problem, Daniel," Judd was trying to make ends meet, literally. "Now, let's define mine and those of the U.S. Government. We no longer have Russia as our largest threat to national security. It stands to reason that having won the cold war, we need to move on to the second largest threat to our national security. Our problems are domestic. Our war is with drug manufacturers and distributors. We've got to throw every resource available into defeating this threat. We must! Can you see that?"

"What you say makes sense to you," Daniel replied, waiting to see where Judd would wind up on the subject.

"Daniel, I know we are closing in on La Cosa Nostra from every possible avenue. We've added twelve hundred new FBI agents and four hundred prosecutors to concentrate strictly on organized crime within the U.S. We've put most of your major crime bosses in jail."

"We have felt your effort to come after us. We've been able to deal with your increased aggression. You will hurt us, but you will never destroy us!" Daniel exclaimed defiantly.

"If we take this to be true, we both exist, but we both lose!"

"I may or may not agree with your point, Mr. Rayburn. So where do we go from here?"

"We lay our cards on the table, Daniel! We tell each other exactly what we both want. Then, we figure the path to that solution. I'll start off. The U.S. government wants a drug-free society, a society living within our system of justice. We want to eliminate organized crime. No more 'hit man' killings, no more protection rackets, no more prostitution or finagling union pension funds, or laundering illegally obtained money. That, Daniel, is what we want. What do you want?"

"Maybe the conversation ends here. You are talking about my families' way of life, our livelihood, our business."

"Don't stop here, Daniel! Think! Boil it down! What does your family really want? Talk to me!"

Daniel took a deep breath.

"We want a good quality of life for ourselves and our families. That is why La Cosa Nostra was originally formed. In the early days no one wanted to hire Italian immigrants. They wanted to treat us like dirt when our forefathers came to America. They called us 'Wops' and 'Dagos.' They degraded our very existence. The turn of the century Americans deprived our fathers of their rights as newly sworn U.S. citizens. They did not come over here with the intention of killing, controlling, and prostituting the American way of life. They came to be a part of it, to share in it! To be happy and raise their families in a better place than where they had come. But 'the land of the free' sent them an early message upon their arrival. Nothing is free!

"Mr. Rayburn, we Italians have a saying, 'La famiglia e tutto' which means 'The family is everything.' Drugs kill kids. We want nothing to do with them and that's *our* truth."

Daniel had fire in his eyes. The decades of frustration of not being accepted, not being allowed, fighting for the "Italian acre" on U.S. soil exploded from him with all the truth, honesty, and dignity he could muster. He was speaking for decades of immigrants, for his father and his father's father.

"We want to live, be respected and to provide for our children! Can't you see that Mr. United States Government? Can't you see that?" Daniel was standing, the veins in his red face about to pop out of his head.

Judd was genuinely touched by the anger, the frustration and the honesty Daniel displayed. This was not the answer he had expected, it was an answer that set the basis for finding solutions, more than he could have asked. They had found common ground—life, liberty and the pursuit of happiness. Not unlike other men's dreams. Somehow America had overlooked one segment of its multi-national society. America allowed and created the conditions for La Cosa Nostra to be born. Now it must find the circumstance to dismantle it or to legitimize it.

"You know, Daniel," Judd was now the one taking a deep breath, "La Cosa Nostra and its members have many charges pending, many atrocities have been committed and are still being committed. The same thing happened in World War II. Deep hatreds formed against the unspeakable acts committed by Germany and Japan. We both know what they were. Today, both Germany and Japan are some of our closest allies. The point I'm making is that their atrocities were forgiven."

"Pardon my ignorance, Mr. Rayburn. I do not follow you. Are you willing to let all the bygones be bygones? Explain."

"You help me, I help you! That simple, Daniel. It really is that simple." Judd reached for a tablet lying on the nightstand next to his bunk. "Look!

Government figures project the illegal drug business within the U.S. to be worth one hundred billion dollars a year in sales. That's the demand the American people have created for their drug habit."

"Your figures are accurate. Go on," Daniel looked over Judd's shoulders at the numbers he wrote on the tablet.

"The La Cosa Nostra only gets a small percentage of the one hundred billion because you don't have exclusive control of the distribution of drugs in the U.S. You sell some, but mostly, you take your percentage from laundering the drug money made by others through organization-owned, semi-legitimate businesses such as casinos and hotels."

Daniel was amazed at how well Judd had grasped the real truth about his family's involvement in drugs.

"La Cosa Nostra's income from drugs, directly, is very small compared to your annual net income derived from other businesses. Am I very far off the mark, Daniel?" Judd was partly telling and partly asking, fishing.

Daniel was following but not committing.

"Continue."

"I figure net income from all of your operations, including drugs, will not come to seven billion dollars per year? The United States is spending approximately three hundred billion dollars to combat drugs in one form or another."

"That figure is way high!" Daniel remarked.

"Not when you figure all the money being spent. It's not only what the government itself sets aside in the official budget, Daniel. The federal budget for the war on drugs is seventeen billion, substantially less than three hundred billion. I'm talking about the whole ball of wax. Let me itemize it for you."

Judd began writing vigorously on the tablet. Daniel watched every stroke of Judd's pen, two businessmen on separate sides of a problem, seeking a solution, in their skivvies.

"Daniel, it is statistical fact that eighty percent of all crime in the U.S. is drug related. Let's determine how many dollars that is." Judd began his figures. "Besides the federal budget of seventeen billion dollars, what about every U.S. city and state police budget? Add another thirty-seven and a half billion. Then we have eighty percent of the people in our prisons convicted because of drugs. It costs to run those prisons, and build more to house the growing number of convicted felons. Add another ten billion.

"Next area is drug-related arson damage, ten billion. That causes insurance premiums to go up. Another problem area is the medical programs to fight drugs, both rehab and critical care of people who OD. This year alone there has been a thirty-five percent increase in cocaine-related emergency response calls by EMT companies, a seventeen percent increase in response calls in cases concerning heroin. We are talking government and private funding now, Daniel. Add twenty-five big ones!

"Speaking of medical, Daniel. How about the money that's being demanded for AIDS research? AIDS is not only being transmitted by homosexuals, it's being transmitted by heterosexuals hopped up on drugs, by junkies sharing needles. Put down another fourteen billion for research and critical care."

Judd finally handed Daniel the tablet. He walked three paces up the cabin and three paces back, dictating numbers to him. Numbers that were so important. After all, what is business other than numbers?

"Daniel, for expediency's sake let's just group the other categories together. We'll come up with a total figure, okay?"

Daniel agreed.

"Lost production of America's workers. U.S. military budgets to fight drugs, credit card fraud related to drugs, stolen cars, stolen household goods, liability insurance and medical policy premiums carried by every private company in the U.S. Think of it, Daniel. The numbers are staggering! Want to agree on a grand total of about three hundred billion in cost to the U.S. government and private sector combined? Would you say I'm close?"

"Close." Daniel could add quite well. "So what you are saying is that the United States is spending three hundred billion to do away with a hundred billion problem. And the fact of the matter is, Mr. Rayburn, you're losing."

"I rest my case. The only way to win the war is stop the manufacture of drugs. As long as they are around, there'll always be people to sell them and to buy them. It's not a matter of throwing more money at the prevention of drug distribution. These figures prove that. I've got to stop the manufacture of them. That's where my problem comes home, hard!

"The drugs are manufactured in other countries. Their governments have either been bought off or killed off by the drug lords. Look at what happened to Colombia. The U.S. is powerless to cross sovereign borders and destroy the drug growing and manufacturing facilities. The rest of the free world would look upon that as an act of aggression. It goes against everything the United States stands for. Now, Daniel, can you see my frustration?"

Judd's face was red. His veins popped out across his forehead.

"But La Cosa Nostra has never been bound by such rules. We go where we want and do what we want," Daniel said in a very relaxed voice.

A plan was beginning to gel, a multi-billion dollar plan. "You have entered into an area of family expertise. What would it be worth to the U.S. government if drugs, such as cocaine, were no longer grown or manufactured?

That is the question we have been searching for, Mr. U.S. Government!" Daniel smiled a twelve-figure smile.

What was the price tag on America's freedom from drugs? Judd thought. Not only in dollars, but in crossing basic ideology that forbids the government from fraternizing with the enemy. Congress would never allow it. The American people would not condone it. Yet, it was a solution…the U.S. *did* forgive the Japanese and German atrocities. Could America forgive once again without unconditional surrender? A failsafe point had been reached in this conversation.

"The cost would be high for both of us," Judd said, overwhelmed by the awesome thought of the U.S. government and La Cosa Nostra working together. "On the one side, you and your father would accomplish the dream of legitimacy. On the other side, you would have to reorganize the Machiavellian way of life you've enjoyed for the last sixty-five years."

"All the members of La Cosa Nostra would not agree to such a deal, I can promise you that," Daniel interrupted.

"I can appreciate that. You didn't let me finish. The cost to La Cosa Nostra goes higher."

"How much higher?"

"The Nuremberg trials, Daniel! Sins cannot be completely forgiven against La Cosa Nostra without some restitution."

"What restitution?"

"Justice! The American people would demand justice!"

"In simple language, you are saying that some of our members would have to be prosecuted and sent away? Is that the final cost to which you refer?"

"Yes. But what if it pertained only to those members who would not go along with the plan?"

"But they would know the plan and go to the press. They would influence the congressmen they have on their payrolls. The whole thing could blow up in our faces." Daniel was being realistic.

"Not if I had a list of the government officials who have been associated with La Cosa Nostra along with dossiers containing incriminating evidence against them like documented payoffs and photos, solid evidence against those law makers and public officials that would keep their knowledge of the deal silent and their mouths shut."

"Interesting. I may have such information. But who would be in charge of putting this plan together?"

"I would."

"No disrespect intended, Mr. Rayburn." Daniel leaned back against the bulkhead in the cabin. "I have sufficient power on my side to make this happen. You do not have the stroke or the power to pull off your side of the plan. Unfortunate, but true."

Judd felt he was close to a solution. He couldn't let the plan be scuttled. He knew he had to think fast.

"Armed with those dossiers, Daniel, I could gain the power rather quickly," Judd said intently.

"How could you accomplish this in such a short amount of time?"

"Get me the dossiers and stay close to the newspapers. I'll show you!"

"I'll discuss the preface of the plan with my father. Neither of us is ready to commit to a plan that is not finalized. The concept has merit, many fallacies, but it could work. I suggest we get dressed before people begin to talk," Daniel said with a smile on his face, finally realizing his embarrassment. "Where can I contact you in the near future?"

Judd wrote a number on the tablet and gave it to Daniel. Both had some heavy soul-searching and planning to do.

"Daniel, I know this is premature, but I have a very important piece to my current puzzle missing. Maybe you can help me?"

"Maybe. Ask. I won't guarantee an answer."

"My puzzle is the involvement of the three U.S. Congressmen in this whole mess. Can you help me?"

"Many people have thought Senator Capriatti from Illinois has been on our payroll for years. Fact is, Capriatti has been unapproachable by any of our families. He is an honorable man. So are Zapata and Fuselier. I cannot help you, believe me. I wish I could. They are clean with us. If they won't accept it from us, it is my thought that they cannot be bribed by the Sicilians or the Cartel, yet they are involved in this Puerto Rican/Russian affair. I haven't a clue. Sorry."

"Thanks, I appreciate your honesty. Are you and Robin going back to New York?"

"Immediately. I believe it is best until this battle in the jungle thing clears." Daniel was putting on his pants and shirt. "One favor I would like to ask of you, Mr. Rayburn."

"Shoot."

"No good-byes with Robin. Let me just take her off the ship now. No good-byes, okay?"

"Only if you express my profound thanks for her nursing me back to health. I mean, she saved my life."

"I will. You have my word on that." Daniel left the cabin.

The launch containing Daniel, Robin, Mario, Erica and Carlo pulled away from the ship. The coolness of the morning was giving way to the heat and humidity of the noonday sun. Judd stood at the edge of the flight deck above the launch looking down at his departing friends. They waved as the launch pulled away. Judd's eyes were on Robin. Robin blew a kiss and a whisper containing her heart as the launch faded out of sight. Erica and Carlo had their footage of the jungle assault and no one knew…

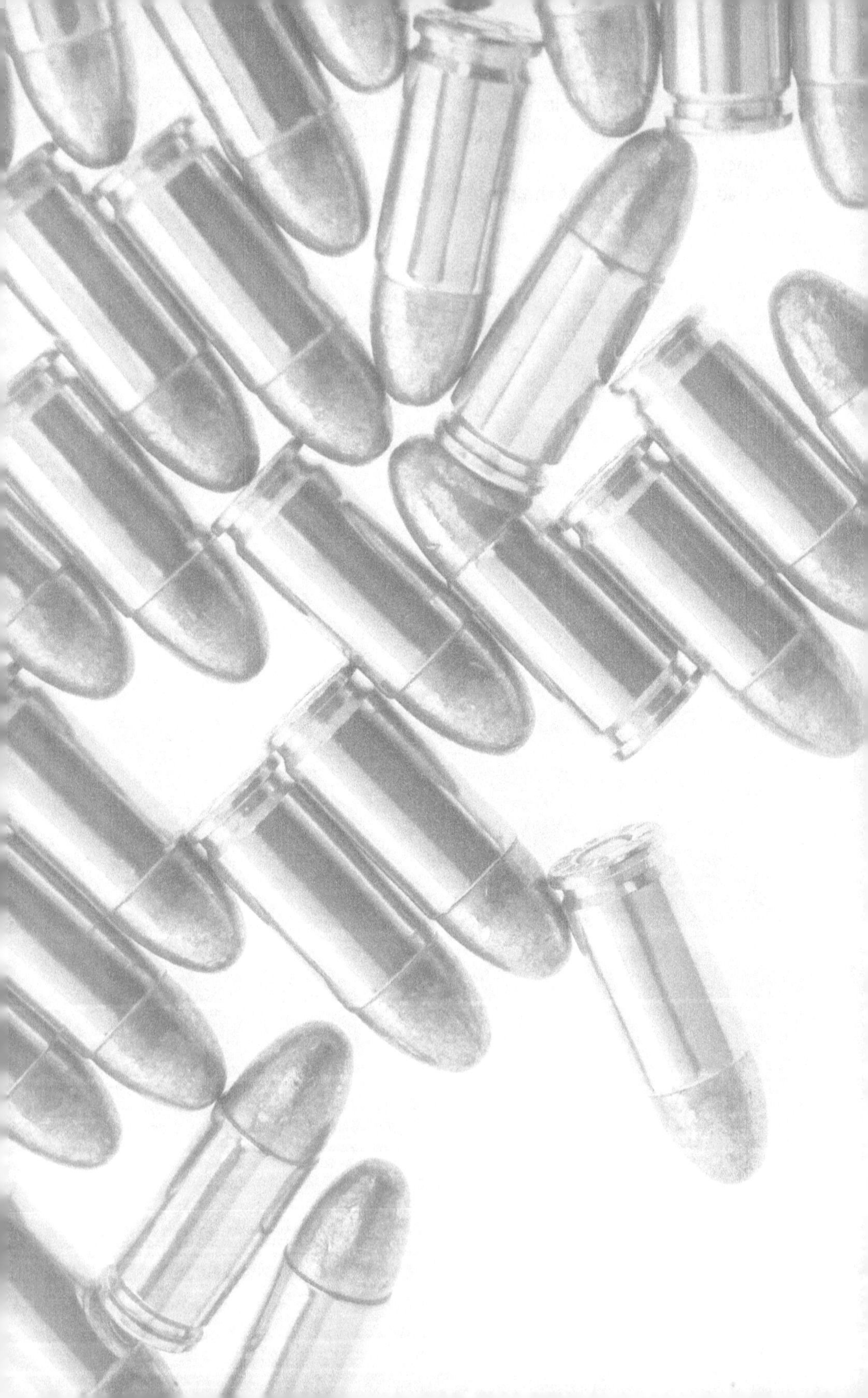

21

IF MIRACLES EXIST?

The C-130 carrying The Jury landed back at their base near Con Can, Texas. No one knew they had even been to Puerto Rico. The Delta Force would say nothing, neither would Perrone. José, Leti and *El Prevision* buried the victims in the jungle. Miguel Torres and his son Tito were on the burial list and had made their last deal. Looma returned to New York with Daniel. A short time later, Rikki, Judd, and Captain Bennett were standing on the flight deck just before her take-off. After good-byes, Rikki catapulted off the carrier deck with Judd as her "rear."

Late Saturday afternoon. Ft. Bliss, El Paso.

Erin, Feather, Jake Ramsey and Maureen were on the flight line at Fort Bliss to welcome Judd back.

Rikki remained with her aircraft to check out some electronic glitches as the rest of the group piled into the van for the ride back to BOQ 17.

"I'm lying low for a while so you lawyer guys can do your thing. Call me when you need me." Rikki crawled up under the F-18 and proceeded to look for the wiring glitch.

"How do you feel, boss? Baby, you look terrible." Maureen wiped the sweat off Judd's forehead. She just wanted to touch him and make sure he was okay.

"I look good now, Maureen. You should've seen me a few days ago. I'm gettin' too old for this…!"

Erin laughed. "So far everything's been quiet, Judd. For once this has been leak-proof."

"Did Erica make it back okay?" Judd asked matter-of-factly.

"Haven't seen her, bro. She's not inside the fort," Feather said with an alarmed, concerned expression. "I'll call the press barracks."

"We may have problems, gang!" Feather said putting down the phone. "Erica's editor said she was in New York. He also said we may want to catch the national news in about three minutes."

Maureen led Erin, Judd and the others to Judd's room and turned on the TV.

The commentator wasted no time in getting right to the lead story.

"…We now go live to our ABC studios in New York for a copyrighted story by Erica Stone, ABC reporter from our affiliate station in El Paso…"

"What you are about to see was filmed live earlier this week over the jungles of Puerto Rico…" Erica's hair and make-up were perfect. She had hit the big time. She looked confident sitting behind the desk at the news studios in New York, as if she had finally found home.

"…Mr. Judd Rayburn, now Special Assistant U.S. Attorney in charge of prosecution in the much-publicized Julio Cortez drug case that will begin later this month, was doing follow-up investigation in Puerto Rico when factions from the Sicilian mob abducted him almost a week ago at a hotel in San Juan. The following is the daring rescue of Mr. Rayburn by the elite Delta Force ordered into Puerto Rico by the President of the United States."

Stunned, the group in Judd's room hung on every word Erica spoke. They were all going to have a lot of explaining to do.

During the next three minutes, there was little narration of the clip. Carlo had filmed the Delta Forces' parasail jump into the jungle, the tracer bullets from the M-60 machine guns piercing the low light conditions of the jungle floor, and finally the medics loading Judd onto the awaiting chopper in the jungle clearing near the area where he had been held. No markings could be seen on the chopper. No faces were clearly visible except that of Judd lying on the stretcher with an I.V. in his arm, surrounded by members of the Delta Force with their backs to the aerial camera.

Switching back to the New York studios, Erica continued her commentary of the unprecedented event.

"Mr. Rayburn, badly beaten during several torture sessions administered by his Sicilian captors, gave out no information. In a live interview with this reporter shortly after his rescue, Mr. Rayburn admitted spitting in their eyes during the beatings."

The TV showed a grainy, obviously blown-up full frame shot of Judd's battered face.

"It is not known what information Mr. Rayburn obtained during his investigation on the island of Puerto Rico or how it will figure into the

Cortez case. Mr. Rayburn is listed in fair condition by naval doctors now caring for him. State Department spokesmen are releasing no information as to casualties suffered by the Sicilian Mafia abductors. Spokesmen did confirm that there were no casualties within the Delta Force. This is Erica Stone reporting live from New York."

After a brief follow-up and bio of Erica Stone by the ABC anchor, Maureen turned off the set.

For a few moments the silence continued in the room while everyone gathered their thoughts about the broadcast.

"I think she covered our butts on this one!" Feather spoke first. "What do you think, Judd?"

"She didn't show Rikki or any of the rest of our group. She didn't show the faces of Perrone, the Jury or *El Prevision*," Judd said, doing a mental damage report in his mind.

"It could have been a lot worse," Erin added. "She could have blown this whole thing wide open. I think so far, so good. We're safe if it doesn't go any further than this. Judd, I can almost feel the ground rumbling. The press corps is sure to be on their way over here, en masse. We'd better prepare a statement, quickly!"

Casey, Erin's secretary, knocked on Judd's door and stuck her head inside, "Judd, Erica Stone is calling you long distance from New York. Line 2."

"Erica! How the…"

"Slow down, handsome," Erica said in a calm, confident voice. "Can't you see, I didn't tell them anything about your little secret vigilante group and I won't."

"I've got to have your word on that, Erica. I want that footage!" Judd blurted out.

"I've destroyed the rest, Judd. Carlo won't say anything either. We've been in with the ABC lawyers all night. We know we can have charges filed against us if we release anything else. There is no more footage. It's been destroyed."

"Erica, I guess you finally got what you wanted."

"Judd, you have no idea. I almost did. I'll settle for an Emmy. What I wanted was you. However, I believe a 'little Robin' won first prize in that department. I'll use you, Judd, but I won't do anything to harm you. You should know that."

Judd hung up the phone. "We're okay, guys. Erica destroyed the rest of the footage."

Finally convincing themselves Erica was telling the truth and hoping nothing would come back to haunt them from the footage, the group got back to the debriefing.

"Judd, were you able to find out anything about the U.S. congressmen while you were being held?" Erin asked.

"All I found out was from Daniel Perrone. He assured me all three are clean, not on anyone's payroll, and I believe him. We're no further along in that department than when I left. Got any ideas?"

"The only thing I can figure is to place Sal on Senator Capriatti's household staff. I have a feeling his current chef is about to come down with an urgent ailment. We need to keep Sal's culinary and bugging skills sharp." Erin was scratching his head. The role of the three congressmen was perplexing. "What about Cortez? Do you think he knows?"

"At this point, Randall, who knows? Cortez hasn't said three words since he's been here. Let's smoke him out a little."

"How so?" Randall asked.

"Arrange for Wiley and Castenada to smuggle in someone who is close to Cortez, a visitor. By now the Mexican Cartel must know that we upset the apple cart down in Puerto Rico. Maybe Cortez won't be so smug knowing things have been turned upside down. Maybe he'll give instructions to his man. We can tape their conversation."

"I'll arrange it," Erin wrote some notes in his pocket notebook. "What came out of the meeting with Perrone?"

"It's going to take a while to brief you on all the details. Let's grab some dinner and I'll fill you in. You will not believe what Perrone and I discussed. It's monumental. Historical. I'll definitely need your help and input on that conversation."

After dinner, the group met back in Judd's room for his debriefing. Upon hearing the conversation between Judd and Daniel, Erin leaned back in his chair and made no other comments for several minutes. Randall was the man in the room who knew politics. He continued to think as the others waited for his reply.

Randall's only reply was, "It could work…"

"Could we pull it off on our end?" Judd asked.

"Doubtful as things stand now," Erin was being practical. "However, if a couple of things could fall into place, like getting the dossiers from Perrone, yeah, we could pull this off, providing miracles do exist!"

"Judd, get some sleep. I'm off to set this meeting up with Wiley and Cortez's man." Randall directed, "Joe, see what you can do to get Sal a chef's job with Senator Capriatti."

"I'm filling out Sal's resume now," Joe said walking out of Judd's room.

Robin didn't sleep well the night before and welcomed the dawn. Sitting in her robe, drinking her first cup of morning coffee, she looked out at the city from her 5th Avenue high-rise condominium bay window. Daniel and Looma were staying with her for the night. Big brother was figuring out a way to introduce Looma to his father, which would take a couple of days, especially since she was Torres' daughter. Nico, "The Bull," did not like Torres.

Looma was very distraught over the news of her father and brother. In his explanation to her, Daniel did not say they had sided with Rigozzi. Instead, he gave her the standard hero's epitaph about how brave they had been in the fight. Looma needed a change of scenery and did not want to attend the funeral. She was not good at funerals, never had been. She didn't attend her own mother's funeral three years before and saw a new life for herself in New York. She wanted to be close to Daniel during her time of grief.

"Sis, you're up early this morning."

Daniel went into the kitchen and poured himself a cup.

"I miss my cowboy. I miss him bad." Robin was near tears. She was not used to not having what she wanted. Her father had raised her as a princess; her wish was his command. "I may fly to Texas."

Daniel wanted to lash out with "no way," but, knowing Robin had a mind of her own, he figured that would only drive her there sooner.

"Robin, I can see your feelings for Mr. Rayburn. But to go to him now would jeopardize something much larger than your relationship."

"Family business! Right, Daniel? Always family business! Well this time brother, I don't care about the family business. I love that man. I want to be near him. I'm going to Texas!"

Daniel walked over and sat down next to her, smoothing her long silky hair with his hand. She began to cry.

"Who always takes good care of you?"

"You do," she sobbed.

"And I always will."

Daniel gently grabbed her by each arm and slowly pushed her back; he wanted to look her in the eyes.

"I know you hate the business our family is in, Robin. Sometimes we all do. Father has had a dream for many years to make our business respectable. That is the reason he sent me to so many schools, to get the knowledge and education to fulfill his dream. With Judd's help, we may just accomplish that dream. It's a long shot, but it is possible.

"As it stands now, I doubt you and Judd could manage a lifetime together when his way of life and ours are so different. Today, we are enemies. Given time, there is a slim chance we can all work together. What I am saying is not only family business; it is our business, our future and maybe your happiness. Please trust me a little longer, Robin. Remain my little sister who listens to her big brother. Please do as I say, okay?"

"But how can this be, Daniel? What did you and Judd talk about on the ship?" Robin wiped the tears from her cheeks.

Daniel had given her an ounce of hope, just enough.

"It is something I must speak to Father about. It is very complex."

Judd and Erin needed to update Judge Ramirez on the new evidence obtained in Puerto Rico that pertained to the Cortez trial. They wouldn't go into detail about the "Jury" rescue even though he was aware. They would inform the judge that no further information had been gathered about the congressmen. They couldn't tell Ramirez about letting Castenada smuggle in a friend of Cortez. Some things judges do not want to know.

As they left the luncheon briefing with Judge Ramirez, they were happy with his decision to begin the trial post haste. Trial would be slated to begin in one week. Satisfied that Wiley and Castenada had exhausted their motions, they would be given one week for *voir dire*, jury selection. The defense would scream, holler and make all kinds of objections. Judge Ramirez was expecting that and would handle it.

The investigation into the U.S. congressmen along with the involvement of public officials from Mexico and Puerto Rico would be ongoing, under secrecy of the Justice Department, Western District only.

22

C Y A!

Sunday, June 21st, New York

Daniel drove past the heavy steel-barred gate surrounding his father's wooded estate. Four La Cosa Nostra soldiers waved him past. As he drove the quarter mile up to the large brick mansion, he knew his father was prepared for the worst. The grounds were crawling with armed men and guard dogs. The layoff of their Sicilian brothers within the organization could end up with no retaliation at all, but being prepared was necessary. Somehow, during the midst of the turmoil created by the mass extermination of the Sicilians within their ranks, La Cosa Nostra members felt a unity they hadn't experienced for many years. Lines were drawn, loyalties chosen, common enemies identified. Instead of disrupting the organization, the elimination of the weak links had strengthened it. Nico Perrone had won an important political battle within the families. He was solidly in command. The other family heads pledged their full support to his wisdom and guidance with every Sicilian that "disappeared" from their ranks.

"I'm so glad you could join me, Daniel. We have much to discuss before the ladies arrive."

"So, Father, what did you think of Looma?"

"Hard to believe, Daniel, that Looma came from the loins of such a spineless man as her father, Miguel. She impressed me. I can tell she loves you deeply and I can see in your eyes that you love her. Be patient, my son. We have many battles in front of us. If she remains loving and loyal to you through these ordeals, I will know her love for you will last. Be patient."

Good, Daniel thought to himself, *Father likes her.* The two of them walked into a large study.

"Sit down Daniel," Nico motioned to a chair across from his. "In my old age, I feel my dream so near, to make respectable our businesses, our members, our families. Ironic, my son, that this dream hinges on trust, not guns.

"More ironic is that the trusted party is our enemy, the U.S. government, not that this is the first time we have worked for them. I am torn on what to do. I risk destroying what has taken three generations to build. However, the reward for such a risk could be that our dreams will come true. No more killing, no more running, no more courtrooms, lawyers or prisons. Our children can play without armed guards watching over them. No more midnight phone calls of sorrow. Do we trust and hope that our dreams will come to fruition, or do we continue our way of life?"

"Father, I know you have many considerations to make. I will carry out your orders as always," Daniel leaned across the coffee table, putting his hand on his father's.

"I know you will, my son. You have been my biggest blessing, my strength. I would like to hear your thoughts in this matter."

"Father, through your leadership, especially in the last few weeks, you have unified our organization in the U.S. It is stronger than ever before. I believe we are now ready to move La Cosa Nostra, *this thing of ours,* in a clear, defined path. As I see it, we have two choices. First, we play along with Rayburn. Secondly, Father, we cover our bases."

"How do you mean, Daniel, cover our bases?"

"Complete trust in Rayburn has many ifs and maybes. If he cannot gain the support for his plan at a high enough level, the twelve hundred additional FBI agents and four hundred new prosecutors all assigned to attacking us will pose a problem we will not be capable of handling without a lot of money. We are stronger now. However, after purging ourselves of Sicilian ties, we are fewer and have one more enemy."

"I follow you Daniel, please continue."

"Either route we choose to take involves a stronger alliance with the Colombian Cartel. If we choose to play this dangerous game with Rayburn, they may expect us to eliminate the entire hierarchy of the Cartel in Colombia. To accomplish this, we must gain the Cartel's confidence, get closer to them. If the support Rayburn needs to muster is unsuccessful, we must continue our family business and expect heavy harassment from the Justice Department. That takes money, Father, a lot of money. The Justice Department will attack and freeze all of our assets they can identify. We must cover this with other sources of income."

"What are you suggesting, Daniel?"

"I am suggesting we meet with the Cartel to put together a deal to buy and control all the cocaine entering the United States, just as the Sicilians are doing in Europe and Russia."

"Daniel!"

"Father, I know you dislike being directly involvement with drugs. I know your reasons, making dope addicts of children. It repulses you! The decision lies with Rayburn and the Executive Branch of the government. If they make the wrong choice, then we will survive. We must diversify in order to do that. Either way, Father, we will be covered. If Rayburn's plan consummates, we pursue our dreams of legitimacy. If they fail, we will have our diversification and the income we need to sustain our way of life. In either situation, we must begin plans to get closer to the Colombian Cartel."

Nico took a slow sip of his Chianti.

"I've always known you would succeed my leadership with strength and wisdom, Daniel. When the time comes, I will go to my grave knowing La Cosa Nostra is in good hands. Contact the Cartel."

FRIDAY, JUNE 26TH, FT. BLISS

Jury selection for the trial was finally complete. Over three hundred prospective jurors had been interviewed by the prosecution and defense teams. Down to the final twenty, twelve would be seated in the last minute. The rest would be alternates.

Judd, Erin and Jake Ramsey allowed the final twenty jurors after extensive interviewing. Trial would begin on Monday, as planned.

"Cortez's visitor just left, Judd."

Randall was walking into BOQ 17 after returning from the stockade on the other side of the fort.

"Did they say anything we can use, Randall? Anything about Capriatti, Zapata or Fuselier?"

"Nothing!" Randall's normally red face was turning crimson, visibly angered. "The guy who came to see Cortez was supposedly his uncle, an older guy we're checking out now. They mentioned no names, nothing about drugs, all idle BS. His 'uncle' acted more concerned with the way Julio was being treated than anything else.

"He did mention the trouble down in the Caribbean. Cortez said he knew all about it. I'd sure like to find out where he gets his information. Cortez was cool during the entire conversation. We taped it and will go back through it, Judd, but, on the surface, there is nothing we can use."

"Well, Randall, there is some good news."

"Put it on me, man. I could use some good news."

"Feather got Sal a job as a chef in Chicago."

"Fantastic! At Capriatti's house?"

"Almost. Sal is working for the senator's next door neighbor. That's as close as we could get."

"We hope, with Sal's gift of gab, he can become chummy with the senator's chef. At least that's our plan," Feather added, walking into the room. "Sal will have Capriatti's house bugged within three days. I'd bet on that, he's pretty good."

"Hello, Cowboy."

Judd knew that whispering, sexy voice.

"Dr. Feel Good. How are you?" he replied, anxiously. Judd wanted to crawl through the phone and wrap his arms around her.

"Want to buy me lunch on Sunday?"

"Sunday? Where? I'd like to, Robin, I'm not sure I can. The trial starts Monday morning."

"I miss you too much, cowboy. I want to see you!"

"I want to see you, too."

"Judd, my brother is standing here. Maybe he can convince you."

"Hello, Judd."

"Nice hearing from you, Daniel. I see you made it home okay."

"Yes, thank you. Judd, I have talked with my father and he wants to meet you. We have much to discuss. Can you be in New York Sunday morning?" Daniel's voice was insistent.

"I'll do my best. Where and when?"

"Fly into Buffalo. We don't want to take the chance of being seen. My father has rented a nice restaurant for the entire day in Sinclairsville. The name of the restaurant is The Granary. Say about eleven a.m. our time?"

"I'll be there, Daniel."

Hanging up the phone, Judd turned to Maureen. "See if you can book me into Buffalo, New York, arriving Saturday night, get me a hotel and a rent car, returning around six-ish Sunday afternoon."

"Oh, the jet-set life of a U.S. Attorney, boss. I'll bet you're going to see your little 'Italian princess.' I know all about it, boss. Erica told me everything about Robin Perrone."

"Shhh! Maureen! Don't mention her name around here. I'm not going to New York to see her, I'm going to speak with her father." Judd realized immediately that was a bad choice of words. Maureen would jump all over that.

"Sounds serious, boss, are you asking him for her hand?"

"Just book the flight and keep that little mind of yours out of the gutter."

"You do like her though, huh, boss?"

SATURDAY MORNING, JUNE 27TH. FT. BLISS

Now that the meeting with the Perrones was set, Erin enlisted the help of top government and private economists, agriculturists and financial experts, giving them a scenario to solve with no explanations.

After receiving their first draft solution, Erin called a meeting with Judd and Feather. Reaching into his briefcase and lifting out his laptop, Erin pulled up a Power Point presentation and began.

"Is there an overhead projector here?"

"There's one in the judges' chambers," Feather left the room to get it.

Randall opened the meeting.

"Judd, do you think La Cosa Nostra has had time to come up with a number? I mean, how much are they going to want to be paid for whacking the Cartel in Colombia and supplying us with those dossiers?"

"I really doubt that they have, Randall. I'm not sure they've even taken the idea to their council of families yet. That's probably what this meeting is going to be about tomorrow. Have you come up with a number?"

"Some of our staff have plugged into IRS files in Washington. We've got a fairly accurate accounting of what each family is worth in terms of yearly income, number of soldiers on the payroll, overhead operating expenses from the hotels and casinos, the whole gamut of businesses they either own or control. There are some 'X' factors, we know that. We've been working on these numbers twenty-four hours a day since your talk with Perrone on the ship and have a pretty good idea of how much they're going to ask."

"So you do have a number?" Judd asked.

"Yes, and no." Erin pulled out several transparencies and placed them on the overhead projector. "We can approach this negotiation, and it will be a negotiated amount, gentlemen, just as a company approaches a public offering or a buy-out. Companies usually hit the public market at ten times the next years' projected net earnings. We believe the La Cosa Nostra net earnings from all their operations is around two billion, as best we can guess. That would put the price tag at twenty billion dollars.

"The obvious answer is whether or not it's worth it," Judd replied. "I hope the answer is a definite yes. I mean, if we can eliminate the federal and private sector price tag of all drug and organized crime related activities, we would save a large part of three hundred billion dollars every year as a nation."

"Not immediately, Judd, but eventually, and not all of that," Erin replied. "We have an embassy in Colombia. We've got legal attaché's in Venezuela that worked in Colombia. We're in the process of incorporating a 'Newco' or new company, under Colombian charter. This company will be in La Cosa Nostra members' names. As we all know, the U.S. government cannot own a company down there. However, we can supply the management of that company, or should I say, we can allow for some of the government's top experts to be 'hired away' by Newco."

"You lost me, Randall," Judd said.

"Think about it for a minute, gentlemen." Erin changed transparencies showing a chain of command chart for Newco. "If we simply eliminate the hierarchy of the Colombian Cartel, thereby taking away the entire income of most of the farmers currently being paid to grow coca leaves, we leave that country open to financial ruin, not to mention, leaving the door wide open for some other group like the Sicilian mob to come in and continue the growing operations down there. We can't allow that to happen.

"We'll form Newco to hire these farmers and reclaim the land to grow coffee beans, soybeans and a variety of other crops. We broker the sale of these crops to the starving nations and continents of the world like Somalia, China and the Russian republics. We can sell food and seed to the UN. That puts the control of the land and the people's loyalty in the pocket of Newco. Furthermore, it partially raises the revenues we need to pay our installment to the La Cosa Nostra on an ongoing basis."

"Randall, who came up with all of this? I'm impressed beyond words!" Judd's head was spinning.

"We rented a small lodge outside of El Paso and brought in some of the country's top economists, accountants, international lawyers and especially, agri-consultants. The best minds we could find to reorganize the economics of a small country. We didn't tell them any of the details or the players. We gave them numbers and a bank of computers.

"They also figured we can shut down twenty-five percent of the U.S. prison system in the near future and renovate those structures for housing.

We can build large, state-of-the-art low income housing facilities in every city in the U.S. where we have prisons. Some of these renovation contracts will go to existing contractors who are currently bidding to the government. Others will be awarded to a U.S. based Newco DBA, further sustaining the income that normally funds the families of La Cosa Nostra. We award Daniel many of the contracts.

"In the future, the organization will earn their payments the hard way. Former La Cosa Nostra employees will act as Drug Police outside the boundaries of the United States. That's their ongoing part of the bargain, keep drugs from entering our borders.

"Newco will be owned by La Cosa Nostra; however, the business end will be operated by some of the most brilliant minds we have in areas such as agriculture, international finance, banking, transportation and marketing. Newco will be subject to taxation on all profits made in the U.S. With the revenues it generates, La Cosa Nostra families will have the necessary profits to live comfortably and carry on their policing actions abroad as well as enough revenues left over for internal investment and vertical integration. Newco will pay taxes!

"They can buy cement companies, lumber companies, steel companies, all for the purpose of building their share of the low-income housing market. Who knows? Newco could become larger than General Motors or AT&T. The possibilities are staggering."

"I've got a question for you, Randall. How are we going to float all this through Congress? I'm really interested in hearing your answer to that question."

"That part is the simplest part of all, Judd," Erin said with a grin on his face. "That's the other half of the bargain!"

"You lost me again, Randall."

"Gentlemen, have you ever studied J. Edgar Hoover politics or the political theories of Lyndon Baines Johnson or former Speaker of the House, Sam Rayburn? They all kept little black books on their political enemies," Erin continued without waiting for answers. "Or, better put, when you got your opponents by the balls, their hearts and minds will follow.

"Armed with those dossiers from Daniel on what congressmen are being paid off, we could spell doom to half the political futures of the people in Congress. If we handle those dossiers correctly, we can scare the hell out of every one on the hill. At the proper time, we'll get the Executive Branch involved.

"What does 'handling them correctly' mean, Randall?" Judd asked.

"We take two or three of the names on the list and leak them to the Washington Post. The media will destroy them. Then the President calls in the Speaker of the House and shows him the dossiers. He'll ask him to set up a series of meetings with the congressmen on whom we have dossiers. The Speaker will let them know in no uncertain terms that what we're doing is for the good of the United States, its people and its future. He will ask many for their resignations and other congress members for their support."

Randall continued his political presentation.

"New elections will be held to fill their positions and *voilà*, as an extra-added benefit to the American public, we've cleaned up graft and corruption in congress, starting anew with fresh faces and fresh ideas. We simply exert the power of the 'gotcha.'"

"Let me play devil's advocate, Randall," Feather remarked. "Some what ifs. What if the Perrone family wants all of this in writing, as in a contractual agreement? We're talking some heavy bucks here, not to mention La Cosa Nostra giving up many of their operations and part of their way of life."

"There can never be written contracts, Joe. The reasons are obvious. We can only show our intentions by putting Newco in place and maybe even issuing a couple of remodeling contracts to them. Once we give the incorporation papers to the Perrone family and lend them our agricultural specialists and their support groups, I suspect that they'll realize the reality that actions speak louder than words. We can plant our people there the minute the Cartel is out of the way. We're also going to have to come up with a substantial amount of cash. Money always talks!"

"Randall, what if the other twenty-three families won't go along with Perrone?"

"Status quo, Judd. We come down on La Cosa Nostra like a five-ton gorilla. We bust every operation they have, we freeze their assets, we put them out of business!"

"The last what if," Feather continued. "What if the American public finds out about this?"

"If they find out, we may lose it all. We'll appeal to the public, to their better sense of judgment. By that I mean, we come clean. We can say to America that we pitted organized crime against drugs to eliminate two violent threats. We tell John Q. Public that we fought fire with fire and we are the winners. Both organized crime and drugs are gone from our shores. What's important now is to get the pledge from La Cosa Nostra that they're willing and able to get on with it."

"Do you want me to present this plan to Daniel and his father tomorrow?" Judd asked.

"Why not? We have to start somewhere," Erin said. "We must know their decision soon. Call me when you get back tomorrow night, no matter how late it is. One last request," Erin looked over at Judd. "Do you think

Judge Ramirez will allow TV cameras in his courtroom? I'd like to get full coverage on this case. It can only help you be more popular with the American public than you already are."

"I believe the judge will allow it. I'll ask him and let you know."

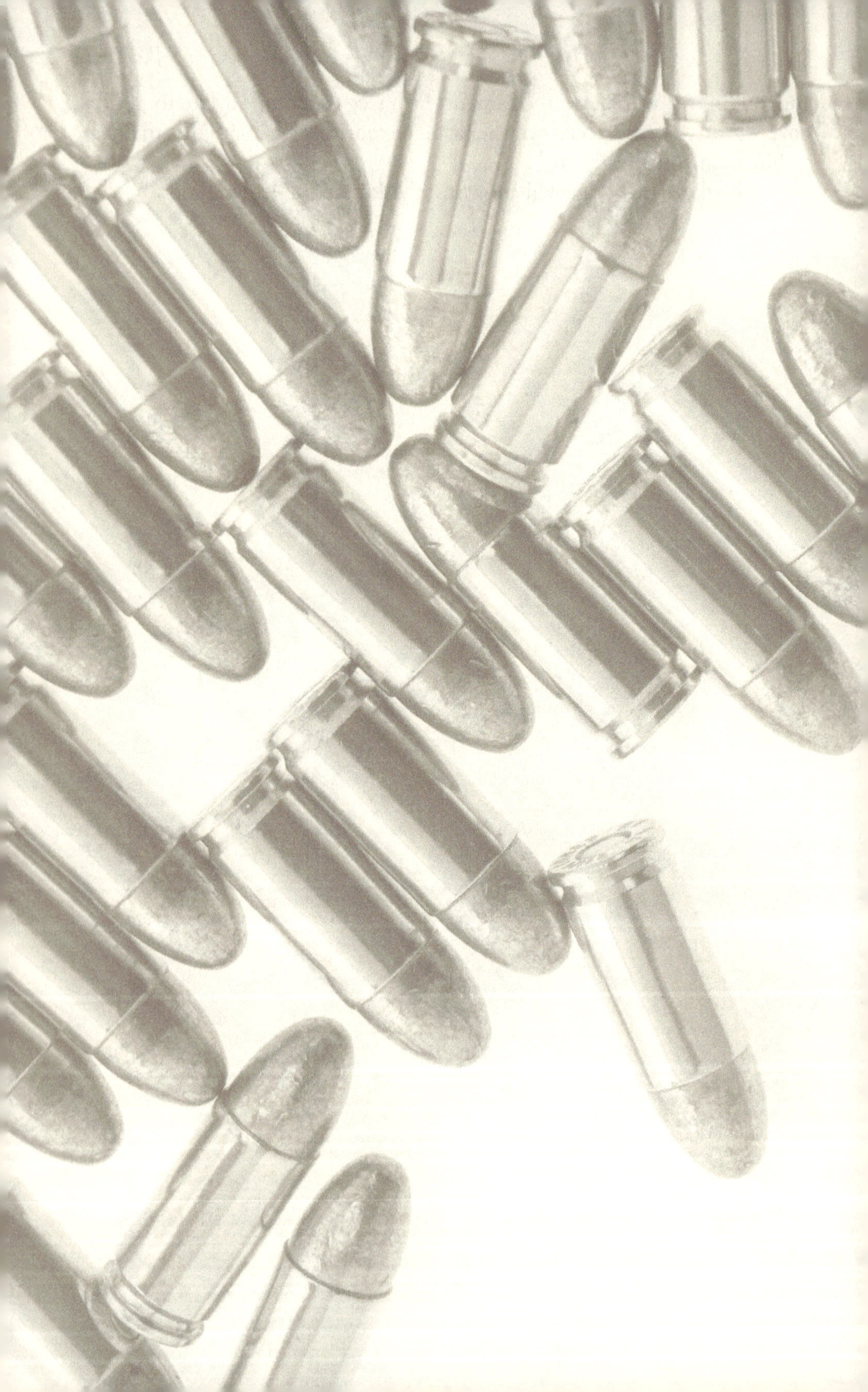

23

THE MEETING

Judd was up early and had coffee sent up to his hotel room. He opened the drapes and looked out over the city of Buffalo. Different from El Paso, greener, more humid yet cooler, outside temperature was sixty-five. In El Paso he had left one hundred six degrees. Judd got out a state map of New York and traced the route to Sinclairsville from the directions Daniel had given him the day before. He went over the notes Erin had compiled on structuring the deal with Nico Perrone. It was going to be a major meeting, a meeting on foreign turf. The only bright spot he could imagine was seeing Robin again, even across the table with her father and brother present. He'd settle for that.

At a little past nine Judd pulled out of the hotel in his rental car and headed toward Sinclairsville. The directions were excellent once he got out of the city and onto the highway. Just before eleven he saw the dark brown, barn-like structure on the left. A sign near the road confirmed he was in the right place. Across from The Granary was a ski slope, now barren of snow but with clear cut paths down the mountain between the tall trees. He could see the inactive ski lifts trailing up the side of the mountain.

As he turned left into the parking lot, he saw several limos, one being a vintage 1952 black Cadillac with running boards. At least twenty men were standing around the cars, no doubt Perrone's body guards. The men came up to his car before he got out, opened his door and politely asked for him to submit to a body search. Judd was not armed. They escorted him into the restaurant.

His eyes met Robin's as she got up from the table near the back of the restaurant and walked over to him.

"Hello, cowboy. Glad you could make it."

Robin kissed him on the cheek. She was dressed in a hunter's green suit with a multicolored silk scarf around her neck. Her long black hair was full and shining against her olive complexion. Judd caught the hint of her perfume as they walked towards her father and Daniel who were still seated at a round table. The smell of eggs, bacon and homemade Belgian waffles filled the room.

Daniel rose to shake hands.

"Judd, I would like to present my father, Nico Perrone."

Nico did not stand, extending his hand. After formalities, Nico motioned for Judd to be seated on the other side of Robin, who was on his right side. Seated next to Daniel was Robert Cotter, Nico's *consiglieri* and Benny "The Hat" Pizulli, Nico's enforcer. Robin squeezed Judd's hand under the table to make him feel more comfortable and to let him know he had a friend at this intimidating brunch bunch.

"These people are my trusted family and friends, Mr. Rayburn. You are free to discuss anything in front of them," Nico spoke in a low, gruff instructive voice. His tone was light, yet adversarial. "Would you like some coffee? Some breakfast? The food here is very good."

"I'll have some black coffee, Mr. Perrone," Judd turned his cup over.

"Judd, you look much better than when I left you," Robin said with a smile, trying to lighten up the atmosphere around the table.

"I feel much better. Thanks for being such an excellent nurse," Judd looked over to Nico. "Your daughter saved my life in Puerto Rico. I'm in her debt."

"I am very proud of her." Nico took Robin's left hand and patted it.

Daniel and the others remained silent. Nico directed the conversation.

"My son, Daniel, tells me you have a problem which I may be of service to remedy, Mr. Rayburn?" Nico wanted Judd to come to him.

"Mr. Perrone, I feel we have a mutual problem. One that can end up as an advantage to both of us if we work together." Judd put the conversation back on an even scale.

"I like to have things to my advantage, Mr. Rayburn. Daniel has informed me about this situation, your side and our position. There may be a way we can benefit each other." Nico opened the door for Judd to go into further detail.

"There would be many details to solidify, Mr. Perrone. We are willing to seek the solutions if we can arrive at an agreement in principle."

"In principle, Mr. Rayburn, we would be talking a large sum of money before we got to the detail stage of an agreement."

"We have a grasp of the money involved, Mr. Perrone. We also realize, as is customary in business, that to join into an alliance, both sides should be within five percent on any cash settlement. We can only guess at that figure, not knowing the details of your business. Can you help us with a figure?"

"Mr. Rayburn, I always like to sort the money issues out very clearly before going forward with details. I am here to listen to your offer, not make one." All eyes were on Judd. He felt as if he were on Nico's center court with no fans of his own in the gallery.

"I would like to show you our 'guestimations' on putting a deal together with your organization, Mr. Perrone." Judd reached into his briefcase and pulled out a small stack of papers, giving them to Daniel for distribution the way Mr. Perrone saw fit.

Daniel gave his father and Robert Cotter a copy and held the rest.

"This balance sheet, if you will allow us to make some assumptions, is where we think your organization is financially, Mr. Perrone. We do not break down your operations individually for obvious reasons to both parties. I would like to think we have done our homework accurately enough to arrive at a point of beginning." Judd waited for Nico's reply.

Cotter entered the conversation after quickly scanning the balance sheet. "Mr. Rayburn, we will neither confirm nor deny your figures. This should be another obvious point. However, let's assume we are at a starting point. What kind of offer are you prepared to make? And what will be our guarantee that you have the authority to make such an offer?"

Judd sensed two things. First, as good negotiators, the Perrone family was not going to be the one to put a dollar figure on the table. Second, Erin's research was close enough to begin negotiations. He could read that from Cotter's expression.

"We have a yearly federal budget allocation of seventeen billion dollars to fight drugs, gentle-men. Add another two billion and we are within a five percent margin of your businesses' estimated one year's net income times ten. This is a standard formula for the purchase of a company." Judd again awaited a reaction.

"Your figures are low, Mr. Rayburn," Cotter replied, still looking at the balance sheet. "I have a question. Are you implying a one-time payoff for our assistance or is this a structured long-term buy out agreement? Is this offer ongoing?"

"I'm offering half down in cash, the balance in one year, and yes, Mr. Cotter, this is an ongoing agreement."

"Define responsibilities for both parties, Mr. Rayburn," Cotter was completely noncommittal.

"Your organization will act as an international police force, Mr. Cotter. Your responsibilities will be to keep the coca plants from being grown and to eliminate the control of the Colombian Cartel over the people and the drugs in Colombia, Peru or any other country where they are active. Also, to make sure that the manufacture of cocaine resin ceases and does not enter the United States. How you accomplish this is your business.

"Let me add something here," Judd continued. "Just as the U.S. government does not take full responsibility for some CIA covert activities, we will not become entangled in any illegal acts you or your organization commit in order to accomplish your side of the bargain.

"In simple terms, you do away with the Cartel. We immediately send our agricultural specialists to Medellin and Cali, Colombia, to begin clearing the coca plants and planning other crops. Our people negotiate the lease of the farmland. We bring in the seed and know-how to cultivate new crops. Our people broker the sale of the crops to Africa, China and Russia through a company we will set up. Let's call it 'Newco' for now. You will own it, the U.S. government will staff it with our experts in all the fields necessary for worldwide distribution. This is phase I, gentlemen.

"Phase II, as you can see from the printed sheets I handed you, consists of building low income housing. We plan one hundred million-dollar plus development in five major cities in every state of the union. We figure forty to fifty percent of the new building contracts will go to Newco. Through Newco's investment and vertical integration—buying cement companies, equip-ment companies and so forth—we believe income paid out to the twenty-four families will total in the neighborhood of ten to twelve billion annually and everything is legitimate and Newco will pay taxes if you want to stay clear of the IRS."

Cotter wrote every number down as Judd spoke. Judd could see no enthusiasm in Cotter's face.

"As you know, Mr. Rayburn, we are very strong in labor, transportation and requisition. Your due diligence has structured this 'Newco' to fit our strengths. We are experts at, should I say, international relations. We have our ways of swaying opinions. A major problem for us to solve would be dissension within our ranks. How do we overcome that?" Cotter asked probingly.

"You give me the names. With the Justice Department's help, we'll re-do the Top One Hundred Most-Wanted list. We'll arrest them, prosecute them and put them away quickly!" Rayburn returned. "We'll back off on the rest of your operations and America gets the justice it seeks. You keep your hotels and gambling facilities.

"In a nutshell, gentlemen, you keep drugs from coming into the U.S., we'll run Newco with the best business minds available, you cease illegal activities in the U.S. and you get the profits from Newco. We send you big checks every year. Everyone wins!"

Judd sat back in his chair.

"Mr. Rayburn, perhaps you and my daughter, Robin, would like to see some of the beautiful forest surrounding the restaurant?" Nico said politely. "This will give us a few minutes to talk among ourselves."

Judd and Robin excused themselves from the table and walked outside. Robin immediately lit a cigarette, took a long puff and laid her head on Judd's shoulder as they walked arm-in-arm across the wooded field that surrounded the restaurant.

"You were magnificent, cowboy!" Robin spoke, looking up at Judd with sleepy, dreamy eyes. "I can read my father better than anyone. I believe you will make his dream come true. He looked pleased when we left."

"I hope so, Robin." Judd put his arm over Robin's shoulder as they walked through the forest. "So much is riding on this decision, La Cosa Nostra's future, America's future, not to mention our own."

"I will let nothing interfere with that, Judd. Nothing!" Robin stopped, threw her arms around Judd and kissed him passionately.

"Robin, I hope you can still say that if the decision goes the other way," Judd was concerned. "If we can't put this deal together, I have to go after Daniel and your father. It's my job to destroy them and their organization. It's difficult to have feelings for someone trying to put your entire family in prison."

"Judd, I know my father. He will make the right decision. I know he will. He must! I also know this few minutes he has asked for will turn into several hours."

Robin squeezed Judd close to her. If the decision went the other way, it may be the last time they would be together. As they talked, they fell deeper and deeper in love. For the moment there was no La Cosa Nostra or Cortez or courtrooms, there was only the other, the trees, the fresh air and their passion. They walked into the forest alone, out of sight of the guards and the restaurant.

"I hoped we would have this time together, Judd." Robin led the way down a path through the forest to a small tree encircled clearing where some quilts were spread out on the ground. Robin had prepared for any moment they may have.

Softly, passionately, slowly holding each other, they slid to the covered ground below. It had been so long since Judd had held a woman in his arms.

"Oh Robin, never has anyone so deeply touched my very soul."

"I know, my love. I feel the same way…"

Robin gently pulled Judd down to cover her body with his. Buttons and cloth kept them apart, too far apart. With their eyes closed, locked in a passionate embrace, they found each button, each piece of thread that separated them until their bodies touched, until their bodies, their tenderness, their spirits became one…

"Mr. Rayburn!" one of the guards shouted from the other side of the grassy hill. "Mr. Perrone asks that you and his daughter rejoin them."

Robin looked up at Judd; "We now face our fate, cowboy. We get to look into the crystal ball and see what lies ahead for us."

They took their time getting dressed, dressing each other. Longing for one more precious moment.

Taking their seats, Judd and Robin held hands under the table, so vulnerable, waiting for Nico Perrone's reply.

24

STICKER SHOCK

"So many details, Mr. Rayburn," Nico said taking a sip of coffee. Judd started to speak. Robin squeezed his hand tightly, stopping his comment.

"My son, Daniel, tells me he thinks you are an honorable man, a man with respect," Nico paused, looking at Cotter. "Now, Mr. Rayburn, you have convinced my *consiglieri*, Mr. Cotter, that you should be given the benefit of my many doubts. Your numbers are close. This is a sign of good faith on your part. They are not accurate, but close. My number is twenty-four billion. Not only accurate, but symbolic, there are twenty-four families in La Cosa Nostra. This meeting is not the time to accept or reject your proposal, Mr. Rayburn. It is a beginning, a beginning that reminds me of 1942 when an associate of mine, Mr. Charles "Lucky" Luciano was enlisted by your government to guard the docks of New York harbor. Maybe this beginning becomes more of a permanent business relationship, maybe not.

Nico stood for the first time during the meeting.

"We will consider your proposal. Daniel will give you our decision at the proper time."

The meeting ended.

Judd walked outside the restaurant accompanied by Robin and Daniel. Stopping at the end of the sidewalk leading up to the restaurant, Daniel spoke.

"Judd, depending on my father's final decision, I will begin compiling the information on the dossiers. They are extensive and accurate. I believe you and Mr. Erin would be surprised at the number of local, state and national government officials we pay off each year."

"It would be even better to serve them a double portion of justice, Daniel," Judd remarked. "I'm optimistic of the events that have taken place today."

"Don't be. We have no deal at this point, Judd. We have a number and many details. The Council of Families must cast their votes. It could go either way."

"Hold me, cowboy!" Robin squeezed Judd hard up against her. "I hope to be seeing much more of you, now. I look forward to that. I miss you already."

Holding her close, Judd whispered softly, "I only hope that nothing will keep us apart. As God is my witness, no matter what the outcome, nothing will keep us apart."

SUNDAY NIGHT, JUNE 28TH, 11:45 P.M. CDT

Feather and Erin drove to El Paso International to wait for Judd's plane to arrive.

Judd walked out of the covered gantry pulling his suitcase, looking very tired from the long day. He smiled as he approached Randall and Joe.

Feather looked at Erin, "I knew he would do it, Randall. He's smiling. He put the deal together."

"Hey, guys, we haven't got a new partner yet, but, we're closer. The Perrones will let us know soon. Let's get to the car and I'll tell you about the meeting."

On the way back to Bliss, Judd gave Erin and Feather a blow-by-blow description of the meeting, leaving out only choice moments he shared with Robin.

"Judd, I've got to ask the question." Erin's voice was now low key and probing. "Do you trust the Perrones?"

"That's a question we're all going to have to answer for ourselves. Do I trust them? Yes. Partly because I want to and partly because I do. You're going to have to develop your own comfort zone with them. Everyone in this is going to have to do that."

"I'll feel a lot more comfort when I see those dossiers, Judd. I think that will be the deciding factor for me." Erin was doggedly direct. "Once we have the dossiers, if they are accurate, La Cosa Nostra opens themselves up to prosecution for tampering with the government; that should prove their trust in us. I'm sure that they're aware of that. At the same time, it gives us the comfort level we seek."

"That's pretty much the way I see it, Randall."

"Now get some sleep and bust Cortez's butt in the morning. Keep me informed."

"Randall, I forgot to tell you. The Perrone's number is twenty-four billion. Have a nice restful night…"

Judd spent another forty-five minutes going over last minute details of the upcoming trial with Jake Ramsey. At two a.m. he set his clock for four hours of sleep and called it a day.

Judd's trial staff had already left BOQ 17 to set up over at the war room turned courtroom. The prisoners would be brought in from the stockade at exactly 8:50 a.m.. The jury would be seated at 8:55. Judd, Randall Erin and Jake Ramsey were on their way to the judge's chambers adjoining the courtroom to meet with Ramirez and the two defense attorneys, Lee Wiley and Alex Castenada. Judge Ramirez was following his usual pattern after years on the bench. He would call the prosecution and defense teams together in chambers to go over "the rules of his court."

"Please come in and be seated gentlemen," Ramirez said to the two teams of lawyers. "As you all know, I have allowed TV cameras in this courtroom. My reasons are simple. I want the American public to see justice administered, carried out in the manner in which our system demands, due process of law."

Ramirez leaned forward over his desk and looked at each lawyer in the room.

"I will not tolerate theatrics because of the extensiveness of the media involved in this case. Is that clear?"

Everyone answered in the affirmative.

MONDAY, JULY 29TH, 8:45 A.M.

Counsel for both sides sat behind their respective tables. Prosecution to the left of the bench, nearest the jury box, defense on the right. The bulletproof booths where the defendants would sit, directly behind the defense table, were outfitted with translation earphones.

At 8:55 a.m. the jury entered the court from the adjoining jury deliberation room. Six men, Six women. The eight back-up jurors were all white, Caucasian males. Hardcore rednecks, every one. Judd had allowed the jury that was seated. The price to Wiley and Castenada was the prosecution's choice of reserve jurists. If any of the seated jurists were harassed or threatened in any way, Judd wanted to make it perfectly clear to Cortez and to the defense team what reserves would take their places.

Five minutes earlier, the defendants were led into the cubicles one by one, each escorted by several U.S. Marshals. Cortez sat under the number "1." As each of the other eleven defendants were led in and chained to their rings, there was a murmur throughout the media gallery.

Judd turned to face Cortez. Cortez looked away.

"All rise!" The bailiff instructed in a loud, authoritative voice.

Judge Ramirez seated the bench. Court was now in session.

"Mr. Bailiff," Ramirez said, "Please read the charges against the defendants."

Each defendant's name was read along with the number assigned to him by the court. A single charge of capital murder followed each name, each number. The charges were read distinctively and loudly by the bailiff with brief pauses in between each defendant. As the last defendant was being named, Judd looked up into the press gallery. There was Erica Stone, front row, center. She nodded down towards Judd. He returned the nod.

Formalities complete, Judd stood to face the jury and began his opening remarks.

"Ladies and gentlemen of the jury, my name is Judd Rayburn. I am hired by you, the American taxpayer, to seek justice. This case meets the criteria for the United States to ask for the death penalty in the event of a guilty verdict.

"Your duty, let me say that word again, your *duty* is not to administer such a penalty. Your duty is to make a decision, a unanimous decision as to whether the evidence presented to you is clear, concise and beyond a reasonable doubt. If, at the end of this trial, you believe that to be the case, you must cast your vote guilty!"

Judd stood directly in front of each juror as he spoke. He presented himself as an educator, a teacher, a warrior and a pillar of fairness. He did not stare or threaten. He did not probe deep into their eyes.

"The evidence you will view may, in some areas, be offensive to you or one of your fellow jurists. The evidence is shocking. It is graphic. If for any reason you may feel ill or sick at your stomachs after viewing such evidence, do not hesitate to raise your hand. The bailiff will escort you into the jury room where medical personnel are standing by to assist you."

Lee Wiley came near to objecting on the grounds of theatrics but held off, not wanting to get his first admonishment from Judge Ramirez. Judd was leading the jurors, true; however, he was more or less instructing the jury of the facilities available to them. *Shrewd*, Wiley thought, but absolutely nothing he could do about it.

"I will close by leaving each one of you with two tasks to complete as your duty in this case. First, to believe your own eyes. Second, to return a verdict of guilty if you do believe your own eyes. Thank you."

Judd turned from the jury after pausing for another look at each one of them. He walked confidently back to his place behind the prosecution's table.

9 A.M. EDT, NEW YORK

"Daniel, you need to join me here at the house immediately. I have news for you that will help you in your dealings with the Colombians." Nico Perrone was insistent as usual.

"I'll be right over, Father." Daniel hung up the phone, got Mario and drove to his father's house.

Within forty-five minutes, the 1955 black vintage Cadillac limo, a gift from his father, delivered Daniel to the front steps of his father's huge, well-guarded estate.

"Come in Daniel." Nico wasted no time. "I have been contacted by the Sicilians. They are putting together a large venture as we suspected. Because of the complexity of their venture, they cannot and do not want to entertain the thought of retaliation or interference from our organization here in the States. To show their good faith, the Sicilians are willing to set up a meeting for us with the Colombians and will use their influence to establish our organization as the sole distribution arm of Cartel drugs within the U.S."

"But sir..."Daniel seldom interrupted his father. "The Sicilians have known about your anti-drug stand for a very long time. Why did they even bother to make the offer to you?"

"Our brothers in Sicily are very wise, Daniel." Nico never wanted his son to underestimate the Sicilian mob bosses. "The venture they are working on is of such large proportion they cannot afford for us to disrupt their proceedings with what we know. Instead of taking the chance of La Cosa Nostra going to the U.S. FBI to bargain, by that I mean asking the FBI to back off on their investigations into our family enterprises in exchange for information leading to the busting up of their venture, they would rather insure our silence by assisting us in putting together a similar large venture to distribute drugs into the U.S.

"They knew I was in a position to change my mind on drug distribution in the States. In order to avoid conflict, they will help us rebuild. They will control drugs into Europe and the Russian republics. We will control drug distribution into the U.S. In the future, they know we will be a good distributor for their heroin. This puts more money and power into their hands. Our organizations will work closer together, we all become stronger. Then, one day, we will take over the Colombian Cartel.

"What we will gain by working together will be world control of drugs and distribution through a unified Mafia organization. The Sicilians have foresight, Daniel. Never forget that. They tolerate the Colombians. They do not like working with them."

"So, Father, when do I go to Medellin, Colombia?"

"The Sicilians will contact me within a couple of days, Daniel. They are making arrangements today."

Robert Cotter, Nico's *consiglieri*, listened to every word. "Daniel, I'll arrange a good faith cash down payment. How much do you think you will need to take down there?"

"I want to impress the Colombians, Robert." Daniel's mind was in high gear to come up with a suitable number. "I want to get their attention, but I do not want to put it all right into their hands. I will take fifty million dollars as a partial down payment with a guarantee of a fifty more when the drugs are delivered."

"That's a lot of cash to raise, Daniel. Maybe you can ask Rayburn to secure it for us...as a token of his good faith..."

25

"He'll Do to Ride the Rivers With"

Lee Wiley was closing his opening remarks to the jury.

"This trial is about the events that took place at Ambush Pass in late April of this year. I will show you how several agencies of the U.S. government had planned to ambush suspected drug dealers from Mexico. How they planned on murdering these men who, according the U.S. Constitution, are innocent until proven guilty. Before we proceed with the presentation of evidence, ladies and gentlemen of the jury, I appeal to your sense of fair play to carefully weigh the facts before you consider sending men to their deaths. Thank you." Wiley returned to his chair at the defense table.

Judd was ready, his path clear. He rose from his chair and addressed the jury.

"For the next twenty-two minutes, ladies and gentlemen of the jury, I want you to view a video shot at the scene of the drug bust. I would ask that you make no notes. I would also ask that you view the film without comment, taking in as many details as you can. We will play it again if any of you request a second showing. As I said in my opening remarks, the video is taken from elements of the news media on the scene and SWAT video teams that took part in the events at Ambush Pass."

Judd turned to the video operators up in the projection booth, as a large screen was unveiled behind the witness stand. Judge Ramirez left the bench to watch the video.

"Please begin," Judd ordered as the lights were lowered.

The video began with film from the El Paso SWAT team cameras focused on the helicopter as it flew over the mountain with a person suspended on a rope beneath it. As the chopper got closer and closer to the SWAT position, more detail came into view. The face of Dee Espinoza was completely clear as the cameraman used a high-powered zoom lens. The anguish, tugging at the rope around his neck, gasping for air was apparent and horrifying. Dee Espinoza appeared to be in obvious pain as the down draft of the chopper blades tossed his long black hair wildly. He kicked desperately to release himself. There was a unified gasp around the courtroom as the jury and media watched the film, partly in horror, partly in disbelief at the macabre overtones they sensed. Cameras focused lower on Dee's body, showing blood streaming from his groin, running down his legs. More gasps from the people inside the courtroom. A reverse angle was dubbed into the video from the news cameras assigned to Erica's team. The helicopter had been videoed from opposite directions between the SWAT cameraman and the news team.

More grasping, more intense pain and horror showed on the grimaced, twisted face of Dee Espinoza as he fought the rope around his neck, the pain of castration, the weight of his own body tugging at his neck. One eyeball had popped out of the socket and thrashed left and right upon Dee's cheek.

Shocking nakedness, the blood and torture was too much for three of the jurors. Hands rose in the jury box, two men and one woman stood, trying to get to the jury deliberation room. One of the men on the far end of the jury box didn't make it, bending over just short of the door. The courtroom became filled with the stench of regurgitated ham and eggs.

Immediately, Judge Ramirez ordered the film stopped and for the lights to be turned on. The pomp and ceremony of a murder trial was quickly reduced to the gut-wrenching reality of terrible, vile death. The smell of vomit added a realness to the video that no one had expected.

Media commentators in the balcony were not spared, as the gagging aroma became worse, spreading throughout the building. One sickness gave way to the next. Hardcore news reporters were heaving their guts out. The balcony was a mess.

Ramirez granted a one-hour recess and ordered the courtroom mopped and deodorized. Twenty armed U.S. Marshals watched the defendants like hawks. Each was released from the handcuff rings and removed to a holding area.

"I knew we'd get a reaction from the jury," Erin said in a whispered voice. "I never thought it would have this much impact on them, even Castenada!"

"We've seen the film a hundred times," Judd whispered back. "To us it has been evidence to convict. Today I believe it's hitting home. We're not looking at it as evidence. We're watching Dee Espinoza die."

Feather sat next to Judd, expressionless, never uttering a word or moving his glance from the screen even though the video had been turned off several minutes before.

Erica left the press balcony with a perfumed handkerchief over her nose. The first three minutes of the video, the vomiting and the stench was news. She headed for the phones to call in a partial report.

TV transmission editors in command studios around the U.S. were using the hour recess to call meetings with senior network officials to see if the American public could stand to see such graphic footage on their TVs, inside their own living rooms? Phone lines to the FCC were jammed by network lawyers.

The much needed hour recess passed. Jurors were again seated in the jury box as the defendants were returned to their cubicles. The press filled their assigned seats. Judge Ramirez emerged from his chambers and instructed the bailiff to leave everyone seated while he made his walk from the bench.

Lights in the courtroom were again lowered as the now infamous video was re-started at the exact point where it had been turned off.

Cameras focused on Cortez in the chopper, showing him cutting the rope with a knife. As the rope loosened around Dee's neck he began his mountain climbing motions trying to grasp anything to keep from falling to the ground. Cameras from two angles followed him down to his death. He bounced a foot off the desert sand when his body hit. The crackle of automatic rifle fire sounded loudly over the speakers in the courtroom, rocket propelled grenades (RPGs) fired from the Cartel soldiers in the mountains above streamed down onto the police cars, striking them and causing ear-shattering explosions.

An out-of-focus figure jumped from behind one of the unmarked police cars and ran, then crawled, in a direct pattern towards the lifeless, rope-entangled body that lay bleeding in the desert. Everyone in the courtroom knew that man was Judd Rayburn, trying desperately to get to his fallen friend, Dee Espinoza.

Numerous, continuous, almost countless explosions boomed through the speakers as jurors and media alike clenched their arms around their midsections, watching in astounding frailty. The ABC crew recorded the Texas Ranger vehicle taking a direct hit from one of the Cartel rockets.

More gasps at the sight of District Attorney Paul Martinez slumping over backwards from a splattering head shot. Judge Ramirez began banging his gavel on the wooden seat next to where he was sitting in an effort to quiet the courtroom and maintain order. The video continued.

Martinez's wife was escorted by friends out of the courtroom. Knowing her husband was dead was one thing. Seeing him die was another. She had seen enough, too much.

Ramirez quickly ordered a second thirty-minute recess.

Minutes later, Ramirez received a note from the jury foreman asking that after the balance of the video was viewed, he adjourn the court for the rest of the day. Half an hour later court was reconvened, the balance of the video was presented and Judge Ramirez complied with the foreman's request, adjourning the court until Tuesday morning at nine a.m.. Reporters streamed out of the upstairs gallery into the news message center adjacent to the foyer of the building.

The silence that surrounded the viewing of the video deteriorated into media mayhem as network reporters began racing outside, standing in front of live feed cameras to tell the world what they had just witnessed.

"Judd," Randall turned in the van to look at Judd sitting in the back seat. "I'm not sure the jury members can assimilate the gamut of evidence that we have prepared. We've shocked the daylights out of them already. I think we need to lighten up on the blood and guts. They can't take the freeze frames. I also don't believe Wiley and Castenada will want to go back into them. They have absolutely no defense. Their only plea is for the mercy of the court for their clients at this point. They're helpless."

"I agree." Judd was a victim of the traumatic videos as well, they had finally sunk in on him. "What do you suggest?"

"I suggest we go directly into the witness phase and bring in the law enforcement officers and Army personnel present, have them give their eyewitness accounts of what went on, then cut directly to the laser experts from NASA tracing the trajectory of the bullets from the Cartel soldiers that killed the officers. I believe that is proof positive for conviction. Any more is case overkill and cruel to the jurors."

"I appreciate your insight," Judd said slowly. "All I've been thinking about is pounding Cortez into the ground. I don't ever want him to forget the death and pain he has caused. I haven't thought much about the grief I'm inflicting on the jurors, not to mention Martinez's wife."

Feather added, "Bro, I've been watching Cortez and the others during the whole trial today. Cortez is scared, I can see it in his eyes. So are the other defendants. Whatever or whomever they expected to bail them out of this trial didn't show up. I believe they realize that they are alone and as Randall said, 'defenseless'. They're defeated and they know it."

"I'd really like to get Cortez on the stand," Judd said clenching his fist.

"Not going to happen, buddy," Randall replied.

"I hear what you're saying, Randall. We'll go to eyewitness testimony in the morning, followed by laser tracing of the bullets by NASA experts in the afternoon. Then, well, I guess the prosecution will rest."

"Judd, I think that's a wise decision," Randall concurred.

The van pulled up to BOQ 17. Judd was somewhat tired, somewhat deflated.

"Boss, a Mr. Tyson Hall, one of the White House's secretaries, called and asked if you and Joe can join the President on this next Saturday, the Fourth of July, for the Presidential Medal of Freedom Award presentation." Maureen read from her steno pad.

Judd looked over to Erin. "Do you think this will be over then, Randall?"

"Yeah, Judd, I do."

Judd turned to Feather. "Looks like we're going to Washington."

7:30 P.M. CDT. FT. BLISS

"Boss, Erica Stone is on line two for you."

"Hey, Erica. How are ya?"

"My stomach is just now settling down, Judd. That was the first time I'd seen what my cameraman shot. You guys really cut a lot of our footage."

"I hope we're not going back to your lost footage, Erica."

"Not important. We would like credit for it though, especially for my cameraman. He'll be awarded for sure. Better his career and all that."

"I'll see he gets the credit, Erica."

"Could you stand a little dinner?"

"I'd love it. What about tomorrow night?"

"I'll settle for that. About eight at the 'O' club?"

"I'll be there..."

TUESDAY, JUNE 30TH.
DAY TWO OF THE CORTEZ TRIAL

Judd studied the faces of each juror as they were seated in the jury box. He could see they were still shaken from the previous day's video and their guarded anticipation was written across each member's face.

Ramirez entered the courtroom and brought the trial to order.

"Ladies and gentlemen of the jury," Judd began slowly, "I must apologize for putting you through the gruesome scenes of yesterday's graphic tape. I had planned on showing it to you again, frame by frame, removing any doubt as to whether the defendants sitting before you were actually at the scene and had committed the atrocities you witnessed. I believe the looks of horror you expressed yesterday created an indelible record of the events in your minds. I'll spare you more gory details."

Judd paused and turned towards the public seating gallery on the ground floor of the theater behind the prosecution table.

"I'm also going to spare additional pain to the widows and families of the fallen officers who are present here today..."

"Objection!" Wiley said furiously.

"Objection sustained! Mr. Rayburn, you will direct your evidence towards the jury, not the gallery."

For the next three hours Judd called eyewitness after eyewitness to the stand. The jury was told about what was supposed to happen, a simple drug bust. They were told over and over again of what did happen, a premeditated slaughter of law enforcement officers trying to do their duty. A massacre, an ambush by the defendants who were on trial.

The last witness called was Texas Ranger Hugh Winsette. The fifty-year-old Ranger walked into the courtroom tall and proud. His boots shone like glass. His gold Ranger belt buckle glistened under the overhead lighting. The Classic Texas Ranger Stetson hat tucked under his left arm revealed the ring it left around his closely cut thinning gray hair.

Winsette's face was sunburned and hard as leather, and his chin appeared to be set in granite. He stood about 5', 10" and carried his one hundred seventy-five pound body on thin legs slightly bowed from years on horseback. His eyes were cold and fixed upon the defendants as he was sworn in and seated in the witness chair.

As Judd asked Ranger Winsette to tell the jury of his recollection of the events at Ambush Pass everyone in the courtroom noticed that Ranger Winsette was a pillar of the old West, representing justice with a big iron around his waist. Ranger Winsette spoke slowly with a heavy Texas drawl. The jurors clung to his every word.

"...then the rocket came streaking down from the mountain. It had a hiss like a mad rattlesnake. I was looking right at my friend and fellow Ranger, Lester Burrows, when the rocket hit. This man, five times decorated for bravery by three different governors, literally exploded right before my eyes. He was just gone...his blood...all over me..."

Ranger Winsette, who was hard as nails, choked. The lump in his throat prevented him from completing the sentence. The courtroom was dead silent as he regained his composure. Handkerchiefs came out of everyone's pockets and purses. Judge Ramirez swiveled his chair around turning his back to the courtroom as he also wiped his eyes.

"…I'd like to show the court a plaque presented by the Captain of the Texas Rangers to Lester Burrows just six months ago…"

Winsette pulled out a small plaque from the witness box. "It will leave everyone with an idea of what kind of man Lester was. The plaque has written on it an old saying from the days when the Texas Rangers were first formed. It reads, '*To Ranger Lester Burrows, He'll Do To Ride The Rivers With*'…" Winsette left the stand.

After lunch, NASA laser experts moved a scale model of the area surrounding Ambush pass in front of the jury box and began pinpointing individual Cartel members through the use of little plastic army figurines. Through physics and geometrical lines, the NASA experts depicted each death, each killer, beyond a reasonable doubt.

With slow, short steps, Judd approached the jury, his arms folded in front of him. Each step he took echoed in the courtroom. There was only silence. Looking at the floor as he neared the jury box, stopping directly in front, Judd looked up, peering at each juror, saying nothing. He walked from one end of the jury box to the other.

"Ladies and gentlemen of the jury," Judd began his summation. "At the beginning of these proceedings, I told you what your job is in this case; to decide if the evidence presented in this trial places the defendants at the scene of the crime, if the evidence shows premeditation, and, if the defendants, in fact, killed the deceased officers. We have proven all those things, beyond a shadow of a doubt. Your task now is simple, listen to the pleas of the defense. Then, return a verdict of guilty. The prosecution rests."

Judd turned and walked briskly back to the prosecution table. The silence was shattered by Judge Ramirez's gavel.

"Court adjourned until tomorrow at nine a.m.."

5:30 P.M. CDT, TUESDAY, JUNE 30TH

"Boss, I know you've had a long one today, but there is a Daniel, that's all the name he gave me, from New York on line 4," Maureen announced. "Do you want me to tell him to call back?"

"No, I'll take it in my room," Judd said. He was waiting for this call.

"Judd, Daniel Perrone. Some trial you got going down there in Texas. You're brutal!"

"It's a brutal business, Daniel. How are things on your end?"

"I have had a meeting with my father. The Sicilians have contacted him. They want to declare a truce with us and go a step further by setting us up with the Colombians for drug distribution here in the U.S."

"Interesting. When does your meeting take place? I'm assuming you will go to Colombia?"

"We are waiting for the details. I believe it will be the latter part of this week. I need a favor."

"If I can, Daniel. What do you need?"

"One hundred million dollars."

"One hundred million!?"

"Actually I only need half of it for now."

"Daniel, are you asking me for one hundred million or fifty million… Like I could do either one?"

"I need fifty million in cash, by Friday. You can see the immediacy of my problem. We have the money. The time element for converting it into cash is the problem. Can you help me?"

"What are you going to do with the money, Daniel?"

"Offer it to the Colombian Cartel as a down payment on our first big drug deal."

"And give them the other half on delivery of the drugs? You're showing good faith, right?"

"Right. We don't want to just hand over that kind of cash to them. Too risky. They would not expect us to do that, either. Our reputation has a habit of preceding us."

"That's a tall order. Let me call you back. I don't happen to have that kind of cash on me. How's Robin?"

"Robin has been like a school girl lately, Judd. I think you may have something to do with that."

"Tell her I said hello. I'll get back to you."

Judd looked into his phone finder for Rikki's office number in Virginia. She had returned shortly after bringing him back to Fort Bliss. If anyone could come up with that kind of money, and keep it quiet, Rikki could.

"Rikki? Judd. How's the spy business?"

"Cute! I was going to call you tonight. Man, what a trial you guys got going down there. CNN showed about a second of some really gruesome stuff."

"I haven't seen TV today. I really don't know what they've shown."

"The lead story on the international news was parts of Ranger Winsette's testimony. Touching! The rest of the story was all Judd Rayburn, Mr. Law and Order."

"Hey, I need a little favor."

"Name it."

"I need fifty million, cash."

"Why fifty million, Judd? Got a hot date?"

"Give me a break, Rikki. Oh yeah, I need it by Friday, in New York."

"Will hundreds be okay?"

"Rikki, can you can do it?"

"Not to worry, as long as good counterfeit Ben Franklins will do."

"Rikki, how good is the counterfeit? Daniel's life will depend on the quality."

"Let me put it this way, only four men in the world could tell it's counterfeit. I put three of them in jail two years ago. The fourth guy is under surveillance in Germany as we speak. Those bills will pass anywhere on this globe. They're even aged, consecutively numbered and sitting in an evidence warehouse outside of Langley, Virginia."

"Sounds good to me, Rikki. At least we won't be getting a bill from Big Brother if something goes wrong?"

"I'll put the cash in a trunk and fly it to New York Friday. It's for Daniel, right?"

"Indirectly. It's a down payment to the Colombians. Daniel will probably meet with them this weekend."

"I get the picture. He's getting close to them with a bunch of cash. That'll get you an invitation to Medellin every time. What do I do with the other fifty million?"

"Why don't you use that as an excuse to come to Bliss. The money will be secure here. I'm sure Daniel will need the other half soon to close his deal."

"Consider it done. Have someone call me with where to deliver the first half, okay?"

"Will do, Rikki. Talk to you soon."

"Daniel? Judd. Commander Rhine will fly the cash to you Friday. Call her and give her the location."

"You guys move fast, thanks. Robin said to tell her `cowboy' hello. I'm assuming she's referring to you."

"Keep me posted, Daniel. We're going out on a limb on this. Call when you've got details, as in how the council votes. By the way, we can offer some protection for you down there in Columbia."

"Thanks again. We can handle that part," Daniel hung up.

"Boss, Erica, line two."

"Thanks, Maureen. Judd."

"I can't make our dinner date tonight. I'm going to be on a conference call with network biggies and lawyers half the night," Erica said with an apologetic tone. "I'll leave the window in my room unlocked if you want to join me later, big guy."

"Thanks for the offer, Erica. I'd better pass."

"See you in court tomorrow, Judd. Today and yesterday offered phenomenal testimony. You should run for president; you'd win! The networks are thinking about running trial footage over the 'soap' shows tomorrow; that in itself almost takes an act of Congress. You're big news, Judd, with a capital 'N'!"

"I'll try not to let it go to my head, Erica. See you tomorrow."

There was a knock on Judd's door followed by Feather.

"Something's bothering me, Judd. Got a minute?"

"I've got all night, Joe. What's the problem?"

"It's Sal, Sal Olivares."

"Mr. Gourmet Cook?"

"Yes, he got that job next door to Senator Capriatti's house too easy."

"Joe, I thought the agency got him the job?"

"No. Sal made two phone calls and was packing his bags for Illinois. When things are that easy, something's usually wrong."

"But, Joe, remember, it was Sal who put us on to the Mexican congressman? That's a biggie in my book."

"Maybe it's nothing, bro, it just arouses my suspicions. Want to get something to eat over at the mess hall?"

"Yeah. Let's ask the whole crew if they want to go with us. We haven't had much time to spend with Maureen and Casey."

"Good idea. I'll round up everyone."

26

MISSING PIECES

Wiley and Castenada spent three hours alternating their time in front of the jury, desperately trying to put up some defense for their clients. They had no defense, the evidence was too incriminating, the crimes too heinous. Against Judge Ramirez's orders, they filed motions of mistrial and second motions to sever, trying anything to deal for at least a couple of their clients' lives. All it got them was brief consideration from Ramirez accompanied by more hand slaps and threats of contempt.

Their last effort at a defense was to plead to the court of illegal seizure on the part of Cortez. Unfortunately, the Immigration and Naturalization Service had videotaped Cortez's staggered walk across the border, right into the hands of waiting agents.

During final summary, Wiley and Castenada pleaded with the jury for leniency, their only hope. The defense rested as the jury received final instructions from Judge Ramirez and retired to the jury deliberation room.

At 4:30 p.m. CDT the bailiff made the call to BOQ 17.

"Mr. Rayburn, this is the bailiff. The jury is bringing in their verdict."

"All rise!" shouted the bailiff.

Ramirez kept the same cold look throughout most of the trial. He dared not show emotion lest the prosecution or defense might accuse him of influencing the jury.

"Has the jury reached a verdict?" Judge Ramirez asked.

The tall African-American jury foreman stood, "Yes, your honor, we have."

"Please pass the verdict to the Bailiff."

Everyone in the courtroom was trying to read the judge's eyes, trying to anticipate the outcome.

"Before I read the jury's verdict, let me first clarify a few points of law," Ramirez addressed the court and gallery. "These twelve defendants are being tried collectively for capital murder. The verdict for one will be the verdict for all..."

"No! Stop Señor Judge! I want to deal! Stop now! Mr. Rayburn, I have information for you! Please stop!" shouted Cortez as U.S. Marshals instinctively leveled rifles at him.

Judge Ramirez banged his gavel vigorously, trying to regain order in the courtroom.

"Remove the prisoner, Marshals!" shouted Ramirez. "Counsels, approach the bench!"

Judd looked over at Erin sitting to his right before walking up to Judge Ramirez. Wiley and Castenada looked back at Cortez to see if he was going to cause the Marshals any further trouble. They quickly walked up to the bench in the center of the courtroom. Network commentators raced to the foyer area to stand in front of their cameras to give the public a detailed description of the disruptive occurrence just moments before.

"The verdict has been delivered in this case, gentlemen," Ramirez said harshly. "I am not at liberty to tell either side what it is as you all well know. Due to the complexity of this trial and due to an ongoing investigation connected to this case, I will allow defense ten minutes to talk to their client, Cortez, to see what information Mr. Cortez may render. Then, Mr. Rayburn, you will have ten minutes after that to reach a decision. Your time starts now, gentlemen, I'll see you in court in twenty minutes."

Wiley and Castenada literally raced to the holding room where Cortez had been taken. Within nine minutes they were at the prosecution table talking to Judd and Erin in muffled voices.

"Cortez says he can tell you about some American congressmen who are involved in a drug scam in Puerto Rico," Wiley said hurriedly.

"Tell Mr. Cortez `not good enough,' Wiley. I already know about them. What details can he give me?"

"Mr. Cortez said nothing about details, Judd. Dammit, man! We're pleading for lives here, give him a chance to tell you what he knows," Wiley said banging his hand on the prosecution table.

"Let's go in and talk to him, Wiley," Judd said. "We've got about seven minutes left."

Judd and Erin accompanied the two defense lawyers into the holding room. Only Cortez and three U.S. Marshals were inside. The other defendants were feverishly squirming around inside their individual cubicles under heavy guard.

"Cortez, you've got three minutes to tell me something I don't already know! Start talking!" Judd looked at Cortez hard.

"Mr. Rayburn, there are U.S. congressmen involved in our company in Puerto Rico, Capriatti, Zavalla and Fuselier!" Cortez blurted out, sweat running down his forehead.

"Cortez, now you have two minutes, I already know that. Give me details. What part do they play?"

"Uh, uh, they, uh. I'm not sure, señor. But I will point them out. Please, help me. I don't want to die!" Cortez was falling apart.

"You've got one minute, Julio. In one minute you get sentenced to death. You'd better think and think fast," Judd spoke slowly, as if he were using up Julio's last minute before being sentenced.

"I will tell you about Mexican congressman Cordova, Señor Rayburn! I will help you!" Cortez spoke as he got down on his knees. "Please don't let me die!"

"I know about him, too, Julio. Your time is up. See you on death row. I'll be there when they strap you down and take your breath away. Count on it! You're gonna die!"

Erin never said a word. Judd knew if his boss would have dealt differently, he would've said something.

Exactly twenty minutes after the outbreak, Cortez was brought back into the courtroom. The two Marshals had to hold him up as they led him back, putting his cuffs through the rings under the cubicle marked Number 1. Cortez was sobbing uncontrollably. His nose was running. He was pitiful.

"Keep your seats," Ramirez instructed. "I will continue with the reading of the verdict. Defendants one through twelve have been found 'Guilty...'"

The courtroom erupted into yelling and applause. Feather, Erin, Ramsey and Judd all formed a huddle hugging one another, Ramirez began banging his gavel.

"Order in this court! There will be order in my court!" Ramirez was shouting. "The next sound out of anyone will land them in jail for thirty days for contempt. I continue. Defendants one through twelve have been found guilty of capital murder. Sentencing to take place in sixty days. Court is adjourned."The ground floor of the makeshift courtroom became flooded with reporters, cameras, and microphones sticking out of the crowd resembling quills on a porcupine. Strobe lights blinded the prosecution staff.

"Mr. Rayburn! What was the new information Cortez wanted to give you?" shouted one of the many reporters pushed up against Judd and his staff.

"No comment!" Judd yelled.

"Will the convicted drug dealers get the death penalty?" shouted another reporter.

"I believe we can count on that," Judd said with confidence in his eyes. "You have witnessed American justice."

"What will you do now, Mr. Rayburn? Will you go back to being the El Paso District Attorney or will you remain with the U.S. Attorney's office?" asked another reporter as the crowd of media pushed and shoved their way nearer to the prosecution staff.

Judd stood up on the prosecution table to keep from getting crushed by the horde of reporters; Feather and Erin joined him. Judd paused before answering the last question.

"Write this down and understand clearly what I am about to tell you."

He waited for the crowd to quiet down.

"I'm giving drug runners and pushers advance warning," Judd pointed with outstretched arm and finger into one of the cameras. "Find another line of work or face me! You've seen what will happen to you. End of statement."

SATURDAY, JULY 4TH, 4 P.M. EDT. WASHINGTON D.C.

Judd and Feather sat in their hotel room near the White House, watching TV, waiting for the awards ceremony. A limo would pick them up at seven p.m.. The phone in their room began to ring.

"Judd Rayburn speaking."

"Judd? Randall Erin, say nothing, just listen. Rikki is amazing. She wouldn't give the money to Daniel Perrone without getting something in exchange. Talk about a stand-off, I can't believe. Rikki got part of the dossiers. Perrone is big-time mad. Rikki figured she could use that leverage and took a chance. Unknown to his father, Perrone advanced some of the dossiers to us. The list is incredible, one third of Congress, Democrats and Republicans, some heavyweights. Pictures, files, copies of checks, voice and videotapes, it's all here. Now powder your nose, stand tall, deliver that speech and get your butt back here. Oh yeah, Judge Ramirez called to offer his congratulations on the way you handled the case. Maureen said to tell you hello. See you tomorrow, Judd."

"Nice talking to you, Randall."

7:45 P.M. EDT. THE WHITE HOUSE

Judd and Joe were surrounded by White House staff giving last minute instructions on the medal ceremony, where to stand, when to talk, the pomp and protocol of the presentation. Thankfully they were, for the present, separated from the network cameras and reporters.

"Don't be nervous, gentlemen. The President will be out in ten minutes to spend a few moments talking to you before we go on the air," instructed one of the White House aides.

They tried their best to remain calm and cool but that was easier said than done. The Oval Office represented such power, Presidents who had worked here, fates had been decided here. The ambiance of the room was indescribable, humbling.

"The President is coming, gentlemen. Stand right here," directed one of the aides as "Hail to the Chief" began to play in the background.

"Congratulations on a precise accounting of the U.S. Justice system, gentlemen. Your country is proud of you and your President is proud of you," spoke the President of the United States as he shook their hands.

"Thank you, sir!" both said in unison, almost overwhelmed.

"I'll save the rest of my speech for the cameras. How much time, Ed?"

"One minute, Mr. President. If you would take your places, gentlemen."

The director counted down with his fingers, three, two, one, and then pointed to the President.

"On this anniversary of our great country's formation on that fateful day in 1776, I have the honored privilege of presenting two of America's finest patriots with our nation's highest civilian award, the Presidential Medal of Freedom. We have all witnessed their heroic actions."

Turning to an assistant, the President continued, "Could I have the medals, please?"

Judd received his medal first as he bowed his head for the red, white and blue ribbon to be placed around his neck. He smiled and shook the President's hand. Feather was next, and he heard the beat of his Indian ancestors' drums.

SUNDAY, JULY 5TH, NEW YORK, NICO PERRONE'S ESTATE

"My brothers of La Cosa Nostra," Nico addressed the council of the twenty-three family bosses gathered at his residence for this unprecedented event. "Ten years ago you showed me great respect by choosing me as head of this esteemed council. This honor has not been taken lightly. Today I will ask you to decide the future of our families, our businesses, and our way of life. We have two great opportunities, which I will outline for you today. At the end of this meeting, we must choose our path by voting. The vote must be unanimous. The high level of secrecy surrounding what I am about to tell you dictates that."

There was an uncanny silence among the rowdy bunch that filled the meeting facilities located fifty yards behind Nico's house. The building was completely without windows and equipped with the latest telecommunications equipment. On the long oval meeting table there were semi-permanent, seating assignments, denoted by solid gold nameplates. At each position was a computer flat screen, secured telephones and two cups of pencils, one with white pencils for affirmative votes, one with black pencils, denoting a negative response.

The council table itself was sunken into the floor. The domed ceiling was illuminated and projected a multi-colored butterfly map of the world. Computer-connected components converted it into a planetarium adding starlight or sunsets at the operator's option. Whatever mood Nico chose could be replicated above the council members.

On the walls opposite each end of the oval table where Nico and Daniel sat were large screens with projector rooms behind each. Adjacent to the long ends of the table were lounges decorated with the finest furniture money could buy. Priceless objects d'art accented the walls. Bars were positioned in all four corners. Thick green sculptured carpet continued down the two steps to the council table area. The table itself was thick, dark walnut surrounded by high-backed black leather swivel chairs. Sophisticated metal detectors mounted at the only entrance to the room were monitored by Nico's men in the main control/projector area. Weapons were not allowed inside the council meetings.

"Recently this council met to deal with a problem concerning our Sicilian brothers," Nico told the men. "We voted; we acted. This is the purpose for our council, to act as one. Because of this unification we have shown, we are no longer threatened by our brothers from the old country. Now, because of our act of solidarity to our twenty-four families, our Sicilian brothers want to help us."

The domed, mapped ceiling projected an enlarged representation of Europe and Russia, on cue, as planned by Nico.

"Our Sicilian brothers are in the final stages of a deal with the Colombian Cartel for exclusive distribution of cocaine and heroin into the areas shown on the map above you…"

Family heads began talking in muffled voices among themselves.

"By showing our strength and independence to them, the Sicilians have arranged a meeting between our organization and the Colombian Cartel for a similar deal, an exclusive distribution agreement for the Colombians' cocaine and the Sicilians' heroin into the United States."

The buzz among the other family heads became louder throughout the room. Questions flew from the men seated around the table as cigar smoke clouded the area.

"Please, my brothers, let me finish. This is not yet an issue to vote upon. We have been offered another option, an option worth, initially, twenty-four billion dollars. Yes, I said billion, my brothers."

"Who wants to give us twenty-four big ones, Nico?" asked the family boss from Chicago.

"The United States government!" Nico shot back, completely quieting the room.

"Nico, I have much respect for you, but I believe you have been drinking too much fine Italian wine, and Lucky Luciano is dead. He's the last member to negotiate with the U.S. government and that was many years ago," said another boss from the Bronx in a joking, raspy voice. Other members around the table laughed.

"Daniel will explain the details of this option," Nico said as Daniel walked around the table to stand beside his father.

"I will go into much more detail in a few moments, gentlemen," Daniel spoke, knowing this would be the most critical selling job of his entire life. "In a nutshell, the U.S. proposal is just the opposite from the first.

"They will pay us twenty-four billion dollars to eliminate the Colombian Cartel and keep drugs out of the U.S. Half the money up front. The balance at the end of the year. One billion cash will go to each family, followed by a guaranteed payment of twelve billion a year thereafter for the twenty-four families, before tax.

"We cease illegal activities in the U.S. and they set up a company for us called Newco, run by the best business minds in America. This company will replace coca plants in Colombia with other crops that are in demand on the global commodity market. They do the growing, packaging and sales, we get the profits."

Comments grew louder, more questions flew.

Daniel couldn't tell the way the room was swaying on the option. He had to influence them quickly.

"I will put up visual displays on the screen in a moment to illustrate possible involvement, projected P&L statements, the whole plan. Our guarantee is this tape recording by U.S. Attorney Randall Erin and his chief prosecutor, Judd Rayburn, the assistant U.S. attorney from Texas who recently won death sentences for the captured Mexican Cartel members. This tape represents their future judicial careers, gentlemen. If they renege on their end of the bargain, we could destroy them now. They have put this trust in our hands, up front."

For the next three and a half hours, Daniel put up visual displays, defined La Cosa Nostra's involvement, their disassociation with existing illegitimate activities, and projected P&L statements. He explained the plan as well as their options to go ahead with the distribution of drugs into the States. Daniel was careful to offer the two options as exactly that, options. He did not try to push one side or the other.

The meeting stretched on into the night. It was agreed no one would leave the meeting room until a final vote was taken. Never had the council been asked to make such a decision, one that would determine their entire future. Either way, La Cosa Nostra, 'This Thing of Ours,' would win.

MONDAY MORNING, 2 A.M. CDT, FT. BLISS

Erin began his briefing to Judd the second he got back to Fort Bliss. "Jake Ramsey and his group have been cataloguing the recipients of the mob payoffs in local, state and national government positions. We've ranked these people by importance and the amount of power they control. The crazy thing about the way the payoffs were made is that some of these guys didn't even know it was mob money."

"Randall, how could they not have known where the money was coming from?" Judd slicked back his thinning blond hair.

"About half the money paid out was through PAC's, political action committees. Legitimate third parties. Some of these congressmen are going to be hard to prosecute, Judd. They had no knowledge of where the money originated."

"Remember, Randall," Judd was speaking as an attorney, "ignorance of the law is no excuse. Do you think we can get to enough of them to make this thing work?"

"I said *half* the money was through third party payoffs," Erin smiled, "you should see some of the names on the other half of the list. To answer your question, we have more than enough names to make it work!"

"We still haven't heard from Daniel Perrone, Judd," Rikki said. "When I saw him Friday and gave him the counterfeit money, he told me his father was calling a council meeting of the families. So far, I figure they have been meeting for the last eight hours in New York. We haven't got the verdict on them yet. Could go either way. They've got that tape you and Randall made for a guarantee. This vote could blow up in our faces!"

"And we've got the dossiers thanks to you, Rikki," Judd said, rubbing his eyes. "I still trust Daniel. He'll make it work. However, if the vote goes the other way, well, it's very simple. We lose our jobs. They get put in jail for tampering."

MONDAY MORNING, 3:30 A.M. EDT, NEW YORK

Five votes had already been taken around the council table. Broken black and white pencils littered the tabletop. The first vote saw the twenty-four families split exactly in half. The fifth vote taken was in favor of making the deal with the U.S. government twenty-one to three. Big money was talking, especially guaranteed big money.

Pressure was mounting on the three dissenting families. They knew the vote had to be unanimous or they would not leave the building alive. A sixth vote would be taken after another hour of explanation.

Daniel focused deeper into the pros and cons of their decision.

"Gentlemen. Consider this. If we choose the drug distribution in the U.S. we create these problems: Turf wars with gangbangers and other drug peddlers that are established. We also incur prosecution on our other ventures from U.S. law enforcement coming down on us. The only way to stop drugs in the U.S. and prevent these obvious wars that will happen is to act as drug police for the government, gentlemen. They pay us to do what we do best…use our influence to get our way. That, gentlemen is poetic justice. Now, do we want greater problems, wars that will kill our members and put others in prison, disrupting family business or do we want to get paid by the government and become legal businessmen? That is the question we are about to vote on…"

Most everything had been explained in detail, over and over and over. They knew they would give up close to hundred members to the FBI for prosecution. They did not know the details of Daniel's plan to eliminate the Cartel heads.

Ties were off, the smell of cigar smoke became heavy in the council room, members were tired, some were getting drunk. If the vote was not unanimous now, the three dissenting family heads knew their fate. Twenty-one for, three against, added up to death.

"We almost have the votes we need to change the course of three generations, gentlemen." Daniel was applying the final pressure. "This will be the absolute last vote. We *will* make a decision. We must."

"Daniel," spoke Paulo Arollo, head of the New Jersey family, "we have seen your documentation, heard your explanations, but as successor to the head of this esteemed council, we have not heard your opinion on these two options. Before the final vote is taken, I would like to know where you stand. You do not have a vote, your father votes for your family."

"I am honored, Mr. Arollo, that you asked," Daniel replied respectfully. "For the first time in many years, this council has come together with the smell of blood on our hands, the blood of our Sicilian brothers. We have killed more in the last three weeks than from the beginning of our organization. Many bodies have disappeared from our ranks and the killing continues. Brothers killing brothers. It has a devastating effect on each of us.

"You asked where I stand? With my own hand, gentlemen, I killed Rigozzi. He was not killed by the Delta Force down in Puerto Rico. I was there. My best friend in the world, Joey Verocchi, my childhood playmate and later trusted confidant, fell by my sister's hand. She killed Joey as he tried to kill me. Joey turned from our family, dishonored us, for what? Rigozzi offered him my father's position at this council.

"Gentlemen, I ask you, would you have allowed Joey Verocchi to lead this council under the direction of Rigozzi? I think not. I believe, instead of joining forces with the Sicilians to take over the world market on drugs, we would have gone to war with them. A war that could have destroyed us all. Then, there is the U.S. government. They have been a worthy opponent. They will make the best ally. They offer what we seek; being legitimate business enterprises, free from prosecution. The Sicilians offer destruction, war, more killing, more drugs that may infect our own children. That is my answer, gentlemen, draw your own conclusions. It is time for the final vote."

One by one, the family heads voted. The first twelve pulled white pencils from the containers and broke them. Number 13 was Ben Pirretti of the Vegas family, one of the three dissenters. In his hand was a pencil of each color. He held the black pencil up and acted as though he would break it. Pirretti broke the white pencil. Other dissenters followed making the vote unanimous. Daniel stood next to his father, shaking hands with each family boss as they left the council room. A basket of antacid tablets sat near the exit.

"Daniel, my son, I am very proud of the way you handled this presentation," Nico said giving Daniel a manly embrace. "It shows me that the council will give you the respect you need when I am gone."

"Your blessing is important to me, Father. During the course of the evening, I have figured out how we can give Rayburn the one hundred men he wants to prosecute without jeopardizing our option to actually distribute the drugs, or if we change our minds at the last minute."

"How will you do that, Daniel?"

"The council knows we must turn over one hundred men for prosecution, basically four from each family. We can hand pick the final four after each family head supplies us with the names of their four expendable people. Our men will take possession of the drugs from the Cartel in Colombia. We will have two plans to get the drugs back to the states.

"One if Rayburn is successful. Another if he is not successful, in which case we will take another vote and go ahead and distribute the drugs. Rayburn will not be in a position to divulge to authorities that he gave us fifty million dollars. We'll make a killing with those free drugs. We contact each family head to send their four representatives to be on board the freighter we use to bring the drugs back to the U.S. These representatives will be instructed by each of the family heads to accompany the drugs back to the states as protection for each family's investment. When the one hundred men and the drugs are on board, we'll alert Rayburn of the freighter's position. Once they get busted, Rayburn gets his one hundred men to prosecute and tells the American public of the largest drug bust in history. We get the second half of our twenty-four billion dollars."

"I see merit to that plan, Daniel. You have covered our options well," Nico said proudly.

"I should call Judd and tell him of the council's decision."

"Make him sweat, Daniel. Morning will be soon enough. Get some sleep."

"Judd? Daniel. The council is unanimous. We're in."

"Best news I've had all day. You guys must have had a long meeting. It obviously went the way you wanted."

"My father has much influence over the council. I could not have done it without him. We need to schedule the transfer of the first half of the money, Judd. These men deal in cash, not talk."

"I understand. I'll get back to you on that. When do you leave for Medellin?"

"Tomorrow. I'll call you when I get back. I may be gone a couple of days."

27

HOCUS POCUS

"Where's the money coming from, anyway?" Feather asked. "Twelve billion! That's a bundle to deliver without anyone knowing where it came from."

"Feather, you don't want to know. James Bond hocus pocus. We'll make the payment. That's all you need to know right now. You might want to get with Perrone to find out the details of his plan with the Cartel. I'm sure he'll need a lot of backup on that operation down there. We've got to keep him honest, too," Judd replied.

"The Jury is getting some really good training down in Texas, Judd. We can be anywhere and do almost anything in a moment's notice." Feather was proud of his elite group. The Puerto Rican operation had sharpened them to a fine edge.

"How're you going to use the dossiers, Randall?" Judd asked.

"Officially, you haven't seen the list yet, okay?" Erin said, hesitating for a moment in deep thought. "Judd, I've got something to tell everyone," Erin said. "I've spoken to the Attorney General in Washington. It was a must move. If we're going to stand a chance of getting twenty-four billion dollars for the payoff, we're going to have to let the President in on this thing. CIA has secret funds that we may be able to use. The Attorney General won't breathe a word of this until he hears from me."

"It was going to have to happen sooner or later, Randall," Judd said, putting his face in his hands." Guess it's that time. I wanted to tell the President when Joe and I were in Washington getting the medal. Time just wasn't right."

"The Attorney General will arrange the meeting with the President," Erin stated. "I've got all the details. How does everyone feel if I go in and do the explanations and try to get the big bucks? It may not be so difficult if I go up there with a handful of these dossiers. I'm sure the President will know what to do with them with the election coming up."

All concurred with Randall making the trip.

"How do you think the President will actually use the dossiers, Randall?" Judd asked.

"He'll probably drop the first bomb immediately after their convention. Another, two weeks later. The final one he'll want to drop a week before the election. After he's won, the President will turn over the dossiers to the Justice Department for prosecution. That would be my best guess. I still need you guys to continue the investigation into Capriatti, Zavalla, and Fuselier."

"We're sure hanging a lot of trust on the Perrones on this one, bro," Feather said.

"It's a little more than just trust," Rikki interrupted. "The way I see it, we both have each other by the throat. They've got the tape you and Erin gave them, but I made a video tape of Perrone handing over the dossiers to me."

Their last night at the fort was spent going over last minute details. They needed to work out how they would communicate with each other, the secured phone numbers they would need to use and where everyone would be. The pucker factor was high and rising as the moment drew near for the final showdown.

WEDNESDAY NIGHT, JULY 8TH, EL PASO

Fort Bliss was getting back to normal. All the news media and trial staff had moved out. Cortez and the other prisoners were scheduled to transfer to Leavenworth Federal Prison in Kansas at 8 p.m. to await sentencing.

"There's the call we've been waiting for." Randall reached for the phone and hit the speaker button.

"Mr. Erin! Have you heard? Did you pick it up on your police scanner?"

"Wait a minute, slow down. Who is this?"

"Mr. Erin, it's Police Chief Rojas. Cortez got away! During the transfer to the airport. We don't know who could have known. The plan was top secret. Four U.S. Marshals killed. It's bad, Mr. Erin. It was terrible! They took him off in a helicopter we think. We don't know where he is…"

"Chief, settle down." Randall turned to Feather, "Joe, turn on the scanner. Someone's got Cortez, he's escaped. Chief, when did this take place and where?"

"Three miles from the airport on a stretch of highway, about forty-five minutes ago. Information is sketchy. We transferred all the prisoners except Cortez in a heavily guarded convoy two hours ago. They've already taken off to Kansas. We decided that if anyone was going to make an attempt on Cortez, they would hit on the convoy. They didn't try anything on the first transfer. We even had one of the Marshals made up to look like Cortez in the first group. We've got another leak. They couldn't have known!"

"How did you transfer Cortez, Chief?" Randall asked, trying desperately to unravel the details of the escape.

"We put him in one of the U.S. Marshall's private cars along with three other officers. The plan was to take Cortez to the private aviation section and fly him to Kansas separately in a small twin-engine aircraft. Three miles from the airport the car carrying Cortez hit a small IED, improvised explosive device, in the middle of the highway, set off by hand activator. The engine of the car was blown right through the hood. The two Marshals in the front seat were killed instantly. The demolition was exact and timed perfectly."

"What about the Marshals in the back seat with Cortez?"

"We found them with gunshot wounds to the head. They're both dead. The concussion must've temporarily knocked them out because they never drew their pistols. We've got APB's out on them now. We can only guess Cortez is in a chopper. By now he's probably across the border."

"Have you got roadblocks set up, Chief?"

"Yes, all over the area. We're not going to find him, though. My guts tell me that much. I know he's across the border. I contacted the Mexican authorities, but that will do no good at all unless someone over there wants Cortez killed. If that happens, we'll still never know. I fear the worst has happened. Cortez is gone for good. We lost him!"

"Dammit!" Randall took a deep breath, staring straight down at his desk. "Keep me posted, Chief."

Randall turned to Rikki and Feather. They heard the whole conversation. Cortez was gone, four more officers killed, more funerals. Back to square one, and Daniel didn't call.

THURSDAY MORNING, JULY 9TH, OUTSIDE MEDELLIN, COLOMBIA

"I love black satin sheets," Looma said stretching, yawning, reaching for the aspirin on the nightstand beside the huge canopy bed.

"Gaudy," Daniel whispered. "Typical Colombian Cartel gaudiness. These people are basically pigs, gluttons. They push everything to extremes. I don't like it!"

"But now, Daniel, my lover, you have worked a very profitable arrangement for your family." Looma also loved money. "My father, rest his soul, made very much money with these gaudy people, as you call them. Now you and your organization will become even more powerful when you control all the drugs in the U.S.."

Daniel hadn't confided in Looma. He had only told her that Plan A would give them sole U.S. distribution of drugs from the Cartel, never mentioning Plan B. He took her to Medellin at the last minute for show. Cartel members liked beautiful women; they used them like tear-off paper towels. Besides, her father was trusted by the Cartel, and gaining their trust was the purpose of his visit.

To show the Colombians strength and sincerity, Robert Cotter, Nico Perrone's own *consiglieri*, accompanied Daniel along with Mario and five other members of the Perrone family. They were well received by the Colombians. The Sicilians lived up to their promises to the Perrone family in arranging a proper introduction.

Camillo Vasquez, undisputed head of the Colombian drug organization, the most powerful man in most of South America, was a more than gracious host for the meeting. He arranged a large dinner the second night of Daniel's visit. All the powerful members of the Cartel were present. Most got very drunk. A couple even hit on Looma, including Camillo's son, Johnnie. Fortunately, most Latin women are very hot-blooded. Johnnie's girlfriend, Rosalinda Quiendo, didn't allow the flirting to get to the point of embarrassment. From that brief incident forward, Looma stuck to Daniel like glue.

On the third day, Vasquez flew Daniel, Mario and Cotter to several of their coca leaf growing sites, constantly guarded by two other choppers full of Cartel soldiers closely following Vasquez's helicopter. No one in Colombia messed with Camillo Vasquez!

After the tour, Vasquez, his son Johnnie, and their head enforcer, Alfonso Garza met privately with Daniel and his group. With the exception of

Camillo, who was partially bald with greasy, gray hair, the other Colombians in the room all looked like Spanish versions of Steven Segal, black hair combed straight back, tied in small pony tails. All had large, single diamonds in their pierced ears. Johnnie was the typical nouveau riche, powerful, only child. He loved to scare people with his position. He liked to kill people and see them die slowly. Cruelty amused him, the gorier the better. Gluttony for death was his thing. He loved women, to beat them and abuse them, sometimes four or five on a good night. He specialized in drunken torture sessions, just for kicks. Johnnie treated Rosalinda well because she was the daughter of his father's best friend.

Daniel handled the negotiations with Camillo Vasquez. He got a price per kilo on cocaine ten percent below normal wholesaler prices and agreed to buy in excess of seven metric tons of cocaine from the Colombians on a yearly basis, knowing this figure represented about half the total production of the Cartel. Daniel figured the Sicilians had negotiated the other half for their plans into Europe and the Russian republics.

It simplified the lives of the Colombian Cartel to have only two worldwide wholesalers that bought their entire production, two clients who could get along with each other. Cotter worked out shipping, delivery, and payment schedules with Camillo's man.

The only thing left to do was deliver the cash. Daniel instructed Mario to bring in the trunks full of cash. Camillo had no idea how much Daniel would bring to the table. He was pleased and incensed at the same time when he saw only half of the agreed upon amount. Daniel carefully explained that La Cosa Nostra was out fifty million dollars for the time being and the Colombian Cartel had a partial payment and gave him details of the balance of payment and how it would be delivered.

Camillo accepted this response. He had dealt with the Sicilians long enough to know just how careful the Mafia could be when it came to large amounts of cash. He took the money and shook hands with Daniel.

Later, Daniel walked down the hall of the luxurious twenty-four bedroom estate. Cotter carried a small case under his arm as they walked down the winding stairs to the ground floor.

They joined Camillo and his son out by the pool. This was the moment that would make or break Plan B.

"You and your son have been extremely hospitable to us during our stay, Mr. Vasquez." Daniel despised Johnnie. "I extend a standing invitation for you and your family to visit us in the States. We would like to return your graciousness at your convenience."

"Thank you for the invitation, Daniel," Camillo returned. "It has been our pleasure to extend our services to you and your esteemed family. It gives me a warm feeling to expand our friendship into a relationship not unlike a brotherhood, even though it would be impossible for us to enter the States. Maybe another location."

Camillo uttered the key word "brotherhood."

"Mr. Vasquez," Daniel spoke depicting the respect of a son talking to his father, "as you probably know, La Cosa Nostra was founded on brotherhood. That brotherhood is sacred to each and every member, each family. I would like to extend this brotherhood from our family to your organization."

Daniel turned to Cotter who handed the small case to him.

"This is a present from my father, Nico Perrone, to you, Mr. Vasquez. It is a first step in becoming a member of our brotherhood."

Daniel handed the red cordovan leather case to Camillo and waited for his reaction.

Camillo opened the case, inside was a 14-carat gold, fully operational 9mm pistol. Engraved on one side of the barrel were the words, "My brother, Camillo Number 1, Nico." Also inside the case was an empty 14-carat gold cartridge clip. The pride and astonishment showed on Camillo's face as he stood and hugged Daniel.

"Truly a sincere gift from such a wonderful man, Daniel," Camillo said, his eyes watering. "Please tell your father I will treasure this gift above all others."

"Mr. Vasquez, there is a highly secret, traditional ceremony that goes with this gift. The ceremony is called the Brotherhood of the Bullet. Only the most trusted elite of our organization are honored with this membership. It goes far beyond family status in La Cosa Nostra. It is a lifetime bond. The highest honor that can be bestowed upon a member of our organization."

"Please give me the details of this ceremony, Daniel. I am honored to be included."

"You will notice there is a clip for the weapon, Mr. Vasquez, but no bullets."

"Yes, I have noticed."

"There is only one bullet that goes with each weapon. Your weapon, your membership into the 'Brotherhood of the Bullet', is gold with the number 1 engraved into the barrel. That is because you are the undisputed head of the Colombian Cartel. The bullet will be presented to you by my father who is the undisputed head of La Cosa Nostra. I have a solid sterling silver pistol, with the number 2 engraved on the barrel. During our ceremony, if you choose to be a part of our brotherhood, I will present an exact duplicate of my pistol to your son, Johnnie."

Camillo parted with the valued gift just long enough for his son to examine it. Johnnie's eyes were full as he held the magnificent weapon.

"One day, my father, Nico, will pass his gold pistol to me. I will then carry his name and his respect with me and will pass my silver pistol to my son," Daniel continued. "However, Mr. Vasquez, the bullet is the important ingredient of the ceremony. Let me explain.

"The single, solid gold bullet represents complete trust. It holds a life in its grip. It represents the ultimate commitment. We have only fifty members of this prestigious brotherhood in all the vast numbers of the entire La Cosa Nostra family. We will extend this membership to you and your top fifty officials of the Colombian Cartel. It is essential that each of our members present each of your chosen men with a replica of their weapon personally, complete with their name on the barrel and their exclusive brother's name within La Cosa Nostra beside it."

"We would be honored to be included in such an exclusive brotherhood, Daniel," Camillo blurted out. "I have fifty key members of my Cartel. Without them we could not function. They are very important to our organization. The number fifty matches perfectly."

"Mr. Vasquez, yours will be the only gold pistol, Johnnie's will be the only solid silver pistol. The others will be of the finest bronze money can buy. Bronze has been a symbolic metal since biblical times. Each will be numbered, given from one brother to another. The ceremony takes place at the stroke of midnight, symbolizing the ending of one day, the beginning of a new day, a new brotherhood. There can be no other people or firearms present during the ceremony or the trust will be broken. Do you wish us to perform this ceremony for your Cartel, Mr. Vasquez?"

Again, Camillo stood and embraced Daniel, overwhelmed by the honor and tradition of belonging to such an exclusive club.

"Yes, Daniel, we are honored! When will we have this ceremony?"

"The manufacture of the custom pistols is not complete, Mr. Vasquez. We'll need the names and the numbers you want to assign to each weapon. Maybe we can combine the balance of the down payment for our merchandise with the ceremony. I will coordinate the shipment of the drugs with the delivery of the pistols with your son, who is soon to become my brother," Daniel said, disgusted at the thought of having Johnnie as a brother. "My father will be here to present you with your bullet, Mr. Vasquez."

"We can use the soccer field near Cali for the presentation, Daniel. It is a beautiful facility. I built it myself."

"I must remind you, there can be no one else near the presentation, Mr. Vasquez. You must realize the secrecy of our brotherhood."

"It will be as you wish. Please extend my thanks to your father. I look forward to your return."

Daniel's plane took off an hour later bound for New York. Daniel was smiling. Plan B was coming to fruition.

MIDNIGHT, THURSDAY, JULY 9TH, ERIN'S OFFICE

"Feather, please," Daniel said, recognizing Erin's voice. He stayed within the prearranged protocol mentioned by Commander Rhine during their visit in New York to speak only to Feather.

"Feather speaking."

"I need to meet with you. Chicago, Saturday night. Domino Bar," Daniel spoke and then hung up.

28

BIG BROTHER

TUESDAY, SEPTEMBER 1ST

The eleven convicted prisoners appeared before Judge Ramirez for sentencing. All received the death penalty. Cortez also received a death sentence pending his recapture. Judd had gotten his convictions, a bittersweet sentence since Cortez had escaped. There was still no news of his whereabouts.

Cortez's picture appeared in every newspaper in the free world. The cutline under his photo read, "Most Wanted Man in the World."

"Of the one hundred eighty-one congressmen's names we got from Perrone, only twenty-two actually received payoffs directly traceable to the mob," Erin said. "Most of the transfers took place through third parties as I said a few months ago. We can still use them as leverage. We have the proof that the monies were received. Our Congress appears to be much cleaner than we speculated. I don't want to go on a witch hunt and destroy the entire confidence of the American public so we'll pop the worst offenders and hold the soiled ones in abeyance."

"This is a pretty tough brand of football, Randall," Judd said realizing the devastation that would come down on the congressmen on the list. "I don't like the dirty part of politics."

"Judd, we didn't take money from the mob. The congressmen made that choice. We're going to bust them for it. What's to feel bad about? That's justice. Let's shift gears for a moment. Where are we with Feather, Commander Rhine, and Perrone?"

"The Perrones aren't taking any unnecessary chances. They won't take possession of the cocaine or make their move until they're positive the President stays President. They've set a date of January 23rd for the transfer, three days after the swearing in ceremony. Daniel's stalling the Cartel by telling them something about some pistols being made. I have no idea what that's all about."

"We still have three loose ends that bother me," Erin said.

"I know, Capriatti, Zapata, and Fuselier," Judd interrupted. "Feather and Rikki are no closer to them now than they were three months ago. We've got absolutely nothing on them. We haven't been able to connect them to stealing a nickel stick of gum in a five and dime store." Later, Erin's voice came over the intercom. "Judd? Randall. I just spoke to the Attorney General. He wants both of us in Washington next week. We're going to meet with the President about this whole mess."

"That was fast. What was their initial reaction?"

"Typical. There was none, just silence. They did have our files couriered straight to the Justice Department. They've been burning the midnight oil."

"They better burn some more. We've got to come up with a chunk of money in a big hurry. Do they realize what we're attempting to do here?"

"That's why we're getting a meeting so fast, Judd. The Attorney General is working thirty hours a day just to verify those dossiers."

THE WHITE HOUSE, ONE WEEK LATER

The White House Chief of Staff greeted Erin and Judd and took them into a waiting area just outside the Oval Office. Neither knew what would take place once on the other side of those two large doors.

"Come in gentlemen. The President and the Attorney General will see you now."

"Good to see you again, Judd," spoke the President cordially, with a bit of a frown on his brow. "I believe both of you know the Attorney General."

"Yes, sir, we've met," Erin responded.

"Men, your secrecy in this matter is of the utmost importance. I know I don't have to remind you of that. This whole scheme is just short of incredible." The President continued his troubled look. "I've taken the liberty to call in several other folks to join us today. The Speaker of the House and the Majority Leader of the Senate. After they arrive, I will call in the three congressmen in question, Capriatti, Fuselier, and Zapata. I met with them earlier in the week. Their story is as astounding as yours."

Judd and Erin said nothing, as they tried to maintain their composure.

"I will let you two in on a little secret, gentlemen." The President wore a stern look. "When it gets to the point that you cannot even trust the Executive Branch of the U.S. government, that is a very sad day. Ever since your Commander Rhine of Naval Intelligence tapped into the Top Secret E.P.I.C. computer, every bell, whistle and alarm installed as safeguards against illegal entry went off. We've been monitoring your activities since that moment."

Erin looked over at Judd with an expression that clearly said, *"We should have expected that."*

"Although I do not approve of some of your methods, being a realist, I can certainly appreciate why you chose the veil of secrecy in your operations. We let you continue because what you were trying to accomplish, originally, was to put Cortez away. We did not want to interfere in your investigations. It was from our monitoring those investigations that we also learned of the private activities of Capriatti, Fuselier, and Zapata. Mr. Erin, your group's activities and those of the three congressmen were paralleling one another. Together, you gentlemen were making history on a grandiose scale.

"They were trying to save the U.S. economically. You were trying to rid our country of drugs and organized crime. Both are endeavors any president would be proud to be a part of. The only problem was that you two were about to destroy what the congressmen were attempting by gathering evidence against them and exposing their actions. They, on the other hand, were willing to put their political careers, not to mention their lives on the line to accomplish their goals.

"That's why I have called them here to tell you their story in their own words. I believe you will be as astonished as I was when I first heard it. There are more details to clarify here today."

"Mr. President, the congressmen have arrived and are waiting to see you."

"Send them in."

The congressmen entered the Oval Office and introductions were exchanged. Judd and Erin had no idea what was about to take place. They didn't know whether they were to be admonished, fired, or worse.

Capriatti remained calm, Fuselier was nearing cardiac arrest, while Zapata sat tight-lipped with a look of defiance written across his face. They shared the same feeling as Judd and Erin. Their fate and future was also unclear.

"Tell us about your involvement with Carolina Pharmaceuticals, gentlemen, and about the guys in these photos…the men right here," the President demanded pointing to the Sicilian mob bosses pictured standing next to the three congressmen.

"Here's another set of pictures for you gentlemen to see. We've identified these five men as Russian businessmen. This guy is in the Russian government."

Capriatti looked at the pictures, showing no reaction whatsoever.

"I give you my word as a member of the Senate of the United States that what I am about to tell you is the truth. I will allow you to form your own opinions when I have finished, but I assure you all, our intentions were for the betterment of our nation."

"Senator, I'll give you the assurance that I and the members of my staff here will listen with an unbiased attitude. Please begin."

Capriatti began his amazing story.

"I'll start with Russia. We have all seen the Russian Republics fall apart. They are in a state of chaos. Chaotic conditions often give rise to very profitable enterprises if the timing is right. Through the Foreign Relations Committee, which I chair, I have been involved with the various Russian republics in meetings to aid their restructuring and re-growth. It is essential that the United States play a major role.

"Mr. President, I know that you see great economic growth potential for both the Russians and the Americans. You have pushed hard for billions in aid."

There was no response from the President.

"That is where Tommy Zapata and I became involved. He's Chairman of the Finance Committee in the House. During these meetings with various government officials in the now-sovereign Russian republics, we met stiff competition for goods and services from the Japanese delegation, not to mention the low interest, no interest loans being offered by them. Japan is in a recession. They offered more money at lower rates. They beat our prices badly on much needed farm machinery essential to getting the Russian agricultural programs back on their feet. In short, gentlemen, this overwhelming opportunity to provide goods and services to the Russian republics, which incidentally, by our estimates would create over half a million U.S. jobs and pump five hundred billion dollars back into the economy of the United

States over a six year period, is being bought away by the Japanese. We were not in a position to compete against their lower interest and labor rates."

"Interesting," said the President.

"We countered by offering U.S. Agricultural Department assistance. That is where we became involved with `Frenchy' Fuselier who chairs the Ag committee in the House. We still couldn't out-perform the Japanese. They beat us at every turn.

"As far as our future foreign relations with the Russian republics were concerned, Mr. President, look at the scenario facing us. The Russians joining forces with the Japanese was completely unacceptable. Hell, the Japanese already own half the U.S. Now they're about to get a solid foothold into Russia. Just think what would happen if the Japanese got Russia back in good working order. Where would that leave the U.S. in the future? Think about that, gentlemen!

"Now let's throw one more future wrench into the gears. The European Economic Community has unified European countries out of the dire necessity to get their own economies back on their feet. The United States is not a member of that exclusive club, either, and Russia is their next door neighbor. Fueled with Japanese money and technical know-how, these two massive economic forces could begin lifting trade barriers between each other and become kissing cousins. Where do you think that leaves the United States, gentlemen?"

The President and the others sat listening to the earnest concerns being expressed by a man they had previously considered to be a dirty senator. This was much larger than personal gain on the part of the three congressmen. They were dealing with the very economic future of the U.S. So far, the scenario Capriatti was drawing out didn't look good. He continued.

"During the meetings with the Russians," Capriatti paused as he took a sip of his now cold coffee, "we met several of their rich entrepreneurs. We were getting nowhere with the government officials over there, so we decided to hit on the people who represented big business, along with several Russian *Mafiya* bosses. They hire all the Russian people, pay their wages and elevate themselves into the government by the sheer number of votes they control due to the masses they employ.

"After literally months of getting on their good side," Capriatti continued his bleak scenario, "two of the entrepreneurial giants confided in me one night, after two bottles of vodka, that they had a plan for complete financial domination of the Russian republics. This plan involved the distribution of drugs to almost three hundred million people. That's where the Russian *Mafiya* comes in. Russia does not currently have a large drug problem. Vodka is their big addiction. Can you imagine the potential drug revenues derived from this untapped market? Especially if the sixth member, Sero Muscovia, of their FDA, allowed the drugs into the country with no heat from inspection!

"That's when the Russians told us about their wishes to meet with the Sicilian mob. Believe it or not, we arranged the meetings between the Russians and the Sicilians through the CIA covert activities group. It was our only chance. We didn't have any options left. Since the Japanese could virtually buy off the Russian government, the game would be all but over for the good ole USA."

"Let me try to finish the story for you, Senator," the President said rocking back in his chair. "If the U.S. set up a deal to get drugs into Russia through the distributorship of the six rather prominent Russians in the pictures, the Russians would be able to twist the arms of their government officials into signing an exclusive contract to buy only U.S. goods and services, sharing profits where necessary. Am I close, Senator?"

"Right on the money, Mr. President," Capriatti said. "We all realize the devastating effects that drugs have on a society, gentlemen. I weighed that effect upon the consequences the United States could face when our children take over from us. We would be leaving them in an almost un-defendable position. I made my choice. I stand in your judgment!"

"Senator Capriatti, to what point has this agreement between the Russian businessmen and the Sicilians progressed?" The President asked.

"The first shipments of heroin will arrive within three months. Cocaine will be thirty days afterwards."

"Gentlemen, I don't know whether to shake your hands or slap them," the President replied after hearing the almost unfathomable story, parts of it for the second time. "I've always thought you were involved with the mob, Capriatti, I'll admit that. For your information, you three gentlemen have been under investigation for five months. We were unable to turn up anything concrete except these pictures. This is all we have."

"It's enough, Sir!" said Capriatti.

"It must've been a difficult decision on your part," the President said as he continued to look towards his one-time political opponent. "Sending one nation into the grip of addiction in order to save your own is beyond my comprehension. The thoughts that must've gone through your mind while making such a choice. I believe your intentions were for the good of the United States, Senator, Congressmen. I'm not going to destroy you. Instead, I am going to tell you about a better plan, one that is already in the final stages.

"We can use your help. I already have plans for the Japanese manufacturers. I'm going to give them more to think about than getting their foot into Russian doors. They are going to be hard pressed to keep them here in our house. I plan to remove the welcome mat with a few well-placed trade embargoes.

"Obviously there are two points we cannot allow," the President continued. "First, we cannot allow an entire nation to be seduced by drug addiction. I want you three guys to work with Randall Erin of the U.S. Justice Department on the details so that we can contact Interpol and crush this distribution plan before it starts. I'll get the State Department involved so we can coordinate with our embassies inside the Russian republics.

"Secondly, we cannot allow the Japanese to sign their financial deal with the Russians. From the information we got from NSA's listening post in Masawa, Japan, the Japanese think they have the Russians over a barrel. They plan to get the Kuril Islands back from the Russians as a partial payment on the loans they will make. The Russians won't go for it. It's that simple."

The President stood and extended his hand to Capriatti. "For once, we're on the same side, Senator. I apologize for my years of mistrust against you. Now let's get to work and stop this big ball from gaining any more momentum. We've got a little ball of our own to get rolling."

"Speaking of trust, Mr. Rayburn," Capriatti mentioned in parting, "your man, Sal Olivares, the DEA chef extraordinaire, is a double agent. He also works for the Mexican Secret Police."

"You're kidding, Senator!" Judd looked as if he'd been struck by lightning. "He got us the information we needed on Cordova."

"I said he *was* a double agent, gentlemen." Capriatti said. "Why do you think I got him the job with my next door neighbor? I wanted to keep an eye on him. I'll get some documentation to you, Mr. Erin, conclusive enough for an indictment against our gourmet friend."

"Thanks, Senator," Erin remarked. "We'll take care of Mr. Salvador Olivares. I have a feeling the cuisine at Leavenworth is going to improve dramatically very soon."

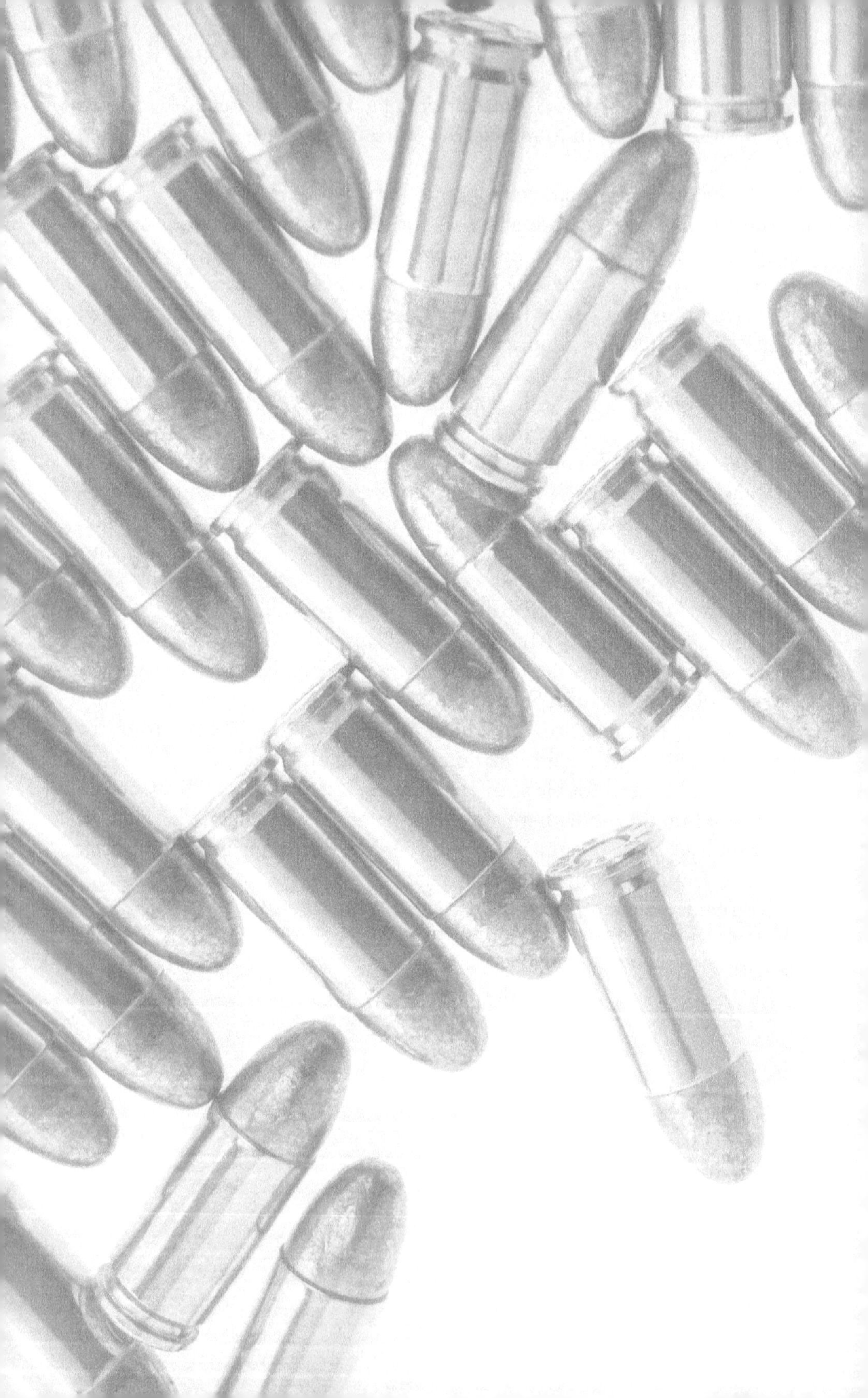

29

BROTHERHOOD OF THE BULLET

"I got a radio message from Rikki and Feather aboard the *Hornet* attack carrier off the coast of Colombia. They've got some seasick Jury members on that ship," Judd noted, knowing Operation Bullet would commence in four days.

"The operation is vital to us," Erin said with a concerned look on his face. "We've got government personnel in place aboard ships down there, agricultural experts, procurement specialists, managers, transportation specialists, commodities brokers, as well as office and heavy equipment. It's imperative that we move like lightning as soon as the Cartel members are removed! How are the Perrones and their men handling their part of the plan?"

"Nico, Daniel, and their other forty-eight men are on board Trump's former yacht which they bought a year ago. They're anchored near Medellin. Commander Rhine got them the other half of the money. The Cartel wouldn't take a check. Daniel said he's ready!"

"What about the one hundred men we're going to bust, are they ready to take possession of the cocaine onto the freighter?"

"Also anchored off the coast just far enough out to be in international waters. We've purposely left the Coast Guard and Navy big brass out of the loop because of possible leaks during ship-to-ship communication. After

Commander Rhine and Feather finish backing up the Perrones' big show with the Jury members, they'll leave again from the carrier and board the freighter, making the bust themselves. That way, we stay in control of the operation."

11:45 P.M. MST, A SOCCER FIELD OUTSIDE CALI, COLOMBIA

"Nico, my friend, and soon-to-be brother, I am honored that you have personally come to be a part of this ceremony. It is the beginning of a very profitable partnership for both of us," Camillo Vasquez said to the La Cosa Nostra senior statesman. "You make me feel proud to be a part of your most high brotherhood. Two family heads becoming one!"

"That is exactly why I am here, Camillo. To make two families one!" stated Nico Perrone, repulsed at the smell of liquor on Vasquez's breath. "If you would direct your men to form a line across the middle of the field, we are ready to begin the ceremony. It is ritual to begin at the stroke of midnight."

Camillo turned to his son, Johnnie. "Get the men ready!"

"Camillo, when your men are in place, my family members will walk in a single file to stand in front of their respective brothers. Please make sure each one of your men are in the right numerical sequence. It would be embarrassing to present the wrong name on the weapon."

"Everyone will be in their place, Nico," Vasquez assured him.

"As I was saying, Camillo, my men will enter the field carrying two silver cases. One with the other half of our down payment. The other with the ceremonial weapons."

"I understand, Nico."

"My son, Daniel, has given you the instructions for the Brotherhood ceremony?

"Yes, Nico, we all know what to do. First, your men take the golden bullet and put it into the clip. Second, they put the clip into the weapon. Third, they chamber the golden bullet into the weapon. These three steps symbolize the power of the bullet.

"Fourth, your men put the muzzle of the weapon to their own head. This symbolizes holding their own lives in their hands, to control their own destiny. Fifth, your men hold the muzzle of the weapon to my men's heads, their newly chosen brothers. This symbolizes holding their brother's life in their hands. Sixth, your men pass the weapons to my men, symbolizing a transfer of the power of the bullet. Seventh, my men hold the weapon to your men's heads. This symbolizes the trust each has in his new brother. Eighth, the weapon is put back in the case, never to have the bullet see daylight again, symbolizing the never-ending brotherhood of the bullet. How did I do, Nico?"

"You have it down perfectly, Camillo. We should now take our positions at the head of the line," Nico said walking towards Daniel, who was standing opposite Johnnie.

"So far so good, Indian," Rikki whispered to Feather as she stood next to him with her black baseball cap turned backwards allowing her to get closer to the laser scope on her sniper's rifle.

Feather never acknowledged Rikki's comment. He stood under the bleachers staring out across the Cali soccer field, focused onto his target with a distant expression on his face that was noticeable. Rikki was concerned. She knew all too well of Feather's dedication to the mission. But he had a far off look that she had never seen before.

"Are you okay, Joe?" Rikki whispered.

Feather never broke his stare.

The fifty members of the Jury were taking no chances. Standing shoulder-to-shoulder underneath the bleachers of the soccer field, each man had been assigned a Cartel target. If Nico's men didn't do the job on the Cartel members, the Jury would.

Perrone's men walked single file onto the soccer field. Each carried two cases, as planned. Each stood facing their new brother with their backs towards the fifty members of the Jury hidden under the stadium bleachers. At the stroke of midnight, the ceremony began.

After step three of the ceremony, cocking the weapons, each member of the Cartel suddenly had a small red spot on their foreheads, spots made by the laser scopes of the Jury. Unseen by Cartel members, noticed by La Cosa Nostra members. Just a small little reminder to La Cosa Nostra that big brother was watching.

Step four, the weapons were held to the heads of the La Cosa Nostra members. Step five, the weapons were held to the heads' of the Colombian Cartel members. Not a word was spoken.

Camillo smiled, standing in front of Nico, anticipating step six, when the golden weapon presented to the head of the Colombian Cartel would finally be his. Johnnie, standing at his father's side, fixed his eyes upon the solid silver pistol as Daniel slowly pulled the weapon from his own head and moved it towards Johnnie's. Fifty weapons were now against the heads of the fifty Colombian Cartel leaders…POW!

The sound of fifty 9mm pistols being fired simultaneously, contained inside of the soccer stadium, resembled the boom of a cannon going off.

In the split second it took to pull the triggers, the twenty-four billion-dollar hit was complete. The Colombian Cartel lieutenants fell to the ground under an ear-shattering echo. No back up from the Jury was necessary. At midnight, January 23rd, the Colombian Cartel went out of business. Cocaine sales ceased.

Six awaiting choppers from the attack carrier *Hornet* swooped down out of the sky onto the blood splattered soccer field. Fifty bodies were loaded immediately and flown out to sea to their final place of rest and disappearance. The custom made weapons were thrust into the belts of the dead, ex-drug peddlers. After all, they were gifts from the Perrone family and the U.S. government.

"It has been many years since I have pulled a trigger and killed a man, Daniel," Nico said walking back to the chopper that would fly them out to their yacht. "I had almost forgotten the terrible feeling it causes, even to kill pigs such as these. This brings back so many memories of the old days. Suddenly I see the faces. They haunt me, Daniel. But no more. We end the old way of life for La Cosa Nostra in the same way it began. We will be happy now…if I can forget the faces."

Rikki tripped the sprinkler system on the soccer field to wash away the blood. Members of the Jury and the Perrone family would never forget the fixed, startled stares on the faces of the lifeless Colombian Cartel members.

As the Jury coptered back to the carrier to refuel and to board the freighter containing the fifty million dollars' worth of pure uncut cocaine,

Rikki, trying to change Joe's attitude, broke out singing, "Turn out the lights, the party's over!"

Feather stared into the clear night sky.

Newco officials were scheduled to begin operations in Colombia at 6 a.m.. Their first duty was to inform the Colombian government of the unfortunate disappearance of the Cartel and to tell them of the new agricultural ventures that Newco, a properly chartered Colombian company, would undertake immediately.

THE WHITE HOUSE, OVAL OFFICE, 3:30 A.M.

The President had gathered the Attorney General, the three congressmen, Judd, Erin, White House Chaplain Kenneth Dykes, and several other cabinet members to wait out the operation down in Colombia. Private conversations were buzzing around the room in several small groups while they waited for the phone to ring on the President's desk.

Judd knew success would mean seeing Robin again, a very narrow thought when he considered the brevity of the entire situation, but it was his thought. He knew failure or a backing out of the Perrones would mean all out war against her family and very possibly an end to their relationship. That part he could not fathom.

"By the way, Judd, while we're waiting, I got a call from Daryl Thompson earlier today from El Paso," Randall said taking a sip of coffee. "He's doing a fine job running the D.A.'s office out there. He called to tell us they discovered who leaked the information to the Mexican Cartel and caused you guys to get whacked at Ambush Pass."

"Who was it? I'll fry the guy!"

"Donald Bonds, Martinez's assistant. But, before you go crazy, Bonds got drunk one night before the bust and went across the border into Juarez. He found some Mexican hooker and shacked up with her. Sometime during the course of the night, he told her everything about the upcoming bust. The girl worked for some of Cortez's men, word got back and the rest is history."

"I'll take that fat slob down, Randall. I promise. We'll take him down for Dee Espinoza, Martinez and the others that died out there."

ON BOARD THE ATTACK CARRIER USS HORNET, OFF THE COAST OF COLOMBIA

The early morning operation to board and seize the drug payload on the freighter *Agua* along with capturing the one hundred La Cosa Nostra dissenters which made up the newly revised F.B.I. Top 100 Most Wanted list was minutes away from commencement. With five Huey loads of Jury members and four Cobra gunships, no complications were expected. For once the odds and the element of surprise rested solely in the hands of the Jury.

Nine choppers took off from the flight deck of the carrier, *U.S.S. Hornet*. The night sky was bright with a full, white moon. Visibility was good, too good, almost like daylight.

"This is Cobra leader to Jury one. Freighter in sight, over."

"Roger, proceed Cobra leader. Jury one out," Feather looked back at his men with a thumbs up. They were ready.

As the squadron of choppers neared the anchored freighter, the deck lights that had so brilliantly directed the choppers to their destination disappeared.

"Jury one, this is Jury two. Be careful Indian. The lights just went off on deck," Rikki said to Feather.

Feather keyed his radio to acknowledge.

The four gunships hovered above the freighter in their assigned positions as Feather's chopper moved over the ship, sideways, inching its way to the drop area over the deck. In less than twenty seconds, Feather and nine of his men rappelled down the ropes to the freighter deck.

"Freighter *Augua*! You are being boarded by the U.S. Navy. Stand to! Do not move! Do not try to resist or you will be fired upon!" Rikki announced over the loudspeakers of her hovering chopper as it flew closer to the ship.

"Movement on the quarterdeck! Above us, high right!" Feather yelled.

Simultaneously, two dual 50-caliber machine guns mounted on swivel turrets were uncovered by La Cosa Nostra mobsters standing on each quarterdeck, fore and aft of the ten Jury members standing amidships below them. The huge 50s, capable of shooting down bombers at twenty thousand feet, opened up on Feather and his men at point-blank range, catching them in a crossfire. Ear-shattering to the gunners, Feather never heard the sound of the first two rounds, half the size of a roll of quarters, that tore through his bullet-proof vest and exited out through his back leaving two holes the size of oranges in his mid-section. The sheer force of the rounds knocked him back twelve feet.

Barely capable of moving his head from the ferocious impact of the two projectiles that almost tore him in half, Feather slowly opened his eyes, trying to regain any motor skills left. All he could do was witness the rest of his men come to the same fate as himself. They never had a chance. The gunships could not return fire for fear of hitting the Jury team on deck. All of them were either dead or near death, it had happened so fast.

As the gunners who were manning the devastating weapons turned them around towards the choppers hovering just above them, Feather caught a glimpse of one of the men firing the guns. It was Cortez. Laughing, yelling, shaking his fist at the choppers above him in jerking, insanely defiant motions. The escaped drug dealer took aim at the closest chopper, squeezed the triggers and exploded the craft, blowing flaming shrapnel all over the deck.

"Jury one! Jury one! Answer me, dammit! Feather are you okay?" screamed Rikki as the chopper she was in backed out of range of the twin 50s. "Feather, this is Rikki! What's your status? We cannot fire! Repeat, we cannot fire!"

Feather's lungs were filling quickly, what was left of them. Seeing that his men were all dead, Feather tried to tighten the grip on his weapon that somehow remained in his hand. He could only focus on one thought, kill Cortez. It was no use. Feather could only witness Cortez fire the twin 50s at the remaining choppers as the convicted murderer howled like a demon in the night. With final, shallow breaths, Joe whispered brokenly into his headset.

"Sink…us. Sink…us. Cortez…"

"God no! Feather!" yelled Rikki, choking back her remorse "I'm coming to get you, baby. Hold on!"

"No…finished. I love…" Feather died. His drums were silent.

Rikki had seen many men die, usually without any emotion. But this was different. Feather was a loner, a warrior, bulletproof, unscheduled for death. Choking the lump down out of her throat, Rikki faced forward to the young lieutenant flying the chopper.

"Lieutenant," her voice was quivering, tears streamed down her face. "I'm taking over the aircraft. Unseat the control."

"But ma'am…"

"I said I'm taking control of the aircraft, lieutenant. Now move!"

Her stoned-faced determined stare through her now darkened, tear-filled eyes left no room for rebuttal from the lieutenant. He unstrapped from the left seat while his co-pilot flew the craft.

In seconds, she was strapped in and took over the chopper.

"This is Jury Two to Cobra Leader, over," she spoke into the headset.

"Jury Two, Cobra Leader, go ahead."

"Cobra Leader, pull your flight to a one mile perimeter of the freighter *Augua*. That is a direct order," she commanded.

"Roger, Jury Two. Cobra flight, this is Cobra leader. Orbit one mile around the freighter *Augua*. Execute on my mark. Mark!"

Commander Rhine pulled the chopper around on a left descending bank away from the freighter. She couldn't get Joe's voice out of her mind. She was dying inside.

Concentrate, she told herself. Sink the ship, sink the ship. Kill Cortez, that heathen bastard.

Rikki hovered the craft just above the calm water about a mile from the ship.

"Lieutenant, put the emergency raft in the water now! You and the rest of the men get out of the aircraft and into the raft." Her voice was firm, unyielding.

"But ma'am…"

"*Now* Lieutenant. I'll bury my husband in my own way! Exit the aircraft immediately." Fire was in her eyes, drying the tears, setting her stare in stone.

"Husband?"

"Out!"

The commander and the rest of the Jury members on Commander Rhine's chopper quickly inflated the raft and exited the aircraft.

"Jury Two, this is Cobra leader."

"Go ahead, Cobra Leader."

"What are your orders, ma'am?"

"Your orders are to stay clear of the freighter *Augua*." Rikki spoke clearly into the headset. "I'll do what must be done."

"Ma'am, with all due respect." The flight leader was unsure what Commander Rhine had in mind. "You can't sink that ship with the armament on your aircraft. It only has mini-guns. No rockets, ma'am, I'll…"

"You'll do as you are ordered, Cobra Leader," she shouted. "Stay clear of the freighter *Augua*."

To gain her composure and to get a feel for the chopper, she began gaining altitude while orbiting the freighter, careful to stay out of visual sight of Cortez and the horrendous dual 50 caliber guns he manned. Her mind stuck on the thought of Joe Feather, her lover, her husband, her secret, no longer a secret. He was dead. His killer was still alive.

Coming around broadside to the ship, Commander Rhine tilted the nose of the chopper downwards just long enough to test the mini-guns with a short burst into the sea below. Now, fully acclimated to her only weapon system, she flicked on the loud speakers mounted underneath the chopper. Moving towards the freighter at full throttle, descending to near sea level, she fixed her stare on the gun emplacement manned by Cortez. Five hundred yards from the ship she began screaming into the loud speakers.

"Cortez, you drug peddling, murderous bastard, get ready to die." Her tears were gone. Her stare fixed. No turning back. "It's just you and me, asshole!"

Cortez clearly heard the invitation to battle, swung the huge 50s around towards Rikki's attacking chopper, let out another banshee yell and began firing at her.

Simultaneously, Commander Rhine squeezed the red firing button as tracers from the mini-guns and the 50s passed each other in the moonlit night sky. Death hung heavily in the air as the chopper closed within two hundred yards of the freighter. Solid streams of light, like red lasers transmitting from the mini-guns on the chopper began searching the deck for her continuously screaming maniacal target.

Bullets ricocheted over the top of the freighter. Huge 50 caliber rounds shattered the windshield of the fast closing chopper, one round finding its mark, tearing deep into Rikki's shoulder, practically severing it from her body.

No turning back, she thought again. Wait for me, my love, I'm coming.

With the trigger of the mini-guns still depressed in a death grip, Commander Rikki Rhine could see the blazoned eyes of Cortez as she rolled the chopper over on its side and crashed upside down, squarely into the 50 caliber gun emplacement. Following its line of deadly tracers to her target, the chopper exploded directly on top of Cortez, silencing the screams, lighting up the night in a huge fireball.

Minutes later, the small freighter *Augua* along with Commander Rikki Rhine's burning chopper, slipped slowly under the surface, hissing and steaming. Mr. and Mrs. Joe Feather delivered their prisoner, Julio Cortez, to the very gates of Hell itself.

After the President briefed everyone on the events at sea, Judd left the President and Erin inside the White House still talking and shaking their heads. It was a somber moment for all. Judd walked outside past the awaiting limo into the darkness of the night, empty, drained, almost lifeless. His two friends, best friends, Rikki and Joe were dead. The price was much too high, he thought. No amount of money was large enough for these two endearing people. This husband and wife who lived a secret, who never got a wedding gift or a congratulation from him, were gone. Cortez or a thousand like him were not worth the price. The war on drugs had been much too expensive.

As he walked past the guard gate adjacent to the front lawn of the White House, he hardly noticed the car parked near the entrance. He was much too deep in thought, wallowing in remorse.

"Judd?"

He looked over to his left to where the voice was calling his name. Robin got out of the car and walked towards him. She could see the tragedy in his swollen eyes, the look of dejection and defeat on his face. She could only think the worst had happened. Fearing for her own father and brother's lives, she asked in a muffled, fearful voice.

"What happened, Judd? Is my father…?"

"No, No," he said, taking her softly into his arms, "they're fine. It's Joe and Rikki, my best friends in the world…" He broke down, no control over his emotions. "They were married…all this time…now they're dead…"

"Oh, Judd, I'm so sorry."

"Robin, it seems that everyone in my life that I have truly loved or cared about has been taken from me. I don't understand it, baby, everyone."

Feeling numb, as if the last ounce of energy he had ever had suddenly left him, Judd slowly slid down to his knees on the sidewalk in front of the White House. Robin held him as she too went to her knees. For a brief time they held each other and cried in each other's arms. Momentarily, lifting her buried head from Judd's slumping shoulder, she placed her hands on his face, gently wiping his tears away.

"Darling, they aren't dead," she said, lowering her hand to take Judd's in hers, placing it on her stomach. Judd looked down at his hand as he felt life move within her. Saying nothing, still unable to talk, he faced her with a questioned look.

"Maybe this is the wrong time to tell you, maybe it is the right time. I've been trying to think of a couple of names, a girl's name and a boy's name."

With a grimace, Judd forced the words from his mouth, unable to put complete sentences together.

"You're…? We're…? Twins?"

"A boy and a girl, Cowboy," Robin said with a sweet smile peeking from beneath the tears in her eyes. "A little Rikki and a little Feather."

For priceless moments they faced each other without uttering a sound. Kneeling in amazement, their thoughts of death turned to thoughts of life, from loneliness to happiness, to loving and to living as the dawn began to peek over the horizon, announcing the arrival of a brand new day.

"Father says you have to make an honest woman of me. Do you think we will get the blessings on our marriage from the Justice Department, my love?"

"That's not important to me anymore, Robin. I lost something almost greater than life itself when Rikki and Feather were killed. But now I have you. I'm…I'm not sure where we'll end up or how I'll support us. Prosecution is all I know."

Robin could see the uncertainty in Judd's eyes. She also saw the love.

"Being together is all that is important, my love. Having a life, raising our children… And who knows, Cowboy, maybe Father has a position for you in his new company."

Judd raised his eyes to meet Robin's, "Imagine that…"

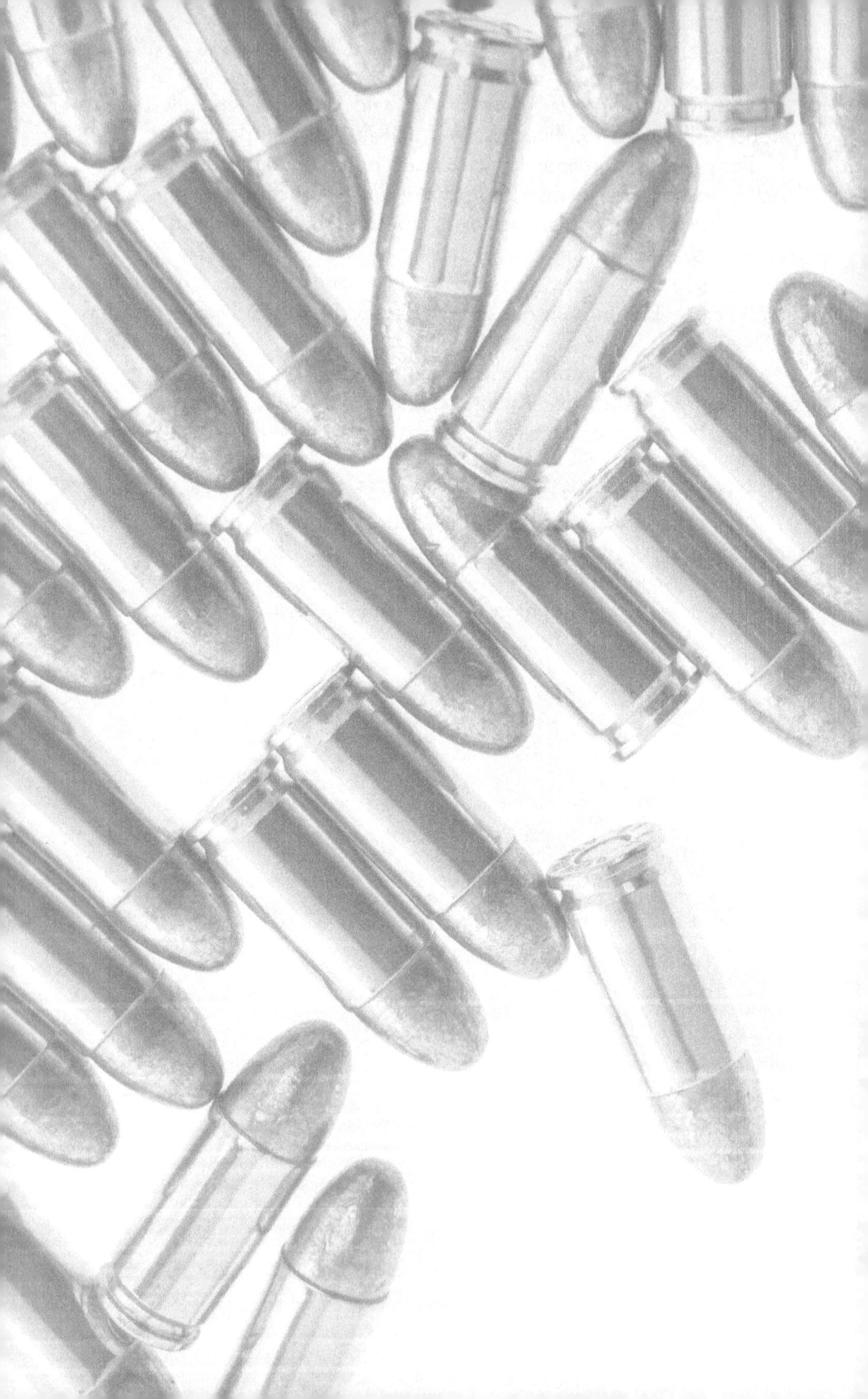

ABOUT THE AUTHOR

Ron Mumford is the author of a non-fiction book, *Finding Your Soul Mate, God's Way*, an action thriller, *Gray Justice*, and a fantasy trilogy which includes *Wayne's Angel*, *Betwixt*, and *Z-Gen*, soon to be published by 3rd Coast Books.

Mumford was a Journalism major at the University of North Texas, worked at two small newspapers as sports editor, as associate editor at a national trade magazine, and has written freelance articles for several newspapers and magazines. After being drafted into the U.S. Army, he was an information specialist (Army Combat Correspondent/Photographer) in Vietnam and Germany, receiving two Bronze Stars for his service in Vietnam. He also wrote for Army Times and Stars & Stripes.

Mumford started his own business as a literary agent in Houston, Texas. He went to New York and Hollywood to pitch his clients' work.

Mumford wants other authors to gain from his experience. One of his first editors, Myra Barnes, Ph.D., from Baytown told him, "Ron, as a writer, if you ever make it big in the book writing business, send the elevator down to your fellow writers!"

He has never forgotten that plea and continues to support fellow Indie writers in any way he can. *IF YOU QUIT, YOU LOSE!* He hopes to spread the word to never quit writing and never give up hope. Someone will come along and send the elevator down...